Parinoush Saniee is a sociologist and psychologist. She ... ... the Iranian government in the ministry ... ... written several novels, of which *The Book of Fa...* ... *the Other One* is the second – also pub... ... Iran; others are awaiting approval by ...

This book has been translated with the assistance of the Sharjah International Book Fair Translation Grant Fund.

THE
BOOK
OF
FATE

Parinoush Saniee

Translated from Persian
by Sara Khalili

ABACUS

ABACUS

First published in Great Britain in 2013 by Little, Brown
This paperback edition published in 2014 by Abacus

3 5 7 9 10 8 6 4

A CIP catalogue record for this book
is available from the British Library.

ISBN 978-0-349-13877-0

Typeset in Goudy by M Rules
Printed and bound in Great Britain by
Clays Ltd, St Ives plc

Papers used by Abacus are from well-managed forests
and other responsible sources.

MIX
Paper from
responsible sources
FSC
www.fsc.org   FSC® C104740

Abacus
An imprint of
Little, Brown Book Group
100 Victoria Embankment
London EC4Y 0DY

An Hachette UK Company
www.hachette.co.uk

www.littlebrown.co.uk

Contents

Cast of Characters

Ahmad	Massoumeh's older brother
Akbar	communist party activist
Ali	Massoumeh's younger brother
Amir-Hossein	old sweetheart of Mrs Parvin
Ardalan	Parvaneh's son
Ardeshir	Mansoureh's son
Asghar Agha	one of Massoumeh's suitors
Atefeh	Massoud's wife and Mr Maghsoudi's daughter
Aunt Ghamar	Massoumeh's maternal aunt
Bahman Khan	Mansoureh's husband
Bibi	Hamid's paternal grandmother
Dariush	Parvaneh's younger brother
Dorna	Siamak and Lili's daughter, Massoumeh's first granddaughter
Dr Ataii	neighbourhood pharmacist
Ehteram-Sadat	Massoumeh's maternal cousin and Mahmoud's wife
Faati	Massoumeh's younger sister
Faramarz Abdollahi	Shirin's fiancé
Farzaneh	Parvaneh's younger sister
Firouzeh	Faati's daughter, Massoumeh's niece
Gholam-Ali	Mahmoud's eldest son
Gholam-Hossein	Mahmoud's second son and youngest child

vii

Grandmother	Massoumeh's paternal grandmother
Granny Aziz	Massoumeh's maternal grandmother
Haji Agha	Mrs Parvin's husband
Hamid Soltani	Massoumeh's husband, communist activist
Khosrow	Parvaneh's husband
Ladan	Massoud's fiancée
Laleh	Parvaneh's second daughter
Lili	Parvaneh's daughter
Mahboubeh	Massoumeh's paternal cousin
Mahmoud	Massoumeh's oldest brother
Manijeh	Hamid's youngest sister, Massoumeh's sister-in-law
Mansoureh	Hamid's older sister, Massoumeh's sister-in-law
Maryam	nosy classmate of Massoumeh
Massoud	Massoumeh's son and second child
Massoumeh (Massoum) Sadeghi	narrator and protagonist of the novel
Mehdi	Shahrzad's husband and co-leader of communist organisation
Mohsen Khan	Mahboubeh's husband
Monir	Hamid's oldest sister, Massoumeh's sister-in-law
Mostafa Sadeghi (Agha Mostafa)	Massoumeh's father
Mr and Mrs Ahmadi	Parvaneh's parents
Mr Maghsoudi	Massoud's fellow soldier at the war front and later his boss and father-in-law
Mr Motamedi	vice president at the government agency where Massoumeh is employed
Mr Shirzadi	a department director at the government agency where Massoumeh works
Mr Zargar	Massoumeh's supervisor at the government agency

Mrs Parvin	next-door neighbour of Massoumeh's family
Nazy	Saiid's wife
Parvaneh Ahmadi	Massoumeh's best friend
Sadegh Khan	Faati's husband, Massoumeh's brother-in-law
Saiid Zareii	Dr Ataii's assistant pharmacist
Shahrzad (Aunt Sheri)	Hamid's friend and co-leader of communist organisation
Shirin	Massoumeh's daughter and youngest child
Siamak	Massoumeh's son and first child
Sohrab	Firouzeh's husband
Tayebeh (Mother)	Massoumeh's mother
Uncle Abbas	Massoumeh's paternal uncle
Uncle Asadollah	Massoumeh's paternal uncle
Uncle Hamid (Hamid Agha)	Massoumeh's maternal uncle
Zahra	Mahmoud's daughter and middle child
Zari	Massoumeh's older sister who died when Massoumeh was eight years old

Locations

Ahvaz – capital city of the western province of Khuzestan and near the Iran–Iraq border

Ghazvin – a major city in northern Iran

Golab-Darreh – a town north of Tehran, in the Alborz mountain range

Kermanshah – the capital city of Kermanshah province in western Iran

Mashad – a city in north-eastern Iran and near the borders of Afghanistan and Turkmenistan; considered holy as the site of the Shrine of Imam Reza

Mount Damavand – the highest peak of the Alborz mountain range, north of Tehran

Qum – a city south-west of Tehran and the centre for Shi'a Islam scholarship. Considered holy as the site of the Fatima al-Massoumeh Shrine

Rezaieh – a city in north-western Iran and the capital of West Azerbaijan province

Shemiran – northern suburb of Tehran

Tabriz – the capital city of East Azerbaijan province in northern Iran

Zahedan – the capital city of Sistan and Baluchestan province, near the border with Pakistan and Afghanistan

Glossary

Agha – an honorific meaning gentleman, sir, mister.

Haft-Seen – Literally meaning 'The Seven 'S's' is a traditional table setting of *Nowruz*, the Iranian new year celebration at the start of spring. The *Haft-Seen* table includes seven items all starting with the letter 's' in the Persian alphabet and they symbolise rebirth, health, happiness, prosperity, joy, patience and beauty. The seven items are apples, sprouts, vinegar, garlic, sumac, *samanu* (a creamy wheat pudding) and *senjed* (a sweet Silver berry or Oleaster fruit). Among other items included are: mirror, candles, painted eggs, coins, goldfish and rose water.

Hijab – refers to both the head-covering worn by Muslim women and modest Islamic styles of dress in general. In Iran, the most common forms of *hijab* have traditionally been the headscarf and the chador. In post-revolution Iran, women are also required to wear a loose-fitting long tunic or manteau.

Khan – obsolescent title of the nobility or tribal chiefs, now used as an honorific corresponding to 'Sir'.

Korsi – traditional furniture of Iranian culture. It is a low table with a heater underneath it and blankets thrown over it. People sit on futons around the *korsi* with the blankets covering their legs. It is a relatively inexpensive way to stay warm in the winter, as the futons and blankets trap the warm air. During the cold months, most family activities take place around the *korsi*.

Wedding *sofreh* – a fine cloth, often with glittering gold and silver threads, is spread out on the floor and adorned with various foods and objects traditionally associated with marriage. These include a mirror flanked by a pair of candelabra, a tray of multi-coloured spices, an assortment of sweets and pastries, a large flatbread, coloured eggs, a platter of feta cheese and fresh herbs, two large sugar cones, a flask of rose water, a small brazier burning wild rue, and an open Qu'ran or a Diwan of Hafez.

SAVAK – Secret Service Police.

CHAPTER ONE

I was always surprised by the things my friend Parvaneh did. She never gave a thought to her father's honour and reputation. She talked loudly on the street, looked at shop windows and sometimes even stopped and pointed things out to me. No matter how many times I said, 'It's not proper, let's go', she just ignored me. Once she even shouted out to me from across the street, and worse yet, she called me by my first name. I was so embarrassed I prayed I would just melt and vanish into the earth. Thank God, none of my brothers were around, or who knows what would have happened.

When we moved from Qum, Father allowed me to continue going to school. Later, when I told him, in Tehran girls don't wear chadors to school and I will be a laughing stock, he even let me wear a headscarf, but I had to promise to be careful and not bring him shame by becoming corrupted and spoiled. I didn't know what he meant and how a girl could get spoiled like stale food, but I did know what I had to do to not bring him shame, even without wearing a chador and proper hijab. I love Uncle Abbas! I heard him tell Father, 'Brother! A girl has to be good inside. It's not about proper hijab. If she's bad, she'll do a thousand things under her chador that would leave a father with no honour at all. Now that you have moved to Tehran, you have to live like Tehranis. The days when girls were locked up at home have passed. Let her

1

go to school and let her dress like everyone else, otherwise she will stand out even more.'

Uncle Abbas was very wise and sensible, and he had to be. At the time, he had been living in Tehran for almost ten years. He came to Qum only when someone died. Whenever he came, Grandmother, God rest her soul, would say, 'Abbas, why don't you come to see me more often?'

And Uncle Abbas, with that loud laugh, would say, 'What can I do? Tell the relatives to die more often.' Grandmother would slap him and pinch his cheek so hard that its mark would stay on his face for a long time.

Uncle Abbas's wife was from Tehran. She always wore a chador when she came to Qum, but everyone knew that in Tehran she didn't keep proper hijab. Her daughters paid no mind to anything at all. They even went to school without hijab.

When Grandmother died, her children sold the family house where we lived and gave everyone their share. Uncle Abbas told Father, 'Brother, this is no longer the place to live. Pack up and come to Tehran. We'll put our shares together and we'll buy a shop. I will rent a house for you near by and we'll work together. Come; start building a life for yourself. The only place you can make money is Tehran.'

At first, my older brother Mahmoud objected. He said, 'In Tehran one's faith and religion fall by the wayside.'

But my brother Ahmad was happy. 'Yes, we have to go,' he insisted. 'After all, we have to make something of ourselves.'

And Mother cautioned, 'But think of the girls. They won't be able to find a decent husband there, no one knows us in Tehran. Our friends and family are all here. Massoumeh has her year six certificate and even studied an extra year. It's time for her to get married. And Faati has to start school this year. God knows how she'll turn out in Tehran. Everyone says a girl who grows up in Tehran isn't all that good.'

Ali, who was in year four, said, 'She wouldn't dare. It's not like I'm dead! I will watch her like a hawk and I won't let her budge.'

2

Then he kicked Faati who was sitting on the floor, playing. She started screaming, but no one paid any attention.

I went and hugged her and said, 'What nonsense. Do you mean to say that all the girls in Tehran are bad?'

Brother Ahmad, who loved Tehran to death, snapped, 'You, shut up!' Then he turned to the others and said, 'The problem is Massoumeh. We'll marry her off here and then move to Tehran. This way, there'll be one less nuisance. And we'll have Ali watch over Faati.' He patted Ali on the back and proudly said that the boy has zeal and honour, and will act responsibly. My heart sank. From the start, Ahmad had been against my going to school. It was all because he himself didn't study and kept failing year eight until he finally dropped out of school, and now he didn't want me to study more than he had.

Grandmother, God rest her soul, was also very unhappy that I was still going to school and constantly harangued Mother. 'Your girl has no skills. When she gets married, they'll send her back within a month.' She told Father, 'Why do you keep spending money on the girl? Girls are useless. They belong to someone else. You work so hard and spend it on her and in the end you'll end up having to spend a lot more to give her away.'

Although Ahmad was almost twenty years old, he didn't have a proper job. He was an errand boy at Uncle Assadollah's store in the bazaar, but he was always roaming around the streets. He wasn't like Mahmoud who was only two years older than him but was serious, dependable and very devout and never missed his prayers or his fasting. Everyone thought Mahmoud was ten years older than Ahmad.

Mother really wanted Mahmoud to marry my maternal cousin, Ehteram-Sadat. She said Ehteram-Sadat was a Seyyed – a descendant of the Prophet. But I knew my brother liked Mahboubeh, my paternal cousin. Every time she came to our house, Mahmoud would blush and start stammering. He would stand in a corner and watch Mahboubeh, especially when her chador slipped off her head. And Mahboubeh, God bless her, was so playful and giddy

3

that she forgot to keep herself properly covered. Whenever Grandmother scolded her to show some shame in front of a man who was not her immediate kin, she would say, 'Forget it, Grandmother, they're like my brothers!' And she would start laughing out loud again.

I had noticed that as soon as Mahboubeh left, Mahmoud would sit and pray for two hours, and then he kept repeating, 'May God have mercy on our soul! May God have mercy on our soul!' I guess in his mind he had committed a sin. God only knows.

Before our move to Tehran, there was plenty of fighting and quarrelling in the house for a long time. The only thing everyone agreed on was that they had to marry me off and be rid of me. It was as if the entire population of Tehran was waiting for me to arrive so that they could corrupt me. I went to Her Holiness Massoumeh's Shrine every day and pleaded for her to do something so that my family would take me with them and let me go to school. I would cry and say I wished I were a boy or that I might get sick and die like Zari. She was three years older than me, but she caught diphtheria and died when she was eight years old.

Thank God my prayers were answered and not a single soul knocked on our door to ask for my hand in marriage. In due course, Father straightened out his affairs and Uncle Abbas rented a house for us near Gorgan Street. And then everyone just sat around waiting to see what would become of me. Whenever Mother found herself in the company of people she considered worthy, she would comment, 'It's time for Massoumeh to get married.' And I would turn red with humiliation and anger.

But Her Holiness was on my side and no one showed up. Finally, the family somehow got word to an old suitor who had since got married and divorced that he should step forward again. He was financially well off and relatively young, but no one knew why he had divorced his wife after only a few months. To me he looked foul-tempered and scary. When I found out what horror lay ahead, I put all ceremony and modesty aside, threw myself at Father's feet and cried a bucketful of tears until he agreed to take me to Tehran

4

with them. Father was tender-hearted and I knew he loved me despite the fact that I was a girl. According to Mother, after Zari died he fretted over me; I was very thin and he was afraid I would die, too. He always believed that because he had been ungrateful when Zari was born, God had punished him by taking her away. Who knows, perhaps he had been ungrateful at the time of my birth as well. But I truly loved him. He was the only person in our house who understood me.

Every day when he came home, I would take a towel and go stand next to the reflecting pool. He would put his hand on my shoulder and dip his feet in the pool a few times. Then he would wash his hands and face. I would give him the towel and while drying his face he would peer at me with his light-brown eyes from over the towel in such a way that I knew he loved me and was pleased with me. I wanted to kiss him, but, well, it was inappropriate for a grown girl to kiss a man, even if he was her father. In any case, Father took pity on me and I swore on everything in the world that I would not become corrupted and I would not bring him shame.

Going to school in Tehran became a whole other story. Ahmad and Mahmoud were both against me continuing my education, and Mother believed that taking sewing classes was more impera-tive. But with my begging, pleading and irrepressible tears I managed to convince Father to stand up to them, and he enrolled me in year eight in secondary school.

Ahmad was so angry he wanted to strangle me and used every excuse to beat me up. But I knew what was really eating away at him and so I kept quiet. My school was not that far from home and a fifteen- to twenty-minute walk. In the beginning Ahmad would secretly follow me, but I would wrap my chador tightly around me and took care not to give him any excuse. Meanwhile, Mahmoud stopped talking to me altogether and completely ignored me.

Eventually, they both found jobs. Mahmoud went to work at a shop in the bazaar that belonged to Mr Mozaffari's brother and Ahmad became an apprentice at a carpenter's workshop in the Shemiran neighbourhood. According to Mr Mozaffari, Mahmoud sat in the store all day and could be counted on, and Father used to say, 'Mahmoud is the one who's really running Mr Mozaffari's shop.' Ahmad, on the other hand, quickly found plenty of friends and started coming home late at night. Eventually, everyone realised that the stench on him was from drinking alcohol, arak to be precise, but no one said anything. Father would hang his head and refuse to return his hello, Mahmoud would turn away and say, 'May God have mercy. May God have mercy,' and Mother would quickly warm up his food and say, 'My child has a toothache and he has put alcohol on it for the pain.' It wasn't clear what sort of a tooth ailment it was that never healed. In all, Mother was in the habit of covering up for Ahmad. After all, he was her favourite.

Mr Ahmad had also found another pastime at home: keeping an eye on our neighbour Mrs Parvin's house from an upstairs window. Mrs Parvin was usually busy doing something in the front yard and, of course, her chador would always fall off. Ahmad wouldn't move from his position in front of the living room window. Once, I even saw them communicating with signs and gestures.

In any case, Ahmad became so distracted that he forgot all about me. Even when Father allowed me to go to school wearing a headscarf instead of the full chador, there was only one day of shouting and fighting. Ahmad didn't forget, he just stopped scolding me and wouldn't talk to me at all. To him I was the personification of sin. He wouldn't even look at me.

But I didn't care. I went to school, had good grades and made friends with everyone. What else did I want from life? I was truly happy, especially after Parvaneh became my best friend and we promised to never keep any secrets from each other.

Parvaneh Ahmadi was a happy and cheerful girl. She was good at volleyball and was on the school team, but she wasn't doing all that well in her classes. I was sure she wasn't a bad girl, but she didn't abide by many principles. I mean she couldn't tell good from bad and right from wrong and had no clue how to be mindful of her father's good name and honour. She did have brothers, but she wasn't afraid of them. Occasionally, she would even fight with them and if they hit her, she would hit them back. Everything made Parvaneh laugh and she did so no matter where she was, even out on the street. It was as if no one had ever told her that when a girl laughs her teeth shouldn't show and no one should hear her. She always found it strange that I would tell her it was improper and that she should stop. With a surprised look on her face she would ask, 'Why?' Sometimes she stared at me as if I was from a different world. (Wasn't that the case?) For instance, she knew the names of all the cars and wished her father would buy a black Chevrolet. I didn't know what kind of car a Chevrolet was and I didn't want to lose face by admitting it.

One day I pointed to a beautiful car that looked new and I asked, 'Parvaneh, is that the Chevrolet you like?'

Parvaneh looked at the car and then at me and she burst into laughter and half-screamed, 'Oh how funny! She thinks a Fiat is a Chevrolet.'

I was red up to my ears and dying of embarrassment, both from her laughter and from my own stupidity in having finally revealed my ignorance.

Parvaneh's family had a radio and a television at home. I had seen a television at Uncle Abbas's house, but we had only a large radio. While Grandmother was alive and whenever my brother Mahmoud was at home, we never listened to music, because it was a sin, especially if the singer was a woman and the song was upbeat. Although Father and Mother were both very religious and knew listening to music was immoral, they weren't as strict as Mahmoud and liked listening to songs. When Mahmoud was out, Mother would turn on the radio. Of course, she kept the volume low so that the neighbours wouldn't hear. She even knew the lyrics to a few songs, especially those by Pouran Shahpouri, and she used to sing quietly in the kitchen.

One day I said, 'Mother, you know a good number of Pouran's songs.'

She jumped like a firecracker and snapped, 'Quiet! What sort of talk is this? Don't you ever let your brother hear you say such things!'

When Father came home for lunch, he would turn on the radio to listen to the news at two o'clock and then he would forget to turn it off. The Golha music programme would start and he would unconsciously start moving his head, nodding in tempo with the music. I don't care what anyone says, I'm sure Father loved Marzieh's voice. When they played her songs, he never said, 'May God have mercy! Turn that thing off.' But when Vighen sang, he would suddenly remember his faith and piety and yell, 'That Armenian is singing again! Turn it off.' Oh, but I loved Vighen's voice. I don't know why, but it always reminded me of Uncle Hamid. From what I can remember, Uncle Hamid was a good-looking man. He was different from his brothers and sisters. He smelled of cologne, which was something rare in my life ... When I was a child he used to take me in his arms and say to Mother, 'Well done, sister! What a beautiful girl you gave birth to. Thank God she didn't turn out looking like her brothers. Otherwise, you would have had to get a big cask and pickle her!'

And Mother would exclaim, 'Oh! What are you saying? What's ugly about my sons? They're as handsome as can be, it's just that they're a little olive-skinned, and that's not bad. A man isn't supposed to be pretty. From back in the old days it has always been said that a man should be uncomely, ugly and bad-tempered!' She would sing these last words and Uncle Hamid would laugh out loud.

I looked like my father and his sister. People always thought Mahboubeh and I were sisters. But she was prettier than me. I was thin and she was plump, and unlike my straight hair that wouldn't curl no matter what I did, she had a mass of ringlets. But we both had dark-green eyes, fair skin and dimples on our cheeks when we laughed. Her teeth were a bit uneven and she always said, 'You're so lucky. Your teeth are so white and straight.'

Mother and the rest of the family looked different. Their skin was olive-toned, they had black eyes and wavy hair, and they were somewhat fat. Though none of them was as portly as Mother's sister, Aunt Ghamar. Of course, they weren't ugly. Especially not Mother. When she threaded off her facial hair and plucked her eyebrows, she looked just like the pictures of Miss Sunshine on our plates and dishes. Mother had a mole on the side of her lip and she used to say, 'The day your father came to ask for my hand, he fell in love with me the instant he caught sight of my mole.'

I was seven or eight when Uncle Hamid left. When he came to say goodbye, he took me in his arms, turned to Mother and said, 'Sister, for the love of God don't marry this flower off too soon. Let her get an education and become a lady.'

Uncle Hamid was the first person in our family to travel to the West. I had no image of lands overseas. I thought it was some place like Tehran, except farther away. Once in a while, he would send a letter and photographs to Granny Aziz. The photos were beautiful. I don't know why he was always standing in a garden, surrounded by plants, trees and flowers. Later, he sent a picture of himself with a blonde woman who wasn't wearing hijab. I will never forget that day. It was late afternoon; Granny Aziz came over so that Father could read the letter to her. Father was sitting next to his mother on the floor cushions. He first read the letter to himself and then he suddenly shouted, 'Wonderful! Congratulations! Hamid Agha has got married and here's a picture of his wife.'

Granny Aziz fainted and Grandmother, who had never got along with her, covered her mouth with her chador and chuckled. Mother hit herself on the head. She didn't know whether to swoon or to revive her mother. Finally, when Granny Aziz came to, she drank plenty of hot water and candied sugar and then she said, 'Aren't those people sinners?'

'No! They're not sinners,' Father said with a shrug. 'After all they're well read. They're Armenian.'

Granny Aziz started hitting herself on the head, but Mother grabbed her hands and said, 'For the love of God, stop it. It's not that bad. He has converted her to Islam. Go ask any man you like. A Muslim man can marry a non-Muslim and convert her. And what's more, it merits God's reward.'

Granny Aziz looked at her with listless eyes and said, 'I know. Some of our prophets and imams took non-Muslim wives.'

9

'Well, God willing, it is a blessing,' Father laughed. 'So, when are you going to celebrate? A foreign wife really calls for a festivity.'

Grandmother frowned and said, 'God forbid, a daughter-in-law is bad enough, now to top it off this one is foreign, ignorant and clueless about purity and impurity in our faith.'

Granny Aziz, who seemed to have regained her energy, collected herself, and as she got up to leave, she said, 'A bride is a home's blessing. We're not like some people who don't appreciate their daughter-in-law and think they've brought a maid to the house. We cherish our daughters-in-law and are proud of them, especially a Western one!'

Grandmother couldn't tolerate her boasting and snidely said, 'Yes, I saw how proud you were of Assadollah Khan's wife.' Then she maliciously added, 'And who knows if she has in fact converted to Islam. Maybe she has made a sinner out of Hamid Agha. In fact, Hamid Agha never had proper faith and practice. Otherwise, he wouldn't have moved to Sin-estan.'

'You see, Mostafa Khan?' Granny Aziz snapped. 'Did you hear what she said to me?'

Finally, Father intervened and put an end to the squabble.

Granny Aziz quickly threw a large party and bragged to everyone about her Western daughter-in-law. She framed the photograph, put it on the mantelpiece and showed it to the women. But up until the moment she died, she kept asking Mother, 'Did Hamid's wife become a Muslim? What if Hamid has become an Armenian?'

After her death, for years we received very little news of Uncle Hamid. Once I took his photographs to school and showed them to my friends. Parvaneh really liked him. 'He's so handsome,' she said. 'He's so lucky to have gone to the West. I wish we could go.'

Parvaneh knew all the songs. She was a fan of Delkash. In school, half the girls were Delkash fans and the other half liked Marzieh. I had to become a Delkash fan. Otherwise, Parvaneh wouldn't stay friends with me. She even knew Western singers. At her home they had a gramophone and they played records on it. One day she showed it to me. It looked like a small suitcase with a red lid. She said it was the portable type.

The school year had not yet ended and I had already learned a lot. Parvaneh always borrowed my notebooks and lecture notes and sometimes we studied together. She didn't care if she had to come to our house. She was very nice and easygoing and paid no attention to what we had and didn't have.

Our house was relatively small. There were three steps at the front door that opened into the front yard, which had a rectangle reflecting pool in the middle. We had put a large wooden bed on one side of it and on the other side there was a long flowerbed parallel to the pool. I mean its long side was parallel to the short side of the pool. The kitchen, which was always dark and black, was separate from the house and at the end of the yard. The bathroom was next to it. There was a sink outside and we didn't have to use the pool's water pump to wash our hands and faces. Inside the house, to the left of the main door, there were four steps that led to a small landing. The doors to the two downstairs rooms opened here. And then there were stairs that led upstairs where there were two other rooms with an adjoining door. The room in the front was the living room and it had two windows. From one side you could see the yard and part of the street and from the other side you could see Mrs Parvin's house. The windows of the other room, where Ahmad and Mahmoud slept, opened on to the rear courtyard with an open view of the backyard of the house behind ours.

Whenever Parvaneh came over, we would go upstairs and sit in the living room. There wasn't much there. Just a large red carpet, a round table and six bentwood chairs, a big heater in the corner and next to it a few floor cushions and backrests. The only decoration on the wall was a framed carpet with the Van Yakad verse from the Quran on it. There was also a mantelpiece, which Mother had covered with a piece of embroidery and on it she had put the mirror and the candelabras from her marriage ceremony.

11

Parvaneh and I would sit on the floor cushions and whisper, giggle and study. Under no circumstances was I allowed to go to her house.

'You're not to step inside that girl's house,' Ahmad would bark. 'First of all, she has a jackass brother; second, she is shameless and fickle. To hell with her, even her mother goes around with no hijab.'

And I would say, 'Who in this city wears hijab?' Of course, I would only mumble it under my breath.

One day when Parvaneh wanted to show me her *Woman's Day* magazines, I snuck over to their house for just five minutes. It was so clean and beautiful and they had so many pretty things. There were paintings of landscapes and women on all the walls. In the living room, there were large navy-blue sofas with tassels on the bottom. The windows that overlooked the front yard had velvet curtains in the same colour. The dining room was on the opposite side and it was separated from the living room by curtains. In the main hall there was a television and a few arm-chairs and sofas. The doors to the kitchen, bathroom and toilet were here. They didn't have to constantly cross the front yard in the cold of winter and the heat of summer. The bedrooms were all upstairs. Parvaneh and her younger sister Farzaneh shared a room.

They were so lucky! We didn't have that much space. Although on the face of it we had four rooms, in reality we all lived in the large room downstairs. We ate lunch and dinner there; in the wintertime we set up the *korsi*, and Faati, Ali and I slept there. Father and Mother slept in the room next door where there was a large wooden bed and a wardrobe for our clothes and odds and ends. We each had one shelf for our books. But I had more books than everyone else, so I took two shelves.

Mother liked looking at the pictures in *Woman's Day*. But we kept the magazines hidden from Father and Mahmoud. I used to read the 'At the Crossroads' section and the serial stories and then I would tell them to Mother. I would exaggerate the details so much

12

that she would come close to tears and I myself would cry all over again. Parvaneh and I had decided that each week, after she and her mother had finished reading the new issue, she would give the magazine to us.

I told Parvaneh that my brothers didn't allow me to go her house. She was surprised and asked, 'Why?'

'Because you have an older brother.'

'Dariush? What's "older" about him? In fact, he's one year younger than us.'

'Still, he's grown up and they say it's not proper.'

She shrugged and said, 'I for one don't understand your customs.' But she stopped insisting that I go over to her house.

I received excellent grades in my end of term exams and the teachers praised me a lot. But at home no one showed any reaction. Mother didn't quite understand what I was telling her.

Mahmoud snapped, 'So what? What do you think you've achieved?'

And Father said, 'Well, why didn't you become the top student in your class?'

With the start of summer, Parvaneh and I were separated. The first few days, she would come over when my brothers were out and we would stand outside the front door and chat. But mother constantly complained. She had forgotten how back in Qum she would spend every afternoon with the women in the neighbourhood, talking and eating watermelon seeds until Father came home. She didn't have any friends or acquaintances in Tehran and the women in the neighbourhood snubbed her. On a few occasions they laughed at her and she got upset. Over time, she forgot her habit of spending the afternoon chit-chatting and so I couldn't talk to my friends either.

On the whole, Mother wasn't happy that we had moved to Tehran. She would say, 'We aren't made for this city. All our friends and relatives are in Qum. I'm all alone here. When your uncle's wife, with all her airs, pays no mind to us, what can we expect of strangers?'

13

She nagged and complained until she finally convinced Father to send us to Qum to spend the summer at her sister's house. I quipped, 'Everyone goes to a country house for the summer, and you want us to go to Qum?'

Mother glared at me and said, 'You are quick to forget where you're from, aren't you? We lived in Qum all year round and you never complained. Now little missy wants to go to a summertime place! I haven't seen my poor sister for an entire year, I have no news of my brother, I haven't visited the grave of my relatives ... The summer will be over by the time we spend just a week at each relative's house.'

Mahmoud agreed to let us go to Qum, but he wanted us to stay with Father's sister so that when he came to visit us on the weekends he would have to see only Mahboubeh and our aunt. 'Just stay with Auntie,' he said. 'There's no need for you to stay at everyone's house. If you do, you'll be leaving the door open for all of them to head down to Tehran to stay with us, and it will be one big headache.' (Wonderful! How hospitable!)

'Right!' Mother replied angrily. 'It's fine if we go to your aunt's house and they come here. But God forbid if my poor sister wants to come for a visit.' (What clout! Whack him on the head and put him in his place.)

We went to Qum. I didn't complain too much because Parvaneh and her family were going to spend the summer at her grandfather's garden estate in Golab-Darreh.

We returned to Tehran in the middle of August. Ali had failed a few classes and had to retake his final exams. I don't know why my brothers were so lazy when it came to studying. Poor Father had so many dreams for his sons. He wanted them to become doctors and engineers. Anyway, I was happy to be back home. I couldn't bear our living like vagabonds, moving from one house to another, going from maternal aunt to paternal uncle and from paternal aunt to maternal uncle ... I especially hated staying with Mother's sister. Her house was like a mosque. She kept asking if we had said our prayers and constantly grumbled that we hadn't said

them properly. And she wouldn't stop bragging about her devoutness and about her husband's relatives who were all mullahs.

A couple of weeks later, Parvaneh and her family also returned to
Tehran. And with the start of the school year, my life was again
happy and pleasant. I was excited to see my friends and teachers.
Unlike the previous year, I was no longer a newcomer and a
novice, I wasn't surprised by everything, I didn't make stupid comments, I wrote better and more literary compositions, I was as
savvy as the Tehrani girls and I could express my opinions. And for
all that, I was grateful to Parvaneh who had been my first and best
teacher. That year, I also discovered the joy of reading books other
than my textbooks. We passed around romantic novels, read them
with many sighs and tears and spent hours discussing them.

Parvaneh made a beautiful opinions scrapbook. Her cousin who
had nice handwriting wrote the subject headings for each page and
Parvaneh pasted an appropriate picture next to them. All the girls
in class, her relatives and a few of her family friends wrote their
answers to each question. The comments in response to questions
such as what is your favourite colour or what is your favourite book
weren't all that interesting. But the answers to what is your opinion about love, have you ever been in love and what key
characteristics should an ideal spouse have, were fascinating. Some
people blatantly wrote whatever they wanted, without considering
what would happen if the scrapbook ended up in the school principal's hands.

I made a poetry scrapbook and I would write my favourite poems
in it in neat handwriting. Sometimes I drew a picture next to them
or pasted in one of the pictures Parvaneh cut out of foreign magazines for me.

One bright autumn afternoon when Parvaneh and I were walking
back from school, she asked me to go to the pharmacy with her so
that she could buy an adhesive bandage. The pharmacy was
midway between school and home. Dr Ataii, the pharmacist, was
a dignified old man whom everyone knew and respected. When we

15

walked in, there was no one behind the counter. Parvaneh called out to the doctor and stood on tiptoes to peer behind the counter. A young man wearing a white uniform was kneeling down, arranging the medicine boxes on the bottom shelves. He got up and asked, 'May I help you?'

Parvaneh said, 'I need an adhesive bandage.'

'Of course. I'll bring one right away.'

Parvaneh jabbed me in the side and whispered, 'Who is he? He's so handsome!'

The young man gave Parvaneh a bandage and as she kneeled down to take money out of her schoolbag she whispered, 'Hey! . . . Look at him. He's so good-looking.'

I looked up at the young man and for an instant our eyes met. A strange sensation ran through my body, I felt my face turn bright red, and I quickly looked down. It was the first time I had experienced such a strange feeling. I turned to Parvaneh and said, 'Come on, let's go.' And I rushed out of the pharmacy.

Parvaneh ran out after me and said, 'What's the matter with you? Haven't seen a human being before?'

'I was embarrassed,' I said.

'Of what?'

'Of the things you say about a man who's a stranger.'

'So what?'

'So what? It's really unseemly. I think he heard you.'

'No he didn't. He heard nothing. And, what exactly did I say that was so bad?'

'That he's handsome and . . .'

'Come on!' Parvaneh said. 'Even if he heard me, he was probably flattered. But between you and me, after I took a better look at him I realised he's not all that good-looking. I have to tell my father that Dr Ataii has hired an assistant.'

The next day we were a little late going to school. But as we hurried past the pharmacy, I saw the young man watching us. On our way back, we looked in through the window. He was busy working, but it seemed as if he could see us. From that day on, in keeping with an unspoken agreement, we saw each other every morning and every afternoon. And Parvaneh and I found a new and exciting subject to talk about. Soon, news of him spread through the school. The girls were all talking about the handsome young man who had started working at the pharmacy and they came up with all sorts of excuses to go there and somehow attract his attention.

Parvaneh and I got used to seeing him every day and I could swear that he, too, waited for us to walk by. We would argue about which actor he resembled the most and in the end decided that he looked like Steve McQueen. I had come a long way. By then, I knew the names of famous foreign actors. Once I forced Mother to go to the cinema with me. She really enjoyed it. From then on, once a week and unbeknownst to Mahmoud, we would go to the cinema at the corner. It mostly featured Indian films, which made Mother and me cry like rain from the clouds.

Parvaneh was quick to find information about the assistant pharmacist. Dr Ataii who was friends with her father had said, 'Saiid is a student of pharmacology at the university. He's a good kid. He's from Rezaieh.'

From then on, the looks we exchanged became more familiar and Parvaneh came up with a nickname for him – Haji Worrywart. She said, 'He looks like he's always waiting and worried, as if he's searching for someone.'

That year was the best year of my life. Everything was going my way. I was studying hard, my friendship with Parvaneh was growing stronger every day and we were gradually becoming one soul in two bodies. The only thing that darkened my bright and happy days was my horror of the whispers around the house that became more frequent as the end of the school year approached and which could put a stop to my education.

'It's impossible,' Parvaneh said. 'They would never do that to you.'

'You don't understand. They don't care whether I am doing well at school or not. They say anything beyond the first three years of secondary school doesn't do a girl any good.'

17

'The first three years?!' Parvaneh said, surprised. 'These days even a school diploma isn't enough any more. All the girls in my family are going to university. Of course, only the ones who passed the entrance exams. You will definitely pass. You're smarter than them.'

'Forget about university! I wish they would just let me finish secondary school.'

'Well, you have to stand up to them.'

The things Parvaneh said! She had no idea what my circumstances were. I could stand up to Mother, talk back to her and defend myself. But I didn't have the courage to be as outspoken in front of my brothers.

At the end of the last term we took our final exams and I became the second top student in my class. Our literature teacher really liked me and when we received our report cards she said, 'Well done! You're very talented. What field of study are you going to pursue?'

'My dream is to study literature,' I said.

'That's excellent. As a matter of fact, I was going to suggest it to you.'

'But ma'am, I can't. My family is against it. They say three years of secondary school is enough for a girl.'

Mrs Bahrami frowned, shook her head and walked into the administration office. A few minutes later she came out with the school principal. The principal took my report card and said, 'Sadeghi, tell your father to come to school tomorrow. I would like to see him. And tell him I won't give you your report card unless he comes. Don't forget!'

That night when I told Father that the school principal wanted to see him, he was surprised. He asked, 'What have you done?'

'I swear, nothing.'

Then he turned to Mother and said, 'Missus, go to the school and see what they want.'

'No, Father, that won't do,' I said. 'They want to see you.'

'What do you mean? I'm not going to walk into a girls' school!'

'Why? All the other fathers come. They said if you don't come, they won't give me my report card.'

18

He knotted his eyebrows in a deep frown. I poured tea for him and tried to endear myself a little. 'Father, do you have a headache? Do you want me to bring you your pills?' I tucked a floor cushion behind him and brought him a glass of water. In the end, he agreed to go to school with me the next day.

When we walked into the principal's office, she got up from behind her desk, greeted Father warmly and offered him a seat close to her. 'I congratulate you, your daughter is very special,' she said. 'Not only is she doing well in her classes, but she is very well mannered and pleasant.' Still standing at the door, I looked down and involuntarily smiled. The principal turned to me and said, 'My dear Massoumeh, please wait outside. I'd like to speak with Mr Sadeghi.'

I don't know what she said to him, but when Father walked out, his face was flushed, his eyes were twinkling and he was looking at me with kindness and pride. He said, 'Let's go to the supervisor's office right now and enrol you for next year. I don't have time to come back later.'

I was so happy I thought I would faint. Walking behind him, I kept saying, 'Thank you, Father. I love you. I promise to be the top student in class. I'll do whatever you ask. May God let me give my life for you.'

He laughed and said, 'Enough! I only wish your indolent brothers had a tiny bit of you in them.'

Parvaneh was waiting outside. She had been so worried she hadn't slept a wink the night before. With signs and gestures she asked, what happened? I put on a sad face, shook my head and shrugged. It was as if her tears were waiting behind her eyes, because all of a sudden they started to roll down her face. I ran over to her, took her in my arms and said, 'No! I lied. It's all right. I'm registered for next year.'

Out in the schoolyard, we were jumping up and down, laughing like lunatics and wiping away our tears.

Father's decision raised havoc at home. Still, he stood firm and said, 'The school principal said she is very talented and will

19

become someone important.' And I, delirious and giddy, didn't care what any of them said. Even Ahmad's hatred-filled leers didn't frighten me.

Summer came and although it meant that Parvaneh and I would again be apart, I was happy with the knowledge that the next school year would bring us together again. We spent only one week in Qum, and every week Parvaneh found some excuse to visit Tehran with her father and came to see me. She kept insisting that I go with them to Golab-Darreh for a few days. I really wanted to go, but I knew my brothers would never agree and so I didn't even bring up the subject. Parvaneh said that if her father spoke to my father, he could convince him to let me go. But I didn't want to create more headaches for Father. I knew saying no to Mr Ahmadi was difficult for him, as was having to deal with the fights and arguments at home. Instead, to gain Mother's favour, I agreed to take sewing classes, so that I would at least have one talent when I went to my husband's house.

Coincidentally, the sewing school was on the road next to the pharmacy. Saiid quickly caught on to my every-other-day schedule and, no matter how, he would make his way to the door on time. One block away from the pharmacy, my heart would start pounding and my breathing would become more rapid. I would try not to look towards the pharmacy and not to blush, but it was no use. Each time our eyes met, I turned red up to my ears. It was so embarrassing. And he, bashfully and with an eager look in his eyes, would greet me with a nod.

One day as I turned the corner, he suddenly appeared in front of me. I became so flustered that I dropped my sewing ruler. He bent down, picked it up and with his eyes cast down quietly said, 'I'm sorry I frightened you.'

I said, 'No,' grabbed the ruler from him and scurried away. For a long time, I wasn't myself. Every time I remembered that moment I would blush and feel a pleasant tremor in my heart. I don't know why, but I was sure he was experiencing the same feelings.

*

20

With the first autumn winds and the early days of September, our long wait came to an end and Parvaneh and I headed back to school. There was no end to all the things we wanted to tell each other. We had to share everything that had happened over the summer, everything we had done and even thought. But ultimately, all our conversations kept coming back to Saiid.

'Tell me the truth,' Parvaneh said. 'How many times did you go to the pharmacy while I was away?'

'I swear I never went there,' I said. 'I was too embarrassed.'

'Why? He has no clue what we think and talk about.'

'So you think!'

'No way. Has he said anything? How do you know?'

'No. I just think so.'

'Well, we can pretend we don't know anything and just do our own thing.'

But the truth was that something had changed. My meetings with Saiid had taken on a different tone and colour and felt more serious. In my heart, I felt a strong, though unspoken, bond with him and hiding it from Parvaneh wasn't easy. We had been going to school for only a week when she found her first excuse to go to the pharmacy and dragged me along with her. I felt so self-conscious. It was as if the entire city knew what was going on in my heart and they were all watching me. When Saiid saw us walk in, he just froze where he stood. Parvaneh asked him for aspirin a few times, but he couldn't hear her. Finally, Dr Ataii came over, said hello to Parvaneh and asked about her father. Then he turned to Saiid and said, 'Why are you just standing there looking dumbfounded? Give the young lady a box of aspirin.'

By the time we walked out, everything had been exposed. 'Did you see the way he was looking at you?' Parvaneh asked, surprised.

I said nothing. She turned and stared into my eyes.

'Why have you turned so pale? You look like you're about to faint!'

'Me? No! There's nothing wrong with me.'

But my voice was shaking. We walked in silence for a few minutes. Parvaneh was deep in thought.

21

'Parvaneh, what is it? Are you all right?'

Suddenly, she exploded like a firecracker and in a voice louder than usual she snapped, 'You are so mean. I am as stupid as you are cunning. Why didn't you tell me?'

'Tell you what? There was nothing to tell.'

'Right! You two have something going on. I would have to be blind not to see it. Tell me the truth; how far have you two gone?'

'How could you say such a thing?'

'Stop it! Stop playing the mouse. You are capable of anything. From that headscarf to now this love affair! Stupid me! And all this time I thought he kept popping up in front of us because of me. You're so sly. Now I understand why they say people from Qum are shrewd. You didn't even tell me, your best friend. I tell you everything. Especially something this important.'

There was a big lump in my throat. I grabbed her arm and pleaded, 'Please, swear that you won't tell anyone. Don't speak so loud on the street, it's not proper. Be quiet, people will hear. I swear on my father's life, I swear on the Quran, there is nothing going on.'

But like a flood gaining force, Parvaneh was getting angrier by the minute.

'You really are a traitor. And you write in my scrapbook that you don't think about such things, that the only thing that's important to you is studying, men are a no-no, they're bad, it's wrong to speak of such things, it's a sin . . .'

'I'm begging you, please stop. I swear on the Quran, there is nothing going on between us.'

We were near her house when I finally broke down and started to cry. My tears brought her back to her senses and like water snuffed out the flames of her anger. In a gentler voice, she said, 'Now why are you crying? And out on the street! I'm just upset because I don't understand why you kept it from me. I tell you everything.'

I swore that I had always been her best friend and that I never had and never would keep secrets from her.

*

Together, Parvaneh and I experienced all the stages of love. She was as excited as I was and kept asking, 'What do you feel now?' As soon as she saw me deep in thought, she would say, 'Tell me, what you are thinking about?' And I would talk about my fantasies, my anxieties, my excitement, my worries about the future and the fear of being forced to marry someone else. She would close her eyes and say, 'Oh, how poetic! So this is what falling in love is like. But I'm not as sensitive and emotional as you. Some of the things people in love do and say make me laugh. And I never blush. So how will I know when I'm in love?'

The beautiful and vibrant autumn days passed as quickly as the autumn winds. Saiid and I had still not exchanged a single word. But now, each time Parvaneh and I walked past the pharmacy, he would quietly murmur a hello and my heart would plunge in my chest like a ripe fruit dropping into a basket.

Every day, Parvaneh unearthed some new information about Saiid. I knew he was from Rezaieh, and his mother and sisters still lived there; he was from a well-respected family; his last name was Zareii; his father had passed away a few years ago; he was in the third year at university studying pharmacology; he was very smart and studious; and Dr Ataii trusted him implicitly and was pleased with his work. Every piece of information was a stamp of approval on my pure and innocent love. I felt as though I had known him all my life and that I would spend the rest of my existence with him alone.

Once or twice a week, Parvaneh would find some excuse to take me to the pharmacy. We would secretly exchange glances. His hands would shake and my cheeks would turn bright red. Parvaneh carefully monitored our every action. Once she said, 'I always wondered what eye-gazing was. Now I know!'

'Parvaneh! What sort of talk is that?'

'What? Am I lying?'

In the mornings, I took particular care doing my hair and I put on my headscarf in a way that my bangs would remain tidy and my long hair could be seen from the back. I tried desperately to put in a few ringlets, but my hair just wouldn't curl. And then one day Parvaneh said, 'You idiot! Your hair is beautiful. Straight hair is the latest fashion. Haven't you heard, the girls at school actually iron their hair to make it straight.'

I regularly washed and ironed my school uniform. I begged Mother to buy more fabric and have a seamstress make a new one for me – what Mother herself sewed was always dowdy and drab. The only thing I had learned in my sewing classes was to find fault with Mother's sewing. Mrs Parvin made a stylish uniform for me and I secretly asked her to shorten the skirt a little. Still, I had the longest uniform in school. I saved my money and Parvaneh and I went shopping. I bought a forest-green silk headscarf. Parvaneh said, 'It really suits you. It makes your eyes look greener.'

We had a cold winter that year. The snow on the streets had yet to melt when it would snow again. In the mornings, there was ice everywhere and we had to take care crossing the street. Every day someone would slip and fall and that day it was my turn. I was near Parvaneh's house when I lost my footing on a patch of ice and fell down hard. I tried to get up, but my ankle hurt terribly. The moment I put my foot on the ground, pain shot all the way up to my waist and I fell back down. Just then, Parvaneh walked out of her house and Ali who was on his way to school also showed up. They helped me get up and walked me back home. Mother bandaged my ankle, but by late afternoon both the pain and the swelling had got much worse. When the men returned home, they each offered an opinion. Ahmad said, 'Forget it ... there's nothing wrong with her. If she had stayed home like a decent girl and hadn't gone out in this blistering cold, this wouldn't have happened.' And he went off to drink.

Father said, 'Let's take her to the hospital.'

'Wait,' Mahmoud said, 'Mr Esmaiil is good at binding broken bones. He lives right at the turn of Shemiran. I'll go bring him. If he says she has broken her leg, then we'll take her to the hospital.'

Mr Esmaiil was about Father's age and famous for splinting fractured bones. That winter, his business was booming. He examined

24

my foot and said I hadn't broken any bones and that it was only a sprain. He put my foot in warm water and started to massage it. He kept talking to me and just as I was about to say something he suddenly twisted my foot. I screamed in pain and fainted. When I came to, he was rubbing my ankle with a concoction of egg yolk, turmeric and a thousand different oils. Then he bandaged it and cautioned me not to walk on it for two weeks.

What a catastrophe. I wept and said, 'But I have to go to school. The second term exams are starting soon.' I knew the exams were a month and a half away and that my tears were flowing for an entirely different reason.

For a few days I really couldn't move. I was sprawled out under the *korsi*, thinking about Saiid. In the mornings, when everyone was at school, I would fold my hands under my head and, with the feeble winter sun shining on my face, I would drown in my sweet fantasies and travel to the town of my dreams, to the blissful days of the future and to a life with Saiid . . .

The only bother in the morning was Mrs Parvin who would find any and all excuses to visit Mother. I really didn't like her and as soon as I heard her voice, I would pretend to be asleep. I don't know why Mother, who went on and on about faith and decency, had become friends with a woman who the entire neighbourhood knew didn't quite walk the straight and narrow, and she hadn't caught on that Mrs Parvin's pandering was all because of Ahmad.

In the afternoon when Faati and Ali came back from school, the calm and quiet of the house would vanish. Ali could singlehandedly wreak hell and havoc in an entire neighbourhood. He had become disobedient and cheeky. He was trying to follow in Ahmad's footsteps and was almost as harsh with me as Ahmad was, especially now that I wasn't going to school. Mother was taking care of me and Father was showing concern, which made Ali jealous. He acted as if I had cheated him out of his rights. He would leap over the *korsi*, harass Faati and make her scream, he would kick my books aside and intentionally or accidently hit my injured ankle and make me shriek in pain. One day, with much begging and crying, I managed to convince Mother to move my bedding upstairs to the living room so that I would be safe from Ali and could study a little.

'Why do you want to go up and down these stairs?' she argued. 'And it's cold upstairs, the large heater is broken.'

'The small heater is enough for me.'

In the end, she gave in and I moved upstairs. I was finally at peace. I studied, I daydreamed, I wrote in my poetry scrapbook, I went on long journeys in my fantasies, I wrote Saiid's name here and there in my notebook in the script I had invented. I found the root of his name in Arabic and I listed its inflectional paradigms – Sa'ad, Saiid, Sa'adat – and I used them in all the examples I had to provide in my homework.

One day Parvaneh came to visit me. While Mother was there, we talked about school and the exams that were due to start on 5 March, but as soon as she left, Parvaneh said, 'You have no idea what has been going on.'

I knew she had news of Saiid. I leaped halfway up and said, 'Tell me, please, how is he? Quick, tell me before someone walks in.'

'Lately, he's been Haji Worrywart. Every day, I saw him standing on the pharmacy steps, peering around, and as soon as he realised I was alone, his face would sag, and looking grief-stricken he would go back inside. Today he showed some courage and came forward. At first he turned red and white a few times, then stammered a hello and finally he said, "Your friend hasn't been going to school for a few days. I'm very worried. Is she well?" I was wicked. I played dumb and said, "Which friend are you referring to?" He looked at me with surprise and said, "The young lady who is always with you. Her house is on Golshan Street." So he even knows where you live! He's a sly one. He has probably followed us. I said, "Oh, you mean Massoumeh Sadeghi. The poor thing fell and sprained her ankle and she can't go to school for two weeks." He turned pale, said it was terrible, then just turned his back to me and walked away. I wanted to call to him and tell him he was very rude, but he had barely taken two steps when he realised how

26

impolite he had been. He turned around and said, "Please tell her I said hello." Then he said goodbye like a normal human being and left.'

My heart and my voice were trembling. 'Oh my God!' I said, panicked. 'You told him my name?'

'Don't be a ninny,' Parvaneh said, 'It's no big deal. To begin with, he already knew it, or at least he knew your last name. You can be sure he has even researched your ancestry. He's so in love. I think one of these days he's going to come and ask for your hand.'

I was delirious. I was so giddy that when Mother walked in with a tray of tea, she looked at me with surprise and said, 'What's going on? You're so chipper!'

'No!' I stammered. 'There's nothing going on.'

Parvaneh quickly jumped in and said, 'You see, today they returned our exam papers and Massoumeh got the highest grades.' And then she winked at me.

'What's the use, my girl? These things are not practical for a girl,' Mother said. 'She's wasting her time. Pretty soon she'll have to go to her husband's house and wash nappies.'

'No, Mother. I'm not going to a husband's house any time soon. For now, I have to get my school diploma.'

Parvaneh mischievously said, 'Yes, and then she'll become Mrs Doctor.'

I glowered at her.

'Oh really?' Mother quipped. 'She's going to continue studying? The more she goes to school the cheekier she gets. It's all her father's fault for doting on her, as if she's so special.'

And still grumbling, Mother walked out and Parvaneh and I burst out laughing.

'Thank God Mother didn't catch on, otherwise she would have said, since when do you become a doctor with a diploma in literature?'

Parvaneh, wiping away the tears of laughter rolling down her cheeks, said, 'My silly girl, I didn't say you are going to be a doctor, I said you will be the missus of a Mr Doctor.'

*

27

In those bright and blissful days, there was no need for a rational reason to laugh. I was so happy that I completely forgot the pain in my ankle. After Parvaneh left, I fell back on my pillow and thought to myself, He is worried, he misses me, I am so content. That day, even Ahmad's shouts as he scolded Mother for Parvaneh's visit didn't bother me. I knew Ali, the spy, had given him a full report, but I didn't care.

Every morning I woke up and while hopping on one leg I tidied up the room. Then, with one hand on the railing and the other holding Grandmother's cane, I slowly climbed down the stairs, washed my hands and face and ate breakfast. And again I laboured back up the stairs. Mother relentlessly complained that I was going to catch pneumonia or fall head first down the stairs, but who was listening? I made do with the small paraffin heater. I wouldn't exchange my privacy for the world and felt so warm inside that I didn't sense the cold at all.

Two days later, Parvaneh came to see me again. I heard her at the front door and quickly made my way to the window. Mother greeted her coldly, but Parvaneh ignored her tone and said, 'I have brought the exams schedule for Massoumeh.' And then she darted up the stairs, ran in, closed the door behind her and stood leaning against the door, gasping for air. Her face was flushed. I didn't know whether it was from the cold or from excitement. Without taking my eyes off her, I went back to bed. I didn't have the nerve to ask any questions.

Finally, she said, 'You're a clever one: lying here in bed and getting wretched me into trouble.'

'What happened?'

'Let me catch my breath. I ran like a madman all the way from the pharmacy.'

'Why? What's going on? Tell me!'

'I was walking with Maryam. When we reached the pharmacy, Saiid was standing at the door. He started nodding and gesturing with his head. And you know how sly Maryam is. She said, "Mr Handsome is motioning to you." I said, "No. What would he want with me?" I ignored him and kept walking. But he ran after us and

28

said, "Excuse me, Miss Ahmadi, would you please come inside for a minute, I need to speak with you." Your Haji Worrywart was as red as a beet. I was terribly nervous and didn't know what to do with that nosy Maryam. I said, "Oh yes, I forgot to pick up my father's medications. Are they ready?" But the idiot just stood there and stared at me. I didn't wait for him to answer. I quickly apologised to Maryam and told her that I had forgotten about my father's medications. I said goodbye and told her I would see her in school tomorrow. But little Miss Nosy wasn't about to give up on such an opportunity. She said she wasn't in a hurry and would come with me.

'The more I said it wasn't necessary the more suspicious she got. Then she said she had forgotten that she, too, had to buy a few things from the pharmacy and walked in with me. Fortunately, Haji Worrywart got wise to the situation. He put a box of medicine and an envelope in a bag, said he had included the prescription and that I should make sure to give it to my father. I quickly stuffed it in my schoolbag. I was afraid Maryam would snatch it from me. I swear, I wouldn't put it past her. You know what a snoop and a snitch she is. Especially now that everyone in school is talking about Saiid. Half the girls who walk this way think he stands outside to see them. Now wait and see what stories they'll make up about me tomorrow. Anyway, Maryam was still in the pharmacy, buying toothpaste, when I hurried out and ran over here.'

'That's awful!' I said. 'Now she's going to be even more suspicious.'

'Come on! She already knows something is going on, with that stupid Saiid putting the so-called prescription in a sealed envelope! Have you ever seen a pharmacist put a prescription in an envelope? And Maryam is no idiot. She was devouring the envelope with her eyes. That's why I got scared and ran off.'

For a few seconds, I lay there as still as a corpse. Everything was muddled in my head. But then I suddenly remembered the envelope and leaped up.

'Give me the letter!' I said. 'But first, check behind the door and make sure no one is there, then close it tight.'

My hands were shaking as I took the envelope from her. There

29

was nothing written on it. I didn't have the nerve to open it. What could he have written? Other than mumbling a hello, we had never spoken to each other. Parvaneh was as excited as I was. Just then, Mother walked in. I quickly slipped the envelope under the quilt and we both sat up straight and looked at her in silence.

'What's going on?' Mother asked, suspicious.

'Nothing!' I stammered.

But Mother's gaze was full of doubt. Once again Parvaneh jumped to my rescue.

'It's nothing,' she said. 'Your daughter is very sensitive. She just blows everything out of proportion.' Then she turned to me and said, 'So what if you didn't get a good grade in English. The hell with it. Your mother isn't like mine. She won't chide you for no good reason.' And looking at Mother, she said, 'Isn't that right, Mrs Sadeghi? Are you going to scold her?'

Mother looked at Parvaneh with surprise, curled the corners of her lips, and said, 'What can I say! So what if your grade isn't good. Actually, it would be better if you failed altogether. That way, you'll go back to the sewing classes, which are far more essential.' Then she put the tea tray in front of Parvaneh and walked out.

We looked at each other in silence for a few minutes and then burst out laughing. Parvaneh said, 'Girl, why are you so dense? The way you acted, anyone would know you're up to no good. Be careful or we'll be found out.'

I felt nauseous with excitement and anxiety. I carefully opened the white envelope, trying not to damage it in any way. My heart-beats sounded like a sledgehammer pounding on an anvil.

'Oh, come on!' Parvaneh said impatiently. 'Hurry up!'

I unfolded the letter. Lines in beautiful penmanship danced before my eyes. I was dizzy. We quickly read the letter, which was no more than a few sentences. Then we looked at each other and in unison asked, 'Did you read it? What did it say?' We read it again, this time more calmly. It started with this verse:

May your body never need the touch of a doctor,
May your delicate being never be harmed.

30

And then, greetings and inquiries about my health and wishes for a speedy recovery.

How polite, how beautiful. I could tell from his handwriting and composition that he was well read. Parvaneh didn't stay long because she hadn't told her mother she was coming to see me. I wasn't paying much attention to her anyway. I was in another world. I couldn't feel my physical presence. I was all spirit, flying in the air. I could even see myself lying there in bed with my eyes open, a big smile on my lips, pressing the letter to my chest. For the very first time, I regretted having often wished that I had died instead of Zari. How pleasant life was. I wanted to embrace the entire universe and kiss it.

The day passed in ecstasy and fantasy and I didn't notice the night go by. What did I eat for dinner? Who came over? What did we talk about? In the middle of the night, I turned on the light and read the letter over and over again. I held it to my chest and dreamed sweet dreams until morning. My instincts told me that this was an experience you have only once in your lifetime and only at the age of sixteen.

The next day, I was impatiently waiting for Parvaneh to come. I sat at the window, staring out at the front yard. Mother was going back and forth to the kitchen and she could see me. She gestured, 'What do you want?'

I opened the window and said, 'Nothing . . . I'm bored. I'm just looking out at the street.' A few minutes later I heard the doorbell. Grumbling, Mother opened the door. When she saw Parvaneh, she turned and gave me a meaningful look: so this is what you were waiting for.

Parvaneh ran up the stairs and tossed her schoolbag in the middle of the room while trying to use one foot to slip the shoe off her other foot.

'Oh come in . . . what are you doing?'

'Damn these lace-up shoes!'

Finally, she took her shoes off, came in and sat down. She said, 'Let me read the letter again. I forgot some parts of it.'

I handed her the book in which I had hidden the letter and said, 'Tell me about today ... Did you see him?'

She laughed and said, 'He saw me first. He was standing on the steps in front of the pharmacy and the way he was looking around, the entire city must have realised he was waiting for someone. When I reached him, he said hello without blushing. He asked, "How is she? Did you give her the letter?" I said, "Yes, she's well and says hello." He sighed with relief and said he was worried you were upset with him. Then he fidgeted a little and said, "She didn't write back?" I told him I didn't know, that I had just handed the letter to you and left. Now what are you going to do? He's waiting for a reply.'

'You mean I should write to him?' I asked nervously. 'No, it's improper. If I do, he will probably think I'm a really cheeky girl.'

Just then, Mother walked in and said, 'And you really are cheeky.'

My heart sank. I didn't know how much of our conversation she had overheard. I looked at Parvaneh. She, too, looked terrified. Mother put down the bowl of fruit she had brought for us and sat down.

'It's good that you have finally realised you are cheeky,' she said.

Parvaneh quickly collected herself and said, 'Oh no, this isn't being cheeky.'

'What isn't being cheeky?'

'You see, I told my mother that Massoumeh wants me to come visit her every day so that I can review the lessons with her. And Massoumeh was just saying that my mother will probably think she is really cheeky.'

Mother shook her head and looked at us warily. Then she slowly got up, walked out and closed the door behind her. I motioned to Parvaneh to keep quiet. I knew Mother was standing behind the door, eavesdropping. We started talking loudly about school and our classes and how far behind I was. And then Parvaneh started reading from our Arabic textbook. Mother really liked the Arabic language and assumed we were reading the Quran. A few minutes later, we heard her walk down the stairs.

'OK, she's gone,' Parvaneh said quietly. 'Be quick and decide what you want to do.'

'I don't know!'

'In the end, you either have to write to him or talk to him. You can't spend the rest of your lives signing and gesturing to each other. We have to at least find out what he has in mind. Is he thinking of marriage or not? Maybe he just wants to deceive us and lead us astray.'

It was interesting. Parvaneh and I were merging and now spoke in the plural.

'I can't,' I said nervously. 'I don't know what to write. You write.'

'Me? I don't know how. You are a lot better than me in composition and you know a lot of poems.'

'Write whatever comes to your mind. I'll do the same. Then we'll put them together and come up with a proper letter.'

Late that afternoon, I was jolted from my thoughts by Ahmad's shouts and hollers out in the yard. 'I hear that vulgar girl is coming over here every day. What's the meaning of this? Didn't I tell you that I don't like her and her airs and pretensions? Why is she constantly here? What does she want?'

'Nothing, my son,' Mother said. 'Why are you making yourself so upset? She just comes to give Massoumeh her homework and she leaves quickly.'

'The hell she does! If I see her here one more time, I'll throw her out with a kick in the ass.'

I wished I could get my hands on Ali and give him a good beating. The little twerp was spying on us and telling Ahmad. I told myself there was nothing Ahmad could do, but still I had to warn Parvaneh to be careful and to come over only when Ali wasn't at home.

I spent the entire day and night writing and crossing out. I had written things to him before, but always in my made-up script and it was all too emotional and familiar for a formal letter. The script was an invention rooted in need. First of all, there was no such thing as privacy and personal space in our house. I didn't even have a drawer all to myself. Second, I needed to write, I couldn't stop, I

33

had to put on paper my feelings and dreams. It was the only way I could organise my thoughts and understand exactly what I wanted.

And yet, I didn't know what to write to Saiid. I didn't even know how to address him in the letter. Dear sir? No, it was too formal. Dear friend? No, it wasn't proper. Should I use his first name? No, that would be too familiar. By Thursday afternoon when Parvaneh came to see me after school, I still hadn't written a single word. She was more excited than ever before and when Faati opened the door for her, she didn't even pat her on the head. She darted up the stairs, threw her bag on the floor, sat right there at the door and started talking while trying to pull off her shoes.

'I was walking back from school just now and he called me and said, "Miss Ahmadi, your father's medication is ready." My poor father, who knows what disease he has that requires so much medicine. Thank God, that nosy Maryam wasn't with me. I went in and he gave me a package. Hurry up and open my bag. It's right there on top.'

My heart was beating out of my chest. I sat on the floor and quickly opened her bag. There was a small package wrapped in white paper. I tore it open. It was a pocket-size book of poetry with an envelope sticking out of it. I was drenched in sweat. I took the letter and leaned against the wall. I felt faint. Parvaneh, who had finally got rid of her shoes, crawled over to me and said, 'Don't swoon now! Read it first, then pass out.'

Just then Faati walked in, clung to me and said, 'Mother wants to know whether Miss Parvaneh would like some tea.'

'No! No!' Parvaneh said. 'Thank you so much. I have to leave soon.'

Then she pulled Faati away from me and kissed her on the cheeks. 'Go now and thank your mother for me. That's a good girl.'

But Faati again came over and clung to me. I realised she had been told not leave us alone. Parvaneh took a piece of candy out of her pocket, gave it to Faati and said, 'Be a good girl and go tell your mother I don't want any tea. Otherwise, she will climb up the stairs and it's bad for her. Her legs will start to ache.'

As soon as Faati left, Parvaneh snatched the letter from me and while saying, 'Hurry up before someone else shows up,' she opened the envelope and started to read.

'Respectable young lady.'

We looked at each other and burst into laughter. 'Oh how funny!' Parvaneh exclaimed. 'Who writes "respectable young lady"?'

'Well, he probably didn't want to be too familiar in his first letters and call me "Miss". To be honest, I have the same dilemma. I don't know how to start my letter.'

'Forget that for now. Read the rest.'

I have yet to allow myself to write your name on paper, although I shout it in my heart a thousand times a day. No name has ever been so becoming and befitting a face. The innocence in your eyes and on your face is so pleasing to the eye. I am addicted to seeing you every day. So much so that when I am deprived of this blessing, I find myself at a loss for what to do with my life.

My heart
Is a mirror hazy with sorrow
Cleanse the dust off this mirror
With your smile.

Not seeing you these days, I am someone lost and adrift. In this solitude, remember me with a word or a message so that I can again find myself. With all my being, I pray that you regain your health. For the love of God, take care of yourself.
Saiid.

Parvaneh and I, dizzy and intoxicated by the beauty of the letter, were deep in fantasy when Ali walked in. I quickly slipped the book and the letter under my legs. With a belligerent look and a bristly tone he said, 'Mother wants to know if Miss Parvaneh is staying for lunch.'

'Oh, no, thank you very much,' Parvaneh said. 'I'm leaving.'

'Very well,' Ali grumbled. 'But we want to eat now.' And he walked out.

I was angry and embarrassed and didn't know what to say to Parvaneh. She had noticed my family's cold attitude towards her and said, 'I've been coming over too often. I think they've had enough of me. When are you coming back to school? You've been in bed for ten days. Isn't that enough?'

'I'm going crazy. I'm tired and bored. I'll probably come back on Saturday.'

'Can you? Is it all right?'

'I'm feeling much better. I will exercise my ankle until Saturday.'

'Then we'll be free. I swear I can't look your mother in the eyes any more. I'll pick you up at exactly seven-thirty on Saturday morning.'

She kissed me on the cheeks and ran down the stairs without bothering to tie her shoelaces. Out in the front yard, I heard her say to Mother, 'I'm so sorry, but I had to come today. You see, we have a test on Saturday and I had to let Massoumeh know so that she can prepare for it. Thank God, it seems her ankle is much better. I'll pick her up on Saturday and we'll slowly walk to school.'

'That won't be necessary,' Mother said. 'Her ankle hasn't healed yet.'

'But we have a test!' Parvaneh insisted.

'So you do. It's not all that important. And Ali tells me there's still a month left until school exams start.'

I opened the window and shouted, 'No, Mother. I definitely have to go. It's a preparatory exam. Its grade gets added to the grade we get on the actual exam.'

Mother angrily turned her back to me and went to the kitchen. Parvaneh glanced up at me, winked and left.

I immediately started exercising my ankle. The instant I felt pain, I would lie down and put my foot up on a pillow. Instead of massaging my ankle with one egg yolk, I used two, and I doubled the amount of the oils. And in between all this, I grasped every opportunity to read the letter that was now my dearest and most valuable possession.

36

I kept asking myself, why is his heart a mirror hazy with sorrow? He must have a difficult life. Obviously, working, supporting his mother and three sisters, and studying is a heavy burden. Perhaps if he didn't have all these responsibilities and if his father was still alive, he would come and ask for my hand right now. The doctor said they are a reputable family. I'm even willing to live with him in a dank room. But why did he write that my name suits my face and my character? Wasn't my accepting his letters proof that I was not innocent? Would I have fallen in love if I were truly innocent? But I couldn't help it. I tried not to think of him, not to have my heart beat so fast when I saw him, not to blush, but I couldn't control any of it.

On Saturday morning I woke up earlier than usual. In truth, I hardly slept all night. I got dressed and made my bed to prove to everyone that I was no longer ailing. I put aside Grandmother's cane, which had served me well, held onto the banister, climbed down the stairs and sat at the breakfast spread.

'Are you sure you can go to school?' Father asked. 'Why don't you let Mahmoud take you there on his motorcycle?'

Mahmoud gave Father a harsh look and said, 'Father, what are you saying? All we were missing was for her to ride without hijab behind a man on a motorcycle!'

'But son, she'll be wearing her headscarf. Won't she?'

'Of course,' I said. 'When have I ever gone to school without a headscarf?'

'And you are her brother, not a stranger,' Father added.

'God have mercy! Father, it seems Tehran has led you astray, too!'

I interrupted Mahmoud and said, 'Don't worry, Father. Parvaneh is picking me up. She'll help me and we'll walk to school together.'

Mother mumbled something under her breath. And Ahmad, his eyes puffy from the previous night's drinking, with his usual anger barked, 'Ha! Parvaneh, of all people. I tell you not to hang out with her and you make her your walking stick?'

'Why? What's wrong with her?'

37

'What's not wrong with her?' he sneered. 'She's vulgar, constantly laughing and giggling, her skirt is too short, and she swings her hips when she walks.'

I turned red and snapped back, 'Her skirt isn't short at all. It's longer than everyone else's in school. She's an athlete and not one of those girls who strut and sashay. And what's more, how do you know she wiggles her hips when she walks? Why are you looking at another man's daughter?'

'Shut up or I'll hit you so hard in the mouth that your teeth will fall out! Mother, do you see how impudent she's become?'

'Enough!' Father roared. 'I know Mr Ahmadi. He is a very respectable and educated man. Uncle Abbas asked him to mediate when he got into an argument with Abol-Ghassem Solati over the store next door. No one goes against what Mr Ahmadi says. Everyone trusts his word.'

Ahmad, who had turned bright red, turned to Mother and said, 'Here you are! And then you wonder why the girl has become so impudent. Why shouldn't she be impudent when everyone always takes her side?' Then he turned to me and growled, 'Go, go with her, sister. As a matter of fact, the girl is decency personified. Go learn respectability from her.'

As luck would have it, just then the doorbell rang. I turned to Faati and said, 'Tell her I'll be right there.' And to bring the argument to an end, I put on my headscarf as quickly as I could, said a hasty goodbye and limped out.

Out on the street, I felt the cold wind on my face and stood for a few seconds to enjoy the fresh air. It smelled of youth, love and happiness. I leaned on Parvaneh. My ankle still hurt, but I didn't care. I tried to curb my excitement and slowly and quietly we set off for school. From a distance, I saw Saiid standing on the second step in front of the pharmacy, peering down the street. When he saw us, he leaped down the steps and came to greet us. I bit my lip and, realising he shouldn't have done that, he went back and stood on the steps. His eager eyes became sad when he saw my bandaged foot and my limp. My heart wanted to flutter out of my chest and go to him. I felt as if I hadn't seen him in years, but I felt closer to

38

him than I had when we last saw each other. Now, I knew him, I knew what his feelings were for me, and I loved him more than ever before.

When we reached the pharmacy, Parvaneh turned to me and said, 'You must be tired. Let's stop for a second.'

I put my hand on the wall and discreetly returned Saiid's hello. 'Does your ankle hurt a lot?' he quietly asked. 'Would you like me to give you a painkiller?'

'Thank you. It's much better.'

'Be careful,' Parvaneh whispered nervously. 'Your brother Ali is coming.'

We quickly said goodbye and continued on our way.

That day we had one hour of physical education, which Parvaneh and I skipped along with another class. We had so much to talk about. When the assistant principal came out into the schoolyard, we ran and hid in the toilets and then we went and sat behind the school's concessions stand. Under the feeble February sun, we read Saiid's letter two or three more times. We praised his gentleness, compassion, civility, penmanship, prose and erudition.

'Parvaneh, I think I have heart disease,' I said.

'Why do you think that?'

'Because my heart doesn't beat normally. I constantly have palpitations.'

'When you see him or when you don't?'

'When I see him my heart beats so fast that I start panting.'

'It isn't heart disease, my dear,' she said laughing. 'It's love disease. If I, a nobody, feel my heart suddenly sink and beat wildly when he pops up in front of me, I can only imagine what you must be feeling.'

'Do you think I will still feel this way when we are married?'

'Silly! If you feel this way after you are married, then you should certainly see a cardiologist, because it will definitely be heart disease.'

'Oh! I have to wait at least two years until he finishes university. Of course, it's not so bad. By then I will have my diploma.'

'But he has two years of military service, too,' Parvaneh said. 'Unless he has already served it.'

'No, I don't think so. How old is he? He may not have to serve. He is the only son, his father has passed away, and he supports the family.'

'Maybe. But still, he will have to find a job. Do you think he could manage the expenses of two households? How much do pharmacists earn?'

'I don't know. But if I have to, I'll go and live with his mother and sisters.'

'You mean you're willing to move to the provinces and live with your mother-in-law and sisters-in-law?'

'Of course I'm willing. I would live in hell with him if I have to. And Rezaieh is a nice city. They say it's clean and pretty.'

'It's better than Tehran?'

'At least it has a better climate than Qum. Have you forgotten that I grew up there?'

What sweet fantasies. Like all romantic sixteen-year-old girls, I was willing to go anywhere and do anything for Saiid.

Parvaneh and I spent much of that day reading the replies we had written to his letters. We reviewed our drafts and tried to come up with a proper letter. But my fingers were freezing and writing with the paper resting on my schoolbag made my handwriting atrocious. In the end, we decided that I should rewrite the letter that night at home and we would give it to Saiid the next day.

That winter day was one of the most pleasant days of my life. I felt I had the world in the palm of my hand. I had everything. A good friend, true love, youth, beauty and a bright future. I was so happy that I even enjoyed the pain in my ankle. After all, if I had not sprained my ankle, I would not have received those beautiful letters.

By late afternoon, the sky became cloudy and it started to snow. Having sat outside in the cold for several hours, my ankle was now throbbing and I had difficulty walking. On the way back home, much of my weight was on Parvaneh's shoulder and every few steps we had to stop and catch our breath. Finally, we arrived in front of the pharmacy. Saiid, seeing the situation I was in, ran out, held me under the arm and led me inside. The pharmacy was warm and bright and through the tall misty windows the street looked dreary and cold. Dr Ataii was busy helping the customers who had lined up in front of the counter. He was calling them one by one and discussing their medications with them. Everyone's attention was on him and no one was looking at us sitting on the couch in the corner.

Saiid kneeled down in front of me, raised my foot and put it up on the low table in front of the couch. He carefully felt my bandaged ankle. Even through all that dressing, the touch of his hand made me shudder as if I had touched a live wire. It was strange. He was trembling, too. He looked at me kindly and said, 'It's still very inflamed. You shouldn't have walked on it. I have set aside some ointment and pain medication for you.'

He got up and went behind the counter. I followed him with my eyes. He returned with a glass of water and a pill. I took the pill and as I returned the glass to him he held out another envelope towards me. Our eyes met. Everything we wanted to say was reflected in them. There was no need for words. I forgot my pain. I saw no one but him. Everyone around us had faded in a fog; their voices were muted and incomprehensible. I was deliriously floating in another world when suddenly Parvaneh jabbed me with her elbow.

'What? What happened?' I asked, confused.

'Look over there!' she said. 'Over there!'

And raising her eyebrows, she nodded towards the pharmacy window. I automatically sat up straight and my heart started to pound. Ali was standing outside, peering through the window with his face up close to the glass and his hands shielding his eyes.

Parvaneh turned to me and said, 'What's the matter? Why are you suddenly as yellow as turmeric?' Then she got up, walked outside and called out, 'Ali, Ali, come, come help me. Massoumeh's ankle is in a bad way and she's in a lot of pain. I can't take her home by myself.' Ali leered at her and ran off. Parvaneh came back inside and said, 'Did you see the look he gave me? He wanted to cut my head off!'

*

41

By the time we made our way home, the sun was setting and it was almost dark. Before I had a chance to ring the doorbell, the door flew open and a hand grabbed me and pulled me in. Parvaneh didn't realise what was happening and tried to follow me. But Mother pounced on her, shoved her back into the street and screamed, 'I don't ever want to see you around here again. Everything we're suffering is because of you!' And she slammed the door shut.

I tumbled down the steps and landed in the middle of the yard. Ali clawed at my hair and dragged me into the house. All I could think of was Parvaneh. I felt so humiliated. I screamed, 'Let go of me, you idiot!'

Mother walked in and while cursing and cussing me she pinched my arm really hard.

'What is the matter?' I cried. 'What has happened? Have you all gone crazy?'

'What do you think has happened, you tramp!' Mother screamed. 'Now you flirt with a stranger right there in public?'

'Which stranger? My ankle ached; the doctor at the pharmacy examined it and gave me some medicine. That's it! I was dying of pain. And besides, in Islam a doctor is not considered a stranger.'

'A doctor! A doctor! Since when is the lackey at a store a doctor? Do you think I'm stupid and don't know that you've been up to something lately?'

'For the love of God, Mother, it's not true.'

Ali kicked me, and with the veins in his neck bulging, he growled hoarsely, 'Yeah, right! I've been following you every day. The lout stands at the door and keeps looking out, waiting for you ladies to show up. All my friends know. They say, "Your sister and her friend are with this guy."'

Mother slapped herself on the head and wailed, 'I pray to God that I see you on the slab in a morgue. Look what shame and dishonour you've brought us. What am I supposed to tell your father and brothers?' And she pinched my arm again.

Just then, the door flew open and Ahmad walked in, glowering at me with bloodshot eyes, his hands knotted in a fist. He had heard everything.

'So you finally did it?' he snarled. 'Here you are, Mother. She's all yours. I knew from the start that if she set foot in Tehran and got gussied up every day and went around the streets with that girl, in the end she'd bring us nothing but shame. Now how are you going to hold your head up in front of friends and neighbours?'

'What have I done wrong?' I screamed. 'I swear on Father's life, I was about to fall on the street, they took me into the pharmacy and gave me a painkiller.'

Mother looked at my foot. It was so swollen it looked like a pillow. She barely touched it and I hollered in pain.

'Don't bother with her,' Ahmad snapped. 'With all the scandal she's created, you still want to pamper her?'

'Scandal? Is it I who have caused a scandal or is it you, coming home drunk every night and carrying on with a married woman?'

Ahmad lunged at me and struck me in the mouth with the back of his hand so hard that my mouth filled with blood. I went crazy. I screamed, 'Am I lying? I saw you with my own eyes. Her husband wasn't home and you snuck into their house. And it wasn't the first time either.' Another blow landed under my eye and made me dizzy. For an instant I thought I had gone blind.

Mother screamed, 'Shut up, girl! Have some shame.'

'Just wait until I tell her husband,' I shouted.

Mother ran over and covered my mouth with her hand. 'Didn't I tell you to shut up?'

I pulled away from her and, filled with rage, I yelled, 'Can't you tell that he comes home drunk every night? Twice the police have taken him to the station because he pulled a knife on someone. These aren't scandals, but if I take a pill at the pharmacy I've brought you shame!'

Two consecutive slaps made my ears ring, but I couldn't control myself, I couldn't quieten down.

'Shut up. May God strike you with diphtheria. The difference is that you're a girl!' Mother burst into tears, held her arms up to the sky and pleaded, 'O God, save me! To whom can I turn? Girl, I pray you suffer. I pray you get torn into pieces.'

I was slumped on the floor in the corner of the room. I felt

43

utterly despondent and tears were welling in my eyes. Ali and Ahmad were out in the front yard, whispering together. Mother's tearful voice interrupted them. 'Ali, that's enough. Shut up.'

But Ali was not finished reporting to Ahmad. I wondered how he had gathered so much information.

Again, Mother barked, 'Ali, I said that's enough! Run out and buy some bread.' And finally, with a smack on the head she ushered him out.

I heard Father's greeting as he walked into the front yard and Mother's usual response.

'Oh! You're home early, Agha Mostafa . . .'

'No one goes shopping in this cold, so I decided to close early,' Father replied. 'What's the matter? You look nervous. I see Ahmad's home, too. How about Mahmoud?'

'No, Mahmoud hasn't come home yet. That's why I'm worried. He always comes home before you do.'

'He didn't take his motorcycle today,' Father said. 'Traffic is bad and he probably can't find a taxi. There's snow and ice everywhere. It seems winter doesn't want to end this year . . . So I see the Armenian closed his place early, too, and somebody decided to come home.'

Father rarely spoke to Ahmad and when he made snide remarks about him it was always as an indirect insinuation.

Sitting on the edge of the reflecting pool, Ahmad retorted, 'As a matter of fact, he didn't close early. But I'm not going out until I know where I stand with all of you.'

Father held on to the door frame and started taking off his shoes. The light from the hallway only partially lit the room. I was on the floor, next to the *korsi*, and he couldn't see me. He quipped, 'So! Instead of us figuring out where we stand with the gentleman, the gentleman wants to determine where he stands with us.'

'Not with you, with that nefarious daughter of yours.'

Father's face turned as white as chalk.

'Watch your mouth,' he warned. 'Your sister's honour is your honour. Have some shame.'

'Forget it! She's made sure we have no honour left. Pull your

44

head out of the snow, Father, and stop hounding me. Your big tub of shame has tumbled to the ground. Everyone in the neighbourhood heard it fall, except for you who have stuffed cotton wool in your ears and don't want to hear.'

Father was visibly shaking. Terrified, Mother pleaded, 'Ahmad, my dear. Ahmad! May God let me sacrifice my life for you, may all that ails and troubles you be inflicted on me, don't say such things. Your father will drop dead. Nothing has happened. Her ankle hurt and they gave her a pill.'

Having regained his composure, Father said, 'Leave him alone. Let me hear what he has to say.'

'Why don't you ask your pampered daughter?' Ahmad said, pointing to the room, and Father's eyes turned searchingly towards me. He couldn't see properly and he reached out and turned on the light. I don't know how I looked, but he suddenly sounded terrified.

'Dear God! What have they done to you?' he gasped as he rushed over and helped me sit up. Then he took his handkerchief from his pocket and wiped the blood from the corners of my mouth. His handkerchief had the cool scent of rosewater.

'Who did this to you?' he asked.

My tears started to flow faster.

'You vile scoundrel, you raised your hand to a woman?' he shouted at Ahmad.

'Here you go,' Ahmad retorted. 'So now I'm the guilty one! Forget about chastity and virtue. We have none. So what if she ends up in the hands of anyone and everyone. From now on, I have to wear a cad's hat.'

I didn't know at what point Mahmoud had arrived home. But just then, I saw him standing midway between the house and the yard, looking confused. Mother intervened and while draping her chador over her shoulders she said, 'That's enough! Now say praise to the Prophet and his descendants. I want to serve dinner. You, stand aside. And you, take this tablecloth and spread it on the floor over there. Faati? Faati? Where are you, you imp?'

Faati had been there the entire time, but no one had noticed her. She emerged from the shadows behind the stack of bedding in the corner of the room and ran to the kitchen. A few minutes later, she walked back carrying the dinner plates and gently put them on top of the *korsi*.

Father finished examining the cut on the side of my mouth, my bruised eye and bloody nose, and asked, 'Who did this to you? Ahmad? Damn him.' Then he turned towards the yard and shouted, 'You lout, am I dead for you to now treat my wife and child like this? Even Shemr who slayed Imam Hossein in Kerbela didn't do this to wives and daughters.'

'Well! Well! So now the lady is all pure and holy and I'm worse than Shemr. Father, your daughter has left you no honour. You may not care, but I do. I still have a reputation among people. Wait until Ali comes back. Ask him what he saw. The lady flirting with the pharmacy lackey for the world to see!'

'Father! Father, I swear to God he's lying,' I pleaded. 'I swear on your life, I swear on Grandmother's grave, my ankle hurt, it was as bad as it was on the first day, I was about to collapse in the street, Parvaneh dragged me to the pharmacy. They put my foot up and gave me a painkiller. Besides, Ali was there, too, but when Parvaneh called him to come and help, he ran off. And then the minute I got home they all attacked me.'

I started to weep. Mother was in the room arranging the dinner plates. Mahmoud was leaning on the shelf above me and observing the commotion with uncharacteristic calm. Ahmad ran inside, stood in the doorway, grabbed hold of the door frame and yelled wildly, 'Say it, say it! The guy put your leg on the table and touched and fondled you. Say that you were laughing the entire time. Flirting. Say that he waits for you on the street every day and says hello to you, plays up to you . . .'

Mahmoud's temper changed. His face flushed and he mumbled something. All I heard was, 'May God have mercy.' Father turned and looked at me questioningly.

'Father, Father, I swear on this blessing' – Ali had just walked in with freshly baked bread and its scent had filled the room – 'he is lying, he is badmouthing me because I found out that he sneaks over to Mrs Parvin's house.'

46

Again Ahmad lunged towards me, but Father shielded me with his arm and warned, 'Don't you raise your hand to her! The things you said can't be true. Her principal told me there is no girl as decent and as innocent as Massoumeh in their school.'

'Yeah!' Ahmad sneered. 'Their school must be a chastity house.'

'Shut up! Watch your mouth.'

'Father, he is right,' Ali said. 'I saw it myself. The guy put her leg up on the table and massaged it.'

'No, Father. I swear. He only held my shoe, and my ankle is so heavily bandaged that no one's hand could possibly touch it. Besides, a doctor isn't considered a stranger. Isn't that right, Father? He just asked me, "Where does it hurt?"'

'Just!' Ahmad said. 'And, of course, we believe you. Look how a scrawny, forty-kilo piece of bird dropping is twirling us on her fingertips. You may fool Father, but I'm shrewder than you think.'

'Shut up, Ahmad, or I will give you a good wallop in the mouth,' Father said.

'Come on! What are you waiting for? All you know how to do is beat us. Ali, why have you kept quiet? Tell them what you told me.'

'I've seen the lackey at the pharmacy stand outside and wait for them every day,' Ali reported. 'And as soon as they come, he says hello and they answer him. And then they whisper and giggle together.'

'He's lying. I haven't been to school in ten days. Why are you making up these lies? Yes, whenever he sees Parvaneh, he says hello to her. He knows her father and prepares his medications and gives them to her.'

'May that girl's grave burn in flames,' Mother said, beating her chest. 'This is all her doing.'

'Then why do you let her in the house?' Ahmad snapped. 'Didn't I tell you not to?'

'What can I do?' Mother said. 'She comes over and they sit and read their books together.'

Ali pulled Ahmad's arm and whispered something in his ear.

'Why are you whispering?' Father asked. 'Say it out loud for everyone to hear.'

47

'They're not reading books, Mother,' Ali said. 'They're reading something else. The other day, I walked in on them and they quickly hid some papers under their legs. They think they're dealing with a child!'

'Go, go and look through her books and see if you can find them,' Ahmad said.

'I looked for them before she came home. They weren't there.'

My heart was beating furiously. What if they found my schoolbag? Everything would be lost. I cautiously turned my eyes and looked around the room. My schoolbag was on the floor behind me. Slowly, carefully, I pushed it under the blanket draped over the *korsi*. Mahmoud's cold voice broke the few seconds of silence.

'Whatever it is, it's in her schoolbag. She just slipped it under the blanket.'

I felt as though a bucket of ice water had poured over my head. I couldn't speak. Ali dove down, pulled the bag out and emptied it out on top of the *korsi*. There was nothing I could do. I felt dizzy and paralysed. He violently shook the books and the letters fell out on the floor. With one leap, Ahmad picked them up and quickly unfolded one. He looked elated. He looked as if he had just received the greatest award in the world.

His voice shaking with excitement, he said, 'Here you are, here you are, Father. Listen and enjoy.'

And he started to read in a mocking tone.

'Respectable young lady, I have yet to allow myself ...'

I was writhing with humiliation, fear and anger. The world was whirling around my head. Ahmad wasn't able to read some parts of the letter. He was halfway through when Mother asked, 'What does that mean, son?'

'It means when he lovingly looks into her eyes ... she is pure and innocent. Right!'

'May God take my life!' Mother gasped.

'Now listen to this. "My heart is I-don't-know-what with sorrow, with your smile ..." You shameless hussy! I'll show him a smile he'll never forget.'

'Look, look, here's another one,' Ali said. 'It's her reply.'

48

Ahmad snatched the letter from him.

'Wonderful! The lady has written back.'

Mahmoud, red in the face and with veins bulging on his neck, yelled, 'Didn't I tell you? Didn't I tell you? A girl who fixes herself up and goes wandering around the streets in a city filled with wolves isn't going to stay pure and untouched. I kept telling you to marry her off, but you said, no, she has to go to school. Yeah, to go to school to learn how to write love letters.'

I had no defence. I had no weapon left. I surrendered. I looked at Father with dread and anxiety. His lips were quivering and he looked so pale that I thought he was about to collapse. He turned his dark, dazed eyes towards me. Contrary to my expectation, there was no anger in them. Instead, I saw profound sorrow rippling in the gleam of an unshed tear. 'Is this how you pay me back?' he muttered. 'You really kept your promise. You really kept my honour.'

That look and those words were more painful than all the beating I had received and they pierced my heart like a dagger. Tears flowed down my cheeks and in a shaky voice I said, 'But I swear, I didn't do anything wrong.'

Father turned his back to me and said, 'That's enough. Shut up!'

And he walked out of the house without his coat. I understood what his walking out meant. He had withdrawn all his support and left me in the hands of the others.

Ahmad was still leafing through the letters. I knew he couldn't read well and Saiid had written in cursive script, which made it all the more difficult. But he acted as if he understood everything and was trying to hide his delight behind a mask of anger. A few minutes later, he turned to Mahmoud and said, 'Now what are we going to do about this scandal? The bastard thinks we're spineless curs. Wait, I'll teach him a lesson he'll never forget. I won't stop until I spill his blood. Run, Ali. Go fetch my knife. His blood is my right, isn't that so, Mahmoud? He has had designs on our sister. Here's proof and evidence. In his own handwriting. Hurry up, Ali. It's in the closet upstairs . . .'

'No, leave him alone!' I screamed in horror. 'He hasn't done anything wrong.'

Ahmad laughed and with a calm I had not seen in him in a long time he turned to Mother and said, 'Mother, do you see, do you see how she is defending her lover? Her blood, too, is my right. Isn't that so, Mahmoud?'

With her eyes brimming with tears, Mother beat her chest and cried, 'God, see what ruin has befallen me? Girl, may God make you suffer. What shamelessness was this? I wish you had died instead of Zari. Look at what you've done to me.'

Ali came running downstairs with the knife. Ahmad nonchalantly got up, as if he was going to run a simple errand. He straightened his trousers, took the knife and held it in front of me.

'What part of him do you want me to bring back for you?'

And he let out a hideous laugh.

'No! No!' I screamed. I threw myself at his feet, wrapped my arms around his legs and begged, 'For the love of God, swear on Mother's life that you won't hurt him.'

Dragging me along, he headed towards the door.

'I beg you, please don't. I did wrong. I repent . . .'

Ahmad was looking at me with savage pleasure. When he reached the front door, he hissed a crude vulgarity, yanked his leg and freed himself from my grip. Ali who had followed us kicked me hard and hurled me down the front door steps.

As he walked out, Ahmad yelled, 'I'll bring you his liver.' And he slammed the door shut behind him.

My ribs had broken. I couldn't breathe. But the real pain was in my heart. I was scared to death of how Ahmad was going to confront Saiid and what he would do to him. I was sitting on the ice and snow next to the reflecting pool and weeping. I was trembling from head to toe, but I couldn't feel the cold. Mother told Mahmoud to bring me into the house and avoid even greater disgrace. But Mahmoud didn't want to touch me. In his eyes, I was now tainted and unclean. In the end, he grabbed me by my clothes and with astonishing rage yanked me away from the pool, dragged me into the house and threw me into the room. My head hit the edge of the door and I felt the warmth of blood on my face.

Mother said, 'Mahmoud, go after Ahmad and make sure he doesn't get himself into trouble.'

'Don't worry, that guy deserves whatever Ahmad does to him. As a matter of fact, we should kill this one, too.'

Still, he went out and quiet was restored in the house. Mother was mumbling to herself and crying. I couldn't stop sobbing. Faati was standing in a corner, biting her nails and staring at me. I was in a strange state of stupor and had no notion of the passage of time. At some point, the sound of the front door brought me back to my senses and I leaped up in fright. Cackling vulgarly, Ahmad walked in and held the bloody knife in front of my eyes. 'Here, look at it carefully. It's your lover's blood.'

The room started spinning around me, Ahmad's face became distorted, and a black curtain came down over my eyes. I was falling down a deep well. The sounds around me turned into a vague, protracted cacophony. I plunged deeper and deeper with no hope of stopping.

Zari was dying. Her face had a strange colour. She was breathing with difficulty, rasping. Her chest and stomach were heaving rapidly. I was biting my nails and watching her from behind the pile of bedding. The sound of voices coming from the front yard intensified my horror.

'Agha Mostafa, I swear she's in a bad way. Go bring a doctor.'

'Enough! Enough! Don't get hysterical. You're upsetting my son. Nothing is going to happen to her. I'm waiting for the decoction to brew. If I give it to her now, she'll be well by the time you come back. Go, don't just stand there ... go, my dear. Rest assured, the girl won't die.'

Zari was holding my hand. We were running through a dark tunnel. Ahmad was chasing us. He had a knife. With every step he took, he came a few metres closer. It was as if he was flying. We were screaming, but it was Ahmad's laughter and voice that echoed in the tunnel.

'Blood. Blood. Look, it's blood.'

Grandmother was trying to make Zari drink the decoction. Mother

51

was holding her head on her lap and squeezing the sides of her mouth with her fingers. Zari was weak and not struggling at all. Grandmother spooned the liquid into her mouth, but it wouldn't go down her throat. Mother blew on her face. Zari stopped breathing, moved her arms and legs, and then breathed again with a strange sound.

Mother cried, 'Mrs Azra said we have to take her to the doctor near the shrine.'

'The hell she did!' Grandmother said. 'Get up and go cook dinner. Your husband and sons will be home any minute.'

Grandmother was hovering over Zari and reciting prayers. Zari's face had turned dark and odd sounds were coming from her throat. Then Grandmother suddenly ran into the yard and screamed, 'Tayebeh, Tayebeh, run and fetch the doctor!'

I took Zari's hand and stroked her hair. Her face was almost black. She opened her eyes. They looked so large and scary. The whites were filled with blood. She squeezed my hand. Then she raised her head from the pillow and it fell back down. I pulled my hand out of hers and ran and hid behind the stack of quilts and pillows. Her arms and legs were moving. I covered my ears with my hands and pressed my face into a pillow.

Out in the yard, Grandmother was twirling the charcoal starter in the air. It kept getting larger and larger until it was as big as the yard. Grandmother's voice resonated in my ears: 'Girls don't die. Girls don't die.'

Zari was sleeping. I stroked her hair and brushed it away from her face, but it was Saiid. His head rolled off the pillow and fell on the floor. I screamed, but no sound came from my throat.

There was no end to my nightmares. Every so often I would wake up to the sound of my own screams, and, drenched in sweat, I would again plunge down the well. I don't know how long I was in that state.

One day I woke up with a burning sensation in my foot. It was morning. The room was filled with the smell of alcohol. Someone turned my face and said, 'She's awake. Missus, look. I swear she's awake. She's looking at me.'

The faces were blurry, but the voices were clear.

'O Imam Moussa bin-Jafar, you who fulfil people's needs, save us!'

'Missus, she's come to. Make a broth and pour it down her throat any way you can. It's almost a week since she ate anything. Her stomach is weak. You have to feed her slowly.'

I closed my eyes. I didn't want to see anyone.

'The chicken broth will be ready in a minute. Thank God a hundred thousand times. All this time, she has vomited everything I made her eat.'

'Yesterday when her fever broke I knew she was going to wake up. The poor thing, how she has suffered. Who knows how all this fever and delirium got into her body.'

'Oh, Mrs Parvin, do you see my agony? In the past few days I have died and come back to life a hundred times. On the one hand, I have to watch my dear child flail and flutter before my eyes, and on the other hand, I have to bear the shame and tolerate her brothers' taunts about the sort of girl I gave birth to. It all burns me up inside.'

I was not in pain. I was just lying in bed, weak and frail. I couldn't move. Simply pulling my hand out from under the blanket felt like a herculean task. I wished I would continue getting weaker and weaker until I died. Why had I woken up? There was nothing for me in this world.

When I again regained consciousness, Mother had laid my head on her knee and was trying to force me to drink some broth. I was shaking my head and resisting the pressure of her fingers squeezing my cheeks.

'May God let me sacrifice my life for you, just one spoonful ... Look what a state you're in. Eat. May all your pain and suffering be mine.'

It was the first time she had spoken such words to me. She had never fawned over me. She was always either busy with my younger siblings or watching over my older brothers whom she loved more than life itself. I was always lost in the middle. I was neither the first

53

nor the last, and not a boy either. If Zari hadn't died, I would surely have been completely forgotten by now; just like Faati, who was usually hiding in a corner and no one ever saw her. I will never forget the day Mother gave birth to her. Grandmother fainted when she heard the child was a girl. But later, Faati came to have another problem as well. They said she was a bad omen, because after she was born, Mother miscarried twice and both times the child was a boy. I really don't know how Mother knew they were boys.

The broth spilled on the sheet. Mother grumbled and walked out of the room.

I opened my eyes. It was late afternoon. Faati was sitting next to me, brushing my hair away from my face with her small hands. She looked so innocent and alone. I looked at her. She was me sitting next to Zari. I felt the warmth of tears on my face.

'I knew you would wake up,' Faati said. 'For the love of God, don't die.'

Mother was walking back into the room. I closed my eyes.

It was night-time. I could hear everyone talking. Mother said, 'This morning she opened her eyes. She was conscious, but no matter how hard I tried to pour a little broth in her mouth, she wouldn't let me. She's so weak she can't move; I don't know where she gets all that energy to fight me. This morning Mrs Parvin was saying we can't keep her going on pills and medicine any longer. If she doesn't eat, she'll die.'

I heard Father say, 'I knew my mother was right. We can't have girls. Even if she recovers, she'll be as good as dead ... with all this shame and dishonour.'

I didn't hear any more. It seemed as though I could control when and what I wanted to see and hear, and just like a radio with an on-off switch, I could turn everything off. But I couldn't control the nightmares. Images danced behind my closed eyelids.

Ahmad, holding a bloody knife and dragging Faati along by her hair, was running towards me. Faati was as small as a doll. I was standing at the edge of a cliff. Ahmad hurled Faati towards me. I tried to catch her, but she slipped through my hands and plunged down the cliff. I looked down. Zari and Saiid's mangled and bloody bodies were down there. My own scream woke me up. My pillow was soaking wet and my mouth felt horribly dry.

'What is the matter? You're not going to let us get a decent night's sleep, are you?'

I was gulping down the water.

I woke up to the sound of the usual morning commotion. They were eating breakfast.

'Last night her fever peaked again. She was hallucinating. Did you hear her scream?'

'No!' Mahmoud said.

'Mother, will you let us eat a lousy bite in peace or not?' Ahmad groused.

His voice was like a dagger piercing my heart. I wished I had the energy to get up and tear him to pieces. I hated him. I hated all of them. I rolled over and pushed my face into the pillow. I wished I might die soon and be free of those selfish, stone-hearted people.

My eyes automatically opened with the sting of the syringe.

'Well, you're finally awake. Don't pretend you're not. Shall I bring a mirror for you to see yourself? You look like a skeleton. Look. I went to the Caravan pastry shop and bought biscuits for you. They're really tasty with tea ... Mrs Sadeghi! ... Massoumeh is awake. She wants some tea. Bring her a tall glass of tea.'

I looked at her with dazed eyes. I couldn't figure her out. Everyone talked behind her back and said that unbeknownst to her husband she has relations with men. I thought of her as a filthy woman. But for some reason, when I saw her I didn't hate her the way I thought I should. I saw no ugliness in her. I just knew that I didn't want to have any contact with her.

Mother walked in with a tall glass of tea filled to the rim.

'Thank God,' she said. 'She wants to drink some tea?'

'Yes,' Mrs Parvin said. 'She's going to have some tea with biscuits. Get up my girl ... get up.'

She slid her hand under me and raised me up. Mother put a few pillows behind me and held the glass up to my mouth. I turned away and clenched my lips, as if I had stored all my energy to do just that.

'It's not going to work. She won't let me. It's all going to spill.'

'Don't trouble yourself. I will give it to her, I'll sit here and I won't leave until she drinks it. Go take care of your chores. Don't worry.'

Mother, looking cranky and irritated, left the room.

'Now, my good girl, just so that I don't lose face, open your mouth and take just one sip. For the love of God, isn't it a shame for that delicate skin to have turned so sallow. You are so thin that you probably weigh as much as Faati. A girl as pretty as you should live, and you won't if you don't eat . . .'

I don't know what Mrs Parvin saw in my eyes or read in the smirk on my lips, but she suddenly grew quiet and stared at me. And then like someone who has made a great discovery, she said, 'Yes! That is exactly what you want . . . you want to die. This is your way of committing suicide. I am such an idiot! Why didn't I see it sooner? Yes, you want to die. But why? Aren't you in love? Who knows, you may end up with him after all. Why do you want to kill yourself? Saiid will be so hurt . . .'

Hearing Saiid's name, I suddenly shuddered and my eyes flew open.

Mrs Parvin looked at me and said, 'What is the matter with you? Do you think he doesn't love you? Don't worry, this is what makes love sweet.'

She held the glass of tea up to my lips. I grabbed her hand with every ounce of energy I had and half rose.

'Tell me the truth, is Saiid alive?'

'What? Of course, he is. Why would you think he is dead?'

'Because Ahmad . . .'

'What about Ahmad?'

'Ahmad stabbed him with his knife.'

'Well, yes, but nothing happened to him . . . Oh . . . you have been unconscious ever since you saw the bloody knife . . . So all

56

these nightmares and screams in the middle of the night are because of this? Poor me, my bedroom is on the other side of this wall. I hear you every night. You keep screaming, "No, no." You shout for Saiid. You probably think Ahmad killed him. Right? Come on, child. Ahmad doesn't have it in him. Did you think someone can just walk out on the street, kill someone and casually go back home? The country has laws. It's not as simple as that. No, my dear, rest assured, all he did that night was put a scratch on Saiid's arm and another one on his face. Then the doctor and the other shop owners intervened. Saiid didn't even go to the police. He is fine. The next day, I myself saw him in front of the pharmacy.'

After an entire week, I could finally breathe. I closed my eyes and from the bottom of my heart I said, 'Thank God.' Then I fell back on the bed, sank my face into the pillow and wept.

It took until the new year holidays in the spring for me to more or less regain my health. My ankle had completely healed, but I was still very thin. I had no news of school and there was no possibility of bringing up the subject. I idled around the house. I couldn't even leave to go to the public bathhouse. Mother would heat some water and I would bathe at home. I was engulfed in a cold and bitter atmosphere. I didn't like to talk. Most of the time I was so sad and drowned in my own thoughts that I didn't know what was going on around me. Mother was very careful not to talk about what had happened. However, she did occasionally slip up and say things that made my heart ache.

Father never looked at me. He acted as though I didn't exist, and he seldom talked to the others. He was sad and nervous and looked much older. Ahmad and Mahmoud tried as far as possible not to come face to face with me. In the morning, they ate their breakfast in a hurry and quickly left the house. At night, Ahmad came home later and more boozed up than ever before and went straight to bed. Mahmoud would quickly eat something and leave to go to the mosque or went up to his room and spent much of the night praying. I was happy not to see them. But Ali was a constant nuisance. He harassed me relentlessly and sometimes said vulgar things to me. Mother often scolded him, but I tried to ignore him.

Faati was the only person whose company I looked forward to and the only welcome presence in the house. Every day when she came back from school, she would come and kiss me and look at me with a strange compassion. Whatever she ate, she brought some of it for me and insisted that I take it. Sometimes she even saved her money and bought chocolate for me. She was still afraid that I was going to die.

I knew going back to school was now an impossible dream. But I was hoping that after the new year they would at least let me take sewing classes. Although I didn't like sewing at all, it was my only hope for gaining a little freedom and stepping outside those four walls. I missed Parvaneh terribly. I didn't know whether I was more desperate to see her or Saiid. It was strange. Despite everything I had gone through, all the pain and humiliation, and all the vile and ugly reflections on my relationship with Saiid, I didn't regret what had come to pass between us. Not only did I not feel guilty, but the purest and most honest emotion in my heart was the love I harboured for him.

Over time, Mrs Parvin told me how events surrounding me had escalated and how it had all affected Parvaneh's family. The night I collapsed, or the following night, Ahmad had gone to their house completely drunk and started cussing and cursing. He told Parvaneh's father, 'Wear your hat a little higher on your head. Your daughter is fast and loose and she was about to lead our girl astray, too.' And he had added a thousand other ugly words, the thought of which made me break into a sweat. How could I ever look Parvaneh and her parents in the face again? How could he say such hateful things to a respectable man?

Having no news of Saiid was driving me mad. Finally, I begged Mrs Parvin to stop by the pharmacy and find out about him. Despite being intimidated by Ahmad, she was always itching for an escapade. I never imagined that one day she would be my confidante. I still didn't like her, but I had no other resources. She was

58

my only connection to the outside world, and to my great surprise, no one in the family objected to her spending time with me.

The next day, Mrs Parvin came to see me. Mother was in the kitchen. Anxious and excited, I asked, 'What news do you have? Did you go there?'

'Yes, I did,' she said. 'I bought a few things and then I asked the doctor why Saiid wasn't there. He said, "Saiid moved back to his home town. This was no place for him any more. The poor guy had no reputation and respect left and his safety wasn't guaranteed. I told him, What if someone pulls a knife on you in the dark and does you in? His youth would have been wasted. And they weren't going to let him marry the girl anyway . . . with that crazy brother! So, for now, he has dropped out of university and gone back to his family in Rezaieh."'

Tears were streaming down my face.

'Enough!' Mrs Parvin scolded. 'Don't start again. Remember, you thought he was dead. You should be thanking God that he's alive. Wait a little. Once the whole incident blows over, he will probably get in touch with you. Although I think it would be better if you forget all about him. They won't give you to him. I mean, there's no way Ahmad would agree . . . unless you manage to convince your father. In any case, we have to wait and see if he shows up.'

The only joy of the new year holidays was that twice they took me out of the house. Once to go to the public bathhouse for the traditional new year's eve bath, during which I didn't see a single soul because they made sure our appointment was very early in the morning, and the second time to visit Uncle Abbas to wish him a happy new year. The weather was still cold. That year spring was late arriving, but the air was filled with the fresh scent of a new year. Being outside the house was so pleasant. The air seemed cleaner and brighter. It was easier to breathe.

Uncle's wife was not on good terms with Mother, and his daughters didn't get along with us. Soraya, Uncle's eldest daughter, said, 'Massoumeh, you've grown taller.'

Uncle's wife jumped in and said, 'But she's thinner. To be honest, I was afraid she had some sort of illness.'

'Absolutely not!' Soraya argued. 'It's because she has been studying too hard. Massoumeh, Father says you study a lot and are the top student in your class.'

I looked down. I didn't know what to say. Mother came to my rescue. 'She broke her leg. That's why she has lost so much weight. After all, none of you ever enquire about anyone's well-being.'

'As a matter of fact, Father and I wanted to come visit you,' Soraya said. 'But Uncle said he wasn't feeling well and didn't want anyone coming to the house. Massoumeh, how did you break your leg?'

'I slipped on ice,' I said quietly.

To change the subject, Mother turned to Uncle's wife and said, 'Miss Soraya has her diploma now. Why don't you find a husband for her?'

'Well, she has to study and go to university. It's too soon.'

'Too soon! Nonsense. As a matter of fact, it's getting too late. I guess now you can't find a decent husband any more.'

'Actually, there are many good candidates around,' Uncle's wife said defiantly. 'But a girl like Soraya doesn't take a fancy to just anyone. In my family everyone is educated: men and women. We're different from people who come from the provinces. Soraya wants study and become a doctor, like my sister's daughters.'

It was impossible for our family visits to end without tension and snide remarks. With her petulance and sharp tongue, Mother always alienated everyone. It wasn't for no reason that Father's sister used to say Mother has a razor for a tongue. I always wanted to build a closer relationship with my relatives, but these deeply rooted animosities made it impossible.

The new year holidays passed and I was still at home. Discreet whispers and hints about my taking sewing classes reaped no result. Ahmad and Mahmoud would not allow me to leave the house under any circumstances. And Father didn't intervene. To him, I was dead.

I was often bored. After finishing the daily household chores, I would go upstairs to the living room and watch the section of the street that was visible from the window. This partial view was my only connection to the outside world. And even that, I had to keep secret. If my brothers found out, they would probably brick up the window. My one dream was to see Parvaneh or Saiid out there on the street.

By then I knew that the only way I could ever leave that house was as someone's wife. In fact, this was the single solution to the dilemma that everyone had voted on and ratified. I hated every corner of that house, but I didn't want to betray my dear Saiid by throwing myself from one prison into another. I wanted to wait for him until the end of my life, even if they were to drag me to the gallows.

A family expressed interest in asking for my hand in marriage. Three women and a man were coming to visit. Mother got busy, diligently cleaning and arranging the house. Mahmoud bought a set of sofas with red upholstery. Ahmad bought fruits and pastries. Their unprecedented cooperation was strange. Like drowning people clinging to a piece of driftwood, they were willing to do anything not to lose the suitor. And once I saw the potential groom, I realised he was indeed nothing but driftwood. He was a heavyset man with no hair on the crown of his head, about thirty years old, and he slurped while eating fruit. He worked with Mahmoud in the bazaar. Fortunately, he and the three women who had accompanied him were looking for a plump and fleshy wife and didn't take a liking to me. That night I went to sleep happy and peaceful. The next morning, Mother told Mrs Parvin all about the event, in great detail and with much embellishment. Her deep disappointment over the end result made me want to laugh.

'What a shame,' she said. 'This poor girl has no luck. He is not only rich, but comes from a good family, too. What's more, he is young and hasn't been married before.' (It was funny, the man was twice my age, but from Mother's viewpoint he was young ... and with that bald head and big paunch!) 'Of course, Mrs Parvin, between you and me, the man was right in his decision. The girl is too scrawny. The man's mother said, "Madam, your daughter needs medical attention." If I'm not wrong, that imp had done something to look even sicklier.'

'Oh, my dear, the way you talk it's as if he was a young man of twenty,' Mrs Parvin argued. 'I saw them out on the street. It's all the better that they didn't take a fancy to her. Massoumeh is too good for you to hand her over to that big-bellied midget.'

'What can I say? We had big dreams for the girl. Forget about me, her father used to say Massoumeh has to marry a man who's a somebody. But after all that disgrace, who's going to come for her? She will either have to marry beneath her or become a second wife.'

'Nonsense! Let things simmer down. People will forget.'

'What will they forget? People investigate, they ask around. The sister and mother of a decent and proper man will never let him marry my ill-fated girl whose mess is known to the entire neighbourhood.'

'Wait,' Mrs Parvin counselled. 'They will forget. Why are you in such a hurry?'

'It's her brothers. They say as long as she is in this house they have no peace of mind and can't hold their heads up in public. People won't forget ... not for a hundred years. And Mahmoud wants to get married, but he says he can't do so as long as this girl is still here. He says he doesn't trust her. He's afraid she will lead his wife astray, too.'

'What drivel!' Mrs Parvin said dismissively. 'This poor thing is as innocent as a child. And what happened wasn't all that serious. All beautiful girls her age have boys falling in love with them. You can't burn them all at the stake because some guy fancied them ... Besides, it wasn't her fault.'

'Yes, I know my daughter well. She may not be all that diligent with her prayers and fasting, but her heart is with God. The day before yesterday she said, "I dream of going on a pilgrimage to the shrine of Imam Abdolazim in Qum." Back then, she used to pray at the shrine of Her Holiness Massoumeh every week. You won't believe how she prayed. That wretched girl, Parvaneh, is the one to blame for all this. Otherwise, my daughter involved in such things? Never!'

'But wait a little longer. Perhaps the guy will come and marry her and everything will end well. He wasn't a bad boy and they want each other. Everyone speaks highly of him. And soon he's going to be a doctor.'

'What are you talking about, Mrs Parvin?' Mother said irately. 'Her brothers say they will give her to Azrael, the angel of death, before they give her to him. And it's not as if he's breaking down our door to come for her. Whatever God wants will happen. Everyone's fate and destiny is written on their forehead from the very first day, and their share has been set aside.'

'Then don't rush into anything. Let fate do its work.'

'But her brothers say they will have to bear the scar of her shame until she gets married and they are no longer responsible for her. How long do you think they can keep her locked up in the house? They're afraid their father will take pity on her and give in.'

'Well, the poor thing does deserve some pity. She's very beautiful. Wait until she is healthy again. You'll see what kind of men will come for her.'

'I swear to God, I cook rice and chicken for her every day. Lamb shank soup, porridge made with wheat and meat. I send Ali out to buy sheep's head and trotters soup for her breakfast. All in the hope that she will gain some weight and not look so sickly so that a decent man can take a liking to her.'

I remembered a fairy tale from my childhood. A monster kidnapped a child. But the child was too thin for the monster to eat. Instead he locked her up and brought her plenty of good food so that she would quickly get fat and become a delectable meal. Now my family wanted to fatten me up and throw me to a monster.

I was put up for sale. Hosting people who came to see me as a potential wife became the only serious event in our house. My brothers and Mother had spread the word that they were searching for a husband for me, and all sorts of people came. Some were so unsuitable that even Ahmad and Mahmoud decided against them. Every night, I prayed for Saiid to show up, and at least once a week I begged Mrs Parvin to go to the pharmacy to see if there was any news of him. The doctor told her Saiid had written to him only once and that the letter the doctor had sent in response had been returned. Apparently the address was wrong. Saiid had melted and vanished in the ground. At night I would sometimes go to the living room to pray and commune with God, and then I would stand at the window and watch the shadows moving along the street. A few times I saw a familiar shadow under the arch of the house across the street, but as soon as I opened the window it disappeared.

The only dream that ushered me to bed at night and made me forget the pain and suffering of my tedious days was that of a life with Saiid. In my mind, I would sketch our small and beautiful house, its furnishings and the decorations in every room. It was my small heaven. I imagined our children, beautiful, healthy and happy. In my dreams I was in eternal love and bliss. Saiid was a model husband. A gentle man, mild-mannered and kind, sensible and intelligent, he never fought with me, he never belittled me. Oh, how I loved him. Has any woman ever loved a man the way I loved Saiid? If only we could live in our fantasies.

In early June, as soon as the final school exams were over, Parvaneh's family moved away from our neighbourhood. I knew they were planning on it, but I didn't think they would leave so soon. Later, I learned that they actually wanted to go sooner, but had decided to wait for the school year to end. For a while, Parvaneh's father had been commenting that the neighbourhood was no longer a good area to live in. He was right. It was good only for the likes of my brothers.

It was a hot morning. I was sweeping the room and I still had not pulled down the wicker blinds when I heard Parvaneh's voice. I ran into the yard. Faati was at the front door. Parvaneh had come to say goodbye. Mother got to the door ahead of me and held it half closed. Then she snatched the envelope Parvaneh had given to Faati, gave it back to her and said, 'Go quickly. Go before her

64

brothers see you and cause another scandal. And don't bring anything here any more.'

With a lump in her throat Parvaneh said, 'But ma'am, I only wrote to say goodbye and to give her our new address. You can read it.'

'That won't be necessary!' Mother snapped.

I grabbed the door with both hands and tried to pull it open. But Mother was holding it tight and kicking me away. 'Parvaneh!' I screamed. 'Parvaneh!'

'For the love of God, don't hurt her so much,' Parvaneh begged. 'I swear she didn't do anything bad.'

Mother slammed the door shut. I sat on the ground and wept. I had lost my guardian, friend and confidante.

The last suitor was Ahmad's friend. I often wondered how my brothers approached these men. For instance, how did Ahmad tell his friend that he had a sister of marrying age? Did they advertise me? Were they making certain promises? Or did they haggle over me like two bazaar merchants? Whatever their approach, I knew it wasn't respectable.

Asghar Agha, the butcher, was just like Ahmad, in age as well as in his crude manners and personality. And he wasn't all that literate. He said, 'A man has to make his bread with the might of his arm, not sit in a corner and scribble away like a half-dead, pencil-pushing clerk.'

'He has money and knows how to straighten out this girl,' Ahmad argued.

And with respect to my being too thin, Asghar Agha said, 'It doesn't matter. I'll give her so much meat and fat to eat that in a month's time she'll be as big as a barrel. Instead, she has sassiness in her eyes.'

His mother was an old, dreadful-looking woman who ate non-stop and endorsed everything her son said. Asghar Agha met with everyone's approval. Mother was happy because he was young and had not been previously married. Ahmad was his friend and supported him because, after a brawl at Jamshid Café, Asghar Agha

65

had vouched for him and he had not been thrown in jail. Father consented because the man's butcher's shop had a decent income. And Mahmoud said, 'It's good, he's a tradesman and he has what it takes to deal with this girl and not let her step out of line. The sooner we wrap things up the better.'

No one cared what I thought and I didn't tell them how much I loathed the thought of living with a filthy, ignorant and illiterate thug who reeked of raw meat and tallow even on the day he came to ask for a girl's hand in marriage.

The next morning, Mrs Parvin rushed over to our house in a state of panic.

'I hear you want to give Massoumeh to Asghar Agha the butcher. For the love of God, don't do it! The man is a knife-wielding hooligan. He's a drinker, a womaniser. I know him. At least ask around and find out about him.'

'Don't blabber, Mrs Parvin,' Mother said. 'Who knows him better, you or Ahmad? And he told us everything about himself. Like Ahmad said, men do a thousand things before they get married, but they put it all aside when they become burdened with a wife and kids. He has sworn on his father's life and even pledged a strand of his moustache that he won't take a single wrong step after he gets married. Besides, we're not going to find anyone better for Massoumeh. He's young, she'll be his first wife, he's rich, he has two butcher's shops and he has mettle. What more could we ask for?'

Mrs Parvin looked at me with such pity and sympathy, as if she was looking at someone sentenced to death. The next day, she said, 'I begged Ahmad not to go through with it, but he's utterly ignorant.' (This was the first time she had confessed to her secret affair with my brother.) 'He said, "It isn't prudent to keep her at home any longer than this." But why aren't you doing something about it? Don't you understand the catastrophe you're facing? Are you really willing to marry this thug?'

'What difference does it make?' I said indifferently. 'Let them do whatever they want. Let them think they're marrying me off. They don't know that any man other than Saiid will touch only my corpse.'

'May God have mercy!' she gasped. 'Don't ever say such things again. It's a sin. You have to get these thoughts out of your head. No man could ever be your Saiid, but not all men are as bad as this lout. Wait, perhaps a better suitor will come along.'

I shrugged and said, 'It makes no difference at all.'

She left looking anxious. On her way out, she stopped in front of the kitchen and said something to Mother. Then Mother slapped herself on the face and from that moment on I was under greater guard. They took away all the medicine bottles and wouldn't let me touch a razor or a knife, and the moment I went upstairs, one of them would hurry after me. It made me laugh. They actually thought I was stupid enough to jump out of a second-floor window! But I had better plans.

Discussions about the marriage ceremony and the wedding slowed down because the groom's sister was absent. She was married and lived in Kermanshah and couldn't travel to Tehran for another ten days. 'I can't do it without my sister's approval and consent,' Asghar Agha said. 'I am as indebted to her as I am to my mother.'

It was eleven in the morning and I was out in the yard when I heard someone banging on the front door. I wasn't allowed to open the door so I called for Faati. Mother shouted from the kitchen, 'This one time, it's all right. Open the door and see who is so impatient.' I had barely opened the door when Mrs Parvin pushed her way in.

'Girl, you are so blessed and lucky,' she half-cried. 'You won't believe what a great suitor I have found for you. As perfect as the moon, as a bouquet of flowers . . .'

I stood there gaping at her. Mother came out of the kitchen and said, 'What's the matter, Mrs Parvin?'

'My dear lady,' she said. 'I have wonderful news. I have found the perfect suitor for her. A real gentleman, from a reputable family, well educated . . . I swear, one strand of his hair is worth more than a hundred of these thugs and hooligans. Shall I ask them to come this afternoon?'

'Wait a second!' Mother said. 'Slow down. Who are they? Where did you find them?'

'They are really upstanding people. I've known them for ten years. I've sewn a lot of dresses for the mother and her daughters. The eldest daughter, Monir, got married a long time ago to one of the landowners in Tabriz and she lives there. Mansoureh, the second daughter, went to university. She got married two years ago and now has a cute, chubby boy. The third daughter is still in school. They are devout people. The father is now retired. He owns a place, a factory, no, the one where they make books. What are they called?'

'What about the guy himself?'

'Oh, wait until you hear about the guy. He is wonderful. He has gone to university. I don't know what he studied, but he is working in that place his father owns. They make books. He is about thirty years old and he is fine looking. When I went for a fitting for the mother, I had a quick look. May God preserve him, he has a nice figure, black eyes and dark eyebrows, slightly olive-skinned ...'

'Well, where did they see Massoumeh?' Mother asked.

'They haven't. I described her to them. I told them what a wonderful girl she is. Pretty, and a good housewife. The mother really wants her son to get married. She had once asked me if I knew of any suitable girls. So, shall I tell them to come this afternoon?'

'No! We've made pledges and promises to Asghar Agha. His sister is coming from Kermanshah next week.'

'Come on!' Mrs Parvin exclaimed. 'You haven't actually done anything yet. You haven't even held the bride's consent ceremony. People change their minds even in the middle of the marriage service.'

'And what about Ahmad? God knows what riot he'll start. And he'll have every right. He will be humiliated. After all, he has made promises to Asghar Agha and he can't just back out of them.'

'Don't worry. I'll deal with Ahmad.'

'You should be ashamed of yourself!' Mother scolded. 'What sort of talk is this? May God forgive you.'

'Don't get the wrong idea. Ahmad is good friends with Haji and listens to him. I'll ask Haji to step in and mediate. Think of this innocent girl. I know that thug has a hand for hitting. When he drinks he loses his mind. And even now, he has a kept woman. Do you think she's going to give him up that easily? Never!'

'He has a what?' Mother asked, confused. 'What did you say he has?'

'Never mind,' Mrs Parvin said. 'I mean he has something going on with another woman.'

'Then what does he want this one for?'

'Well, he wants this one to be his wife and have his kids. The other one can't have children.'

'How do you know?'

'Madam, I know these types of people.'

'How? Who are you to say such things? Have some shame.'

'And you always think the worst. My own brother was like this. I grew up with this sort of man. For the love of God, don't let this poor girl climb out of a hole and fall into a pit. Let this family come, meet them and see how people can be different from each other.'

'First, I have to talk to her father and see what he says. Besides, if these people are so good, why don't they take a bride from their own clan?'

'Honestly, I don't know. I guess it's Massoumeh's luck. God loves her.'

Surprised and sceptical, I watched Mrs Parvin's enthusiasm and persistence. I simply couldn't understand the woman. Her actions were contradictory. I couldn't understand why she was so concerned about my future. I thought there must be another game at play.

Father and Mother debated all afternoon. Mahmoud joined the discussion for a while and then he said, 'The hell with it. Do whatever you want. Just get rid of her soon. Send her off and give us some peace of mind.'

Stranger yet was Ahmad's reaction. He came home late that night and the following morning when Mother opened the subject with him, he didn't object at all. He simply shrugged and said, 'What do I know? Do as you please.'

What a bizarre influence Mrs Parvin had on him.

A day later, the new suitor's family came to the house. Ahmad didn't come home and when Mahmoud found out the visitors were all women and not wearing full hijab he didn't come into the living room at all. Mother and Father looked them up and down and appraised them with a buyer's eye. The suitor himself hadn't come. His mother was wearing a black chador, but his sisters had no hijab. They really were worlds apart from all the others who had come before them.

Mrs Parvin was running the show and eagerly promoting me. When I walked in with a tray of tea, she said, 'See how pretty she is. Imagine how much more beautiful she will be once she plucks her eyebrows. She lost a little weight after she caught a cold and had a fever the other week.' I grimaced and looked at her with surprise.

'Being thin is very fashionable these days,' the eldest sister said. 'Women are killing themselves to lose weight. And my brother hates fat women.'

Mother's eyes gleamed with joy. Mrs Parvin smiled proudly and looked over at Mother. It was as if they had complimented her and not me. As per Mother's orders, I served tea and then went and sat in the room next door. The samovar and tea set had been brought upstairs so that I wouldn't have to go up and down the stairs and risk causing an embarrassment. They were all talking fast. They said their young man had studied through the last year of law at the university but had not yet received his degree.

'For now, he is working at a printing house. In fact, his father is half owner. His salary isn't bad and he can support a wife and children. And he has a house. Of course, it isn't his. It's his grandmother's. She lives downstairs and we've fixed the upstairs for dear Hamid. Young men like to have their own place; and with his being the only son, his father gives him whatever he wants.'

'Well, where is he?' Father asked. 'Will we have the honour of meeting him?'

'To be honest, my son has left everything up to me and his sisters. He said, "If you like her and approve, it will be the same as me approving." And he is now away on a business trip.'

'God willing, when is he coming back?'

The youngest sister jumped in and said, 'God willing, in time for the marriage ceremony and the wedding.'

'What?' Mother said, surprised. 'You mean we're not going to see the groom until the marriage ceremony? Isn't that a little strange? Doesn't he want to at least see his bride-to-be? A quick glimpse is religiously sanctioned and allowed.'

The eldest sister, trying to speak slowly so that Mother would fully understand, said, 'Truth be told, the issue isn't what is permissible and what is not. The issue is that Hamid is travelling right now. We have seen the young lady and our decision is Hamid's decision. And we have brought a photograph of him for the young lady to see.'

'What ... ?' Mother exclaimed, again. 'How could that be? What if the groom has a problem or a defect?'

'Madam, bite your tongue! My son is as good and as healthy as can be. God forbid that he has a problem! Isn't that so, Mrs Parvin? After all, Mrs Parvin has seen him.'

'Yes. Yes. I've seen him. God bless him, there is nothing wrong with him and he is very handsome. Of course, I looked at him with the eyes of a sister.'

The eldest sister took a photograph out of her handbag and gave it to Mrs Parvin who in turn held it up to Mother's eyes and said, 'See how gracious and gentlemanly he looks? May God bless him.'

'Now, please show the photograph to the young lady,' the eldest sister said. 'If, God willing, she takes a fancy to him, we can wrap things up by next week.'

'Please, madam,' Father said. 'I still don't understand the reason for all this rush. Why don't we wait until the young man returns?'

'Well, truth be told, Mr Sadeghi, we really don't have time. His father and I are leaving on a pilgrimage to Mecca next week and we want to settle all our duties and obligations before we go. Hamid pays no mind to himself and if he's not married I will worry and I won't have peace of mind. It has always been said that people who leave for Haj should leave nothing half done. They should settle all their affairs and responsibilities. When we heard about your daughter, I resorted to divination and the result was favourable. It had never turned out this positive for a girl. And I realised that I have to finalise things before I leave, just in case I don't come back.'

'God willing, you will come back healthy and happy.'

Still holding the photograph, Mother got up and said, 'You are so fortunate. I hope visiting God's home will be in our destiny, too.' Then she came into the room next door and held the photograph in front of me. 'Here, take a look. They're not our type of people, but I know you prefer their kind.'

I pushed her hand away.

The discussions took place at a fast pace. Father seemed convinced that the groom's presence was not necessary after all. It was very strange. They wanted to hold a wedding in a week's time. Mother's only worry was how to get everything done in such short a time. But Mrs Parvin came to her aid and volunteered to take care of everything.

'Don't worry at all,' she said. 'We'll go shopping tomorrow. And it will take me only two days to make her dress. I will take care of your other sewing needs as well.'

'But what about her trousseau and dowry? Of course, since the day my girls were born, I have been buying the necessities and setting them aside, but there are still a lot of things missing. And much of what I have for her is back in Qum. We have to go get them.'

The groom's mother said, 'Madam, please don't worry. Let the couple go to their home. We'll celebrate the consummation of their marriage after we return from Haj. By then, we will have time to arrange for whatever they need. Besides, Hamid does have some household things.'

They arranged for us to go and buy my wedding ring the following day, and invited the entire family to visit them any night we were free so that we could see their home and lifestyle at first hand and get to know them. I couldn't believe the speed with which everything had got so serious. I suddenly heard myself say, 'Saiid, save me! How can I put a stop to this?' I was furious with Mrs Parvin and wanted to rip her head off.

As soon as the groom's family left, discussions and arguments started. 'I won't go to buy the ring because his mother isn't going either,' Mother announced. 'And Massoumeh can't go alone. Mrs Parvin, you go with her.'

'Yes, of course. And we also have to buy fabric for her dress. By the way, don't forget, you have to buy the groom's ring.'

'I still don't understand why the groom didn't come and show himself.'

'Don't let bad feelings into your heart. I know the family. You won't believe what nice people they are. They gave you their address, to put your mind at ease, and you can go ask around about them.'

'Mostafa, what are we going to do about her trousseau?' Mother said. 'You and the boys have to go to Qum to bring the chinaware and the several sets of bedding I've put aside for her. They're in the basement at your sister's house. But what are we going to do about the rest of the things she needs?'

'Don't worry,' Mrs Parvin said. 'They did say it isn't important. Besides, it's their own fault for being in such a rush. All the better for you. You can blame them for whatever is missing.'

'I'm not going to send my daughter to her husband's house stripped and naked,' Father snapped. 'We have some of the necessities and we'll buy the rest this week. And everything else we'll provide in good time.'

The only person who had no role in these discussions, who never offered a suggestion, who never asked a question, and whose opinion didn't matter, was me. I sat awake all night overwhelmed with sadness and anxiety. I begged God to take my life and save me from that forced marriage.

The next morning I felt very ill. I pretended to be asleep and waited for everyone to leave the house. I heard Father talking to Mother. He wanted to use his contacts and resources to investigate

73

the groom's family and was not going to work that day. And then he said, 'Missus, I left money on the mantelpiece for the ring. See if it's enough.'

Mother counted the money and said, 'Yes. I don't think it will cost more than this.'

Father left the house with Ali. Fortunately, since the start of the summer he had been taking Ali to work with him, which meant there was calm and quiet in the house. Otherwise, God knows what would have happened to me.

Mother came into the room and said, 'Wake up. You have to get ready. I let you sleep longer so that you will have more energy today.'

I sat up, hugged my knees and said with determination, 'I won't go!' I was bold when the men were not at home.

'Get up and stop acting like a spoiled child.'

'I am not going anywhere.'

'The hell you're not! I'm not about to let you ruin your good luck. Especially not now.'

'What good luck? Do you even know who these people are? Who is this guy? He's not even willing to show himself.'

Just then the doorbell rang and Mrs Parvin walked in, all made up and chipper and wearing a black chador.

'I thought I should come early, just in case you need help with anything. By the way, I found a beautiful pattern for a wedding dress. We have to buy an appropriate fabric. Do you want to see it?'

'Mrs Parvin, help me out,' Mother pleaded. 'This girl is being stubborn again. Come and see if you can get her going.'

Mrs Parvin took off her high-heeled shoes and came into the room. She laughed and said, 'Good morning, Miss Bride. Come on, get up and go wash your face. They will be here any minute and we don't want them to think they have a lazy bride, do we?'

Seeing her, anger flared up inside me and I screamed, 'Who are you anyway? How much are they paying you as the broker?'

Mother slapped herself in the face and cried, 'May God punish you! Shut up! This girl has swallowed shame and vomited modesty.' And she lunged at me.

74

Mrs Parvin held out her arm and blocked her way. 'Please, it's all right. She's just angry. Let me talk to her. You should leave. We'll be ready in half an hour.'

Mother left the room. Mrs Parvin closed the door and stood leaning against it. Her chador slipped off and spilled on the floor. She was staring at me, but she wasn't seeing me. She was looking somewhere else, far from that room. A few minutes passed in silence. I watched her with curiosity. When she finally started to speak her voice sounded unfamiliar. It didn't have its usual ring. She sounded bitter and subdued.

'I was twelve when my father threw my mother out of the house. I was in year six and all of a sudden I found myself mother to my younger brother and three sisters. They expected of me what they expected from their real mother. I ran the household, cooked, washed clothes, cleaned, and tended to the children. My duties were no less after my father remarried. My stepmother was like all stepmothers. I don't mean she tortured us or kept us hungry, but she wanted her own children more than she wanted us. Perhaps she was right.

'Ever since I was a small child, I was told that when they cut my umbilical cord they had spoken my cousin Amir-Hossein's name. I was to become his wife. That's why my uncle always called me his pretty bride. I don't know when it started, but as far back as I can remember, I was in love with Amir. After my mother left, he was my only consolation. Amir loved me, too. He would always find some excuse to come to our house, sit on the edge of the reflecting pool and watch me work. He used to say, "Your hands are so small. How do you wash all these clothes?" I always left my most difficult chores for when he was around. I liked the way he looked at me with concern and compassion. He would tell my uncle and his wife what a difficult life I was living. Every time my uncle came to our house he would tell my father, "My good man, this poor child deserves pity. You are being cruel. Why does she have to suffer just because you and your wife couldn't get along? Stop being so stubborn. Go take your wife by the hand and bring her back home."

'"No, brother. Never. Don't ever speak that hussy's name in front of me. I made sure and divorced her three times so that there would be no way back."

'"Then think of something. This child is wasting away."

'When saying goodbye, my uncle's wife would always take me in her arms and hold me tight against her chest, and my tears would start to flow. She smelled like my mother. I don't know, perhaps I was just acting spoiled. In any case, my father finally came up with a solution and married a woman who had two children from a previous marriage. Our house was like a kindergarten – seven children of every age and size. I was the eldest. I'm not saying I did everything, but I ran around from morning until night and still there was more work to do; especially since my stepmother was very observant of the codes and tenets of purity and impurity. She really disliked my uncle and his wife, because she thought they had sided with my mother. The first thing she did was to put an end to Amir's visits to our house. She told my father, "It's ridiculous for this jackass to come here all the time to sit around and ogle us. And the girl is now old enough to start covering herself."

'A year later, she used us as an excuse to cut off all contact with my uncle's family. I missed them terribly. The only way I could see them was if we all went to my aunt's house. I would beg my cousins to ask my parents' permission for me to spend the night at their house. To make sure my stepmother wouldn't complain, I had to take my brothers and sisters with me. A year passed. Each time I saw Amir he had grown taller. You won't believe how handsome he was. His eyelashes were so long they cast a shadow over his eyes, just like a parasol. He wrote poems for me and bought the lyric sheets to the songs I liked. He would say, "You have a beautiful voice. Learn how to sing this song." Frankly, I couldn't read and write so well, and I had forgotten the little I had learned while I was still going to school. He used to say he would teach me. What wonderful days. But little by little, my aunt got tired of us always staying at her house. Her husband was constantly complaining. And so we were forced to see less of each other. The following new year, I begged for us to go visit my uncle. My father was about to give in, but my stepmother said, "I won't set foot in that witch's house."

'I don't know why my stepmother and my uncle's wife disliked each other so much. Poor me, stuck in the middle. That new year was the last time I saw them. It was at my aunt's house. She arranged it so that my father and my uncle would come face to face. She wanted them to make amends. Everyone was sitting in the upstairs living room. They asked the children to leave. Amir and I went and sat in a room downstairs and the children went to play in the garden. My aunt's daughters were in the kitchen preparing the tea tray. We were alone. Amir took my hand. I suddenly felt hot all over. His hands were warm and his palms were wet. He said, "Parvin, my father and I have talked. This year, after I get my diploma, we will come and ask for your hand. Father said we can get engaged before I go for my military service." I wanted to jump into his arms and cry with joy. I could hardly breathe.

"'You mean this summer?"

"'Yes, if I don't fail any classes, I will graduate."

"'For the love of God, don't fail a single class."

"'I promise. For you, I will study very hard."

'He squeezed my hand and I felt as if he was holding my heart in his grip. He said, "I can't stand being away from you any more."

'Oh . . . ! What can I say? I have relived that scene and those words so many times that every second of it is like a movie playing in front of my eyes. Sitting in that room, we were so drowned in our own world that we didn't realise a fight had broken out. By the time we came out into hallway, my father and stepmother were cursing out loud and walking down the stairs, and my uncle's wife was leaning over the banister and countering their curses. My aunt ran after my father and begged him not to behave that way, that it was unseemly, that he and his brother should put aside their differences and make up. She begged them, for the love of their mother's spirit, for the love of their father's spirit, to remember they were brothers and should support each other. She reminded them of the old saying that even if brothers eat each other's flesh, they will never throw away the bones. My father was slowly calming down, but my stepmother screamed, "Didn't you hear the things they said to us? What sort of a brother is he?"

'My aunt said, "Mrs Aghdass, please stop it. It's not right. They didn't say anything insulting. He is the older brother. If he said something out of kindness and concern, you shouldn't take offence."

"'So what if he is older! It doesn't give him the right to say whatever he wants. And my husband is his brother, not his lackey. What business do they have meddling in our lives? That pop-eyed wife of his can't stand to see anyone better than herself. We don't want relatives like them."

'Then she grabbed one of her children by the arm and stormed out. My uncle's wife screamed after her, "Go take a good look at yourself! If you were a decent woman your first husband wouldn't have thrown you out with two kids."

'My sweet fantasy didn't even last an hour. Like a bubble, it burst and disappeared. My stepmother was determined. She said she would make sure my uncle's family would always bear the grief of my loss in their hearts. She told my father she was already a mother by the time she was my age and that she could no longer tolerate a rival like me in her house. Around that time, Haji Agha came and asked for my hand. He was a distant relative of my step-mother and had already been married twice. He said, "I divorced them because they couldn't get pregnant." Now, he wanted to marry a young, healthy girl to make sure he would have children. The idiot! He wasn't willing to consider for even a second that he was the one who had a problem. Of course, men never have any problems or shortcomings; especially not rich men. He was forty years old and twenty-five years my senior. My father said, "He has a world of money, several shops in the bazaar, and plenty of land and property around Ghazvin." In short, my father's mouth was watering. Haji Agha said, "If she bears my child, I will give her a sea of money." When they took me to the marriage ceremony, I was feeling worse than you do now.'

Mrs Parvin stared at some distant point and two teardrops fell on her cheeks.

'Why didn't you kill yourself?' I asked.

'Do you think it's easy? I didn't have the courage. And you should get these silly thoughts out of your head. We each have a destiny and you can't fight yours. Besides, committing suicide is a great sin. You never know, perhaps this will turn out to be a blessing for you.'

Mother pounded on the door and yelled, 'Mrs Parvin! What are you doing in there? We're going to be late. It's already nine-thirty.'

Mrs Parvin dried her tears and answered, 'Don't worry. We will be ready on time.' Then she came and sat next to me and said, 'I told you all this so that you don't think I don't understand what you are going through.'

'Then why do you want to make me miserable and unhappy, too?'

'They are going to marry you off anyway. You have no idea what Ahmad has planned for you.' And then she asked, 'By the way, why does he hate you so much?'

'Because Father loves me more than he loves Ahmad.'

Suddenly, I grasped the reality behind the words I had impulsively blurted out. I had never understood it that clearly. Yes, Father loved me more.

The first memory I had of his kindness was on the day Zari died. He came home from work and stood frozen in the doorway. Mother was wailing and Grandmother was reading from the Quran. The doctor was shaking his head and walking out with a look of hatred and disgust on his face. When he came face to face with Father, he roared, 'This child has been on the verge of death for at least three days and you waited until now to call a doctor? Would you have done the same if it was one of your sons lying there instead of this innocent girl?'

Father's face was as white as plaster. He was about to collapse. I ran over to him and wrapped my tiny arms around his legs and called Grandmother. He sat down on the floor, held me tight, pressed his face in my hair and sobbed. Grandmother said, 'Get up, son. You're a man. You shouldn't cry like a woman. What God gave, God has taken away. You shouldn't challenge his will.'

79

'You said it was nothing serious,' Father yelled. 'You said she would get well soon. You didn't let me bring a doctor.'

'It would have made no difference. If she was meant to live, she would have lived. Even the greatest sage and physician would not have made a difference. This is our fate. We are not meant to have girls.'

'This is all nonsense,' Father cried. 'It's all your fault!'

It was the first time I saw Father shout at his mother. In truth, I liked it. After that day, Father would often hold me in his arms and silently cry. I knew from the way his shoulders would start to shake. And from then on, he showered me with the love and attention he had denied Zari. Ahmad never forgot nor forgave this favouritism. His angry looks always followed me and as soon as Father went out he would beat me up. Now, Ahmad had reached his heart's desire. I had lost favour in Father's eyes, I had broken his trust, and Father, disappointed and heartbroken, had abandoned me. It was the best opportunity for Ahmad to take his revenge.

Mrs Parvin's voice brought me back. 'You have no idea what he was going to do to you. You don't know what a vile and disgusting man he is. And don't think anyone would have come to your rescue. You won't believe the performance I had to put on to finally convince him to say no to that louse and to let this suitor's family come and see you. My heart was breaking for you. You are just like me fifteen or twenty years ago. I saw how your family just wanted to marry you off and there was no sign of that incompetent Saiid. I thought you should at least marry someone who won't turn you black and blue with his fists the day after the wedding. Someone who is decent and, God willing, you may grow to like. And even if you don't, he should be someone who will let you live your own life.'

'Just like you?' I said in a stinging and bitter tone.

She looked at me with reproach. 'I don't know. Do as you wish. We all find a way to take revenge on life and to make our existence tolerable.'

*

I didn't go with them to shop for a ring. Mrs Parvin told the groom's family that I had a cold and she took the silver ring I was wearing so that she would know what size the wedding ring should be.

Two days later, Father, Ahmad and Mahmoud went to Qum and came back with a carload of household furnishings. Mother said, 'Wait. Wait. Don't bring these things in here. Take them straight to her own house. Mrs Parvin will go with you and show you the way.' Then she turned to me and said, 'Come, girl. Get up and go take a look at your home and see what you're missing and tell them where you want them to put everything. Come on, be a good girl and get up.'

'There's no need,' I said with a shrug. 'Tell Mrs Parvin to go. I have no intention of getting married. It seems she's the one who is all excited.'

The next day, Mrs Parvin brought the wedding dress for a fitting. I refused to try it on. 'That's all right,' she said. 'I have your measurements. I'll make it based on your other dresses. I'm sure it will turn out fine.'

I didn't know what to do. I was constantly restless and agitated. I couldn't eat. I couldn't sleep. And even when I did fall asleep for a few hours, I had so many nightmares that by the time I woke up I was more tired than before. I was like someone sentenced to death and approaching the hour of her execution. Finally, as difficult as it was, I decided to talk to Father. I wanted to throw myself at his feet and weep until he took pity on me. But everyone was careful to not leave us alone together for even a minute. And it was obvious that Father, too, was doing everything he could to avoid me. Subconsciously, I was expecting a miracle. I thought a hand would appear out of the sky and steal me away at the last moment. But nothing happened.

Everything progressed on schedule and the promised day arrived. From early in the morning the front door was open and Mahmoud, Ahmad and Ali were coming and going. They arranged a row of chairs around the front yard and prepared platters of pastries. Of course, they were expecting very few guests. Mother had asked that no one in Qum be told about the wedding. She didn't want any of our relatives to show up and see the sorry state of affairs. They told Father's sister that the wedding was going to be a few weeks later, but they had to invite Uncle Abbas. In fact, he was our only relative present at the ceremony. With the exception of a few of our neighbours, the guests were all related to the groom.

Everyone kept insisting that I go to the beauty parlour, but I refused. Mrs Parvin faked this, too. She threaded my face, plucked my eyebrows and put curlers in my hair. All the while, tears were streaming down my face. Uncle Abbas's wife had come over in the morning to help, or, according to Mother, to spy. 'Oh you're such a sensitive sissy?' she said. 'There is hardly any hair on your face for you to cry like this.'

'My child has become so weak that she can't bear it,' Mother said.

Mrs Parvin had tears in her eyes, too. Every so often, she pretended she needed a new piece of thread and she turned away to wipe her eyes.

The marriage ceremony was to be held at five o'clock when the weather had cooled off a little. At four, the groom's family arrived. Although it was still very hot, the men stayed outside and sat in the shade of the tall mulberry tree. The women went upstairs to the living room where the wedding *sofreh* had been laid out. I was in the room next door.

Mother burst into the room and scolded, 'You're still not dressed? Hurry up. The gentleman will be here in an hour!'

I was shaking from head to toe. I threw myself at her feet and begged her not to force me to go through with the marriage. 'I don't want a husband,' I pleaded. 'I don't even know who this lout is. For the love of God, don't make me. I swear on the Quran, I will kill myself. Go and break this up. Let me talk to my father. Wait and see, I will not say yes. Just watch me! Either you put an end to this, or I will say in front of everyone that I do not consent to getting married.'

'May God take my life!' she gasped. 'Be quiet! What sort of talk is this? Now you want to shame us in front of all these people? This time, your brother will cut you into tiny pieces. Ahmad has been carrying his knife in his pocket all day. He said, "If she says one word out of line, I will finish her off right here." Think about your poor father's reputation. He will have a heart attack and drop dead.'

'I don't want to get married and you can't force me.'

'Shut your trap and don't raise your voice. People will hear.'

She came at me, but I dove under the bed and huddled in the farthest corner. The curlers had all come loose and scattered around the room.

'May you meet your death!' Mother hissed. 'Come out of there! May God let me see you on a slab at the morgue. Come out!'.

Someone was knocking on the door. It was Father. 'Missus, what are you doing?' he asked. 'The gentleman will be here any minute.'

'Nothing, nothing,' Mother said. 'She's getting dressed. Just tell Mrs Parvin to come here quick.'

And then she snarled, 'Come out, you miserable wretch. Come out before I kill you. Stop creating so much scandal.'

'I won't. I won't get married. For the love of brother Mahmoud, for the love of Ahmad whom you love so much, don't force me to get married. Tell them we have changed our minds.'

Mother couldn't crawl under the bed. She clawed at me, grabbed me by the hair and dragged me out. Just then, Mrs Parvin walked in.

'May God have mercy! What are you doing? You are tearing out all her hair!'

Mother wheezed, 'See what she's doing? She wants to put us to shame at the last minute.'

Still curled up on the floor, I glared at her with hatred. She still had a cluster of my hair in her fist.

I don't remember saying yes during the marriage ceremony. Mother kept squeezing my arm with all her might and whispering, 'Say yes. Say yes.' Finally, someone said yes and everyone cheered. Mahmoud and a few of the men were sitting in the next room and they chanted praise to the Prophet and his descendants. A few things were exchanged, but I was oblivious to it all. There was a veil across my eyes. Everything was floating in a fog, a haze. People's voices blended into a confusing and incomprehensible clamour. Like someone transfixed, I sat staring at a distant point. I didn't care that the man sitting next to me was now my husband. Who was he? What did he look like? Everything was over. And Saiid didn't come. My hopes and dreams had reached a bitter end. Saiid, what did you do to me?

When I came to, I was in that man's house, in the bedroom. He was sitting on the edge of the bed with his back to me, taking off his tie. It was obvious that he was not used to wearing one and it had bothered him. I stood in a corner and gripped the white chador they had made me wear to come to that house, tight against my chest. I was trembling like an autumn leaf. My heart was pounding. I was trying not to make a sound so that he wouldn't notice my presence in the room. In total silence, tears were falling on my chest. God, what sort of tradition was this? One day they wanted to kill me because I had exchanged a few words with a man I had known for two years, knew a lot about, loved and was ready to go to the ends of the earth with, and the next day they wanted me to climb into bed with a stranger whom I knew nothing about and for whom I felt nothing but fear.

The thought of his hand touching me made my skin crawl. I felt I was in danger of being raped and there was no one to save me. The room was half dark. As if my stare had burned the back of his neck, he turned and looked at me, and sounding surprised, he quietly said, 'What's the matter? What are you afraid of . . . ? Of me?' Then he smiled sarcastically and said, 'Please don't look at me like that. You look like a lamb gaping at its slaughterer.'

I wanted to say something, but I couldn't speak.

'Calm down,' he said. 'Don't be afraid. You're about to have a heart attack. I won't touch you. I'm not an animal!'

My tense muscles relaxed a little. My breath, which had been caged in my chest for I don't remember how long, was set free. But he stood up and again my body contracted and I pressed myself tightly into the corner.

'Listen, my dear girl, there are things I have to do tonight. I have to go see my friends. I will leave now. Change into something comfortable and get some sleep. I promise you, if I come back home tonight, I will not come to you. I swear on my honour.' Then he picked up his shoes, held his arms up in surrender and said, 'See! I'm leaving.'

At the sound of the front door closing, I crumpled like a rag and sank to the floor. I was so exhausted that my legs could no longer bear my weight. I felt as though I had carried a mountain. I sat in that position until my breath regained its normal rhythm. I could see my reflection in the dressing table mirror. My image kept distorting. Was that really me? There was a ridiculous veil sitting lopsided on my dishevelled hair and despite the remnants of the repulsively heavy make-up, my face looked terribly pale. I tore the veil off my head. I tried to unfasten the buttons on the back of my dress. It was useless. I yanked on the collar until the buttons ripped out. I wanted to tear that dress off and be rid of anything that symbolised that absurd marriage.

I looked around for something comfortable to wear. There was a bright red nightgown with masses of pleats and lace laid out on the bed. I said to myself, This is Mrs Parvin's shopping. I saw my suitcase sitting in a corner. It was large and heavy. I moved it with great difficulty and opened it. I took out one of my house dresses and put it on. I walked out of the bedroom. I didn't know where the bathroom was. I switched on all the lights and opened all the doors until I found it. I held my head under the sink faucet and soaped my face several times. The shaving kit on the side of the sink looked foreign. My eyes remained fixed on the razor. Yes, that was my only escape. I had to set myself free. I imagined them finding my lifeless corpse on the floor. For sure, the stranger would be the first person to discover it. He would be terrified, but he would certainly not be sad. But when Mother found out I was dead, she would wail and weep, she would remember how she clawed at my hair and dragged me out from under the bed, she would remember how I begged and pleaded, and her conscience would suffer. I felt

85

a certain chill and pleasure in my heart. I went on with my imaginings.

What would Father do? He would put his hand on the wall, lean his head on his arm and cry. He would remember how much I loved him, how I wished to study and didn't want to get married, he would be tormented by the cruelty he had shown me, and perhaps he would become ill. I was smiling at the mirror. What satisfying revenge!

Well, what would the others do?

Saiid. Oh, Saiid would be shocked. He would holler, cry and curse himself. Why didn't he come to ask for my hand in time? Why didn't he steal me away one night and help me escape? He will live the rest of his life with sorrow and regret. I didn't want him to have so much grief, but it was his own fault. Why did he disappear? Why did he not try to find me?

Ahmad! ... Ahmad would not be sad, but he would feel guilty. After he heard the news, he would be in a daze for a while. He would feel ashamed. Then he would run to Mrs Parvin's house and drink morning and night for an entire week. And from then on, he would spend all his drunken nights under my scolding gaze. My spirit would never leave him in peace.

Brother Mahmoud would shake his head and say, 'That wretched girl, sin after sin, what flames she must be burning in now.' He would not blame himself the slightest bit, but still, he would read a few *suras* from the Quran, he would pray for me on a few Friday nights, and he would be proud of himself for being such a compassionate and forgiving brother. A brother who despite my having been a bad girl had asked God to forgive me and who had lessened the burden of my sins with his prayers.

What about Ali? What would he do? He would probably be sad and become a bit reticent, but the minute the neighbourhood kids came for him, he would run out and play and forget everything. But poor little Faati, she was the only one who would cry for me with no sense of guilt. She would feel just as I did when Zari died, and she would be plagued by a destiny similar to mine. How sad that I won't be there to help her. She, too, would find herself friendless and alone. Mrs Parvin would praise me for having preferred death to an undignified life. She would regret that she had lacked the courage to do the same and had betrayed her great love. Parvaneh would learn about my death very late. She would cry and surround herself with the souvenirs she had of me and she would always remain sad. Alas! Parvaneh, how I miss you, how I need you.

I started to cry. The fantasies faded away. I picked up the razor and held it against my wrist. It wasn't very sharp. I had to press hard. I didn't have the heart, I was afraid. I tried to remember my rage, anger and hopelessness. I reminded myself of the wounds Ahmad had inflicted on Saiid. I counted, 'One, two, three,' and I pressed down. A strong burning sensation made me drop the razor. Blood gushed out. Pleased, I said, 'Well, that's one. Now how am I going to slash my other wrist?' The cut burned so much that I couldn't hold the razor with that hand. I said, 'It doesn't matter. It will just take longer, but in the end all the blood will drain out of this one wrist.'

Again, I drowned in my fantasies. I felt less pain. I looked at my wrist; it had stopped bleeding. I squeezed the wound and groaned in excruciating pain. A few drops of blood fell into the sink, but again the bleeding stopped. It was no use; the cut wasn't deep enough. I can't have reached the vein. I picked up the razor. The cut on my wrist was throbbing; how could I cut the same place again? I wished there was a better way that didn't involve so much pain and blood.

My mind instinctively went on the defence. I remembered the woman who had spoken at a ladies' Quran reading session. She had talked about the sin and the unseemliness of committing suicide, about how God would never forgive you if you took your own life, and about how you would spend eternity in the flames of hell, in the company of snakes with fiery fangs and torturers who flog the humans' burned bodies. There, you would have to drink rancid water and suffer the hot spears they would stab into your body. I remembered that for a week I had nightmares and had screamed in my sleep. No, I didn't want to go to hell. But what about my revenge? How could I make them suffer? How could I make them understand how ruthless they had been with me?

I thought to myself, I have to do this; otherwise I will lose my mind. I must torment them the way they tormented me. I must make them wear black and mourn my death for the rest of their lives. But will they really have tears in their eyes for the rest of their days? How long did they cry for Zari? She hadn't even committed a sin and now, from one year to the next, no one ever mentioned her name. Barely a week had passed when they all gathered around and said it was God's will and they should not question it, that it was divine providence and they should not be ungrateful. They said God was testing them and as his servants they must pass the test with honour. God had given and God had taken away. And in the end, they were all convinced that they had done no wrong and had played no role in Zari's death. I thought, it will be the same for me. After a few weeks they will quieten down and after two years, at the most, they will forget. But I will remain in eternal torment and I won't be there to remind them of what they did to me. And in the middle of all this, those who truly love me and need me will be left alone and grieving.

I threw down the razor. I couldn't do it. Just like Mrs Parvin, I had to give in to my destiny.

My wrist had stopped bleeding. I wrapped a handkerchief around it and returned to the bedroom. I went to bed, buried my head under the sheets and wept. I had to accept the fact that I had lost Saiid, that he did not want me. Just like someone burying a loved one, I buried Saiid in the deepest corner of my heart. I stood over his grave and cried for hours. Now, I had to leave him. I had to let time bring me indifference and forgetfulness and erase his memory from my mind. Would that day ever come?

CHAPTER TWO

The sun was high in the sky when I woke up from a deep and dreamless sleep. I looked around, confused and disoriented. Everything seemed unfamiliar. Where was I? It took a few seconds for me to remember everything that had happened. I was in that stranger's house. I leaped up and looked around the room. The door was open and the utter silence suggested I was alone. I was relieved. It was strange; a sort of indifference and coldness had spread through my whole being. The anger and rebellion that had raged inside me for the past several months seemed to have died down. I felt no sorrow and no yearning for the house I had lived in and the family from whom I had been separated. I felt no sense of belonging to them or to that house. I didn't even feel hatred. Even though it felt as cold as ice, my heart beat slowly and regularly. I wondered whether there was anything in the world that could one day make me feel happy again.

I got out of bed. The room was larger than it had seemed the night before. The bed and the dressing table were new. They still smelled of varnish. They were probably the ones Father said he had bought. My suitcase was open and in disarray. A carton stood in the corner of the room. I opened it. There were some sheets, pillowcases, oven mitts, kitchen linen, towels and a few other odds and ends that my family had not had time to unpack.

I walked out of the bedroom and into a square hall. There was another room on the far side. It looked like a storage room. To the left of the hall there was a large glass door with honeycomb panes. The kitchen and the bathroom were to the right. There was a red carpet on the floor of the hall and floor cushions and backrests made of carpet were arranged on either side. On one wall there were a few shelves full of books. Next to the glass door was another shelf with an old sugar bowl, the statue of the bust of a man I did not recognise, and a few more books.

I peeked into the kitchen. It was relatively small. On one side of the brick counter there was a navy-blue wicker lamp and on the other side a new gas range with two burners; the gas tank was under the counter. A set of china plates and platters with a red floral design were stacked on a small wooden table. I remembered them well. When I was young, Mother had bought them during a trip to Tehran for the trousseau Zari and I would need. A large carton sat in the middle of the kitchen. It was full of newly polished copper pots of different sizes, several spatulas and a large heavy copper tub. Obviously, they had not found an appropriate place to put them.

Everything that was new belonged to me and everything else belonged to the stranger. I was standing there surrounded by the dowry that had been prepared for me from the day I was born. The entire objective of my life was reflected in those kitchen and bedroom furnishings. Each piece revealed that the only thing expected of me was to work in the kitchen and to serve in the bedroom. What onerous duties. Would I be able to manage the tedious task of cooking in such a disorganised kitchen and tolerate my unpleasant duties in the bedroom with a stranger?

Everything was repulsive to me, but I didn't even have the energy to feel agitated.

I continued with my exploration and opened the glass door. One of our carpets was spread on the floor and sitting on the mantelpiece were two crystal candelabras with red pendants and a mirror with a clear frame. They were probably from my marriage ceremony, but I couldn't remember having seen them. In one corner was a rectangular table with an old faded tablecloth, on which sat a large brown radio with two big, bone-coloured knobs that looked like a pair of bulging eyes staring at me.

Next to the radio was a strange square box. I walked over to the table. There were a number of small and large envelopes with pictures of orchestras on them. I recognised the box. It was a gramophone, just like the one Parvaneh's family had. I opened the lid and ran my fingers over the black, round rings nestling inside one another. Too bad, I didn't know how to turn it on. I looked at the envelopes. It was fascinating; the stranger listened to foreign music. If only Mahmoud knew! ... The books and the gramophone were the only interesting items in the house. I wished they would just leave me alone there with those few things.

Well, there was nothing else in the apartment. I opened the front door and found myself on a small terrace. There were stairs that led down to the front yard and up to the rooftop. I went downstairs. In the middle of the brick-paved yard was a round reflecting pool with old blue paint and fresh clean water. Two long and narrow flowerbeds flanked either side of the pool, a relatively large cherry tree in the middle of one and another tree in the middle of the other. When autumn eventually came, I realised it was a persimmon. A few Damascus rose bushes with dusty, thirsty-looking leaves had been planted around the trees. Next to the wall, an old withered grapevine hung from a time-worn trellis.

The façade of the house and the walls surrounding the yard were made of red bricks. I could see the bedroom and living room windows of the upstairs apartment. There was a toilet at the far end of the yard, the kind we used to have in Qum and that I was always afraid of using. A few steps separated the yard from the wraparound terrace of the ground floor, which had tall windows with rolled-up wicker shades. The curtain at one of the windows was open. I walked over to it, shielded my eyes with my hands and peered inside. The furnishings consisted of a deep red carpet, several floor cushions and a bedding set that was folded up and stacked next to the wall. There was a samovar and a tea set next to one of the floor cushions.

The front door of the ground-floor apartment looked older than the front door of the apartment upstairs and there was a large pad-lock on it. I assumed this was where the stranger's grandmother lived. She was probably at some social gathering. I remembered seeing at the marriage ceremony an old, slightly bent woman wear-ing a white chador with tiny black flowers on it. I remembered she had put something in my hand; perhaps a gold coin. The stranger's family must have taken her somewhere else so that the bride and groom could be alone for a few days. The bride and groom! ... I snickered and went back to the yard.

A staircase led down to the cellar. Its door was locked. Narrow windows below the ground-floor veranda cast some light into the underground room. I peered through them. The cellar looked clut-tered and dusty. It was obvious that no one had gone down there in a long time. I turned to go back upstairs when my eyes again caught sight of the dusty Damascus rose bushes. I felt sorry for them. A watering can stood next to the reflecting pool. I filled it and watered the plants.

It was around one o'clock and I was starting to feel hungry. I went to the kitchen and found a box of pastries from the marriage cer-emony. I tasted one. It was very dry. I wanted something cold. There was a small, white refrigerator in the corner, containing cheese, butter, some fruit and a few other things. I took a bottle of water and a peach, sat on the kitchen windowsill and ate. I looked around; what a cluttered and messy kitchen.

I took a book from the shelves in the hall, went back to the unmade bed and lay down. I read a few lines, but I had no idea what I had read. I couldn't concentrate. I tossed the book aside and tried to sleep, but I couldn't. Thoughts kept dancing around in my head: now, what should I do? Do I have to spend the rest of my life with the stranger? Where had he gone in the middle of the night? He must have gone to his parents' house. He may have even com-plained to them about me. What should I say if his mother scolds me for having kicked her son out of his own home?

I tossed and turned for a while until the thought of Saiid erased all other thoughts from my head. I tried to push it aside. I chided myself that I should not think about him ever again. Now that I had failed to kill myself, I had to watch how I behaved. This was how it had started for Mrs Parvin, and now she was comfortably cheating on her husband. If I didn't want to turn out like her, I had to stop thinking about Saiid. But my memories of him wouldn't leave me alone. I decided the only solution was to start collecting pills so that if one day life seemed unbearable and I found myself being drawn down immoral roads, I would have an easy and painless means of suicide. Surely, God would understand that I had taken my life to escape from sin and would not assign me a horrifying punishment.

I felt as if I had been in bed for hours and had even dozed off, but when I looked at the large, round clock on the wall, I saw that it was only three-thirty. What could I do? I was terribly bored. I wondered, where did the stranger go? What does he plan to do with me? I wished I could live in that apartment without him having anything to do with me. There was music, a radio, plenty of books and, most important of all, there was peace, seclusion and independence. I had no desire at all to see my family. I could take care of all the household chores, and the stranger and I could live our separate lives. Oh, if only he would agree.

I remembered Mrs Parvin saying, 'Perhaps you will grow to like him. And if not, you can have your own life.' I shuddered. I knew exactly what she meant. But was she really guilty and at fault? Would I be an unfaithful woman if I were to do the same? Unfaithful to whom? Unfaithful to what? Which is the greater disloyalty: sleeping with a stranger whom I don't love, whom I don't want to touch me, to whom I was married after someone spoke a few words and I was forced to say yes or someone else said it on my behalf; or making love with a man I love, who is everything to me and with whom I dream of living, but no one has spoken those few words for us?

What strange thoughts were spinning around in my head. I had to do something, I had to keep busy; otherwise, I would lose my mind. I switched on the radio and turned up the volume. I had to hear voices other than my own. I went back to the bedroom and made the bed. I crumpled up the red nightgown and stuffed it in the carton that was there. I looked in the closet; it was untidy and many of the clothes had fallen off their hangers. I tossed everything out and arranged my clothes on one side and the stranger's clothes on the other. I tidied up the odds and ends in the dresser drawers and organised the items that were sitting on top of it. I dragged the heavy carton into the storage room across the hall, which contained only a few boxes of books. I tidied that room, too, and then I took the unnecessary items from the bedroom and stored them there. By the time I finished rearranging these two rooms it was dark outside. Now I knew where everything was.

I was hungry again. I washed my hands and went to the kitchen. Oh, it was in such a state, but I didn't have the energy to tidy it up. I boiled some water and brewed some tea. There was no bread. I smeared some butter and cheese on the dry pastries and ate them with a cup of tea. I went over to where the books were in the hall. Some had strange titles that I didn't quite understand; there were several law books, clearly the stranger's textbooks, and there were a number of novels and volumes of poetry – the works of Akhavan Saless, Forough Farokhzad and a few other poets that I really liked. I remembered the poetry book that Saiid had given to me. My small book, with an ink drawing on its cover of a stem of morning glory in a vase. I would have to remember to bring it. I leafed through Forough's *The Captive*. What courage she had and how boldly she had expressed her emotions. I felt some of her verses with my entire being, as if I had composed them myself. I marked a few of the poems so that later I could copy them in my poetry scrapbook. And I read out loud:

I am thinking of taking wing from this dark prison in a
moment of neglect,
To laugh in the face of the prison-keeper and to start life
anew beside you.

And again, I scolded myself to have some shame.

It was past ten o'clock when I picked up a novel and went to

94

bed. I was exhausted. The title of the book was *The Horsefly*. It described terrible and horrifying events but I couldn't put it down. It helped me to not think and to not be afraid of being alone in the stranger's home. I don't know what time it was when I finally fell asleep. The book fell from my hands and the light stayed on.

It was close to noon when I woke up. The apartment was still drowned in silence and solitude. I thought, What a blessing to live without being bothered by anyone; I can sleep as late as I want. I got up, washed my face, brewed some tea and again ate a few of the pastries. I said to myself, Today is Saturday and all the shops are open. If the stranger doesn't come back, I will have to go out and do a little shopping. But with what money? In fact, what am I going to do if he doesn't come back? He must have gone to work today and, God willing, he will come back late in the afternoon. I wanted to laugh; I had said God willing, meaning I would like him to come back. I wondered, Do I really value him in some way?

I remembered one of the stories in *Woman's Day* magazine. A young woman is forced into a marriage, just like me. On her wedding night she tells her husband that she loves another man and cannot go to bed with him. The husband promises not to touch her. After a few months, the woman starts to discover the man's virtues and gradually forgets her past love and develops feelings for her husband, but he is not willing to forget the promise he has made and never touches her. Could the stranger have made a similar promise? Excellent! I had no feelings for him; I just wanted him to come home. First, I needed to clarify where we stood with each other; second, I needed money; and third, I had to make it clear to him that under no circumstances was I willing to return to my family. The truth was that I had found a refuge and I liked living without being pestered and plagued by them.

I turned the radio on loud and went to work. I spent many long hours in the kitchen. I cleaned out the cabinets, lined their shelves with sheets of newspaper and neatly arranged the dishes and other odds and ends in them. I stacked the large copper pots under the countertop near the gas range. In the carton of towels and linens, I found some loose fabric. I cut it into different-sized tablecloths and since I didn't have a sewing machine I hand-stitched the borders. I spread one on the kitchen table and the others on the kitchen counter and cabinets. I put the new samovar, which was obviously part of my dowry, on one of the cabinets and set the tea tray next to it. I washed the gas range and the refrigerator, which were both very grimy, and spent a long time scrubbing the kitchen floor until it looked clean. There were a few embroidered tablecloths among my things. I took them to the living room and spread them on the mantelpiece, on the table where the radio and gramophone were, and on the bookshelves. I rearranged the records and books according to height and I fiddled with the gramophone a little, but I still couldn't turn it on.

I looked around me. The apartment had taken on a different look. I liked it. A noise out in the front yard drew me to the window, but I didn't see anyone there. The flowerbeds looked parched and thirsty. I went outside and watered them, and then I poured water in the yard and on the stairs and washed them. It was dark outside when, tired and drenched in sweat, I finally finished the work. I remembered that we had a bath in the apartment. Although there was no hot water and I didn't know how to turn on the large kerosene water heater in the corner of the bathroom, it was still a welcome prize. I washed the bathtub and the sink and then I took a cold shower. I quickly washed my hair, lathered my body and got out. I put on the floral house dress Mrs Parvin had made for me, gathered my hair in a ponytail and looked at myself in the mirror. I thought I looked very different. I was no longer a child. It was as if I had aged several years in just a few days.

At the sound of the door to the street my heart sank. I ran over to the window. The stranger's parents, his youngest sister Manijeh, and his grandmother Bibi were in the front yard. His sister was holding his grandmother under the arm and helping her up the steps to the ground-floor veranda. His father was walking ahead to unlock the door. I heard his mother panting up the stairs to the first floor. With trembling hands and legs, I opened the door and after taking a deep breath I said hello.

'Well! Well! Hello, madam bride. How are you? Where's the groom?' And before I had a chance to answer, his mother walked in and called out, 'Hamid? Son, where are you?'

I sighed with relief; they didn't know he had left on our wedding night and had not come back to the apartment. 'He is not home,' I said quietly.

'Where did he go?' his mother asked.

'He said he was going to visit his friends.'

His mother shook her head and started inspecting the apartment. She poked her head into every nook and cranny. I didn't know how to interpret the way she kept shaking her head. I felt as though a tough teacher was reviewing my exam paper. I was nervous, waiting for her final judgment. She ran her hand over the embroidered tablecloth I had spread on the mantelpiece in the living room and asked, 'Did you embroider this?'

'No.'

She went to the bedroom and opened the closet door. I liked how neat and tidy it was. Again she shook her head. In the kitchen, she looked inside the cabinets and examined the plates and platters. She picked one up and turned it over. 'Is it a Massoud?'

'Yes!'

Finally, the inspection ended and she returned to the hall. She sat down on a floor cushion and leaned against a backrest. I went to prepare some tea. I put some pastries on a platter and took it to the hall.

'My girl, come sit down,' she said. 'I am so very pleased. Just like Mrs Parvin said, you are pretty, meticulous, have excellent taste, and in just two days you have managed to straighten up this apartment. Your mother said a day or two after the marriage we would have to come and help you clean your home, but that doesn't seem necessary. I can tell you are a great homemaker and my mind is at ease. Now, my girl, where did you say Hamid is?'

'With his friends.'

'Look here, my girl, a wife must be a woman. She must keep a tight grip on her husband and manage him. You have to keep your eyes open. My Hamid has thorns and his thorns are his friends. You have to make sure he cuts himself off from them. And let me warn you, his friends aren't meek and obedient. Everyone said, if we get Hamid busy with a wife and kids, he will lose interest in them. Now it's up to you to keep him so distracted that he won't feel time fly by. And in nine months you should hand him his first child and nine months later the second one. In short, you have to keep him so busy that he will lose interest in all that other stuff. I did my best; by weeping, fainting and praying I finally managed to marry him off. Now it's your turn.'

It was as if a veil had suddenly been lifted from before my eyes. Aha! So just like me, the poor stranger had been forced to sit through that marriage ceremony. He was not interested in his spouse or married life. Perhaps he, too, was in love with someone else. But if that was the case, why didn't his family ask for that girl's hand? After all, their son and his desires were very important to them. Unlike me, he didn't have to sit and wait for suitors to come calling; he could choose anyone he wanted. His parents were so desperate to see him get married that they would not have objected to his choice. Perhaps he was altogether against marriage and didn't want to be burdened by it. But why? After all, he was a man of a certain age. Could it have been just because of his friends? His mother's voice pulled me out of my thoughts.

'I cooked herb stew with lamb shank. Hamid loves it. I didn't have the heart not to give him some. I brought you a pot. I know you're not going to have time to wash and clean herbs for quite a while ... By the way, do you have any rice here?'

Surprised, I shrugged.

'It's in the cellar. Every year his father buys rice for us and he always buys a few sacks for Bibi and Hamid as well. Make some smothered rice tonight; it will go well with the stew. Hamid doesn't like steamed rice. We are leaving tomorrow and I had to bring Bibi back home; otherwise, I would have kept her with us for a few more days. She is a harmless old woman. Look in on her once in a while.

She usually takes care of her own cooking, but it would be nice if you could drop in on her and take her some food. It would please God.'

Just then, Manijeh and her father walked in. I got up and said hello. Hamid's father smiled at me and said, 'Hello, my girl. How are you?' Then he turned to his wife and said, 'You were right. She looks much prettier than she did at the marriage ceremony.'

'Look and see what a home she has made in just a single day. See how she has cleaned and organised everything. Now let's see what excuse our son will come up with this time.'

Manijeh peeked around and said, 'How much time did you have? You two were probably sleeping all day yesterday and you had to go to the mother-in-law greeting.'

'We had to go to what?' I asked.

'The mother-in-law greeting. Isn't that right, Mother? Don't the married couple have to go visit the bride's mother the day after the marriage?'

'Well, yes. You should have gone. Didn't you?'

'No,' I said. 'I didn't know we had to.'

They all laughed.

'Of course, Hamid has no clue about these customs and traditions, and how would this poor girl know?' his mother said. 'But now that you do know, the two of you must go visit your mother. They are expecting you.'

'Yes, and they will give you gifts,' Manijeh said. 'Mother, remember the beautiful Allah pendant you gave Bahman Khan when he and Mansoureh came for the mother-in-law greeting?'

'Yes, I remember. By the way, my girl, what would you like me to bring for you from Mecca? And don't stand on ceremony.'

'Nothing, thank you.'

'And we've decided to hold the bedside ceremony after we return. Well, give it some thought until tomorrow and see if there is anything you would like from Mecca.'

'Missus, let's go,' his father said. 'I don't think this boy is going to show up and I'm tired. God willing, he will come to see us tomorrow or he will come to the airport to see us off. Well, my girl, let's leave the goodbyes for tomorrow.'

His mother hugged and kissed me and with a lump in her throat she said, 'Swear on your life and his that you will take care and not let anything bad happen to him. And do look in on Manijeh while we're away, although Mansoureh will take care of her.'

They left and I breathed a sigh of relief. I gathered the tea glasses and dessert plates and then went downstairs to look for the rice. I heard Bibi calling me from her apartment so I went over and said hello to her. She carefully looked me up and down and said, 'Hello to your beautiful face. God willing you will have a happy marriage, my girl, and you will straighten out this boy.'

'I'm sorry, but do you have the key to the cellar?' I asked.

'It's right there on top of the door frame, my girl.'

'Thank you. I'll prepare dinner right away.'

'Good girl. Cook, cook.'

'I'll bring some for you. Don't bother preparing anything for yourself.'

'No my girl, I don't eat dinner. But if you go to buy bread tomorrow, get some for me as well.'

'Of course!'

And I thought, If the stranger doesn't come back home, how am I going to buy bread?

The scent of smothered rice and fresh herb stew stirred my appetite. I couldn't remember the last time I had had a proper meal. Dinner was ready around ten o'clock, but there was no sign of the stranger. No, I couldn't and didn't want to wait for him. I ate ravenously, washed the dishes and put the leftovers, which were enough for four meals, in the refrigerator. Then I took my book and went to bed. Unlike the previous night, I fell asleep quickly.

I woke up at eight. My sleep hours were slowly returning to normal and the bedroom no longer felt unfamiliar. The peace that I felt after such a short time in that apartment I had never experienced in my own crowded and unsafe home. I lazily tossed around in bed for a while and then I got up and made the bed. I walked out of the bedroom and suddenly froze where I stood. The stranger was sleeping on a blanket on the floor, next to the floor cushions. I had not heard him come in the night before.

I stood still for a while. He was in a deep sleep. His figure wasn't as burly as I had imagined. His forearm was resting over his eyes and forehead. He had a bushy moustache that completely covered his upper lip and part of his lower lip as well. His hair was curly and tousled. He was somewhat olive-skinned and seemed to be tall. I said to myself, This man is my husband, but if I had run into him on the street, I would not have recognised him. How ridiculous. I quietly washed up and turned on the samovar. But what was I going to do about bread? Finally, I had an idea. I put on my chador and soundlessly walked out of the apartment. Bibi was at the reflecting pool, filling the watering can.

'Hello, Mrs Bride. Has that lazy Hamid not woken up yet?'

'No. I am going to go buy some bread. You still haven't had breakfast, have you?'

'No, my girl, and I'm not in a hurry.'

'Where is the bakery?'

'When you walk out the door, turn right, at the end of the road, turn left, go one hundred steps and you'll be right in front of the bakery.'

I fidgeted a bit and then I said, 'I'm sorry, do you have any small change? I don't want to wake Hamid and I'm afraid the bakery won't have any change.'

'Yes, my dear. It's on the mantelpiece.'

When I returned, Hamid was still asleep. I went to the kitchen and started preparing breakfast. I turned to take the cheese out of the refrigerator and suddenly came face to face with the stranger standing in the doorway. I instinctively gasped. He quickly stepped back, raised his arms in surrender, and said, 'No! No! For the love of God, don't be afraid. Do I look like the bogeyman! Am I really that scary?'

I wanted to laugh. Seeing me smile, he relaxed and raised his arms higher to rest his hands on top of the door frame.

'It looks like you are feeling better today,' he said.

'Yes, thank you. Breakfast will be ready in a few minutes.'

'Wow! Breakfast! And you've cleaned the place. I guess Mother was right when she said, with a woman in the house everything will be neat and tidy. I just hope I can still find my things. I'm not used to all this order.'

He went into the bathroom. A few minutes later, he called out, 'Hey ... there was a bathtowel here. Where did you put it?'

I took a folded towel to the bathroom door. He popped his head out and said, 'By the way, what is your name?'

I was stunned. He didn't even know my name. After all, my name had been spoken several times during the marriage cere-mony. How indifferent he must have been, or how deeply drowned in his own thoughts.

Coldly, I said, 'Massoum.'

'Ah, Massoum. But is it Massoum or Massoumeh?'

'It makes no difference. Most people call me Massoum.'

He peered more carefully into my face and said, 'It's good ... it suits you.'

My heart ached. He had said the same thing. What a difference between his love and affection and this one's indifference. He once told me he repeated my name a thousand times a day. Tears welled up in my eyes. I turned and went back to the kitchen, took the breakfast tray to the hall and spread the cloth on the floor. With his curly hair still wet and a towel slung around his neck, the stranger walked over. His dark eyes were kind and cheerful. I no longer felt any fear.

'Excellent! What a great breakfast. And we have fresh bread, too. Another benefit of being married.'

I thought he only said this for my benefit. He probably wanted to make up for the fact that he didn't know my name. He sat down cross-legged and I put a tea glass in front of him. He spread some cheese on a piece of bread and said, 'Well, tell me, why were you so afraid of me? Am I scary or would you have been frightened no matter who walked into your bedroom that night as your husband?'

'I would have been scared no matter who it was.'

And in my heart I continued, Except Saiid. If it were him, I would have leaped into his arms with my heart and soul.

102

'Then why did you get married?' he asked.

'I had to.'

'Why?'

'My family believed it was time.'

'But you are still very young. Did you think it was time?'

'No, I wanted to go to school.'

'Then why didn't you?'

'They said a year six certificate is enough for a girl,' I explained. 'I begged so much that they actually let me study a few more years.'

'So they forced you to sit through that marriage ceremony and they refused to let you go to school, which was your legitimate right.'

'Yes.'

'Why didn't you resist? Why didn't you stand up to them? Why didn't you rebel?'

He looked flushed.

'You should have claimed your right, even if by force. If people refused to submit to coercion, there wouldn't be so many oppressors in the world. It is this submissiveness that strengthens the foundations of tyranny.'

I was amazed; he had no notion of reality. I stifled my laugh and with a smile that must have been sarcastic, I said, 'So you didn't submit to coercion?'

He gaped at me and said, 'Who? Me?'

'Yes, you. They forced you to sit through that marriage ceremony, didn't they?'

'Who said such a thing?'

'It's obvious. You can't say you were counting the minutes to get married. Your poor mother worked so hard, swooned and pleaded so much, until you finally gave in.'

'My mother said all this, didn't she? Well, she told you the truth. And you are right, I was forced into it. Beating and torturing people isn't the only means of oppression; sometimes people use love and affection to disarm you. But when I agreed to get married, I didn't think any girl would want to marry me under these circumstances.'

103

For a while, we ate in silence. Then he picked up his tea glass, leaned against a floor cushion and said, 'You are really good at cutting someone down to size ... I like it. You didn't waste a minute.' Then he laughed and I started laughing, too.

'Do you know why I didn't want a wife?' he asked.

'No. Why?'

'Because when a man gets married his life is no longer his. His hands and feet are tied and he gets so tangled up that he can't think about his ideals or try to reach them. Someone once said, "When a man gets married, he stands still. When his first child is born, he drops to his knees. When the second child comes, he lies prostrate. And with the third one, he is destroyed." Or something along those lines ... Of course, I don't mind having my breakfast ready and my home clean, having someone to wash my clothes and take care of me. But this is all human selfishness and it is rooted in the incorrect way we are brought up in a male-dominated society. I believe we shouldn't think about women like this. Women are the most oppressed people in history. They were the first group of humans to be exploited by another group. They have always been used as a tool and they continue to be used as a tool.'

Although his comments sounded a little like they came straight from a book and I didn't understand a few of the words, such as 'exploited', I still liked what he had said. The phrase 'Women are the most oppressed people in history' became etched in my mind.

'Is that why you didn't want to get married?' I asked.

'Yes, I didn't want to be restricted and confined, because that is the inescapable nature of traditional marriages. Perhaps if we were friends and of the same mind and outlook, it would be different.'

'So why didn't you marry someone like that?'

'The girls in our group don't opt for marriage all that easily. They, too, have dedicated themselves to the cause. Besides, my mother hates everyone in our group. She used to say, "If you marry one of them, I will kill myself."'

'Did you love her?'

'Love who? ... Oh, no. Don't misunderstand. I don't mean I was

104

in love with someone and my mother was against it. No! My parents were insisting that I get married and I decided to put an end to the whole issue by marrying someone in our group. That way, she wouldn't become an obstacle to my activities, but my mother read my hand.'

'In your group? Which group do you mean?'

'It is not a formal group,' he said. 'We're just a bunch of people who get together to take valuable actions that benefit the disadvantaged. After all, everyone has goals and ideals in life and strives to achieve them. What are your goals? What direction do you want to take?'

'My goal was to continue my education. But now ... I don't know.'

'Don't tell me you want to spend the rest of your life scrubbing this apartment.'

'No!'

'Then what? If your goal is to get an education, do it. Why are you giving up?'

'Because they don't allow married people in secondary school,' I said.

'You mean to tell me you don't know there are other ways of getting an education?'

'Like what?'

'Go to night school and take the standardised tests. Not everyone has to go to an ordinary school.'

'I know, but wouldn't you object?'

'Why would I object? As a matter of fact, I would rather be with an educated and intelligent person. Besides, it's your right. Who am I to stand in your way? I'm not your jailer.'

I was stunned. I couldn't believe what I was hearing. What sort of a man was he? How different he was from all the other men I knew. I felt as though a light as bright as the sun had been turned on in my life. I was so happy I could barely talk. I said, 'Are you telling the truth? Oh, if you would only let me go to school ...'

He wanted to laugh at my reaction but instead he kindly said, 'Of course I'm telling the truth. It is your right and you don't need

105

to thank anyone for it. Everyone should be able to pursue what they like and believe to be the right path for them. Being married doesn't mean impeding your spouse's interests. On the contrary, it means supporting them. Isn't that so?'

I nodded enthusiastically. I understood his inference that I, too, should not impede his activities. From that day on, our agreement became the unwritten rule of our life together; and although because of it I gained some of my human rights, in the end it was a rule that proved not to my benefit.

He didn't go to work that day and, naturally, I didn't ask why. He decided we should go to his parents' house for lunch. They were leaving on their trip that evening. It took me a while to get ready. I didn't know how I should dress. I decided to wear my headscarf as I usually did and if he disapproved then I would put on my chador. When I walked out of the bedroom, he pointed to my headscarf and said, 'What is that? Does it have to stay?'

'Well, ever since my father gave me permission, I have only worn a headscarf. But if you prefer, I will wear a chador.'

'Oh, no! No!' he exclaimed. 'Even the headscarf is too much. Of course, it's up to you. Dress any way you like. This is a human right, too.'

After a very long time, that day I felt cheerful. I felt I had a supporter I could rely on, I felt the dreams that only a few hours ago had seemed impossible were now within my reach. And I walked beside him with tranquillity. We talked. He talked more than I did. At times, he was too bookish and sounded like a teacher lecturing a stupid student. But I didn't mind. He was truly well read and when it came to experience and education, I wouldn't even be considered his student. I was in awe of him.

At his parents' house everyone gathered around us. His oldest sister, Monir, and her two sons had come from Tabriz. The two boys were somewhat distant and didn't mingle with the others that much. They mostly spoke to each other and only in Turkish. Monir was very different from her sisters and looked much older than them. To me, she looked more like their aunt than their sister. Everyone was happy to see that Hamid and I were getting along with each other. Hamid was constantly joking with his mother and sisters. He kept teasing them and, stranger yet, he would kiss them on the cheek. To me it was all funny and surprising. In the house where I grew up, the men rarely spoke to the women, much less joked and laughed with them. I liked the atmosphere in their home. Ardeshir, Mansoureh's son, had started crawling. He was very sweet and kept throwing himself into my arms. I felt well and I laughed from the bottom of my heart.

'Well, thank God, the bride knows how to laugh,' Hamid's mother said joyfully. 'We hadn't seen her laughter.'

'In fact, she looks so much more beautiful when she laughs, with those dimples in her cheeks,' Mansoureh added. 'I swear, if I were you I would always laugh.' I blushed and looked down. Mansoureh went on, 'See, brother. See what a beautiful girl we found for you. Say thank you.'

Hamid laughed. 'I am much obliged.'

'What is the matter with all of you?' Manijeh said, sulking. 'Why are you acting like you've never seen a human being before?'

Then she walked out of the living room and her mother said, 'Leave her alone. After all, she was always her brother's pet. Oh, I am so happy. Now that I see you two together, I feel so relieved. I thank God a hundred thousand times. Now I can fulfil my pledge at the house of God.'

Just then, Hamid's father walked in and we stood up to greet him. He kissed me on the forehead and gently said, 'Well, Miss Bride. How are you? I hope my son hasn't been bothering you.'

I blushed and looked down and quietly said, 'No, he hasn't.'

'If he ever does, come and tell me. I will pull his ear so hard that he won't dare ever upset you again.'

'Dear Dad, please don't,' Hamid said, laughing. 'You've pulled our ears so much that we are all long-eared.'

While we were saying our goodbyes, his mother drew me aside and said, 'Listen, my dear, ever since the olden days it has been said that you have to establish the terms of your marriage from the

107

very first night. Stand firm. I don't mean fight with him; instead, use good humour and kindness. You will find the way. After all, you are a woman. Flirt, coquette, sulk and charm. In short, don't let him stay out late at night and in the morning send him to work on time. You have to cut his friends out of your life. And, God willing, get pregnant soon. Don't give him a break. Once he has a couple of kids around him, he will forget all about his tomfooleries. Show me your grit.'

On the way back home, Hamid asked, 'Well, what was Mother telling you?'

'Nothing. She just said I should take care of you.'

'Yes, I know; to take care of me so that I stop socialising with my friends. Right?'

'Something like that . . .'

'Any what did you say?'

'What could I say?'

'You should have said, I'm not a watch-guard in hell to want to make his life miserable.'

'How could I possibly say such a thing to my mother-in-law on the very first day?'

'God save us from these old-fashioned women!' he groaned. 'They don't understand the concept of marriage. They think a wife is a shackle around a wretched man's ankles, when in fact the meaning of marriage is companionship, collaboration, understanding, acceptance of each other's desires and equal rights. Do you think marriage means anything other than this?'

'No. You are absolutely right.' And in my heart, I praised all that wisdom and selflessness.

'I can't tolerate women who constantly ask their husband, where were you, who were you with and why did you come home late? Among us, men and women have equal and clearly defined rights, and neither has the right to fetter the hands and feet of the other or to force them to do things they don't like. And they don't have the right to cross-examine each other either.'

'How wonderful!'

I got the message loud and clear. I must never ask why, where and with whom ... The truth is that, at the time, it really wasn't important to me. After all, he was much older than me, much better educated and far more experienced. Surely he knew better how one should live. Besides, what did I care what he did and where he went? It was more than enough for me that he believed in women's rights and would allow me to continue my education and pursue my interests.

We returned home late in the evening. Without saying a word, he took a pillow and a sheet and started preparing a place to sleep. I was ill at ease. It was embarrassing for me to sleep on the bed and to make someone as kind as him sleep on the floor. I hesitated for a while and finally said, 'This is really not right. Go sleep on the bed and I will sleep on the floor.'

'No, I don't mind. I can sleep anywhere.'

'But I'm used to sleeping on the floor.'

'Me, too.'

I went into the bedroom and wondered how long we could continue living like that. I had no amorous feelings or instinctive desire for him, but I did feel indebted to him. He had saved me from my parents' house and he was extending the greatest kindness to me by allowing me to go back to school. And that first day's feeling of repulsion at the thought of him touching me had disappeared. I went back to the hall, stood over him and said, 'Please come and sleep in your place.'

He looked at me with curious, probing eyes. With a faint smile, he reached out and I helped him get up; and he took his place as my husband.

That night, after he fell into a deep sleep, I cried for hours and paced up and down the apartment. I didn't know what was wrong with me. I had no clear thoughts. I was just sad.

A few days later, Mrs Parvin came to see me. She was all excited. 'I waited all this time for you to come and see me, but you didn't, so I decided to come myself and see how you are.'

'I'm fine!'

'So how is he? He hasn't bothered you, has he? Tell me, what did you have to suffer on the first night? The state you were in, I thought you would surely have a heart attack.'

'Yes, I felt terrible that day. But he understood. Seeing the way I was, he went out and let me sleep comfortably.'

'Wow! What a sweetheart!' she said, surprised. 'Thank God. You can't imagine how worried I was. Now do you see how wise he is? If you had married that butcher, Asghar, God knows what he would have done to you. So, all in all, are you pleased with him?'

'Yes, he's a very nice man. His family is nice, too.'

'Thank God! Now you see how different they are from your other suitors.'

'Yes, and I owe it all to you. I am only now realising what a great service you have done for me.'

'Oh, come on ... it was nothing. You are so good yourself that they liked you, and thank God you are now comfortable. It was your good fortune. Miserable me, I didn't have any such luck.'

'But you don't have any problems with Haji Agha,' I said. 'The poor man leaves you alone.'

'Huh! You see him now that he's old and sick and has lost his pluck. You don't know what a wolf he was, how he attacked me that first night, how I was shaking and crying, how he beat me. Back then, he was rich and he still believed that if a woman doesn't get pregnant it is because there is something wrong with her. He was a big shot and really full of himself. He did unspeakable things to me. The moment I heard the front door and knew that he was home, I would start shaking from head to toe. I was just a child and I was terrified of him. But when by the grace of God he went bankrupt, lost everything, and the doctors told him he had a problem and could never have any children, it was like taking a needle to a balloon, all the air went out of him. Overnight, he aged twenty years and everyone abandoned him. By then I was older and stronger and had more courage. I could stand up to him or walk out on him. Now, he's afraid that I, too, will desert him and so he leaves me alone. Today, it's my turn to run wild; but what about the youth and health that he stole from me? I can never get them back ...'

We sat in silence for a while. She shook her head as if she wanted to rid herself of her memories. And then she said, 'By the way, why haven't you gone to visit your parents?'

'Why should I visit them? What good did they do for me?'

'What? After all, they're your parents.'

'They threw me out of the house. I will never go there again.'

'Don't say that; it's sinful. They are expecting you.'

'No, Mrs Parvin. I can't. Don't talk about it any more.'

Three weeks had passed of my married life when one morning the doorbell rang. I was surprised. I had no one who would come to visit me. I ran to the door and saw Mother and Mrs Parvin standing there. I was taken aback and coldly said hello.

'Hello, madam!' Mrs Parvin said. 'It seems you're having a really good time, the way you left and never looked back. Your mother was dying of sorrow. I told her, "Let's go so you can see for yourself that your daughter is well."'

'Where have you been, girl?' Mother asked, crossly. 'I've been worried sick. For three weeks we've had our eyes glued to the door, waiting for you. Don't you ever tell yourself that you have a mother and a father? That there are customs and traditions?'

'Really!' I said. 'Which customs and traditions do you mean?'

Mrs Parvin motioned with her head for me to keep quiet and then she said, 'At least invite us in. This poor woman has walked a long way in this heat.'

'Very well,' I said. 'Please come in.'

As she climbed the stairs, Mother grumbled, 'The day after the marriage ceremony, we sat up until all hours of the night waiting for our groom to come visit us. No one came. Then we said maybe you'll come the next day, we said maybe this Friday, we said maybe next Friday. Finally, I said the girl must be dead, something has happened to her. How could someone leave her father's house and never look back? As if she never had a father and a mother to whom she is indebted.'

We were in the middle of the hall when I suddenly couldn't stand listening to her any more.

'Indebted?' I snapped. 'Why am I indebted to you? Because you made me? Did I ask to be conceived for me to now feel obligated to you? It was all for your own pleasure, and when you found out I was a girl, you mourned and grieved and regretted having had me. What have you ever done for me? I begged you to let me go to school. Did you? I begged you not to force me into marriage, to let me live in that miserable house for another year or two. Did you? How much did you beat me? How many times did I come close to dying? How many months did you keep me locked up in that house?'

Mother was weeping and Mrs Parvin was looking at me with horror. But the anger and frustration in my heart had erupted and I couldn't suppress it.

'From as far back as I can remember, you have said a girl belongs to others, and you were quick to hand me over to others. You were so desperate to get rid of me that you didn't even care who you were handing me over to. Wasn't it you who dragged me out from under the bed so that you could throw me out all the quicker? Wasn't it you who said that I had to leave that house so Mahmoud could get married? Well, you threw me out. I now belong to others. And you expect me to kiss your hand? Excellent! Well done!'

'That's enough, Massoumeh!' Mrs Parvin scolded. 'You should be ashamed of yourself. Look at what you're doing to this poor woman. No matter what, they are your parents, they raised you. Doesn't your father love you enough? He wanted everything for you. Did he not worry enough for you? I saw what this woman went through while you were sick. She sat with you every night until dawn and she cried and prayed for you. You were never an ungrateful girl. All parents, even the worst ones, deserve their child's gratitude. Whether you like it or not, you are indebted to them and it is your duty to observe and recognise this; otherwise, God will be offended and he will turn his anger on you.'

I felt calmer, I felt unburdened. The hatred and spite that had been bothering me like a pus-filled boil was draining out and Mother's tears soothed my pain like a salve.

'My duty as their child? Very well; I will observe my duties as

112

their child. I don't want to end up being the guilty party.' Then I turned to Mother and said, 'If you ever need me to do anything for you, I will do it, but don't expect me to forget what you did to me.'

Weeping even harder, Mother said, 'Go bring a knife and cut this hand that dragged you by your hair out from under the bed. I swear to God I will feel better, I will suffer less. A hundred times a day, I tell myself, May God break your arm, woman; how could you beat that innocent child like that? But my girl, if I hadn't done what I did, do you know what would have happened? Your brothers would have cut you into tiny pieces. On the one hand, from early that morning, Ahmad kept telling me, "If this girl starts acting up and embarrassing us, I will set her on fire." And on the other hand, your father's heart had been aching all week. It was thanks to pills and medications that he made it through that day. I was terrified he was going to have a heart attack. What was I to do? I swear, my heart was breaking, but I didn't know what else to do.'

'You mean you didn't want to marry me off?'

'Yes, I did. I prayed a thousand times a day that a decent man would show up, take your hand and save you from that house. Do you think I didn't know how sad and unhappy you were in that prison? You were getting thinner and sallower by the day. My heart broke every time I looked at you. I prayed and made pledges to God for you to find a good husband and to be set free. Grieving for you was killing me.'

The kindness of her words was thawing the ice of my stubborn anger. I said, 'Now, stop crying.' And I went and brought three glasses of chilled sherbet.

To change the mood, Mrs Parvin said, 'Well, well! What a clean and organised home you have. By the way, did you like your bed and dressing table? I chose them myself.'

'Yes, Mrs Parvin worked very hard during that time,' Mother said. 'We are all grateful to her.'

'I am, too.'

'Oh, please stop! Don't embarrass me. What hard work? It was a pleasure. No matter what I chose for you, your father bought it without a moment's hesitation. I had never shopped like that. If I

113

had asked him to buy the Shah's furniture for you, he would have bought it. It's obvious the dear man truly loves you. Ahmad was constantly yelling, why I was racking up so many expenses, but your father wanted to do it for you. He kept saying, "I want everything to be respectable. I want her to be able to hold her head up high in front her husband's family. I don't want them to say she didn't have a proper dowry."'

Still sniffling, Mother said, 'The sofas he ordered for you are ready. He is waiting to see when would be a convenient time for you so that he can have them delivered.'

I sighed. 'Well, how is he feeling now?'

'What can I say? He's not well.'

She wiped her eyes with the tip of her headscarf and said, 'That's what I wanted to talk to you about. It's all right if you don't want to see me, but your father is dying of sorrow. He doesn't talk to anyone in the house and he has started smoking again, one cigarette after the other, and he is coughing non-stop. I'm afraid for him, I'm afraid something bad is going to happen to him. Just for his sake, stop by the house. I don't want you to regret not having seen him.'

'God forbid! Don't be a naysayer. I'll come. I'll come this week. I'll see when Hamid has time; and if he doesn't have time, I'll come myself.'

'No my dear, that's not right. You have to do as your husband wishes. I don't want him to get upset.'

'No, he won't be upset. Don't worry, I'll arrange it.'

Hamid made it clear to me that he had no interest in or patience for family visits and he encouraged me to build an independent social life for myself. He even wrote down a bus guide, sketched out the various routes and explained when it would be best to take a taxi. A few days later, on an afternoon in mid-August when I knew Hamid was not going to be home, I got dressed and went to my parents' house. It was strange; the house had so soon become 'theirs' and no longer 'mine'. Do other girls become strangers in their family homes this quickly?

It was the first time I had gone out alone and travelled a long distance by bus. Although I was a bit nervous, I liked that sense of independence. I felt I was an adult. When I reached my old neighbourhood, different emotions stirred up in me. The thought of Saiid made my heart ache and walking past Parvaneh's old house made me miss her all the more. Worried that I might start crying in the middle of the street, I started to walk faster, but the closer I got to Father's house, the weaker my legs felt. I didn't want to come face to face with the people in the neighbourhood. I was embarrassed.

Tears welled up in my eyes when Faati greeted me at the door, jumped into my arms and started to cry. She begged me to move back to the house or take her away with me. When I walked in, Ali didn't move from where he was sitting. He just shouted at Faati, 'Stop snivelling! Didn't I tell you to go fetch my socks?'

It was close to dusk when Ahmad came home. He was already drunk and in a stupor. Completely ignoring the fact that it had been almost a month since he had last seen me, he took whatever it was he had left behind and went out again. When Mahmoud arrived, he scowled, mumbled something in answer to my hello and went upstairs.

'You see, Mother, I shouldn't have come. Even if I visit once a year, it will still upset them.'

'No, my girl, it's not about you. Mahmoud is angry over something else. He hasn't talked to anyone in a week.'

'Why? What's the matter with him?'

'Don't you know? The other week we got all dressed up, bought pastries, fruit and a few lengths of fabric, and went to Qum to see your father's sister to ask for Mahboubeh's hand for our Mahmoud.'

'Well?'

'Nothing came of it. It wasn't meant to be. A week earlier, she had given her consent to marry someone else. They hadn't told us out of spite, because we hadn't invited them to your marriage ceremony. Of course, it's all for the best. I wasn't happy about the two of them getting married ... with that witch of a mother. It was Mahmoud who kept talking about his cousin – Mahboubeh this and Mahboubeh that.'

I felt a kind of joy fill my entire being and I understood the meaning of 'sweet revenge' with every cell in my body. I said to myself, You are so vindictive! And someone inside me replied, He deserves it; let him suffer.

'You can't imagine how your aunt bragged about the groom. She said he's the son of an ayatollah, but he has gone to university and is modern thinking. Then she went on and on about his wealth and property. Poor Mahmoud, he was so angry he wouldn't have bled even if you had stabbed him with a knife. His face was so red I thought he was going to have a heart attack. And then they made a few snide remarks about how they were going to trim the house with lights and celebrate the wedding for seven days and seven nights, that one should marry off a girl with pride, not in secret and in a rush, and that if an aunt isn't going to be invited to her niece's wedding, then who is . . .'

I was in the room when Father came home. I went and stood by the wall so he wouldn't see me; it was darker inside than it was outside. He held on to the door frame with one hand, leaned his left ankle on his right knee and started to untie his shoelace.

'Hello,' I said, gently.

His foot dropped to the floor and he peered around in the dimness. For a few seconds he looked at me with a smile full of kindness and then he raised his foot back up to his knee and as he continued to take his shoes off, he said, 'What a surprise! You remembered us?'

'I always remember you.'

He shook his head, put on his slippers and, just like old times, I handed him his towel. He looked at me with reproachful eyes and said, 'I never thought you would be this unfaithful.' There was a big lump in my throat. These were the kindest words he could have spoken.

During dinner, he kept putting everything in front of me and talking fast. I had never known him to be this talkative. Mahmoud didn't come down to eat.

'Well, tell me,' Father said, laughing. 'What do you feed your husband for lunch and dinner? Do you even know how to cook? I heard he wants to come and complain about you!'

'Who? Hamid? The poor man never complains about food. He eats whatever I put in front of him. As a matter of fact, he says, "I don't want you to waste your time cooking."'

'Huh! Then what are you supposed to do?'

'He says I have to continue my education.'

There was silence. I saw a glint in Father's eyes and everyone else gaped at me.

'What about taking care of the house?' Mother asked.

'It's easy. I can do both. Besides, Hamid says, "I don't care at all about lunch and dinner and household chores. You have to do what interests you; especially going to school, which in fact is very important."'

'Forget it!' Ali said. 'They won't let you in school any more.'

'Yes, they will. I went and spoke to them. I'm going to go to night school and I can take the standardised exams. By the way, I should remember to take my books with me.'

'Thank God!' Father exclaimed. And Mother looked at him with surprise.

'Well, where are my books?'

'I put them all in the blue duffel bag; it's in the basement,' Mother said. 'Ali, son, go fetch the bag.'

'Why should I? Doesn't she have arms and legs?'

Father turned to him with unprecedented anger and, with his hand raised ready to strike Ali in the mouth, he shouted, 'Quiet! I don't ever want to hear you talk to your sister like that ... If you ever make that mistake again, I will crush every tooth in your mouth.'

We were all staring at Father. Ali, looking irked and intimidated, got up and walked out. Faati sat tight against me and quietly chuckled. I could sense her satisfaction.

When I got up to leave, Father walked me to the door and quietly whispered, 'Will you come again?'

It was too late to enrol in night school for the summer term. I registered for autumn and waited impatiently for classes to start. I had plenty of free time and spent most of it reading Hamid's books. I started with works of fiction and moved on to the poetry books, which I read carefully. Then I read the philosophy books, which were very boring and difficult. Eventually, having nothing else to do, I even read his old textbooks. But as pleasant as reading was, it wasn't enough to make my life fulfilling.

Hamid hardly ever came home early and sometimes he would not show up at all for several days. At first, I would cook dinner, spread out the tablecloth and sit and wait for him. Many times I fell asleep waiting, but continued the same routine. I hated eating alone.

Once, he came home around midnight and found me asleep on the floor next to the dinner spread. He woke me up and snapped, 'Don't you have anything better to do than to waste time cooking?' Startled at having been jolted awake and wounded by his reaction, I went to bed and quietly cried until I fell asleep. The next morning, like a lecturer addressing an audience of idiots, he delivered a lengthy speech about the role of women in society, and then with controlled anger he said, 'Don't act like illiterate, traditional women or exploited, shackled women and try to trap me with foolish love and kindness.'

Angry and hurt, I retorted, 'I wasn't trying to do anything. It's just that I get tired of being alone and I don't like eating by myself. I thought since you don't come home for lunch and who knows what you eat, I could prepare a proper meal for your dinner.'

'Perhaps consciously your intention is not to trap me, but subconsciously that is your goal. It's an old trick women use. They try to snare a man through his stomach.'

'Forget it! Who wants to trap you? After all we are husband and wife. It's true that we don't love each other, but we are not enemies either. I would enjoy talking with you, learning from you and hearing a voice other than my own in the house. And you would eat at least one home-cooked meal a day. Besides, your mother insisted on it. She worries a lot about you eating properly.'

'Aha! I was right to try to find my mother's footprints in all this. I know it's not your fault; you're just following her instructions.

118

From day one, you intelligently and rationally agreed to never be an obstacle to my life, my duties and my ideals. So please tell Mother on my behalf, she shouldn't worry at all about my meals. We have meetings every night and a couple of the guys are responsible for food and they are pretty good cooks.'

From that day on, I never waited for him at night. He spent his life with invisible friends, in an environment that I knew nothing about. I didn't know who his friends were, where they came from and what those ideals were that they were so proud of. All I knew was that their influence over Hamid was a hundred times more than mine or his family's.

With the start of night school, my days took on a regular schedule. I spent much of my time studying, but loneliness and the empty house, especially in the early darkness of cold and silent autumn nights, still weighed on me. Our life continued based on mutual respect, without fights and arguments and without any excitement. My only outing was on Fridays when Hamid would make sure to come home in time for us to go visit his parents. I was content to settle for even these brief opportunities to be with him.

I knew he didn't like me wearing a headscarf, especially when we went out together. In the hope that he would take me out more often, I put all my headscarves away. But his friends left him no free time to spend with me and, given his strange sensitivity, I didn't dare complain or mention them.

Hamid's grandmother Bibi, who lived just below us, was my only companion. I took care of her and prepared her meals. She was a kind and quiet woman and far more hard of hearing than I had originally thought. When I wanted to talk to her, I had to scream so much that in the end I would get exhausted and give up. She asked me every day, 'My dear, did Hamid come home early last night?'

And I would answer, 'Yes.'

To my surprise, she always believed me and never asked why she never saw him. She couldn't hear, but she acted as if she couldn't see either. Once in a while when she was feeling lively, she would tell me about the past, about her husband who was a good and pious man and whose death had left a chill in her heart even in the summertime. She talked about her children who were busy with their own lives and seldom visited her. Sometimes she told me about my father-in-law's childhood mischiefs. He was her first and favourite child. And now and then, she reminisced about people I didn't know and most of whom had died. Bibi had been a happy and fortunate woman, but now it seemed she had nothing to do but wait for death, even though she wasn't all that old. What was strange was that the others were waiting for the same thing. Not that they ever said anything or neglected her in any way, but there was something in their behaviour that conveyed this.

Loneliness resulted in my picking up my old habit of talking to the mirror. I would sit and talk to my reflection for hours. I loved doing this when I was a child despite the fact that my brothers always made fun of me and called me crazy. I had tried hard and broken the habit; but in reality, the desire had never left me, it had just been suppressed. Now that I had no one to talk to and no reason to hide anything, it had again surfaced. Talking to her, or to myself, however one should describe it, helped me organise my thoughts. Sometimes we visited past memories and cried together. I would tell her how much I missed Parvaneh. If only I could find her; there was so much for us to talk about.

One day I finally decided to try to find Parvaneh. But how? Again, I had to ask Mrs Parvin for help. On one of my visits to Mother's house, I also stopped by to see her, and I asked her to enquire around the neighbourhood and see whether anyone knew where the Ahmadi family was living. I was too embarrassed to talk to those people myself; I always felt they looked at me in a special way. Mrs Parvin asked around, but no one had any information, or perhaps because they knew about her relationship with Ahmad, they didn't want to give her the Ahmadi's address. One person even asked her if she wanted the address so that a knife-wielding thug could pay the family another visit. I decided to stop by my old school, but they no longer had Parvaneh's file. She had changed schools. My literature teacher was happy to see me.

When I told her I was continuing my education she very much encouraged me.

One cold and dark winter evening when I was bored and had nothing to do, Hamid came home early and gave me the honour of having dinner with me. I was beside myself with joy. Fortunately, that morning Mother had come to see me and she had brought some white fish for us. She had said, 'Your father bought fish, but he just couldn't swallow a bite of it unless he shared it with you. I brought some so he could rest easy.'

I had put the fish in the refrigerator, but I wasn't in the mood to cook it just for myself. When I realised Hamid was staying home for dinner, I used some dried herbs and made herb rice to go with the fish. It was the first time I had cooked it, but it didn't turn out bad. In truth, I mustered all my cooking skills to prepare it. The smell of fried fish had whetted Hamid's appetite. He was idling around the kitchen and picking at the food and I was laughing and telling him off. When everything was ready, I asked him to take Bibi's dinner downstairs for her. Then I spread the tablecloth and adorned it with everything we had available. It was as if there was a formal feast in the house and in my heart. Oh, how easy it was to make me happy and how they denied it to me.

Hamid came back, quickly washed his hands and we sat down to eat. While picking the bones out of the fish for both of us, he said, 'You have to eat herb rice and fish with your fingers.'

And I spontaneously said, 'Oh, what a wonderful evening! On this cold and dark night, I would have gone crazy with loneliness if you hadn't come home ...'

He was quiet for a while and then he said, 'Don't take it so hard. Take advantage of your time. You have your classes to study for and there are all these books here. Read them. I wish I had the time to sit and read.'

'There are no books left for me to read. I have even read some of them twice.'

'Are you serious? Which ones have you read?'

'All of them; even your textbooks.'

121

'You are joking! Did you understand any of them?'

'Some of them not very well. As a matter of fact, I do have a few questions I would like to ask you when you have some time.'

'That's strange! How about the short-story collections?'

'Oh, I love them. I cry every time I read them. They are so sad. There is so much pain and suffering and so many tragedies.'

'They reveal only a small corner of the realities of life,' he said. 'To gain greater power and wealth, governments have always forced the deprived and defenceless masses to toil and they have pocketed the fruits of their labour. The end result is injustice, misery and poverty for the people.'

'It is so heartbreaking. When will all this despair end? What can one do?'

'Resist! The one who understands must stand up against tyranny. If every freeborn man fights against injustice, the system will collapse. It is inevitable. In the end, the oppressed of the world will unite and eradicate all this injustice and treachery. We must help pave the way for this unity and uprising.'

He sounded as if he was reading from a document, but I was fascinated. I was in awe of the things he was saying and, instinctively, I recited a poem:

If you rise, if I rise
everyone will rise.
If you sit, if I sit, who will rise?
Who will fight the foe?

'Wow! Bravo!' he said, surprised. 'I guess you do understand a thing or two. Sometimes you say things that one doesn't expect hearing from someone your age and with your education. It seems we can put you on the path.'

I didn't know whether I should take his words as a compliment or an insult. But I didn't want a single dark shadow to fall across our cosy evening and decided to ignore what he had said.

After dinner, he leaned against the backrest and said, 'It was really delicious and I ate so much. It's been a long time since I had a meal this good. The poor guys, who knows what they had to eat tonight. Probably the usual bread and cheese.'

Taking advantage of his good mood and the comment he had made, I said, 'Why don't you invite your friends for dinner one night?' He looked at me pensively. He was weighing things in his mind, but he wasn't frowning. So I continued, 'Didn't you say every night a different person is responsible for food? Well, why can't I be responsible for food one night? Let your poor friends have a real dinner for once.'

'As a matter of fact, some time ago Shahrzad said she would like to meet you.'

'Shahrzad?'

'Yes, she's a very good friend. Smart, brave, a true believer and she can analyse and summarise many of the issues much better than the rest of us.'

'She's a girl?'

'What do you mean? I said her name is Shahrzad. Do they ever name a boy Shahrzad?'

'No, I mean is she married or single?'

'Oh, the way you all talk ... yes, she's married. I mean she didn't have a choice; she had to get out from under her family's control so that she could dedicate all her time and energy to the cause. Unfortunately, in this country no matter what position women have in society, they can never be free of social customs and their restrictions and obligations.'

'But doesn't her husband mind that she's with you and your friends all the time?'

'Who? Mehdi? No, he's one of us. It was an inside marriage. We decided on it because in many ways it was to the benefit of the group's cause.'

It was the first time he was talking to me about his friends and their group and I knew that any strong or rash reaction on my part would make him grow silent again. I had to be a good listener and remain quiet even when confronted with a subject this strange.

'I, too, would like to meet Shahrzad,' I said. 'She must be an interesting person. Promise me you will invite them over some day.'

'I have to think about it. I will discuss it with them and we will see.'

Two weeks later, I was finally given the honour and it was decided that Hamid's friends would come for lunch on the following Saturday, which was an official holiday. I was busy all week. I washed the curtains and the windows and I kept rearranging the furniture. We didn't have a dining room table. Hamid said, 'Forget it, what do they need a dining room table for? Spread the table-cloth on the floor. It's better. They will be more comfortable and there will be more room for everyone.'

He had invited only twelve people: his closest friends. I didn't know what to cook. I was so excited that I asked him several times. 'Cook anything you like,' he said. 'It's not important.'

'Yes, it is important. I want to cook dishes that they like. Tell me who likes what.'

'How would I know? Everyone likes something different. You don't have to cook every single dish.'

'Well, not all of them. For example, what does Shahrzad like?'

'Herb stew. But Mehdi loves split pea stew and Akbar is still craving the herb rice and fish that I told him about. And late after-noon, when the weather gets cold, everyone gets a hankering for noodle soup. In short, they like everything ... But you shouldn't go to too much trouble. Cook whatever is easier for you.'

I started shopping on Tuesday. The temperature had dropped and there was a gentle breeze. I shopped so much and hauled so many heavy bags up the stairs that even Bibi got fed up and said, 'My girl, even a feast for seven kings doesn't require so much prim-ing and preparing.'

On Thursday, I did some of the preliminary cooking. On Friday, we came back a little sooner from visiting Hamid's parents and again I got busy cooking. I prepared so much food that simply reheating it all would take from morning until noon. Fortunately, the weather was cold and I had lined up all the pots and pans out

124

on the terrace. Late afternoon, as Hamid was getting ready to leave, he said, 'If I'm delayed, I'll come back with the guys tomorrow around noon.'

I got up early in the morning and again dusted the entire apartment, boiled and rinsed the rice, and when everything was done, I took a quick shower. I didn't wet my hair; I had washed and set it with curlers the night before. I put on my yellow dress, which was my best one, dabbed on a little lipstick, took the curlers out of my hair and let the beautiful curls cascade down my back. I wanted to look flawless and not cause Hamid any embarrassment. I wanted to be so perfect that he would stop hiding me in the house like a backward, illegitimate child. I wanted to be someone his friends would consider deserving of joining their group.

Close to noon, my heart sank at the sound of the doorbell. The ring was a signal; Hamid had a key. I quickly took off my apron and ran to the top of the stairs to greet them. There was a cold wind blowing, but I didn't care. Right there at the top of the stairs, Hamid introduced me to everyone. There were four women and the rest were all men, and they were all about the same age. Inside the apartment, I took their coats and looked at the women with curiosity. They didn't look all that different from the men. They were all wearing trousers and oversized sweaters that were mostly old and didn't match the rest of their outfits. They had treated their hair as if it was a nuisance; they had either cut it so short that from behind they could be mistaken for a man, or they had tied it up with a rubber band. None of them was wearing any make-up.

Although everyone was polite and courteous, other than Shahrzad, no one paid much attention to me. She was the only one who kissed me on the cheeks, looked me up and down, and said, 'Beautiful! Hamid, what a gorgeous wife you have. You never told us how attractive and well dressed she is.'

It was only then that everyone turned and looked at me more carefully. I sensed an invisible sarcastic smile on some of their faces. Although no one said anything impolite, there was something in their behaviour that not only made me blush and feel embarrassed, but Hamid, too, seemed uncomfortable. Trying to change the subject, he said, 'Enough for now! Go in the living room and we will bring the tea.' A few of them sat on the sofas and the others on the floor. Almost half of them smoked. Hamid quickly said, 'Ashtrays; give me as many ashtrays as we have.' I went to the kitchen and fetched the ashtrays and gave them to him. Then I went back to the kitchen and started pouring the tea. Hamid followed me there and said, 'What sort of a get-up is that?'

'Why? What do you mean?' I asked, confused.

'What kind of dress is that? You look like a Western doll. Go put on something simple; a shirt and a pair of trousers or a skirt. And wash your face and tie back your hair.'

'But I'm not wearing any make-up. It's just a little lipstick, and it's a very light colour.'

'I don't know what you've done; just do something so you don't stand out so much.'

'Shall I rub coal on my face?'

'Yes, do it!' he snapped.

My eyes were brimming with tears. I could never tell what was good or bad in his eyes. I suddenly felt drained. It was as if in that one moment the exhaustion of the entire week suddenly over-whelmed me. The head cold that had started a few days ago and that I had chosen to ignore suddenly got worse and I felt dizzy. I heard one of them say, 'What happened to the tea?' I pulled myself together and finished pouring the tea and Hamid carried the tray to the living room.

I went to the bedroom, took off my dress and sat on the bed for a while. There was no particular thought in my head. I was just sad. I put on the long pleated skirt that I usually wore around the house and grabbed the first shirt I saw in the closet. I put my hair up with a pin and used a cotton ball to wipe off what was left of my lipstick. I was trying to swallow the lump in my throat. I was afraid that if I caught sight of myself in the mirror my tears would start to flow. I tried to distract myself. I remembered that I hadn't poured any clarified butter over the rice. I walked out of the bed-room and ran into one of the girls who was just then walking out of the living room. The moment she saw me, she said, 'Oh, why the change in decoration?'

They all craned their neck to peek out and take a look at me. I was red up to my ears. Hamid poked his head out of the kitchen and said, 'She's more comfortable this way.'

I stayed in the kitchen the entire time and everyone left me alone. It was around two when everything was finally ready and I spread the tablecloth in the hall. Although I had closed the living room door so that I could comfortably prepare the lunch spread, I could hear them talking loudly. I couldn't understand half of what they were saying. It was as if they were speaking a foreign language. For a while, they talked about something called the Dialectic and they repeatedly used the terms 'the populace' and 'the masses'. I couldn't understand why they didn't just say 'the people'. Lunch was finally ready. I had a terrible backache and my throat burned. Hamid inspected the lunch spread and then invited the guests to eat. Everyone was surprised by the variety, colour and scent of the dishes and they kept telling each other which dish to try.

Shahrzad said, 'I hope you're not too tired. You have really gone to a lot of trouble. We would have been satisfied with bread and cheese. You didn't have to work so hard.'

'Forget it!' one of the men said. 'Bread and cheese is what we eat every day. Now that we've come to a bourgeois home, let's see how they eat.'

Everyone laughed, but I thought Hamid didn't like the comment. After lunch, they all went back to the living room. Hamid carried a stack of plates to the kitchen and irately said, 'Did you have to cook so much food?'

'Why? Was it bad?'

'No, but now I have to listen to their jibes until the end of the world.'

Hamid served a few rounds of tea. I gathered up the lunch spread, washed the dishes, put away the leftovers and tidied up the kitchen. It was past four-thirty. My back still hurt and I felt as if I had a fever. No one was asking for me, I had been forgotten. I understood very well that I didn't fit in with them. I felt like a schoolgirl at her teachers' party. I was not the same age as them, I didn't have their education and experience, I couldn't debate the way they did, and I wasn't even bold enough to interrupt them and ask what they wanted to drink or eat.

I poured another round of tea, prepared a platter of cream puffs and carried the tray to the living room. Again, everyone thanked me and Shahrzad said, 'You must be tired. I'm sorry none of us helped you clean up. The truth is, we really are no good at these sorts of things.'

'You're welcome, it was nothing.'

'Nothing? We couldn't do any of what you did today. Now, come and sit next to me.'

'Of course, I'll be right back. Just let me say my prayers before it is too late and then I can come and sit comfortably.'

Again, they all gave me a strange look and Hamid frowned; and again, I didn't know what I had said that was so strange and out of the ordinary. Akbar, who had earlier called Hamid a bourgeois and I sensed some rivalry or tension between them, said, 'Wonderful! There are still people who say their prayers. I am delighted! Madam, since you have preserved your ancestors' beliefs, would you explain to me why you pray?'

Flustered and vexed, I said, 'Why? Because I am a Muslim and every Muslim must pray. It is God's command.'

'How did God give you this command?'

'Not just to me, to everyone. He did it through his messenger and the Quran that was descended to him.'

'You mean to say there was someone sitting up there who wrote down God's commands and threw them down into the arms of the Prophet?'

I was getting angrier and more confused by the minute. I turned to Hamid and with my gaze appealed to him for help, but there was no kindness or compassion in his eyes, only fury.

One of the girls said, 'Now, what happens if you don't say your prayers?'

'Well, it would be a sin.'

'What happens to someone who sins? For instance, we don't

pray and, according to you, we are sinners. What will happen to us?'

I clenched my teeth and said, 'After death, you will suffer, you will go to hell.'

'Aha! Hell. Tell me, what sort of a place is hell?'

My entire body was shaking. They were mocking my beliefs.

'Hell is made of fire,' I stammered.

'It probably has snakes and scorpions, too?'

'Yes.'

Everyone laughed. I looked beseechingly at Hamid. I needed help, but he had hung his head down, and although he wasn't laughing like the others, he wasn't saying anything either. Akbar turned to him and said, 'Hamid, you haven't even managed to enlighten your own wife, how are you going to save the masses from their superstitions?'

'I'm not superstitious,' I snapped angrily.

'Yes, my dear, you are. And it's not your fault. They have ingrained these notions in your head so well that you have come to believe them. The things you say and waste your time on are in fact superstitions. They are all things that are of no value to the masses. They are elements that make you dependent on someone other than yourself. And they are all meant to scare you into being content with what you have and to stop you from fighting for what you don't have, all in the hope that in another world you will receive everything. You believe in things that have been created to exploit you. This is exactly what superstition is.'

I was dizzy and felt like I was going to vomit. 'Do not revile God!' I said furiously.

'See, kids! See how they brainwash people? It's not their fault. These ideas are planted in their heads from the time they are small children. See what a difficult road we have ahead of us in fighting against the "opium of the masses"? This is exactly why I say we must include the campaign against religion in our mandate.'

I could no longer hear them. The entire room was spinning around my head. I thought if I stayed another minute, I would be sick right there. I ran to the toilet and threw up. I felt a dreadful pressure inside me. There was a stabbing pain in my back and lower abdomen, and then my legs were wet. I looked down. There was a pool of blood on the floor.

I was burning up. Below me, flames were dragging me towards them. I tried to escape, but my legs wouldn't move. Terrifying, hideous-looking witches were stabbing pitchforks in my stomach and pushing me towards the fire. Snakes with human heads were laughing at me. A vile creature was trying to pour rancid water down my throat.

With a child in my arms, I was locked in a room that was burning in flames. I ran towards different doors, but each one I opened I found myself facing more flames. I looked at my child. He was drenched in blood.

When I opened my eyes, I was in a strange, white room. A sharp chill ran through me and I closed my eyes again, curled up and shivered. Someone pulled a blanket over me and a warm hand felt my forehead. Someone said, 'The danger has passed and the bleeding has almost stopped. But she is very weak. She must grow stronger.'

I heard Mother's voice. 'You see, Hamid Khan. Let her come to our house at least for a week so that she can regain some of her strength.'

I was confined to bed for five days at Mother's house. Faati fluttered around me like a butterfly. Father was constantly shopping for strange things that he claimed were nutritious and restorative, and every time I opened my eyes, Mother would make me eat something. Mrs Parvin sat by my side and talked all day long, but I had no patience for her. Hamid came to visit me every afternoon. He looked depressed and embarrassed. I didn't want to look at him. Talking to the people around me had again become difficult for me. There was a profound sadness inside me.

Mother kept saying, 'My girl, why didn't you tell me you were pregnant? Why did you work so hard? Why didn't you ask me to come and help you? Why did you let yourself catch such a bad cold? After all, you have to be careful during the first few months. Well, everything is going to be fine. You shouldn't grieve so much for an unborn child. Do you know how many times I miscarried? This, too, is God's will and wisdom. They say a child that is miscarried must have had some defect; a healthy child doesn't die that easily. You should be grateful. God willing, the next ones will be healthy.'

The day I returned home, Hamid came to pick me up in Mansoureh's car. Before I left, Father put a gold Van Yakad prayer pendant around my neck. He didn't know any other way to express his love. I understood him well, but I just wasn't in the mood to talk and to thank him; all I did was wipe away my tears. Hamid stayed home for two days and took care of me. I knew what a great sacrifice he thought he was making, but I felt no gratitude towards him.

His mother and sisters came to see me. 'I miscarried my second child, the one after Monir,' his mother said. 'But then I gave birth to three healthy children. Don't grieve for no good reason; you have plenty of time, you are both young.'

The truth was that I didn't know the cause of my deep depression. It was certainly not because of the miscarriage. Although I had sensed some changes in me during the previous few weeks and somewhere in my mind I knew what had happened, I had not admitted to myself that I was becoming a mother. I had no clear understanding of what it meant to have a child and to call it mine. I still thought of myself as a schoolgirl whose first obligation was to study. Yet, my sorrow was tinged with a painful feeling of guilt. The foundation of my beliefs had been shaken and I felt disgusted by those who had caused it. I was terrified of the doubt that had infested my mind and I believed God had punished me by taking my child.

'Why didn't you tell me you were pregnant?' Hamid said.

'I wasn't sure, and I didn't think the news would make you happy.'

131

'Is having a child really important to you?'

'I don't know.'

'I know your problem isn't just the child; something else is troubling you, it was obvious from your hallucinations. Shahrzad, Mehdi and I discussed it a lot. That day you were under pressure from all sides. You were physically tired and had a bad cold and the things the guys said delivered the last blow.'

My eyes were brimming with tears.

'And you didn't defend me. They made fun of me, they laughed at me, they treated me like an idiot, and you sided with them.'

'No! Believe me, none of them meant to hurt or insult you. After that day, you don't know how Shahrzad fought with everyone, especially with Akbar. And it all resulted in us adding to our mandate the need to develop a proper approach to presenting and promoting our principles. Shahrzad said, "The way you guys talk, you offend people and make them wary; you scare them away." That day, Shahrzad stayed with me at your bedside the entire time. She kept saying, "We are the reason this poor girl ended up like this." Everyone is worried about you. Akbar wants to come and apologise.'

The next day, Shahrzad and Mehdi came to visit me and brought a box of pastries. Shahrzad sat next to my bed and said, 'I am so happy you are feeling better. You really gave us a scare.'

'I'm sorry; I didn't mean to.'

'No, don't say that. We are the ones who should be apologising. It was our fault. We argue so harshly and vehemently and are so immersed in our beliefs that we forget people are not used to this sort of confrontation and it shocks them. Akbar always argues like an ass, but he didn't mean anything by it. He was really upset afterwards. He wanted to come today, but I told him not to bother, that seeing him would make you sick again.'

'No, it's not his fault. It's my fault for being so weak that a few words can shake my faith and beliefs and I can't answer back and argue as I should.'

'Well, you're still very young. When I was your age, I didn't have the confidence to even argue with my father. With time, you'll grow older and more experienced and your beliefs will develop a more solid foundation, one that is based on your own perception, research and knowledge, and not on what others memorise and repeat like a parrot. But let me confess something to you. Don't give too much credence to all this intellectual high-brow talk. Don't take these guys too seriously. In their heart, they still have their faith and in difficult times they still unconsciously turn to God and seek his protection.'

Hamid who was standing in the doorway, holding the tea tray, started to laugh. Shahrzad turned, looked at him and said, 'Isn't that so, Hamid? Let's be honest. Have you been able to completely forget your religious beliefs? To eliminate God from your convictions? To not mention his name under any circumstance?'

'No, and I don't see why it would be necessary. This was the subject of our discussion the day before you all came here for lunch, and that's why Akbar went on like that. I don't understand why the guys all insist on this so vehemently. In my view, people who have religious beliefs are more peaceful, more hopeful, and they seldom feel abandoned and alone.'

'You mean you don't make fun of my praying and my faith and you don't consider it to be a superstition?' I asked.

'No! Sometimes when I see you pray with such calm and emotional confidence, I even envy you.'

With an approving smile, Shahrzad said, 'Just remember to pray for us, too!' And I instinctively hugged her and kissed her on the cheeks.

From then on, I saw very little of Hamid's friends, and even that limited contact took place in a well-defined framework. They respected me, but they didn't consider me one of them and tried not to talk about God and religion in front of me. They were not comfortable in my company and I was no longer all that interested in seeing them.

Once in a while, Shahrzad and Mehdi would stop by and visit us as friends, but I still didn't feel any closeness towards them. My feelings for Shahrzad were a combination of respect, kindness and envy. She was a complete woman; even men respected her. She was well educated, intelligent and eloquent. She wasn't afraid of anyone, and not only did she not need to lean on anyone, she was the one their entire group relied on. What was interesting was that despite all her strong characteristics, she had soft and tender emotions. When faced with certain human tragedies, tears would quickly well up in her dark eyes.

Her relationship with Mehdi was a mystery to me. Hamid had told me that they had got married for the benefit of their organisation, but there was something far deeper and more human between them. Mehdi was a very quiet and intelligent man. He rarely took part in their debates and hardly ever displayed his knowledge and skills. Like a teacher listening to his students review their lessons, he remained silent and only observed and listened. It didn't take long for me to realise that Shahrzad played the role of his spokesperson. During their discussions, she always kept a subtle eye on him. A nod from Mehdi was a sign of approval for her to continue with what she was saying, and a slightly raised eyebrow would leave her pensive in the middle of a debate. I thought, No, it was impossible to develop such a bond without love. I knew that Hamid's ideal wife was someone like her, not like me. Still, I felt no resentment. I had placed her so far above myself that I believed I didn't even deserve to be jealous of her. I just desperately wanted to be like her.

Towards the end of spring, during the final exams for year ten, feelings of weakness, fatigue and nausea made me realise I was pregnant. As difficult as it was, I did well in my exams, and this time, with mindfulness and enthusiasm, I sat waiting for the birth of my child; a child whose smallest gift to me would be an escape from infinite loneliness.

Hamid's family was very excited at the news of my pregnancy and considered it a sign that Hamid had finally changed his ways and settled down. I let them believe what they wanted to; I knew if I complained about his long absences, I would not only betray Hamid and risk losing him for ever, but his family would blame me and consider me to be the guilty party. His mother truly believed and used every excuse to remind me that a capable wife can keep her husband duty-bound to his home and family; as proof, she would tell me how when they were young she had saved her husband from the snare of the communist Tudeh Party.

That summer, Mahmoud married my maternal cousin, Ehteram-Sadat. I was neither eager nor interested in helping with the preparations and my pregnancy provided the perfect excuse. The truth was that I didn't like either one of them. But Mother was as happy as you would expect her to be and constantly listed the new bride's merits over Mahboubeh. With the help of my aunt, who didn't know whether she should forgo her strict hijab to make her work easier, Mother was busy attending to all that needed to be done.

On the wedding day, Mahmoud looked like he was attending a funeral. Scowling and with a surly expression on his face, he kept his head down and didn't exchange pleasantries with anyone. The festivities were taking place both at Father's house and at Mrs Parvin's. The men gathered at Father's house while the women went next door. Contrary to what had been decided, Mahmoud didn't stay for even a day at Father's house. He had rented a house near the bazaar and the bride was taken there on the wedding night.

There were colourful string lights hanging on all the walls and between the trees, and pedestal lamps flanked the doors. The cooking was being done in Mrs Parvin's front yard, which was larger than ours. There was no music or singing. Mahmoud and Ehteram-Sadat's father had stipulated that no one was allowed to engage in any irreligious activities.

I was sitting with the other women in Mrs Parvin's front yard and fanning myself. The women were busy cheerfully chatting and eating fruit and pastries. I was wondering what the men were doing. There was no sound coming from next door, except occasionally when someone would urge everyone to say praise to the Prophet and his descendants. It seemed they were all waiting for dinner to be served so that they could complete their obligations and shake off their boredom.

'What kind of a wedding is this?' Mrs Parvin kept complaining. 'It's just like my late father's funeral!'

And my aunt would silence her by puckering her brow and saying, 'May God have mercy!'

My aunt believed that, other than herself, everyone in the world was a sinner and no one practised their faith properly. But her dislike of Mrs Parvin was of a different nature. That night she repeatedly groused, 'What is that hussy doing here?' If we had been anywhere other than at Mrs Parvin's house, my aunt would have certainly thrown her out by now.

Ahmad never showed up at the wedding. Mother kept asking Ali who was standing by the front door, 'Did your brother Ahmad come?' And then she would slap the back of her hand and say, 'You see! It's his brother's wedding after all, and your poor father is left with no one to help him. Ahmad cares about no one other than those unsavoury friends of his. He thinks the world will come to an end if he doesn't go out with them one single night.'

Mother's words made Mrs Parvin air her grievances, too. 'Your mother is right. Ever since you left, Ahmad has got even worse. He's hanging out with a bunch of strange people. May God lead him to a happy end.'

'He is so stupid that he deserves whatever happens to him,' I said.

'Oh, don't say that, Massoumeh! How could you? Perhaps he wouldn't be like this if the rest of you paid some attention to him.'

'Like how?'

'I don't know. But it isn't right the way you have all abandoned him. Your father won't even look at him.'

That night Father's sister arrived at the wedding alone. Up until that moment, Mother kept saying, 'You see what an uncaring aunt you have? She didn't even bother coming to her eldest nephew's wedding.' And when she saw my aunt walk in, she puckered her lips and said, 'The lady has graced us.' Then she quickly got busy doing something so that she could pretend not to have seen her arrive.

My aunt came and sat next to me and exclaimed, 'Oh, I almost

136

died on the way coming here! The car broke down and I was delayed for two hours. I wish you had held the wedding in Qum so that the entire family could come and I wouldn't have to suffer so much travelling back and forth.'

'Oh, dear Auntie, we didn't want you to go to any trouble.'

'What trouble? How many times does one's eldest nephew get married for one to not want to take two steps?'

Then she turned to Mother and said, 'Hello, madam. You see that I did finally come; and this is how you greet me?'

'Is this the time to come?' Mother grumbled. 'Like a stranger?'

Hoping to change the subject, I said, 'By the way, dear Auntie, how is Mahboubeh? I really miss her. I wish she had come.'

Mother glowered at me.

'Frankly, my girl, Mahboubeh is away. She sends her apologies. She and her husband left for Syria and Beirut yesterday. God bless him, what a husband. He adores Mahboubeh.'

'How interesting. Why Syria and Beirut?'

'Well, where else would they go? They say it is beautiful there. They call Beirut the Bride of the Middle East.'

Mother petulantly said, 'My dear, not everyone can go to the West like my brother.'

'As a matter of fact, they could,' my aunt retorted. 'But Mahboubeh wanted to go to a place of pilgrimage. You see, she is obliged to go to Haj, but because she is with child, her husband said for now they should visit the shrine of Her Holiness Zeynab and postpone a pilgrimage to Mecca until a later time, God willing.'

'Well, as far as I know, you have to take care of all your obligations, organise your life and then go to Haj,' Mother continued to argue.

'No, my dear Tayebeh, these are all excuses made by people who can't go to Haj,' my aunt countered. 'In fact, Mahboubeh's father-in-law, who is a scholar and a cleric and has ten seminarians in his pay, says when someone has the financial means, he is obliged to go.'

Mother was sizzling like wild rue over fire. She always became

137

like this when she couldn't come up with an appropriate retort. She finally found one and said, 'Absolutely not! My brother-in-law's brother, our bride's paternal uncle, is a much more accomplished scholar and he says that going to Mecca has many conditions and requirements. It's not as simple as that. Not just your family, but even your seven neighbours to the right and your seven neighbours to the left should not be needy for you to be obliged to go to Haj. And in your case, well, with your son being out of work—'

'What out of work? A thousand people are beholden to him. His father wanted to open a store for him, but my son didn't want one. He said, "I don't like the bazaar and I don't want to be a shop-keeper. I want to study and become a doctor." Mahboubeh's husband who is educated says my son is very talented and he has made us promise to leave the boy alone until he takes the university entrance exams.'

Mother opened her mouth to say something, but I jumped in and again tried to change the subject. I was afraid the wedding would turn into a battleground if their bickering continued.

'By the way, Auntie, how far along is Mahboubeh? Did she have any cravings?'

'Only during the first two months. Now she's feeling very well and has no problems. The doctor has even allowed her to travel.'

'My doctor said I shouldn't walk too much and I'm not allowed to bend over too often.'

'Then don't, my girl. You have to be very careful during the first few months, especially because you're weak. May God let me give my life for you, they probably don't take care of you the way they should. In the beginning, I wouldn't let Mahboubeh make a move. Every day, I cooked whatever she was craving and sent it to her house. It's a mother's duty. Tell me, have they cooked mixed grain and vegetable soup for you?'

My aunt was not willing to call a ceasefire.

'Yes, Auntie,' I said, quickly. 'They're constantly bringing food for me, but I don't have an appetite.'

'My dear, they're probably not cooking it properly. I'll prepare

138

such a delicious dish for your cravings that you'll want to eat your fingers, too.'

Mother was so angry that she had turned the colour of beetroot. She was about to say something when Mrs Parvin called her and told her that it was time to serve the men's dinner. With Mother gone, I breathed a sigh of relief. My aunt calmed down like a volcano that had suddenly stopped erupting and started looking around, exchanging greetings with a few guests by nodding to them. Then she turned her attention back to me.

'God bless you, my dear, you look beautiful. You are definitely having a boy. Now, tell me, are you pleased with your husband? We never did see the prince, the way they rushed the marriage . . . as if the soup was hot and they didn't want it to lose flavour. Now, is he really a soup to savour?'

'What can I say, Auntie? He's not bad. His parents were leaving for Mecca and there was no time. They wanted to take care of everything and go to Haj with peace of mind. That's why there was such a rush.'

'But with no investigation and no enquiries? I heard you hadn't even seen the groom until the marriage ceremony. Is it true?'

'Yes, but I had seen a photograph of him.'

'What? My dear, one does not marry a photograph. You mean you developed feelings for him and realised he's the man of your life just by looking at his picture? Even in Qum they don't marry girls off like that. Mahboubeh's father-in-law is a mullah, not one of those phoney mullahs, he's a well-respected cleric and he is more devout than all of Qum. When he came to ask for Mahboubeh's hand for his son, he said a boy and a girl should talk to each other and make sure they want one another before they give their answer. Mahboubeh spoke with Mohsen Khan all alone on at least five occasions. They invited us to dinner several times and we did the same. And although the entire city knows them and there was no need for an investigation, we still asked around and made enquiries. You don't just hand over your daughter to a stranger as if you had found her on the side of a street.'

'I don't know, Auntie. To be honest, I wasn't willing, but my brothers were in a rush.'

'How dare they? Was your presence taking up their space? From the very start your mother spoiled these boys too much. All Mahmoud does is fake piety and God knows where that Ahmad is.'

'But Auntie, I'm not unhappy now. This was my fate. Hamid is a good man and his family takes good care of me.'

'How is he financially?'

'Not bad. I don't lack for anything.'

'What does he do anyway?'

'They have a printing house. His father owns half of the business and Hamid works there.'

'Does he love you? Are you having fun together? Do you know what I mean?'

Her words made me think. I had never asked myself whether I loved Hamid or whether he loved me. Of course, I wasn't indifferent towards him. In general, he was a pleasant and likeable man. Even Father who had seen very little of Hamid liked him. But the sort of love I had felt for Saiid didn't exist between us. Even our conjugal relationship was more out of a sense of duty and based on physical need rather than an expression of love.

'What is it, my dear? You're suddenly deep in thought. Do you love him or not?'

'You know, Auntie, he's a good man. He tells me to go to school and to do whatever I want. I can go to the cinema, to parties, to fun outings; the poor thing doesn't say a word.'

'If you're going to be roaming around the streets all the time, then when are you going to see to the house and cook lunch and dinner?'

'Oh, Auntie, there's plenty of time. Besides, Hamid doesn't care about lunch and dinner. If I feed him bread and cheese for an entire week, he will never complain. He is really a harmless man.'

'Of all impossible things … a harmless man! You make me worry. The things you say!'

'Why, Auntie?'

'Look here, my girl. God has yet to create a harmless man.

140

Either he is up to no good and just wants to keep you busy so that you don't interfere with his life, or he is so deeply in love that he can't say no to you, which is very unlikely and even if it is true, it will be short-lived. Wait a little, then see what song he sings.'

'I really don't know.'

'My girl, I know men. Our Mahboubeh's husband is not only pious, but educated and modern. He adores Mahboubeh and doesn't take his eyes off her. Ever since he found out she's pregnant, he pampers her like a child, but he also watches her like a hawk to see where she goes, what she does and when she comes back. Between you and me, sometimes he is even a little jealous. After all, it's love. There should be a little jealousy. Your husband must have his own little jealousies. Does he?'

Hamid jealous? Over me? I was certain there wasn't an ounce of jealousy in him. If I had told him right then that I wanted to leave him, he would probably be overjoyed. Even though he had absolute freedom to live his life and to go and come as he wished, and I never dared complain about my round-the-clock loneliness, he still considered marriage to be a headache and a shackle, and grumbled about the constraints of family life. Perhaps I had taken over a corner of his mind that he would have otherwise dedicated to his goals. No, Hamid was never jealous when it came to me.

As these thoughts flashed through my mind like bolts of electricity, I caught sight of Faati and quickly called her over. 'Faati, my dear, come clear away these plates. Is Mother serving dinner? Tell her I will be right there to put the dressing on the salad.' And with that excuse, I left Auntie and the merciless mirror she had held up to my life. I felt strangely depressed.

By the start of autumn, I was feeling much better and my belly was slowly growing bigger. I registered in night school for year eleven classes. Every day, late in the afternoon, I would walk to school, and every morning I would open the curtains, sit under the sun that shined in the middle of the room, stretch out my legs, and study while eating the fruit rolls my aunt had made. I knew that soon I would not have much time to study.

One day Hamid came home at ten in the morning. I couldn't believe my eyes. He hadn't been home for two entire days and nights. I thought perhaps he was ill, or could it be that he was worried about me?

'How come you're home at this hour of the day?'

He laughed and said, 'If you don't like it, I can leave.'

'No . . . I just got worried. Are you feeling well?'

'Yes, of course. The telephone company called to say they are coming to instal the phone. I didn't know how to get hold of you and I knew you didn't have any money at home, so I had to come.'

'A telephone? Really? They're going to instal a telephone for us? Oh, how wonderful!'

'Didn't you know? I paid for it a long time ago.'

'How would I know? You hardly ever talk to me. But it's great; now I can call everyone and feel less lonely.'

'No, Mrs Massoumeh! That won't do. A telephone is for necessary occasions only; it's not for women's silly chatter. I have to have a telephone for certain important communications and the line has to be free. We will be receiving more calls than making them. And remember, you are not to give the number to anyone.'

'What do you mean? Mother and Father can't have our telephone number? And here I was, thinking the gentleman bought a telephone because he was worried about me, because he's gone for days and wants to at least know how I am feeling, or so that I can call someone if I suddenly go into labour.'

'Now, don't get upset. Of course you can use the telephone when necessary. I meant I don't want you to talk on the phone twenty-four hours a day and keep the line busy.'

'At any rate, who would I call? I don't have any friends, and Mother and Father don't have a telephone and have to go to Mrs Parvin's house to make a call. That leaves only your mother and sisters.'

'No! No! Don't you dare give them the number. Otherwise, they will use it to keep tabs on me all day long.'

The telephone was installed and my link to the outside world, which had been limited because of my advancing pregnancy and the cold winter weather, was again restored. I spoke with Mrs Parvin every day. She would often invite Mother over to her house to talk to me. And if Mother was busy, Faati would chat with me. In the end, Hamid's mother found out about the telephone and, piqued and cantankerous, she asked me for the number. She assumed I had not wanted her to have it, and I couldn't tell her that it was what her son had ordered. From that day on, she called at least twice a day. Gradually, I picked up on the timing of her calls and when I was certain it was her, I wouldn't answer the telephone. I was too embarrassed to continue lying to her that Hamid was sleeping, or had run out to buy something, or that he was in the bathroom.

In the middle of a cold winter night, I felt the first shocking stab of labour pains. I was overwhelmed with fear and anxiety. How could I let Hamid know? My mind was in a muddle. I had to get a grip and remember the instructions the doctor had given me. I had to organise myself, I had to write down the time interval between the contractions, and I had to find Hamid. His telephone number at work was the only number I had for him, and although I knew no one was there at that hour of the night, I dialled the number. There was no answer. I didn't have any of his friends' telephone numbers. He was always strangely careful not to write down any telephone numbers or addresses; he tried to memorise them. He said it was safer that way.

My only option was to call Mrs Parvin. At first, I was uncomfortable waking them up at that hour, but the pain of the contractions erased my hesitation. I dialled the number. The sound of the ringing echoed in the receiver, but no one answered. I knew she slept soundly and her husband was hard of hearing. I hung up.

It was two in the morning. I sat and stared at the second hand of the clock. The contractions were now coming at regular intervals, but they were not as I had expected them. With every minute that passed, I became more frightened. I thought of calling Hamid's mother. But what would I say? How could I tell her Hamid was not at home? Earlier that evening, I had told her Hamid had come home from work and was downstairs visiting Bibi. Later, Hamid called from somewhere and I told him to telephone his mother and tell her that he had gone to see Bibi. If I called now and told her Hamid had not come home at all, she would scold me and lose her mind with worry over her son. She would go to every hospital and wander around the streets, looking for him. Her concern for her son verged on obsession and was void of any reason and logic.

Stupid thoughts ran through my mind. I was holding my hands under my stomach and pacing up and down the room. I was so panicked that I thought I was going to faint. Each time the contractions came, I froze where I stood and tried hard not to make a sound, but then I remembered that even if I hollered, no one would hear me. Bibi was almost deaf and slept deeply, and if I did manage to wake her, there was nothing she could do to help me. I remembered my aunt telling me that when Mahboubeh's contractions started, her husband became so nervous that he began running around in circles, telling her how much he loved and adored her. My entire being filled with hatred and disgust. Our child's life and mine were not worth anything to Hamid.

I looked at the clock, it was three-thirty. Again, I called Mrs Parvin. I let the telephone ring for a long time, but it was no use. I thought I should get dressed and go out into the street; eventually someone would drive by and take me to the hospital. Ten days earlier, I had prepared a suitcase for myself and the baby. I opened it, emptied it out and looked for the list the doctor and Mansoureh had written for me. Again, I folded everything and packed the suitcase. I had a few more contractions, but the intervals now seemed irregular. I lay down on the bed and thought I had made a mistake. I had to concentrate.

I looked at the clock. It was four-twenty. The next time I jolted up with stabbing pain it was six-thirty in the morning. The contractions had stopped for a while and I had fallen asleep. I was nervous. I went over to the telephone and dialled Mrs Parvin's number. This time, I was going to let it ring until someone finally answered. The telephone rang about twelve times when on the other side of the line Mrs Parvin's sleepy voice said hello. Hearing her, I burst into tears and cried, 'Mrs Parvin, help me! The baby is coming.'

'Oh my God! Go to the hospital. Go! We're on our way.'

'How? With all this stuff?'

'Isn't Hamid there?'

'No. He didn't come home last night. I must have called you a hundred times during the night. It's God's will that the child still hasn't come.'

'Get dressed. We'll be right there. I'll get your mother and we'll come right over.'

Half an hour later, Mrs Parvin and Mother arrived and rushed me to the hospital in a taxi. Despite the intensifying pain, I felt calmer. At the hospital, the doctor said it was still too soon for the child to come. Mother took my hand and said, 'When a woman in labour prays during a contraction, her prayer will come true. Pray for God to forgive your sins.'

My sins? What sins had I committed? My only sin was that I had once loved someone; it was the sweetest memory I had of my life and I did not want anyone to erase it.

It was past noon, but there was no sign of the baby. They gave me injections, but they were useless. Each time Mrs Parvin came to the room, she looked at me with dread and just to have something to say, she would ask, 'But where is Hamid Agha? Let me call his mother. Perhaps they know where he is.'

I would groan and in broken words tell her, 'No, don't. He will call the hospital when he goes home.'

Seething with anger, Mother said, 'What is the meaning of this? After all, shouldn't his mother come and see what has become of her daughter-in-law and her grandchild? Why are they all so uncaring?' Her constant grousing was making me even more stressed.

By four in the afternoon, worry was rippling over Mother's face and I could hear Father's voice outside the door. 'But where is this doctor? What is this nonsense about him being kept aware of the patient's condition over the telephone? He should be at her bedside!'

'Where are our own precious midwives?' Mother said. 'My child has been in pain all day. Do something!'

Now and then, I fainted in pain. I no longer had the energy to even moan.

Mrs Parvin wiped the sweat from my face and told Mother, 'Don't cry. Childbirth is always painful.'

'No, you don't understand. I was there when many of our relatives gave birth. My other sister, God rest her soul, was the same way. She died in childbirth. When I look at Massoumeh lying there and suffering, it's as if I'm looking at Marzieh.'

It was strange that, despite all the pain, I was still aware of everything that was going on around me. Mother went on and on about how I resembled Marzieh, and I kept getting weaker and losing more hope with every passing second. I thought to myself, I'm a goner, too.

It was after five o'clock when Hamid came. Seeing him, I suddenly felt safe, I felt stronger. How truly odd that in trying times a woman's closest and best support is her husband, even if he is unkind. I didn't notice when his mother and sisters arrived, but I heard the commotion. His mother was fighting with the nurse.

'But where is the doctor? We are losing the baby!' I knew her concern was for her grandchild, not for me.

The nurse who was examining me said, 'Oh my, what hissy fits! Madam, the doctor said he will come when it is time.'

It was eleven at night. I had no energy left. They took me to a different room. From the conversations around me, I understood there was a problem with the baby's breathing. The doctor was quickly pulling on his gloves and shouting at the nurse who couldn't find my vein. And then everything went dark.

I woke up in a clean and bright room. Mother was sitting next to my bed, napping. I was not in pain, but I felt profoundly weak and tired.

'Is the baby dead?' I asked.

'Bite your tongue! You have a baby boy as handsome as can be. You can't imagine how happy I was when I found out it's a boy and how proud I felt in front of your mother-in-law.'

'He's healthy?'

'Yes.'

The next time I opened my eyes, Hamid was in the room. He laughed and said, 'Congratulations! It was really difficult, wasn't it?'

I burst into tears and said, 'Being alone was more difficult.'

He put his arm around my head and stroked my hair. All my resentment was forgotten.

'Is the baby healthy?' I asked.

'Yes, but he is very small.'

'How much does he weigh?'

'Two kilos and seven hundred grams.'

'Did you count his fingers and toes? Are they all there?'

'Of course, they are all there,' he said, laughing.

'Then why won't they bring him to me?'

'Because he is in an incubator. The birth was long and exhausting. They will keep him in the incubator until his breathing becomes normal. But I can already tell he is very playful. He is constantly moving his arms and legs and boohooing.'

I felt much better the next day and they brought the baby to me. The poor thing had scratches all over his face. They said it was because of the forceps. I thanked God that he had not been harmed, but he was constantly crying and refused to take my breast. I felt faint with exhaustion.

There was a huge crowd in my room that afternoon. No one agreed on whom the baby resembled. Hamid's mother said he looked exactly like Hamid, but Mother believed he looked like his uncles.

'What will you name him?' Mother asked Hamid.

Without a pause, he said, 'It's obvious, Siamak.' And he cast a meaningful glance at his father who laughed and nodded in approval. I was stunned. We had never discussed baby names. Siamak was a name that I had never considered and was not on the long list of the ones I had thought of.

'What did you say? Siamak? Why Siamak?'

147

Mother added, 'What sort of a name is Siamak? One should name a child after the prophets so that he will be blessed in life.'

Father motioned to her to keep quiet and not to interfere.

Sounding resolute, Hamid firmly said, 'Siamak is a good name. One should name a child after a great man.'

Mother looked at me quizzically and I shrugged, suggesting I didn't know who he was referring to. Later, I discovered that among his group, most of the men had similar names. According to them, they had been named after true communists.

After I was released from the hospital, I went to Mother's house and stayed there for ten days, until I felt stronger and had learned how to take care of my child.

I returned home. My son was healthy, but he cried all the time. I would hold him in my arms and walk all night until dawn. In the morning, he would sleep for a few hours here and there, but I had a thousand things to take care of and could not rest. Mrs Parvin came to see me almost every day and sometimes she brought Mother with her. She helped me a lot. I could not leave the apart-ment and she did all my household shopping for me.

Hamid felt no sense of responsibility. The only change in his life was that on nights when he did come home, he would take a pillow and a blanket and sleep in the living room. And then he would complain that he had not slept well and that he had no peace and quiet at home. I took my son to the doctor a few times. He said children who are delivered with forceps and experience a difficult birth are often nervous and ill-tempered, but they don't have any specific problems and my child was perfectly healthy. Another doctor said perhaps my son was hungry and my breast milk was not enough for him. He suggested I supplement his food and give him formula as well.

Fatigue, weakness, lack of sleep, my son's constant crying and, most important of all, loneliness made me more depressed every day. I couldn't confide in anyone. I believed it was my fault that Hamid had no interest in being at home. I had lost my self-confidence, I shunned everyone, and my old disappointments and defeats revealed themselves to me more forcefully than ever before. I felt the world had ended for me and that I would never be free of the burden of that heavy responsibility. Often my tears flowed as my son cried.

Hamid paid no attention to me or to our child. He was busy with his own daily routine. It had been four months since I had left the apartment except to take my child to the doctor. Mother kept saying, 'Everyone has children, but no one sits at home the way you do.'

With the weather getting warmer and the child growing older, I started to feel better. I was fed up with being tired and depressed. And finally, on a beautiful May day, I reclaimed my ability to make decisions. I told myself that I was a mother and had responsibilities, that I had to be strong and stand on my own two feet, and that I had to raise my son in a happy and healthy environment.

Everything changed. The joy of life flowed inside me. And it was as if my son, too, had sensed the transformation in me. He cried less and sometimes even laughed and reached out to me when he saw me. Seeing him like that made me forget all my sorrows. He still kept me up many nights, but I had grown accustomed to it. Sometimes I would sit and watch him for hours. Every move he made had a special significance for me. It was as if he was a world I had just discovered. From one day to the next, I grew stronger, and from one day to the next, I loved him more. Maternal love was slowly seeping into every cell of my body. I kept telling myself, I love him so much more today than I did yesterday; a love stronger than this is impossible. But the next day I would feel he was even more dear to me. I no longer felt the need to talk to myself. I talked and sang to him. With his large, intelligent eyes, he made me understand which song he liked more, and when I sang a rhythmic song, he clapped his hands in tune with it. Every afternoon, I took him out in his pram and walked under the old trees along the roads and alleys in the neighbourhood. He loved our outings.

Faati used every excuse to come over and hold Siamak in her arms. After the school year ended, she would sometimes spend the night with me. Her presence was a huge comfort. Again, the Friday lunches at my in-laws' house resumed. Although Siamak wasn't a well-tempered child and didn't easily go from one person's arms to the next, Hamid's family truly loved him and refused to accept any excuse to cancel a lunch.

The gentlest and most beautiful relationship was between Father and Siamak. During the previous two years, Father had come to our home no more than three times. But now, once or twice a week, he would stop by after closing the store. At first, he would try to come up with a reason for his visits; he would bring milk or baby food. But soon, he no longer felt he needed an excuse. He would come, play with Siamak for a while, and then leave.

Yes, Siamak had given my life a new scent and colour. With him in my life, I sensed Hamid's absence less than I did before. My days were taken up by feeding him, bathing him and singing to him. And wisely, he refused to allow me to spend a moment without paying full attention to him. The little rascal demanded all my love and attention. I had completely put aside school, classes and exams. The fascinating device that kept us very entertained during that time was the television that Hamid's father had bought as a gift for Siamak.

Towards the end of the summer, we went on a trip with Hamid's parents. What a miracle! And what a pleasant week. Hamid was completely disarmed with his mother around. He came up with a thousand excuses for us not to go, but none of them worked. It was my first visit to the Caspian coast. I was like an excited child. Seeing all that beauty and lushness and, at last, the roaring waves of the sea, left me amazed and awestruck. I could sit for hours on the seashore and revel in all that beauty. Siamak, too, seemed to love being among family and in that environment. He kept leaping into Hamid's arms and would come to me only if he was tired or hungry. He would clasp Hamid's hands in his own tiny ones and his grandparents would become ecstatic watching them together. One day Hamid's mother gleefully whispered to me, 'You see!

Hamid will no longer be able to leave this child and go after the things he does. Put the second one in his arms as soon as possible. Thank God!'

Hamid bought a straw hat, which we used to try to keep Siamak and his fair skin shielded from the sun, but I had turned the colour of copper. One day I noticed Hamid and his mother whispering together and he kept turning and looking at me. I pulled myself together. I had stopped wearing headscarves and chadors a long time ago, but I was always careful how I dressed. That day I was wearing a short-sleeved dress that was relatively thin and had an open collar. Although it was very conventional compared to the bathing suits women were wearing, still it was too much for me. I thought, They are right to criticise me; I have become too bold.

Later, when Hamid joined me, I anxiously asked, 'What was your mother telling you?'

'Nothing!'

'What do you mean nothing? She was talking about me. Tell me, what have I done to upset her?'

'Come on! They have really planted the seeds of tales of brides and mothers-in-law deep in your mind! She isn't upset at all. Why are you so cynical?'

'Then tell me what she said.'

'Nothing. She just said, "Your wife is much more beautiful now that she is suntanned."'

'Really? And what did you say?'

'Me? What did you want me to say?'

'I mean, what do you think?'

He looked me up and down with a probing, appreciative look and jauntily said, 'She's right. You are very beautiful, and you are becoming even more beautiful every day.'

I felt a special joy in my heart and smiled involuntarily. I was so pleased with his compliment. It was the first time he had openly admired me. With some modesty, I said, 'No! It's just the sun. Otherwise, I'm always so pale. Don't you remember last year you used to tell me I looked like sick people?'

'No, not like sick people; you just looked like a child. Now you're older, you've gained some weight, and with this sun you have a more beautiful colour. Your eyes are lighter and brighter. In short, you are turning into a beautiful and complete woman ... '

That was one of the best weeks of my life. The memory of those warm, sunny days made bearable many of the cold, dark nights that were to come.

My Siamak was an intelligent, playful, restless and beautiful child; at least, in my eyes. Hamid would laugh and say, 'There is a foreign proverb that says, There is only one beautiful child in the world and every mother has him!'

Siamak started walking and talking very early and with broken words managed to express himself. I can confidently say that from the day he took his first steps, he never sat quietly again. Whatever he wanted, he would try to force you to give it to him, and if that didn't work, he would scream and cry until he got his way. Contrary to my mother-in-law's predictions, even a child's love and needs did not bind Hamid to his home and family.

A year later, I again thought of going back to school, but caring for my son left me with little free time. By the time I managed to take the final exams for my penultimate year, Siamak was two years old. Now, there was only one year left before I could receive my secondary-school diploma and achieve my dream. But a few months later, I was troubled to find out I was pregnant again. I knew the news would not make Hamid happy, but I didn't expect the anger and disgust he expressed. He flew into a rage over why I had not been more careful taking my contraceptive pills. The more I explained that the pills did not agree with me and made me ill, the angrier he got.

'No, the problem is your idiotic mentality,' he shouted. 'Everyone takes the pill, how come you are the only one who gets sick taking them? Why don't you just admit that you like being a baby machine? In the end, you all choose this as your mission in life. Do you think by having a baby a year you can trap me into giving up my fight?'

'It is not as if you have helped raise our son or spent any time

152

with him that now you are afraid you will have to invest even more time. When were you ever concerned with your wife and son to now think your worries will be greater with a second child?'

'Even your existence is a hindrance to me. You are suffocating me. I don't have the patience for all the whining and whimpering of a second one. You have to figure this out before it's too late.'

'Figure what out?'

'Have an abortion. There is a doctor I know.'

'You mean, kill my child? A child just like Siamak?'

'Enough!' he yelled. 'I am sick of this nonsense. What child? Right now, it's only a few cells, a fetus. You say "my child" as if the kid is crawling on all fours in front of you.'

'Of course, it exists. It is a human being, with a human soul.'

'Who taught you this drivel? The old fuddy-duddy matrons in Qum?'

Crying and furious, I said, 'I will not kill my child! It's your child, too. How could you?'

'You are right. It's my fault. From day one, I should have never touched you. Even if I come to you once a year, you are sure to get pregnant. I promise you, I will never make that mistake again. And you can do whatever you want. But let me make it clear, do not count on me and do not have any expectations of me.'

'It is not as if I have ever expected anything from you. What have you ever done for me? Which responsibility did you ever live up to for me to now expect even more of you?'

'At any rate, just pretend I don't exist.'

This time, I knew what to expect and prepared everything ahead of time. Mrs Parvin ran a telephone cable to Mother's house so that I could contact them more easily and not panic like I had done the last time. Fortunately, the baby was due at the end of summer and during school holidays. We planned for Faati to come and stay with me the last few weeks so that she could take care of Siamak in case I had to unexpectedly go to the hospital. I prepared what I would need for the baby. Siamak's old clothes were still usable and I didn't need to buy too many.

'Isn't Hamid Agha around?' Mother constantly asked.

'You see, Hamid doesn't have a regular schedule. Some nights he has to stay at the printing house and he often has to go on last-minute business trips.'

Unlike my first pregnancy, this time everything went well and on schedule. Knowing that I had only myself to rely on, I carefully planned and organised everything. I wasn't nervous or worried. As I anticipated, Hamid was not there when the contractions started and he didn't find out I had given birth until two days later.

Mother was exasperated. 'This is ridiculous,' she said. 'It wasn't our custom for our husbands to be at our bedside when we gave birth, but they would come to see us afterwards and they would show some affection and concern. But this husband of yours has really gone too far, acting as if nothing has happened.'

'Forget it, Mother. Why do you bother? It's best that he is not around. He has a thousand and one worries and responsibilities.'

I was much stronger and more experienced than the first time. Even though I was in labour and in terrible pain for many hours, the birth was normal and I was conscious throughout. I had a strange feeling when I heard the baby cry. 'Congratulations!' the doctor said. 'He's a chubby little boy.'

I didn't need time to experience maternal feelings; I sensed them in every cell of my body. Unlike last time, nothing about this baby was strange or unusual to me. I didn't get nervous when he cried, I didn't panic when he coughed or sneezed, and I wasn't irritated when he wouldn't sleep at night. He, too, was calmer and more tolerant than Siamak. My children's temperaments were an exact reflection of my emotional state during childbirth.

After I was released from the hospital, I went to my own home; it was easier for the children. I started taking care of two boys with different needs and I immediately took up the housework. I knew I could not count on Hamid. He had finally found the excuse he had been searching for. By finding me guilty, he had freed himself and relinquished the last of his responsibilities to me. He even behaved as if I was indebted to him. He rarely came home at night, and when he did, he slept in a different room and completely ignored me and the children. My pride would not allow me to ever want or expect anything from him; perhaps I knew it would be futile.

My biggest problem was Siamak. He was not the type of child who was going to easily forgive me for having brought a rival into his life. When I walked into the house with a baby in my arms, he acted as if I had committed the greatest betrayal. Not only did he not run to me and cling to my skirt, but he ran away and hid behind the bed. I handed the baby to Faati and followed Siamak. With sweet words and promises, I took him in my arms, kissed him and told him how much I loved him. I gave him the toy car I had bought earlier and said that his little brother had brought it for him. He looked at it with scepticism and reluctantly agreed to come and see the baby.

But my tactics didn't work. With every day that passed, Siamak became more cantankerous and highly strung. Although his speech was almost fully developed by the time he was two and he could easily express himself, now he rarely talked and when he did, he mixed up his words or used the wrong ones. Occasionally, he would even wet his pants. It had been almost a year that he no longer needed to wear nappies, but now I had to force him to wear them again.

Siamak was so sad and depressed that my heart ached every time I looked at him. The shoulders of that three-year-old boy looked even more fragile under the burden of his sorrow. I didn't know what to do. The paediatrician had told me to involve Siamak in taking care of his little brother and to try not to hold the baby in my arms in front of him. But how? I didn't have anyone to keep Siamak away so that I could breastfeed the baby and he refused to be near his brother without being violent with him. I couldn't single-handedly fill the void he was feeling in his life. He desperately needed his father.

A month passed and we still hadn't picked a name for the baby. One day when Mother came for a visit, she said, 'Doesn't that spineless father want to give his son a name? Why don't you do something about it? The poor child . . . People throw parties to celebrate the naming of their child, they seek advice and divination to select a proper name, and you two don't care at all.'

'It isn't too late.'

'It isn't too late? The boy is almost forty days old! In the end, you have to give him a name. How long do you want to keep calling him Baby?'

'I don't call him Baby.'

'Then what do you call him?'

'Saiid!' I said impulsively.

Mrs Parvin gave me a piercing look. There was concern and the glint of a tear in her eyes. Oblivious to it all, Mother said, 'It's a nice name and it goes well with Siamak.'

An hour later when I was in the bedroom breastfeeding the baby, Mrs Parvin came in, sat next to me and said, 'Don't do it.'

'Don't do what?'

'Don't name your son Saiid.'

'Why? Don't you think it's a nice name?'

'Don't play dumb with me. You know very well what I mean. Why would you want to bring back sad memories?'

'I don't know. Maybe I want to call him by a familiar name in this ice-cold home. You can't imagine how lonely I am and how thirsty I am for affection. If there was the tiniest bit of love in this house, I would have even forgotten his name.'

'If you do this, each time you call your son, you will think of Saiid and your life will become even more difficult.'

'I know.'

'Then choose a different name.'

A few days later, I took advantage of an opportunity and asked Hamid, 'Aren't you planning on getting a birth certificate for this child? We have to give him a name. Have you thought about it at all?'

'Of course. His name is Rouzbeh.'

I knew who Rouzbeh was and regardless of whether he was a hero or a traitor, under no circumstances was I going to allow Hamid to force me into naming my child after him. My son had to have his own name, so that he could give it meaning with his own personality.

'Absolutely not! This time, I will not let you name my child after your own idols. I want my son to have a name that I will enjoy every time I call him by it, not a name that will remind everyone of a dead person or of an agonising death.'

'A dead person? He was a champion of self-sacrifice and resistance.'

'Good for him. I don't want my son to be a champion of self-sacrifice and resistance; I want him to have a normal, happy life.'

'You really are common. You have no understanding of the significance of revolution and the true heroes who travelled the road to freedom. You think only of yourself.'

'For the love of God, stop it! I cannot stand your memorised lectures any more. Yes, I am common and self-centred. I think only about myself and my children because no one else thinks about us. Besides, for someone who accepts no responsibility whatsoever for this child, why is it that when it comes to naming him you suddenly remember you are a father? No, this time, I choose. His name is Massoud.'

Siamak was three years and four months old and Massoud was eight months old when Hamid disappeared. Of course, at first this wasn't how I perceived his absence.

'I'm going to Rezaieh with the guys for a couple of weeks,' he said.

'Rezaieh? Why there?' I asked. 'Then I guess you will also go to Tabriz to visit Monir. Right?'

'No! As a matter of fact, I don't want anyone to know where I am.'

'Your father will know you are not going to work.'

'I know. That's why I told him I am going out of town to see someone who has a collection of old books and wants to sell some of them and reprint the others. I asked for ten days off. By then I will come up with some other excuse.'

'You mean you don't know how long you will be away?'

'No, and don't make a fuss. If we are successful, we will stay longer. If not, we might be back in less than a week.'

157

'What is going on? Who are you going with?'

'You are so nosy! Stop interrogating me.'

'I'm sorry,' I said. 'You certainly don't need to tell me where you are going. Who am I to know about your plans?'

'Come on, you don't need to be indignant about it,' he said. 'And don't create chaos. If anyone asks, just tell them I'm on a business trip. And around my mother, you have to act in a way that will put her mind at ease and not make her worry for no good reason.'

The first two or three weeks passed quietly. We were used to Hamid not being there and didn't have any difficulties when he was away. He had given me enough money to cover one month's expenses and I had some money of my own, too. A month later, his parents started getting worried, but I would calm them down and tell them that I had heard from him, that he had just called, that he was well and that his work was taking a little longer, and other such lies.

In early June, the weather suddenly turned hot and an illness similar to cholera spread among children. Despite all my efforts to keep my sons safe, they both became ill. The instant I noticed Massoud had a low fever and a stomach ache, I didn't wait for Mrs Parvin to come and keep an eye on Siamak, I rushed both boys to the doctor. I bought the medications he prescribed and returned home. But late at night, they both took a turn for the worse. They vomited any medicine I gave them and their fever was rising from one minute to the next. Massoud's condition was worse. He was panting like a frightened sparrow and his small stomach and chest were heaving. Siamak's face was flushed and he kept asking me to take him to the bathroom. I was running around in circles. I put their feet in iced water, laid cold towels on their foreheads, but none of these made any difference. I noticed Massoud's lips were white and dry and I remembered the last thing the doctor told me. 'Children become dehydrated much faster than you think and it can lead to death.'

A voice inside me said that if I waited another minute I would lose my children. I looked at the clock. It was almost two-thirty in

158

the morning. I didn't know what to do. My brain was not functioning. I was biting my nails and tears were rolling on to my hand. My children, my beloved children, all I had in this world, I had to save them, I had to do something, I had to be strong. Whom could I call? Whoever I called would need time to come to us and there was no time to waste.

I knew there was a children's hospital on Takht-e Jamshid Avenue. I had to hurry. I put nappies on both boys, took all the money I had at home, carried Massoud in one arm, took Siamak by the hand and set off. The streets were deserted. Poor little Siamak, weak and burning with fever, could hardly walk. I tried carrying both of them, but the heavy bag I had packed made it impossible and every few steps I took, I had to stop and put Siamak down. My innocent children didn't even have the energy to cry. The distance from the house to the corner of the street seemed endless. Siamak had almost fainted. I was pulling him along by the arm and his feet were dragging on the ground. I kept thinking, If anything happens to my children, I will kill myself. This was the only conscious thought going through my mind.

A car pulled up next to me. Without uttering a word, I swung open the rear door and climbed in with the children. All I could manage was, 'The children's hospital. Takht-e Jamshid. For the love of God, hurry.'

The driver was a dignified-looking man. He looked at me in the rear-view mirror and asked, 'What happened?'

'They were a little sick this afternoon. They had diarrhoea. But it suddenly got much worse. Their fever is very high. I beg you, please hurry.'

My heart was pounding and I was gasping for air. The car was tearing through the empty streets. 'Why are you alone?' the man asked. 'Where is their father? You won't be able to put the children in the hospital all by yourself.'

'Yes, I can. I mean I have to, or I will lose them.'

'You mean they don't have a father?'

'No, they don't,' I snapped.

And I angrily looked away.

In front of the hospital, the man jumped out of the car and took Siamak in his arms, I took Massoud, and we ran inside. The moment the emergency room doctor saw the children, he frowned and said, 'Why did you wait so long?' He took Massoud, who by now was unconscious, from my arms.

'Doctor,' I pleaded, 'for the love of God, do something.'

'We will do what we can,' he said. 'Go to the admissions office and take care of the paperwork. The rest is in God's hands.'

The man who had driven us to the hospital was looking at me with such pity that I could no longer hold back my tears. I sat down on a bench, held my head in my hands and wept. I caught sight of my feet. My God! I was wearing house slippers. No wonder I almost fell a hundred times on the street.

The hospital required payment to admit the children. The man said he had money with him, but I didn't accept. I gave the admissions clerk all the cash I had and I told him I would pay the balance first thing in the morning. The sleepy clerk complained a little, but in the end he agreed. I thanked the man who had helped me and told him he should leave. Then I hurried back to the emergency room.

Lying on hospital beds, my children looked small and frail. Siamak had an IV attached to him, but they couldn't find Massoud's vein. They were sticking needles all over his body, but my unconscious son wasn't making a sound. Every time they pierced him with a needle, I felt as if they were stabbing a dagger in my heart. I covered my mouth with my hand so that my cries wouldn't distract the doctor and the nurses. From behind my veil of tears, I was witnessing my beloved child slowly dying. I don't know what I did that attracted the doctor's attention, but he motioned to a nurse to take me out of the room. The nurse put her hand on my shoulder and kindly yet firmly ushered me out.

'Nurse, what is happening? Have I lost my son?'

'No, madam. Don't upset yourself. Pray. God willing, he will recover.'

'For the love of God, tell me the truth. Is his condition very critical?'

160

'Of course, his condition isn't good, but if we can find a vein and connect the IV, there will be room for hope.'

'You mean all these doctors and nurses can't find this child's vein?'

'Madam, children's veins are very delicate, and it is even harder to find one when they have a fever and have lost so much water.'

'What can I do?'

'Nothing. Just sit here and pray.'

This entire time, with every heartbeat I had been calling out to God, but until that moment I had not been able to utter a complete sentence or to recite a single prayer. I needed to breathe fresh air, I needed to see the sky. I couldn't talk to God without looking up at the heavens. It seemed as if it was only then that I would be facing him.

I walked outside and felt the cool morning breeze on my face. I looked up at the sky. There was still more darkness in it than light. I could see a few stars. I leaned against the wall. My knees were shaking under my weight. Gazing out at the horizon, I said, 'God, I don't know why you brought us into this world. I have always tried to be content with that which pleases you, but if you take my children from me, I will have nothing left to thank you for. I don't want to speak blasphemy, but it would be an injustice. I beg you to not take them from me. Spare them.' I didn't know what I was saying, but I knew he could hear and understand me.

I went back inside and opened the door to the room. An IV was attached to Massoud's foot and there was a cast on his leg.

'What happened? Is his leg broken?'

The doctor laughed and said, 'No, madam. We put the cast on so that he won't be able to move it.'

'How is he? Will he get well?'

'We have to wait and see.'

I was going back and forth between their beds. Seeing Massoud move his head and hearing Siamak quietly moan gave me hope. At eight-thirty in the morning, they moved the children to an ordinary hospital unit.

'God be praised, they are out of danger,' the doctor said. 'But we have to be very careful and make sure the IVs don't come out.'

Keeping the IV in Siamak's arm was by far the most difficult.

Mother, Mrs Parvin and Faati burst into the hospital room in a state of panic. Seeing the children, Mother burst into tears. Siamak was testy and someone had to constantly hold his arm in place. Massoud was still very weak. An hour later, Father arrived. He looked at Siamak with such sadness that my heart ached. As soon as Siamak saw Father, he reached out to him and started to cry. But a few minutes later, Father's caresses calmed him down and he fell asleep.

Hamid's parents arrived together with Mansoureh and Manijeh. Mother greeted them with angry looks and snide remarks. I had to glower at her to put a stop to it; they were embarrassed and upset enough. Mansoureh, Faati, Mrs Parvin and Manijeh all volunteered to stay with me, but I preferred to have Mrs Parvin at my side. Faati was herself just a child, Mansoureh had a son to care for, and Manijeh and I didn't have all that warm a relationship.

Mrs Parvin and I stayed up all night. She held Siamak's hand while I sat on Massoud's bed with my arms wrapped around him and my head on his legs. He, too had grown restless since that afternoon.

After three difficult and exhausting days, we returned home. All three of us had lost a lot of weight. I hadn't slept in four nights. I looked at myself in the mirror; there were dark circles under my eyes and my cheeks were sunken. Mrs Parvin said I looked like an opium addict. She and Faati stayed with me. I bathed the children and took a long shower. I wanted to wash away the agony I had suffered, but I knew its memory would stay with me for ever and that I would never forgive Hamid for not having been there.

Two weeks later, life was almost back to normal. Siamak was again being naughty, ill-tempered and stubborn. He had grown to accept Massoud's presence and he would allow me to embrace him. But still, I somehow felt that in his heart he remained angry with me. Massoud was pleasant and cheerful; he leaped into everyone's arms, didn't shy away from anyone, and became sweeter and more delightful by the day. He would wrap his arms around my neck, kiss my cheek and with his few tiny teeth he would bite my face as if he wanted to devour me. His expressions of love were endearing. Siamak had never been as affectionate with me, not even when he was very small. His expressions of love always seemed constrained. And I wondered, How could two children of the same parents be so different?

Hamid had been gone for two months and I had no news of him. Of course, given the warnings he had offered before he left, I was not worried. But his parents were starting to be nervous again. I was forced to tell them that he had called, that he was well and that he didn't know how much longer his project would keep him away.

'But what sort of work is this?' his mother asked angrily. Then she turned to her husband and said, 'Stop by the printing house and find out where they have sent him and why it is taking so long.'

Another two weeks went by. One day a man telephoned and said, 'I'm sorry to disturb you, but I wanted to know if you have any news of Shahrzad and Mehdi.'

'Shahrzad? No. Who are you?' I asked.

'I am her brother. We are very worried. They said they were going to Mashad for two weeks, but it has been two and a half months and we have not heard from them. My mother is terribly anxious.'

'Mashad?'

'Were they going somewhere else?'

'I don't know. I thought they went to Rezaieh.'

'Rezaieh? What does Rezaieh have to do with Mashad?'

I regretted what I had said and uneasily replied, 'No, I must have made a mistake. By the way, who gave you this telephone number?'

'Don't be frightened,' he said. 'Shahrzad gave me the number and said that in case of an emergency this is the only telephone that someone might answer. Isn't that the home of Hamid Soltani?'

'Yes, it is. But I have no information either.'

'Please, if you find out anything, call me. My mother is sick with worry. I wouldn't have troubled you if I didn't have to.'

I was starting to get anxious. Where had they gone? Where were they that they couldn't even make a telephone call and put an end to their families' worries? Perhaps Hamid didn't care, but Shahrzad didn't seem to be that thoughtless and uncaring.

I ran out of money. I had spent the sum Hamid had given me as well as the money I had saved. I had already borrowed from Father to pay for the children's hospitalisation and I couldn't say anything to Hamid's father and make him more worried than he was. I had even borrowed some money from Mrs Parvin, but that was all gone, too.

Didn't Hamid think about how we were supposed to live? Or had something really happened to him?

Three months passed. I could no longer keep his mother calm by coming up with new lies. With each day that passed, I become more and more worried. His mother was constantly crying and saying, 'I know something terrible has happened to my son; otherwise, he would have called me or written to me.'

She tried not to say anything that would upset me, but I knew she somehow blamed me. None of us dared say that Hamid might have been arrested.

'Let's call the police,' Manijeh said.

Terrified, Hamid's father and I snapped, 'No, no, it will only make matters worse!' And we looked at each other. And his mother continued cursing and damning Hamid's unsavoury friends.

'My dear Massoum,' his father said, 'do you have an address or a telephone number for any of his friends?'

'No,' I said. 'It seems they are all together. Some time ago, a man called and said he was Shahrzad's brother. He, too, was worried and looking for information. But he said something strange. He said Shahrzad and Mehdi had gone to Mashad, while Hamid told me they were going to Rezaieh.'

'Then maybe they are not together. Maybe they are on different missions.'

164

'Missions?'

'Oh, I don't know. Something like that.'

Then his father found an excuse, pulled me aside and said, 'Don't ever talk to anyone about Hamid.'

'But everyone knows he has gone on a trip.'

'Yes, but don't say anything about him being missing. Just say that he is still in Rezaieh, that his work assignment is taking longer, that he is in regular contact with you. Don't ever say you have not heard from him. It will create suspicion. I will go to Rezaieh and see what I can find out. By the way, do you have money? Did Hamid leave enough to cover your expenses?'

I looked down and said, 'No, the children's hospital bills wiped out everything I had.'

'Then why didn't you say something?'

'I didn't want to upset you. I borrowed some money from my parents.'

'Oh, you shouldn't have done that. You should have told me.' He gave me some money and said, 'Repay what you owe your family immediately and tell them Hamid sent the money.'

A week later, tired and despondent, Hamid's father returned from his futile trip. Together with Monir's husband, he had searched every town in Azerbaijan province as far as the border with the Soviet Union and they had found no trace of Hamid. Now I was truly anxious. I never thought I would feel that worried for Hamid. Early in our marriage, he had broken that habit in me, but this time it was different. He had been gone for too long and the circumstances were suspicious.

Towards the end of August, one night I was jolted awake by a strange noise. The weather was still warm and I had left the windows open. I listened carefully. There was a sound coming from the front yard. I looked at the clock. It was ten minutes past three in the morning. Bibi would not be outside at that hour. Terrified, I thought a burglar had broken in.

I took a few deep breaths, gathered my courage and tiptoed to the window. In the pale moonlight, I saw the shadow of a car and three men in the front yard. They were rushing back and forth, carrying some things. I tried to scream, but I couldn't. I just stood there staring at them. After a few minutes, I realised that they were not taking anything out of the house. On the contrary, they were transferring things from the car to the cellar. No, they were not thieves. I knew I had to stay calm and quiet.

Ten minutes later, the three men finished moving the goods and a fourth man emerged from the cellar. Even in the dark, I could recognise Hamid. In utter silence, they pushed the car out of the yard, Hamid closed the door to the street and he climbed up the stairs. I had strange and conflicting emotions. Rage and anger had combined with joy and relief over his return. I felt like a mother who, after finding her missing child, first slaps him hard on the face, then holds him tight in her arms and weeps. He was trying to unlock the upstairs door as quietly as possible. I wanted to rile him. The instant he stepped inside, I turned on the lights. He leaped back and looked at me with horror. A few seconds later, he said, 'You are awake?'

'Well! What a surprise to see you here. Did you lose your way?' I said snidely.

'Great!' he retorted. 'What a warm welcome.'

'Were you expecting a welcome? You have some nerve! Where have you been all this time? You didn't even bother calling. Would it have killed you to send a message, a short letter, or something? Didn't you think we would die of worry?'

'I can see how worried you were for me!'

'Yes, the idiot that I am, I was worried. But forget about me; didn't you think about your poor mother and father who have been sick with worry?'

'I told you not to make a fuss, that our work might take longer than expected.'

'Yes, fifteen days could turn into a month, but not four months. The poor old man looked for you everywhere. I was scared something would happen to him.'

'Looked for me? Where did he look for me?'

'Everywhere! Hospitals, coroners' offices, police departments.'

Horror-struck, he exclaimed, 'Police departments?'

Mischief simmered in me. I wanted to hurt him.

'Yes, with Shahrzad's brother and your other friends' relatives they sent photographs of all of you to the newspapers.'

His face was as white as chalk.

'You are a lunatic! Couldn't you do one thing right and manage things here?'

And he quickly started to put his dusty shoes back on.

'Where are you off to now? Well, I can just tell the police you've come back, and not empty-handed.'

He was gaping at me with such dread that I wanted to laugh.

'What are you saying? Do you want to get us all killed? This place is no longer safe. I have to get word to the guys. I have to see what the hell we are supposed to do now.'

He had opened the door and was about to walk out when I said, 'There's no need. I lied. No one called the police. Your father just went to Rezaieh and came back without finding any trace of you.'

He breathed with relief and said, 'Are you sick? I almost had a heart attack.'

'You deserved it . . . Why should it be just us who get scared half to death?'

I arranged his bedding in the living room. 'I will just sleep in my room,' he said. 'In the back room.'

'I have turned it into the children's room.'

I had hardly finished my sentence and his head had barely reached the pillow when he fell fast asleep, still dressed in his dusty clothes.

CHAPTER THREE

Months were speeding by. The children were growing up and their personalities were taking shape, becoming more distinct. Siamak was a proud, belligerent and mischievous boy who had a certain reserve in expressing affection. The slightest adversity agitated him and he would try to crush any obstacle in his way with the might of his fists. In contrast, Massoud was gentle, kind and mild-mannered. He expressed his love to the people around him and even showed affection for nature and the objects that surrounded him. His caresses soothed the pain left in me by the lack of Hamid's love.

In their relationship, the two boys strangely complemented each other. Siamak gave the orders and Massoud implemented them. Siamak daydreamed and invented stories and Massoud believed them. Siamak would joke and Massoud would laugh. Siamak would hit out and Massoud would take the beating. I was often afraid that Massoud's gentle and loving nature would be crushed by Siamak's hostile and powerful personality. But I could never openly protect Massoud. The slightest move on my part was enough for Siamak's rage and jealousy to explode and lead to even more fist fights. The only way to avoid these clashes was to distract him by something more interesting.

But Siamak was also an impenetrable shield that protected Massoud against others. He would so wildly and strongly attack anyone who posed a threat to his brother that Massoud himself would plead and beg to save his enemy from Siamak's hands. Often the enemy was my brother Mahmoud's son, Gholam-Ali, who age-wise fell right between Siamak and Massoud. I don't know why the three of them would start to fight the instant they came together. Hamid believed this was how boys played and communicated with each other. But I couldn't understand or accept his reasoning.

Although Mahmoud had married three years after me, he already had three children. His first child was Gholam-Ali, the second was Zahra who was one year younger than Massoud, and his last child was Gholam-Hossein who was only one year old. Mahmoud was still foul-tempered and reclusive, and his obsessive nature was growing more pronounced from one day to the next. Ehteram-Sadat was constantly complaining to Mother about him. 'Lately he has become even more confused and daft,' she would say. 'He repeats his prayers several times and he still wonders if he said them properly.'

In my opinion, Mahmoud was not suffering from anything. His mind was as sharp as ever; he was especially savvy when it came to work and financial matters and had made a success of his business. He had a store in the bazaar where he worked independently, and people considered him a first-rate expert in carpets. He was never uncertain or obsessive in his work, and the only role religion played in his professional life was his careful observation of a Muslim's obligation to contribute one-fifth of his income to charity. Therefore, at the end of each month he would send his entire earnings to Ehteram's father in Qum, who would take a small portion of it for almsgiving and return the rest to Mahmoud. By this 'change of hands', as they called it, all of Mahmoud's money would become halal and he would have no reason to worry.

Ahmad had long since left the family. No one was more worried about him than Mrs Parvin who constantly said, 'We have to do something. If he continues like this, he will not survive.'

His problem was no longer limited to his nightly drinking and drunken rowdiness on the streets. Mrs Parvin said he was using drugs as well. But Mother refused to believe her and tried to save him from the devil and bad friends by praying and resorting to superstitious mumbo jumbo. Father, on the other hand, had completely given up hope for him.

Ali had grown up, but he hadn't managed to get his secondary-school diploma. For a while he worked in Ahmad's carpentry workshop, but Father thought it wise not to delay matters and used all his power and influence to get him away from Ahmad. 'If I leave him alone and don't stop him right now, he will be lost to us like the other one,' Father used to say.

Ali himself had gradually become disillusioned by Ahmad. He had built his brother into a strong and capable idol, and now he suffered to see him constantly drunk and in a stupor. Apparently this idol was finally shattered when one of the thugs at Café Jamshid gave Ahmad a good beating and threw him out into street; Ahmad was so drunk that he couldn't even lift a finger to defend himself. And at the workshop, Ali's colleagues, who not too long ago would have competed with each other for the honour of being Ahmad's apprentice, now ridiculed and harassed him. In any case, given all this, Ali willingly, but ostensibly under pressure from Father, left Ahmad and went to work for Mahmoud, so that he too would turn out to be a pious and wealthy merchant.

Faati turned into a demure, shy and mild-mannered girl. She stayed in school until the end of year three and then, as prescribed for decent girls, she started going to sewing classes. She herself was not all that interested in continuing her formal education.

I went to extreme lengths to enrol Siamak in school a year earlier than the law required. I knew that he was mentally ready. I was hoping that school would instil discipline in him and he would expend his boundless energy with children his own age and be less difficult at home. But like everything else, his going to school became a trying experience. At first, I had to sit in the classroom with him and only after he was comfortable being there would he allow me to leave; then I would have to stand for hours out in the schoolyard so that he could see me from the window. He was scared, but he expressed his fear with violence. On the first day of school, when the school supervisor took him by the hand to walk him to his classroom, he bit her hand.

When Siamak's rage peaked, the only way I could calm him down was to make myself the target of the waves of his anger. I would hold him in my arms and tolerate the blows of his kicks and small fists until he calmed down and started to cry. It was only on these occasions that he would allow me to hold, caress and kiss him. At all other times, he tried to pretend that he had no need for kindness. But I knew how deeply he hungered for affection and attention. I felt sorry for him. I knew he was suffering, but I didn't know why. I knew he loved his father and his absence pained him. But why wasn't he getting used to that situation? Could the absence of a father have that great an effect on a child?

I persistently read books on psychology and observed Siamak's behaviour. When Hamid was home, Siamak behaved differently. He listened only to his father. Although he could not sit still for a moment, he would sit on Hamid's lap for long periods of time and listen to him talk. And I learned too late that his refusal to sleep was because he was waiting up for his father. When Hamid was home, at bedtime he would stroke Siamak's hair and he would fall asleep quietly and peacefully. Accordingly, I gave Hamid the nickname 'Sleeping Pill'.

Fortunately, Father's presence and the deep affection he and Siamak shared somewhat made up for Hamid's absence. Even though Siamak didn't like to cling to anyone, when Father came to visit he would stay close to him and occasionally sit on his lap. Father treated Siamak with great calm and like an adult. In return, Siamak listened to him and accepted whatever he said without any reluctance. At the same time, Siamak could not bear to see Hamid or Father express any affection towards Massoud. He had accepted the fact that others, even me, divided their attention between him and his brother, and might even show greater affection for Massoud, but he wanted his father's and grandfather's love all for himself and could not tolerate the presence of a rival. In Hamid's case, this was not a problem; he never paid any particular attention to Massoud. But Father, who had a very clear understanding of this child, had to try hard not to express any love for Massoud in front of Siamak. This in itself made Siamak even more grateful to his grandfather and deepened his love for him.

Eventually, Siamak got used to going to school, even though not a month went by when I wasn't summoned by the principal because he had got into a fight. Still, with his new schedule set, I again started thinking about my own education. I was unhappy that I still had not received my school diploma and had left such an important matter unfinished. I started waking up early in the morning to take care of my household chores. When Siamak left for school, Massoud would keep himself busy with his games and spend hours drawing with his coloured pencils, or if the weather was nice, he would ride his tricycle in the yard. And I would sit and quietly study. I didn't feel the need to attend classes ...

Every afternoon when Siamak came home from school it felt as if an earthquake had struck the house. Doing homework had become yet another problem. He would drive me to desperation until he finally finished his schoolwork. Over time, I understood that the more sensitivity I showed, the more stubborn he became. As a result, I tried hard to be patient and not to pressure him. And late at night or the following morning, he would start to write his homework.

One morning when I was home with Massoud, Mrs Parvin came to see me. She seemed excited. I immediately realised she had come to share some news. She liked delivering first-hand news in person. She would highly embellish it and relate it in great detail, then wait to see my reaction. If the news was ordinary, she would simply tell me over the telephone.

'Well, what is the news?' I asked.

'The news? Who said I have any news?'

'Your expression, your manner, your face, they all scream that you have some hot news!'

Excited, she sat down and said, 'Yes! You won't believe it; it's so interesting ... but first bring some tea. My throat is dry.'

This, too, was one of her habits. She would torture me to death before she told me what had happened and the hotter the news, the more she would prolong sharing it. I quickly put the kettle on the stove and hurried back.

'Well, tell me, it's going to take a while for the tea to brew.'

'Oh my, I am choking with thirst, I can hardly talk.'

Annoyed, I went back to the kitchen and brought a glass of water for her and said, 'Well? Tell me.'

'Let us have our tea first.'

'Ugh ... as a matter of fact, don't tell me. I don't want to know,' I said with a pout, and I went back to the kitchen.

She followed me and said, 'Now don't sulk. Guess who I saw this morning.'

My heart sank, my eyes grew wide and I said, 'Saiid?'

'Oh come on, you still haven't given up? I thought with two kids you would have even forgotten the guy's name.'

I had thought so, too. I felt embarrassed. His name had just popped out of my mouth. I wondered, Does this mean he is still in my thoughts?

'Never mind,' I said. 'Now tell me, who did you see?'

'Parvaneh's mother!'

'For the love of God, are you being honest? Where did you see her?'

'Everything at its proper time. The water is boiling. Brew the tea and I will tell you everything. This morning, I went to the street behind Sepahsalar Park to buy shoes. Through a shop window I saw a woman who looked like Mrs Ahmadi. At first I wasn't sure. To be honest, she has aged a lot. By the way, how long has it been since we last saw their family?'

'About seven years.'

'I walked into the shop and looked at her. It was Mrs Ahmadi. At first she didn't remember me, but I thought at least for your sake I should talk to her. I said hello and finally she recognised me. We chatted for quite a long time. She asked about everyone in the neighbourhood.'

'Did she ask about me?' I asked, excited.

'Honestly, no. But I led the conversation around to you and told

173

her that I see you regularly, that you are married and have children. She said, "In that house, she was the only person worth socialising with. Of course, my husband says their father is a good, honourable man, but I will never forget what her brother did to us. He left us with no honour in the neighbourhood. No one had ever talked to my husband like that, and you can't imagine the things he accused poor Parvaneh of. My poor husband was about to faint. We couldn't hold our heads up in that area any more. That's why we moved so quickly. But Parvaneh would have given her life for that girl. You have no idea how much she cried. She kept saying, They will kill Massoum. Parvaneh went over to their house a few times, but Massoumeh's mother didn't let her see the girl. My poor child; she suffered a hard blow."'

'I was there once when she came to the door and Mother didn't let me see her,' I said. 'But I don't know about the other times.'

'It seems she even came to invite you to her wedding. She had brought an invitation card for you.'

'Really? They didn't give it to me. My God, I am so fed up with these people. Why didn't they tell me?'

'Your mother was probably afraid you would again live through the crush you had on that boy.'

'A crush? With two kids?' I said, exasperated. 'I will show them. They are still treating me like a child.'

'Oh, no,' Mrs Parvin said. 'Back then you still didn't have Massoud. This was a long time ago; perhaps four years ago.'

'You mean Parvaneh has been married for four years?'

'Well, of course, otherwise they would have had to pickle her!'

'What rubbish! How old could she be?'

'Well, she is about the same age as you and you have been married for seven years.'

'Wretched as I am, I was forced into it. They threw me down a well. But not everyone has to live through that hell. Well, whom did she marry?'

'She is married to the grandson of her father's aunt. Her mother said she had many suitors after she graduated from school, but in the end she married this guy. He is a doctor and lives in Germany.'

'You mean she now lives in Germany?'

'Yes, she moved there after they got married, but she spends most summers here with her family.'

'Does she have children?'

'Yes, her mother said she has a three-year-old daughter. I told Mrs Ahmadi how long you searched for Parvaneh, how terribly you missed her, and that your brother has lost his spunk and no longer poses a danger to anyone except to himself. Finally, I managed to get her telephone number, although she wasn't very comfortable giving it to me.'

My mind travelled back to seven years earlier. The camaraderie and deep friendship that I had shared with Parvaneh, I had never developed with anyone else. I knew I would never have another friend like her.

I was too embarrassed to call her mother. I didn't know what to tell her. But in the end, I did. I felt a lump in my throat the moment I heard her voice. I introduced myself and told her that I knew it was audacious of me to be calling her. I told her that Parvaneh had been my dearest friend, my only friend. I told her that I was ashamed of what had happened and asked her to forgive my family. I told her that I wished I could see Parvaneh again, that I still spent hours talking to her, that not a day went by without my thinking about her. I gave Mrs Ahmadi my telephone number so that Parvaneh could call me the next time she came to Iran to visit her family.

With two noisy children at home and a thousand chores and responsibilities, preparing for my final exams wasn't easy. I had to study at night, after the children went to bed. Near dawn, when Hamid came home and found me still awake and studying, he would look surprised and comment on my tenacity and determination. I took my final exams after Siamak had taken his, and the dream I had had for so many years finally came true; a simple dream that girls my age had attained as their natural right, without having to become so obsessed with it.

*

Hamid's activities were becoming more serious and dangerous. He had even come up with a security arrangement and had planned escape routes out of the house. Although I didn't know what his group was doing or planning, I sensed constant danger around me. After his strange trip and long absence, their organisation seemed to be more cohesive, their goals more defined and their work more structured. At the same time, there were news reports of incidents around the city that I felt were somehow connected to them. But the fact was that I didn't know and I didn't want to know. My ignorance made life bearable and lessened my fear, especially for the children.

At six o'clock on a summer morning, the telephone rang. Hamid reached it before I did. He hardly said two words and hung up, but suddenly he looked pale and terrified. It took almost a minute for him to regain his composure. I stood staring at him with horror and didn't have the nerve to ask what had happened. He rushed around, packed a few necessities in a duffel bag and took all the money we had at home. Trying to remain calm, I quietly asked, 'Hamid, have you been betrayed?'

'I think so,' he said. 'I'm not sure what has happened. One of the guys has been arrested. Everyone is relocating.'

'Who was arrested?'

'You don't know him. He is a new member.'

'Does he know you?'

'Not by my real name.'

'Does he know where we live?'

'Fortunately not. We didn't have any meetings here. But others may have been arrested, too. Don't panic. You know nothing. Go to your parents' house if you think you will be more comfortable there.'

Siamak had woken up at the sound of the telephone and looking worried and startled he was following Hamid around. He had sensed our anxiety.

'Where will you go?' I asked.

'I don't know. For now, I just have to leave. I don't know where I will be. I will not contact you at all for a week.'

Siamak wrapped his arms around Hamid's legs and begged, 'I want to go with you!'

Hamid pushed him away and said, 'If they come here, no matter what they find, just tell them it doesn't belong to us. Luckily you don't know anything that could put us in even greater danger.'

Again, Siamak clung to him and cried, 'I am coming with you!'

Hamid angrily ripped him off his leg and said, 'Gather your kids and take care of yourselves. Go to my father if you need money and don't talk to anyone about this.'

After he left, I stood there in a daze for some time. Terrified, I wondered what destiny had in store for us. Siamak was in a rage. He was throwing himself against the walls and doors and then I saw him running towards Massoud who had just woken up. I ran and picked him up in my arms. He tried to break away by kicking and punching me. It was useless to try to pretend that everything was fine and nothing had happened. That perceptive and sensitive child could sense my anxiety with every breath that I took.

'Listen to me, Siamak,' I whispered in his ear. 'We have to be calm and not tell anyone our secret; otherwise it will be very bad for Daddy.'

He suddenly grew quiet and said, 'Not tell anyone what?'

'Don't tell anyone that Daddy had to leave like this today. And make sure Massoud doesn't find out either.'

He looked at me with fear and disbelief.

'And we shouldn't be afraid. We have to be brave and strong. Daddy is very strong and he knows what to do. Don't worry, no one will find him. We are his soldiers. We have to be calm and keep his secret. He needs our help. Do you agree?'

'Yes.'

'So let us promise each other that we will not say anything to anyone and we will not make a fuss. All right?'

'All right.'

I knew he couldn't really understand the weight of what I was telling him, but it didn't matter. With his young and imaginative mind, he filled the gaps and exaggerated the heroic aspects of the story to his liking.

We never again talked about any of it. Sometimes when he saw me lost in thought, he would quietly take my hand and without saying a word he would look at me. I would try to banish my worries, and I would smile confidently and whisper in his ear, 'Don't worry. He is in a safe place.' And he would run off, raise a racket and pick up his game where he had left off. He would leap behind the sofa at the speed of lightning and make strange noises while shooting his water pistol in every direction. He was the only one capable of changing his mood and behaviour so dramatically.

Those anxiety-filled days seemed endless. I tried hard not to do anything rash and I didn't tell anyone what had happened. I had a little money in my wallet and I did my best to make do with it. I constantly asked myself, What will they do to him if they catch him? What has his group been involved in? What if the destruction I read about in the newspaper was their doing? I had never felt fear that close and that serious. In the beginning, I had thought of their meetings as an intellectual game, a pastime, a means for childish self-aggrandisement, but now everything had changed. The memory of that summer night when they had stashed things in the cellar amplified my fear. After that night, there was always a large padlock on the door of the room at the back of the cellar.

A few times I complained to Hamid about it, but he would only retort, 'Why are you constantly nagging? Why is this bothering you? You hardly ever go down to the cellar. It is not as if your space has been cramped.'

'But I'm afraid. What is down there? What if it puts us in danger?'

Hamid kept reassuring me that there was no need to worry and that whatever was down there was not dangerous. But before he left, he had said that if they found anything in the house I should just say it was not ours and that I knew nothing about it. Then, there were things down there that he did not want discovered.

A week later, in the middle of the night, the sound of the front door woke me from my light and troubled sleep. I ran into the

178

hall and turned on the light. Hamid whispered, 'Turn it off, turn it off!'

He wasn't alone. Two strange-looking women, tightly clad in chadors, were standing behind him. I caught sight of their feet. They were wearing rugged men's boots. The three of them went into the living room. Then Hamid came back out, closed the door behind him, and said, 'Now you can turn on that small lamp and give me the news.'

'There is no news,' I said. 'Nothing has happened here.'

'I know that. But have you noticed anything suspicious?'

'No . . . '

'Have you gone out?'

'Yes, almost every day.'

'And you didn't feel you were being followed? Do we have any new neighbours?'

'No, I haven't noticed anything.'

'Are you sure?'

'I don't know; I haven't sensed anything out of the ordinary.'

'All right. Now if you can, go bring something for us to eat. Tea, bread and cheese, last night's leftovers, whatever you have.'

I put the kettle on the stove. Even though I knew danger was still hovering around him, I felt a certain joy; I was relieved that he was unharmed. As soon as the tea was ready, I put cheese, butter, fresh herbs, the preserves I had recently made, and all the bread we had at home on a tray and took it to the living room door. I quietly called Hamid. I knew I should not go in. He opened the door, quickly took the tray and said, 'Thanks; now go to bed.'

He seemed to have lost some weight and his beard looked slightly salt and pepper. I wanted to kiss him.

I went to the bedroom and closed the door. I wanted them to be able to comfortably use the bathroom. Again, I thanked God that once more I was seeing him alive and well. But a sense of foreboding gnawed at me. Drowned in vague imaginings, I finally fell asleep.

The sun had just risen when I woke up. I remembered that we had no bread. I got dressed, washed my face, went to the kitchen to

179

turn on the samovar and returned to the hall. The children had woken up, but the door to the living room was still closed.

Siamak followed me back into the kitchen and quietly whispered, 'Is Daddy back?'

Taken aback, I asked, 'How did you know?'

'It's weird here. The living room door is locked and there are shadows behind the glass.'

The living room door was made of matte, honeycomb glass.

'Yes, my dear. But he doesn't want anyone to know, so we shouldn't say anything.'

'He is not alone, is he?'

'No, he has two friends with him.'

'I will make sure Massoud doesn't find out.'

'That's good, my son. You are a man now, but Massoud is still young and he may say something to others.'

'I know. I won't let him go near the living room door.'

Siamak stood guard at the living room door with such determination that Massoud grew more and more curious, wanting to know what was going on. They were about to get into a fight when Hamid walked out of the living room. Massoud stood there looking stunned while Siamak ran to him and clung to his legs. Hamid hugged and kissed them both.

'Sit with your children while I prepare breakfast,' I said.

'All right, let me wash first. And prepare something for our friends, too.'

When the four of us sat together at the breakfast spread, I suddenly felt like crying.

'Thank God,' I sighed. 'I was afraid we would never be together again.'

Hamid looked at me tenderly and said, 'For now, everything is fine. You haven't talked to anyone, have you?'

'No, I haven't even told your parents. But they have been very curious. They keep asking about you. Remember to call them; otherwise, as you like to say, there is going to be a big fuss.'

'Daddy,' Siamak said, 'I didn't tell anyone either. And I was careful for Massoud not to find out.'

Hamid looked at me with surprise. I gestured to him that there was nothing to worry about, and I said, 'Yes, Siamak has been a big help. He is great at keeping secrets.'

In his sweet, childish tone Massoud said, 'I have a secret, too. I have a secret, too.'

'Forget it,' Siamak snapped. 'You are still a kid, you don't understand.'

'I'm not a kid, I understand.'

'Boys, be quiet!' Hamid chided. Then he turned to me and said, 'Look here, Massoum, put something on the stove for lunch, then go to your father's house. I will call you and let you know when to come back home.'

'When will you call?'

'You will definitely have to stay there tonight.'

'But what am I going to tell them? They will think we have had a fight.'

'It doesn't matter. Let them think you are sulking. But you are not to come back under any circumstances until I call you. Do you understand?'

'Yes, I understand. But all this is finally going to get us into real trouble. I have been sick with worry all week. For the love of God, whatever you have stashed in this house take it all away. I am afraid.'

'Leave the house and we will do just that.'

Angry and upset, Siamak said, 'Daddy, let me stay.'

I motioned to Hamid to talk to him and took Massoud with me to the kitchen. The two of them sat facing each other. Hamid was talking in a serious tone and Siamak was listening intently. That day my six-and-a-half-year-old son behaved like a responsible adult who knew he had a duty to perform.

We said goodbye to Hamid and left to go to Father's house. Calm and quiet, Siamak struggled to carry the heavy duffel bag I had packed. I wondered what was going through his young mind. At Father's house, too, Siamak neither played nor made a sound. He sat on the edge of the reflecting pool and watched the red fish in the water. He didn't even get excited when Ehteram-Sadat brought Gholam-Ali to the house that afternoon; he didn't start a fight or create mischief.

'What is wrong with him?' Father asked.

'Nothing, Father. He has become a gentleman!'

I looked at Siamak and smiled. He looked up and smiled back at me. There was such serenity on his face. Now Siamak, Hamid and I shared a secret, a very important secret. We were a close family and Massoud was our child.

As I had expected, Mother was surprised by our unannounced visit. All the way there, I had thought about what I should tell her and what excuse I should offer for wanting to stay the night. The moment we walked in, she said, 'God willing, it is good news. What brings you here? And with luggage?'

'Hamid has a men's gathering,' I explained. 'Some of his friends and the printing house employees are coming over. He said they would all be more comfortable if I'm not there. And a few of them are coming from the provinces and staying for a few days. Hamid said I shouldn't go back as long as they are there. He will come and pick us up after they leave.'

'Really?' Mother said. 'I didn't know Hamid Agha is so honour-bound that he doesn't want his wife in the house when unfamiliar men are present!'

'Well, when men get together they want to feel free and talk about things they can't discuss in front of women. Besides, I have a few lengths of fabric and I have been meaning to ask Faati to make a dress for me; this will be the perfect opportunity.'

My stay at Father's house lasted three days and two nights. Although I was worried, I still had a pleasant time. Mrs Parvin made an elegant shirt and skirt for me and Faati made two floral house dresses. We talked and laughed. Mother, who had returned from Qum a week earlier, had plenty of fresh news about the family, our old neighbours and acquaintances. I found out that Mahboubeh had a daughter and was pregnant with her second child.

'This one is probably a girl, too,' Mother said. 'I can tell by the way she looks and acts. You can't believe how jealous they all were when I talked about your sons and Mahmoud's sons. And Mahboubeh's daughter looks just like Mahboubeh when she was that age, pale and plain.'

'Oh, Mother!' I chided. 'Mahboubeh was adorable when she was young; remember those blonde ringlets! And in this day and age there is no difference between sons and daughters for them to be jealous because Mahmoud and I have boys.'

'What do you mean there is no difference? This is so typical of you; you don't value what you have. In any case, they were as arrogant as you can imagine. Now that they are rich, they put on such airs that I wouldn't be surprised if they give fancy names to the lice that crawl on them! They almost burst with envy when I told them about Mahmoud Agha's success and the money he makes.'

'Come on, Mother. Why would they be jealous? You just said they are very rich.'

'True, but they still can't stand the sight of us; they want us to go without. By the way, your aunt was saying that Mahboubeh's husband wanted to take her on a trip to the West this year, but Mahboubeh didn't want to go.'

'Why? What an idiot!'

'Not at all. Why would she want to go? Over there everything is impure. How would she say her prayers? By the way, you should know that Ehteram-Sadat's uncle has been arrested. Mahmoud is very upset. He is afraid it might be bad for business.'

'What? Who arrested him?'

'It's obvious! The secret police ... it seems he gave a talk at the mosque.'

'Are you serious? Bravo! I didn't think he was that brave. When did they take him?'

'It has been a couple of weeks. They say they are tearing his flesh into tiny pieces with a pair of tweezers.'

A chill ran up my spine and I thought, God have mercy on Hamid.

*

Late in the afternoon on the third day, Hamid came to pick us up in a yellow Citroën 2CV. The boys were excited to see him and the car. Unlike other times, Hamid was not in a hurry for us to leave. He sat with Father on the wooden bed out in the yard and they drank tea and talked.

While saying our goodbyes, Father said, 'Thank God, my mind is at ease. I thought perhaps you two had had a fight, God forbid. I was worried. But I have to say, I really enjoyed these three days. Seeing you all in this house restored my soul.'

Father wasn't in the habit of saying such things. His words deeply moved me. On the drive back home, I gave Hamid the news about my relatives, especially about Ehteram-Sadat's uncle having been arrested.

'The damned SAVAK has got so strong,' he said. 'They are going after all the organisations.'

Not wanting the conversation to continue in front of Siamak, I said, 'Where did you get the car?'

'For now, it's mine to use. We have to purge a few locations.'

'Then, please start with your own home.'

'It's all done. I'm not worried about the house any more. I was really nervous ... If they had raided the house, we would have all been tagged for execution.'

'For the love of God, Hamid! Have pity on these innocent children.'

'I have taken every possible precaution. For the time being, our house is the only safe site.'

Although the car's engine was loud and we were whispering, I noticed Siamak listening intently.

'Sh! The kids ...'

Hamid turned and glanced at Siamak, then smiled and said, 'He is not a kid any more. He is a man. He is going to take care of you when I'm away.'

There was a glint in Siamak's eyes; his entire being had swelled with pride.

As soon as we arrived home, I went down to the cellar. There was no sign of the padlock on the door and there was nothing in

184

the back room other than ordinary household odds and ends. I thought to myself, Tomorrow morning I must do a thorough inspection, just in case they have left something behind.

Siamak was constantly following Hamid around. He wouldn't even let me give him a bath.

'I am a man,' he said. 'I will take a bath with Dad.'

Hamid and I looked at each other and laughed. The two of them took a bath after Massoud and me. Their voices echoed in the bathroom and I could hear some of what they were talking about. It was so pleasant. Although Hamid had spent little time with us, the father and son had a deeply intimate relationship.

Hamid was very busy for several days, but then he started spending much of his free time at home. It seemed he had nowhere to go and there was no sign of his friends. Like all men, he spent his days at work and his evenings at home. He was getting bored and frustrated. I took advantage of the opportunity and often asked him to take the boys to the park or out for a walk – something he had never done. I think those were the best days of my children's lives. The experience of having a father and a mother and a normal life, which for other children was not something extraordinary or something to be especially grateful for, meant the world to them, and to me. Gradually, I became so bold that one day I even suggested we go on a trip for a few days.

'Let's go to the Caspian coast,' I said, 'like we did the year Siamak was born.'

Hamid looked at me gravely and said, 'No, we can't. I'm waiting for news. I have to be either at home or at the printing house.'

'Just for two days,' I insisted. 'It's been two months and there has been no news, and schools open next week. Let the kids have some fond memories. Let them at least go on one trip with their parents.'

The boys clung to him. Massoud begged Hamid to take us on a trip, even though he didn't know what a trip was. Siamak didn't say anything, but he held Hamid's hand and looked at him with hope-filled eyes. I knew that look would weaken Hamid's resolve.

'Did you know Mansoureh's husband has bought a villa on the

Caspian coast?' I persisted. 'Mansoureh is always telling me that everyone has gone and stayed there except us. If you want, we can take your parents with us. After all, they deserve it, too. They dream of going on a short trip with their son. And we can drive there.'

'No, the car isn't sturdy enough for the Chalous road!'

'Then we will take the Haraz road. You said the car is new; why wouldn't it be sturdy enough? We will drive slowly.'

The children were still pleading with him, but it was all over when Siamak kissed Hamid's hand. We had won.

Hamid's parents didn't join us, but they were happy to see that after all these years we were going on a family trip. Mansoureh was already up north. She spoke on the telephone with Hamid and happily gave him the address. And finally, we set off.

Leaving the city, we felt as though we were stepping into a different world. The children were so mesmerised by the mountains, valleys and meadows that for a long time they each remained glued to a window and didn't make a sound. Hamid was humming a song and I was singing along with him. My heart was brimming with joy. I said the prayer that is customarily recited prior to travelling and I asked God not to take away the good fortune of our being together. The car struggled up the steep inclines, but it didn't matter. I wanted that trip to last for ever.

I had made meat cutlets for lunch. We stopped in a scenic area and ate. The children chased after each other and I relished the sound of their laughter.

'It's strange,' I said. 'Siamak's behaviour has changed so dramatically. Have you noticed how calm he is? He has become obedient and pleasant. I can't remember the last time I scolded him, while in the past, not a day would go by without us having a big fight.'

'I really don't understand what your problem is with this child,' Hamid said. 'To me he is a wonderful boy. I think I understand him better than you do.'

'No, my dear. You only see the way he is when you are at home.

His personality is completely different when you are not there. He is worlds apart from the boy you have seen every day for the past two months. You are like a sedative for him, a tranquilliser.'

'Ugh ... don't say that! No one should be that dependent on me.'

'But a lot of people are,' I said. 'It isn't something you can control.'

'Even the thought of it bothers me and makes me feel anxious.'

'Well, let's not dwell on it. We won't talk about it, we will just enjoy the beautiful days we have together.'

Mansoureh had prepared an airy room with a view of the sea for us. With her there, Hamid couldn't move his bedding to a different room and had to sleep next to me. We were all enjoying the sun and the sea. I wanted to get sunburned. I left my hair down and wore the colourful open-necked dresses I had recently made for myself. I wanted to again attract Hamid's admiring looks. I wanted his affection and attention. On the third night, he finally caved in, broke his years-old promise and took me in his arms.

That memorable trip brought us closer together than ever before. I knew Hamid expected more of me than just being a housewife. I read as much as I could and started discussing with him what I had learned from his books over the years. I tried to fill the empty place of his friends by sharing ideas and talking about social and political issues. Little by little, he realised that I, too, had an awareness of politics and societal issues, and he even came to appreciate my intelligence and good memory. To him, I was no longer a backward child or uneducated woman.

One day when I recited a section of a book he had forgotten, he said, 'It is such a shame that with all your talent you didn't pursue your education. Why don't you take the university entrance exams? I am sure if you continue studying you will make huge progress.'

'I don't think I will pass the exams,' I said. 'My English is poor. And besides, what would I do with the children if I were to go to university?'

'The same thing you did when you were preparing for your

school diploma. What's more, the children are older now and you have more time to yourself. Take English classes, or, better yet, enrol in the preparatory classes for the university entrance exams. You can do anything you want.'

After eight years, I was finally experiencing a real family life and I was savouring every pleasant moment of it. That autumn I took advantage of Hamid being at home in the afternoons and I signed up for the preparatory classes. I didn't know how long his circumstances would stay the same, but I tried to take full advantage of those precious days. I kept telling myself that their group had disbanded and that we could live as a real family for ever. Hamid was still constantly nervous, waiting for a telephone call, but I thought that, too, would soon end.

I still knew nothing about their organisation. Once, in the middle of a discussion, I asked him about it. 'No, don't ask about the guys and our activities,' he said. 'It's not that I don't trust you or that you wouldn't understand, it's simply that the less you know the safer you are.'

I never again expressed any curiosity about their group.

Autumn and winter passed quietly. Hamid's schedule gradually took on a different rhythm. Once a week or once every two weeks, telephone calls would be exchanged and he would disappear for a day or two. In the spring, he assured me that the danger had passed, that none of the members of his group could be traced, and that almost all of them had relocated to safe houses.

'You mean, all this time they were practically homeless?' I asked.

'No,' he said. 'They were on the run. After those early arrests, a lot of addresses were discovered and many were forced to abandon their homes.'

'Even Shahrzad and Mehdi abandoned their home?'

'They were among the first. They lost everything they had. All they had time to do was to save the records and documents.'

'Did they have many things?'

'Oh, Shahrzad's family had given her so much in dowry that you

188

could furnish two homes with it. Of course, over time she had given away many things, but there was still a lot left.'

'After they left their home, where did they go, what did they do?'

'Slow down! Don't get into details and serious subjects.'

During the spring and summer, Hamid went on a few extended trips. He was in good spirits and I was careful to not let anyone find out about his absences. Meanwhile, I was studying hard and getting ready for the university entrance exams. As much as my passing the exams made Hamid and me happy, it took our families by surprise. Their reactions were all very different.

'What are you going to university for?' Mother asked. 'It's not like you want to become a doctor.'

In her mind, the only reason anyone would go to university was to become a doctor.

Father was happy, proud and astonished.

'Your school principal told me how talented you are, but I already knew it,' he said. 'I only wish at least one of these boys had turned out like you.'

Ali and Mahmoud were of the belief that I still hadn't given up my childish silliness and that my husband couldn't control me because he didn't have enough backbone, wasn't man enough and lacked a sense of honour.

I was soaring. I felt proud and confident. Everything was going my way.

I threw a large party for Manijeh who had got married some time ago and I had not had time to have a celebration in her and her husband's honour. After many years of estrangement, our families gathered together. Of course, Mahmoud and Ali used the excuse that women without hijab were going to be present at the party and they didn't come, but Ehteram-Sadat came with her loud and boisterous children.

I was so happy that nothing could bother me or take that smile off my face.

*

189

My life took on a new direction. I enrolled Massoud in a kinder-garten close to home and took care of most of my responsibilities at night so that in the morning I could go to the university with peace of mind, and without Hamid and the children lacking any-thing.

The weather had turned cold. The autumn wind was knocking the tree branches against the windows. The drizzling rain that had started that afternoon was now mixed with snow and it was coming down harder. Hamid had just fallen asleep. I was thinking to myself, Winter has arrived so suddenly; it is good that I have already got out my warm clothes.

It was almost one o'clock in the morning and I was getting ready for bed when the sound of the doorbell made me freeze to the spot. My heart started pounding in my chest. I waited for a few seconds and told myself I had misheard, but just then I saw Hamid stand-ing in the middle of the hall looking panic-stricken. We stared at each other.

With a voice that barely rose from my throat, I said, 'Did you hear it, too?'

'Yes!'

'What should we do?'

As he pulled his trousers on over his pyjamas, he said, 'Hold them off as long as you can. I will get out over the rooftop and take the route I had planned; then open the door. If there is any danger, turn on all the lights.'

He quickly put on a shirt and a jacket and ran towards the stairs.

'Wait! Take a coat, a sweater, something . . .'

The doorbell was ringing incessantly.

'There's no time. Go!'

He was halfway through the door that led to the rooftop when I grabbed a sweater that was within my reach and tossed it to him. I tried to regain my calm and look sleepy. I wrapped a coat around me and went down the stairs into the front yard. I was shivering uncontrollably.

By then whoever it was was pounding on the door. I turned on the light in the yard so that Hamid could see us better from the

190

rooftop and I opened the door. Someone shoved the door open, dashed into the yard and closed the door. It was a woman wearing a floral chador that was clearly not hers, as it barely reached her ankles. Terrified, I glared at her. Her wet chador slipped down to her shoulders and I gasped, 'Shahrzad!'

She quickly raised her finger to her lips for me to keep quiet and whispered, 'Turn off the light. Why is it that the first thing you two think to do is to turn on the lights?'

I looked up at the rooftop and turned out the light.

She was drenched to the skin.

'Come inside, you will catch a cold,' I said quietly.

'Shh! Quiet!'

We stood there behind the door and listened to see if there were any sounds coming from the street. There was only silence. After a few minutes, like someone suddenly drained of all energy, Shahrzad leaned against the door and slid down to the ground. Her chador spilled out around her. She put her arms on her knees and buried her head in them. Water was dripping from her hair. I held her under the arm and struggled to help her get up. She couldn't walk. I picked up her chador and took her by the hand; it was surprisingly hot. Helpless and weak, she followed me and we climbed up the stairs.

'You have to dry yourself off,' I said. 'You're very sick, aren't you?'

She nodded.

'There is plenty of hot water; go and take a shower. I will bring you some clothes.'

Without saying a word, she went to the bathroom and stood under the shower for some time. I put together some clothes that I thought would fit her and took some bedding to the living room and prepared a place for her to sleep on the floor.. She came out of the bathroom and got dressed. She wasn't speaking and had the lost look of a desperate child.

'You must be hungry.'

She shook her head.

'I have warmed up some milk. You must drink it.'

Silent and submissive, she drank the milk. I led her to the living room and she fell asleep before she could even make herself comfortable under the bedclothes. I pulled the blanket over her, walked out and closed the door.

It was only then that I remembered Hamid. Could he still be up on the roof? I quietly climbed up the stairs to the rooftop. He was hunkered down under the awning of the small alcove on top of the stairs.

'Did you see who it was?' I whispered.

'Yes, Shahrzad!'

'Then why are you still up here? She doesn't pose any danger.'

'As a matter of fact she poses a great danger. I have to wait and see if she was followed. How long has it been since she arrived?'

'Half an hour ... no, forty-five minutes. If she was being followed, something would have happened by now. Right?'

'Not necessarily. Sometimes they wait for everyone to gather. They don't raid a group house without plenty of planning and preparation.'

I was trembling again. 'What if they raid our house? Will they arrest us, too?'

'Don't be afraid, you're not involved. Even if they arrest you, you don't know anything. They will let you go.'

'But how would they find out that I don't know anything? I guess by plenty of torture!'

'Get these stupid thoughts out of your head,' he said. 'It's not that simple. You must stay strong. You will lose your confidence if you keep thinking along these lines. Now tell me, how is she? What did she say?'

'Nothing. She couldn't talk. I think she is very sick. I think she has a terrible flu.'

'Shahrzad and Mehdi had become too conspicuous. They had been identified. Their house was the first one that was raided. They have been living underground for a year and a half. They stayed in the provinces for a long time until we arranged a safe house for them. They must have been exposed again.'

'You mean the poor things have been homeless for a year and a half?'

192

'Yes!'

'Where is her husband?'

'I don't know. They were together. Something must have happened to force them to separate . . . he might have been arrested.'

My heart sank. The first thought that crossed my mind was that Mehdi knew where we lived.

That night Hamid stood guard up on the roof until dawn. I took him warm clothes and hot tea. In the morning, I woke the children up a little earlier than usual, gave them breakfast and walked them to their school and kindergarten. On the way, I looked around me carefully to check for anything suspicious or unusual, searching for a hidden agenda in every glance and movement. After I dropped off the children, I bought some groceries and returned to the house. Hamid had come downstairs.

'I don't know what to do,' he said. 'Should I go to the printing house or not?'

'I think it is better if we act normally and not attract any attention,' I said.

'Did you notice anything out of the ordinary on the street?'

'No, everything seemed normal. Maybe everything being normal is what is not normal. Maybe they don't want us to be cautious and on our guard.'

'Stop imagining things,' Hamid said. 'I think I have to wait and talk to Shahrzad and find out exactly what has happened. She may need me to do something for her. Aren't you going to wake her?'

'No, the poor girl is really exhausted and sick. Do you want me to call the printing house and tell them you are not going to work today? You can rest a little until she wakes up.'

'No, you don't need to call. They are used to me not showing up at work now and then. I never call to let them know.'

Shahrzad lay in bed looking almost unconscious until one in the afternoon. I cooked a large pot of turnip soup and marinated some meat for kebab. She clearly needed to regain her strength. She was half the size she had been the last time I had seen her. I went out and bought some sedatives, cough syrup and something to reduce fever. It was almost time for the children to come home. I went to her and gently put my hand on her forehead. She still had a fever. She woke with a fright and sat up with a jolt. For a few seconds she stared at me and her surroundings. She had no notion of place and time.

'Don't be afraid,' I gently said. 'Calm down. It's me, Massoumeh. You are safe.'

Suddenly, she remembered everything. She took a deep breath and fell back on her pillow.

'You have become too weak,' I said. 'Sit up. I have made some soup. Eat a little, take the medication and go back to sleep. You have a very bad case of flu.'

Her large eyes filled with sorrow and her lips trembled. I pretended I hadn't noticed and walked out. Hamid was pacing the hall.

'Is she awake?' he asked. 'I have to talk to her.'

'Wait; let her pull herself together and eat something first ...'

I took the soup and the medicine to the living room. She was sitting up. I took off the towel I had wrapped around her hair the night before. Her hair was still a little damp.

'Start eating,' I said. 'I will go get a comb or a brush.'

She put a spoonful of soup in her mouth, closed her eyes and savoured it.

'Hot food! Soup! Do you know how long it has been since I had something hot to eat?'

My heart ached. I said nothing and walked out. Hamid was still impatiently pacing up and down the hall.

'What is the matter?' I snapped. 'Why are you in such a hurry? Wait a few minutes. I won't let you talk to her until she has eaten something.'

I took a comb and returned to the living room. It was difficult combing her tangled hair.

'A hundred times I wanted to go and cut it all off and be rid of it,' she said. 'But I never found the time.'

'What? Why would you want to cut off all this beautiful, lush hair? A bald woman is really ugly.'

'Woman!' she said thoughtfully. 'Yes, you are right. I had forgotten I am a woman.'

She laughed sarcastically and ate the rest of her soup.

'I have made kebab, too. You have to eat some meat to gain strength.'

'No, not now. I haven't eaten in forty-eight hours. I have to eat slowly and in small portions. Give me some more soup later on ... Is Hamid home?'

'Yes, he is waiting to talk to you. I think he is running out of patience.'

'Tell him to come in. I feel much better. I feel alive again.'

I gathered the dishes, opened the door and asked Hamid to come in. He greeted her so eagerly and yet so politely and ceremoniously that it was like he was talking to his boss. I walked out and closed the door.

They talked quietly for more than an hour.

When the children came home from school, Siamak walked in and like a dog that has smelled a stranger in the house he asked, 'Mum, who is here?'

'One of your father's friends,' I said. 'Make sure you don't tell anyone!'

'I know!'

And then he started to observe everything carefully. He pretended he was playing in the hall, right behind the living room door, but he was all ears, hoping to hear something. I called him and said, 'Go buy a couple of bottles of milk.'

'No, not now.'

And he quickly resumed his game behind the closed door.

Hamid walked out of the living room, tucked the sheets of paper he was holding into his jacket pocket and while putting on his shoes he said, 'Shahrzad is going to stay here for now. I have to go out. Don't worry if I'm late or if I don't come home tonight. I will definitely be back by late afternoon tomorrow.'

I went to the living room. Shahrzad was lying down.

'Did you take the medication?' I asked.

Looking embarrassed, she sat up and said, 'Please forgive me; I know I am intruding. I will try to leave as soon as possible.'

'Please! You need to rest. Consider this your own home. I will not let you leave until you have fully recovered.'

'I'm afraid I may cause problems for you. All these years, we have tried to keep this house safe for you and your children, but last night I put that safety at risk. I had spent two entire days going from one hole to another and, as luck would have it, the weather suddenly turned cold. It started to rain and snow. And I wasn't feeling well. I had a fever and it was getting worse by the hour. I was afraid I would collapse on the street. I had no other options; otherwise, I would not have come here.'

'You did well to come. For now, please don't worry about anything; just sleep and rest assured that nothing has happened here.'

'For the love of God, don't be so formal with me.'

'All right!'

But I couldn't help it. I didn't quite know where I stood with her and what the nature of our relationship was. The children were peeking through the door and eyeing Shahrzad with curiosity. She laughed, wiggled her fingers and said hello to them.

'God bless them,' she said. 'Your sons have grown so much.'

'Yes! Mr Siamak is now in year three and Massoud is five years old.'

I handed her the pills and a glass of water.

'I thought they were closer in age,' she said.

'We enrolled Siamak in school a year early. Come here, boys, come here and say hello to Sha—' I suddenly noticed the alarmed look on Shahrzad's face and realised that I should not mention her name. I hesitated a moment and said, 'Come and say hello to Aunt Sheri.'

Shahrzad raised her eyebrows and laughed as if the name sounded silly to her.

The children came in and said hello to her. Siamak was scrutinising her with such curiosity that Shahrzad grew nervous. She even looked down to make sure her shirt buttons hadn't come undone.

'All right, that's enough,' I said. 'Everyone out. Auntie has to rest.'

And outside the door, I told the boys, 'Don't make any noise and don't tell anyone Auntie is visiting.'

'I know!' Siamak snapped.

'Yes, son. But now Massoud has to know, too. Do you understand, dear? This is our secret. You cannot tell anyone.'

'OK,' Massoud said cheerfully.

A few days later, Shahrzad had almost recovered, except that she still had a dry cough which kept her awake at night. I tried to stimulate her appetite by cooking various tasty dishes, hoping that she would regain some of the weight she had lost. Hamid was constantly coming and going, reporting to Shahrzad behind closed doors, and leaving again with new instructions.

A week went by. Shahrzad paced the rooms and tried to stay away from the windows. I had stopped going to my classes at the university and we were not sending Massoud to the kindergarten for fear that he would inadvertently say something about what was going on at home. He spent the days quietly playing, making houses with the new Lego Hamid had bought for him, and drawing beautiful pictures that were too advanced for his age and reflected a special talent. Emotionally, too, he was displaying the creative spirit of an artist. He looked at objects intently and discovered things in them that none of us had noticed. When the weather was nice, he would keep himself busy for hours with the plants and flowers in the yard. He would even plant seeds and, surprisingly, they would all grow. He lived in a different world. It was as if earthly matters had no value for him. Unlike Siamak, he was quick to forgive and adapted to any situation. He reacted with his entire being to the smallest kindness. He was aware of all my emotions and if he sensed that I was upset, he would try to cheer me up with a sweet kiss.

Massoud's relationship with Shahrzad quickly escalated to a deeply loving tenderness. They liked to spend all their time together. Massoud watched over her like a guard and constantly drew pictures and built houses for her. He would sit on her lap for long periods of time and in his sweet childish language weave strange stories about the things he had built. Shahrzad would laugh wholeheartedly and Massoud, feeling encouraged, would continue with his sweet-talking.

197

Siamak, on the other hand, treated Shahrzad with respect and reserve; the same way Hamid and I treated her. I liked her very much and tried to be relaxed and friendly with her, but for some reason I always felt like a schoolgirl around her. To me she was the symbol of competence, political astuteness, courage and self-reliance. All these characteristics had escalated her to a superhuman in my mind. She was always kind and comfortable with me, but I couldn't forget that she was twice as perceptive and intelligent as my husband, even giving him orders.

Hamid and Shahrzad were constantly talking, and I would try not to disturb them or show any curiosity. One night after I put the children to bed, I went to the bedroom and sat down to read. Thinking that I, too, had gone to bed, they sat in the hall and talked comfortably.

'We are very lucky that Abbas never came to this house,' Hamid said. 'The rascal didn't even resist for forty-eight hours.'

'I knew from the start that he was weak,' Shahrzad responded. 'Remember how he was constantly nagging during training? It was as clear as daylight that his conviction wasn't strong.'

'Why didn't you tell Mehdi?'

'I did, but he said it was too late to put him aside, Abbas knew everything. Mehdi said we should try to bring him around, that he had the right foundation. But deep in my gut, I was always wary.'

'Yes, I remember,' Hamid said. 'Even when we had gone as far as the border, you objected to his going with us.'

'That's why Mehdi never gave him any sensitive information and I tried to have him meet as few people as possible. Just the fact that he knows nothing about you, not even your real name, or where you live and where you work, has really helped us.'

'Yes, but our greatest luck was that he didn't live in Tehran. Otherwise, he would have eventually figured it all out.'

'If the good-for-nothing had held out for just forty-eight hours, we could have saved everything. Still, thank God the central nucleus and the guys in Tehran weren't caught. And what's left of the ammunitions should be enough. If the operation goes well and according to plan, we can seize the enemy's weapons.'

I felt a chill run up my spine and cold sweat settled on my forehead. Questions rushed through my mind. What were they planning to do? Where had they been? My God, where and with whom had I been living? Of course, I knew they were working against the Shah's regime, but I didn't know that the scope of their activities had widened to that extent. I always imagined their actions to be limited to intellectual debates, printing leaflets, writing articles, newsletters and books, and giving lectures.

That night when Hamid came to the bedroom, I told him I had overheard their conversation. I broke into tears and begged him to give it all up, to think about his life and his children.

'It's too late,' he said. 'I should have never built a family. I told you this in a thousand different ways, but you didn't accept it. I am alive because of my ideals and my duty to live up to them. I can't just think about my own kids and forget about the thousands of wretched children living under the tyranny of this executioner. We have sworn to save the people and to set them free.'

'But what you are planning is very dangerous. Do you really think that with a handful of people you can go up against the army, the police force and the SAVAK, destroy them all and save the people?' I asked.

'We have to do something so that the world will stop believing that this country is an island of peace and stability. We have to shake the foundations so that the masses wake up, stop being afraid and start believing that even this mighty power can fall. Then, they will gradually join us.'

'You are all too idealistic. I don't believe that any of what you say will ever happen. You will all be destroyed. Hamid, I am terrified.'

'Because you don't believe. Now stop making a big fuss. What you overheard was just talk. We have had hundreds of these plans and none of them were ever carried out. Don't ruin your own and the children's peace of mind over nothing. Go to sleep; and don't ever mention this to Shahrzad.'

After ten days of Hamid going and coming, taking messages and orders to unknown people and places, the decision was made that Shahrzad was not to leave our house until further notice and that we should try and resume our normal life. The only problem was that we had to find a way to stop people from coming to the house.

Although we usually didn't have that many callers, the occasional visits by our parents, Mrs Parvin and Faati could still create difficulties. We decided to take Bibi and the boys to visit Hamid's parents regularly so that they wouldn't want to come to the house to see them. And I told my own family that I had classes at the university every day and that I would visit them whenever I could. I also told them that I would leave the children with them when I had afternoon classes. Despite all this, we did occasionally have unannounced visitors. On these occasions, Shahrzad would stay in the living room and lock the door from the inside, and we would tell our visitor that we had lost the key and couldn't use that room.

Shahrzad stayed with us. She tried to help me around the house, but she knew nothing about housekeeping and laughed at her own incompetence more than anyone else. Instead, having grown close to the children, she took care of Massoud with love and affection. And in the afternoon when Siamak came home from school, she worked with him on his homework, reviewed his lessons and practised dictation with him. In the meantime, I went to my classes at the university and started taking driving lessons. We had agreed that if I learned how to drive, it would be helpful in emergencies as well as vital to the children's safety. The Citroën was still covered and parked in the yard. Shahrzad and Hamid believed that there was no suspicion directed at the car and that it was safe for me to drive it.

Massoud hardly left Shahrzad's side and was constantly busy doing something for her. He drew a picture of a house and told her that it was their house, that when he grew up he would build it so that they could get married and live there together. Shahrzad pinned the drawing to the wall. Whenever Massoud came shopping with me, he would ask me to buy all his favourite foods so that he could give them to Shahrzad. On sunny days, he would search around the yard for interesting gifts for her. Since there were hardly any flowers in bloom at that time of year, he would often pluck a few blossoms from the thorny wintersweet bush and with bloody fingers offer them to Auntie Sheri who kept them as one would keep a precious object.

The longer she lived with us, the more I learned about her. She was a very simple woman. One could not describe her as beautiful, but she was attractive and charming. One day after she had taken a shower she asked me to cut her hair short.

'Let me instead blow-dry it for you,' I said. 'It will dry faster and it will look beautiful.'

She didn't object. Massoud stood and watched intently as I styled Shahrzad's hair. He loved beauty and enjoyed observing women tend to themselves. Even when I wore the lightest shade of lipstick, he would notice and say something nice about it, but he preferred it when I wore red lipstick. After I finished blow-drying Shahrzad's hair, he picked up a red lipstick and said, 'Auntie Sheri, put this on.'

Shahrzad looked at me.

'Well, put it on,' I said. 'It's not a big deal.'

'No, I'm too embarrassed.'

'Embarrassed in front of whom? Me? Massoud? Besides, what is wrong with wearing a little lipstick?'

'I don't know. There is nothing wrong with it, but it's inappropriate for me. It's a bit too frivolous.'

'What rubbish! You mean you have never worn make-up?'

'I used to, when I was younger. And I liked it, but it's been years . . .'

Massoud again insisted, 'Auntie, put it on, put it on. If you don't know how, I will put it on for you.' He took the lipstick and put some on Shahrzad's lips. Then he stood back and looked at her, his eyes full of admiration and joy. He clapped, laughed and said, 'She looks so pretty! Look how pretty!' And he leaped into her arms and gave her a big kiss on the cheek.

Shahrzad and I burst out laughing, but suddenly she grew quiet, put Massoud back down on the floor, and with utter simplicity and innocence she said, 'I am jealous of you. You are a fortunate woman.'

'Jealous of me?' I said, surprised. 'You are jealous of me?'

'Yes! I think it is the first time I have felt this way.'

'You must be joking. I am the one who should be jealous of you. I have always wished I was like you. You are an amazing woman: well educated, brave, a capable decision maker ... I always think Hamid wishes he had a wife like you. And then you say ... Oh, no! You must be joking. I am the one who should be jealous, but I don't think I even deserve to be envious of you. I would be like the commoner who is jealous of the Queen of England.'

'Nonsense. I am a nobody. You are far better and more complete than me. You are a lady, a good and loving wife, a kind and wise mother, eager to read and learn, and willing to make sacrifices for your family.'

Looking terribly sad, she sighed and got up from the chair. Instinctively, I knew she was longing to see her husband.

'How is Mr Mehdi?' I asked. 'Has it been a long time since you saw him?'

'Yes, almost two months. The last time was two weeks before I came here. Given the situation, we had to take two different escape routes.'

'Do you have news of him?'

'Yes, poor Hamid is constantly taking our messages back and forth.'

'Why doesn't he come here one night, in the middle of the night, so that you can see each other?'

'It's too dangerous. His coming here could make this house no longer safe. We have to be careful.'

I threw caution to the winds and said, 'Hamid says your marriage was arranged by the organisation, but I don't believe him.'

'Why not?'

'You two love each other like a husband and wife, not like colleagues.'

'How do you know?'

'I am a woman, I can recognise love, I can sense it. And you are not the type of woman who could share a bed with a man you don't love.'

'Yes,' she said. 'I have always loved him.'

'Did you meet through the organisation?... Oh, I am sorry, I am being nosy. I take it back.'

'No... it's all right. I don't mind. I haven't had a friend to talk to in years. Of course, there were people close to me, but I was always the listener. It seems the need to talk is always there. You are perhaps the only friend I have had in recent years with whom I can talk about myself.'

'I have had only one true friend in my life and I lost her years ago.'

'Then it seems we need each other; me more so than you. At least you have your family, I don't even have that. You cannot imagine how much I miss them, how much I miss the gossip, the family news, the simple chit-chat and the everyday issues. How long can one talk about politics and philosophy? Sometimes I wonder what is going on in our house and I realise that I have forgotten the names of some of the children in the family. They must have forgotten me, too. I am no longer a member of any family.'

'But don't you all believe that you belong to the masses and to the global family of the working class?'

She laughed and said, 'You have learned quite a lot, haven't you! Still, I miss my own family. But what was the question you asked?'

'I asked, where did you and Mehdi meet?'

'At the university. Of course, Mehdi was two years ahead of me. He had a great ability to lead and an astute, analytical mind. When I found out that the leaflets that were being distributed and the slogans that were appearing on the dormitory walls were his handiwork, he became my hero.'

'You were not interested in politics at the time?'

'Yes, I was. How could a university student claiming to be an intellectual not be interested in politics? Being a leftist and opposed to the regime was almost like an official duty for the students. Even those who weren't true believers used politics to pose as intellectuals. There were very few real devotees like Mehdi. I still hadn't read and learned enough. I didn't really know what I believed in. Mehdi shaped my thoughts and beliefs. Although he came from a religious family, he had read the works of Marx, Engels and others, and he analysed them very well.'

'So he tempted you to join the organisation?'

'At the time, there was no organisation. We started it together much later. Perhaps if it wasn't for Mehdi, I would have chosen a different path. But I am sure I would not have veered too far from politics.'

'How did you end up getting married?'

'The group was starting to take shape. I was from a traditional family and, like most Iranian girls, I couldn't go out whenever I wanted to and I couldn't stay out until late at night. One of the guys suggested that for me to be able to dedicate all my time to the cause, I should marry someone in the group. Mehdi agreed and like a real suitor he came to our house with his family and asked for my hand in marriage.'

'Were you happy in your marriage?'

'What can I say? Perhaps I did want to marry him, but I didn't want the reason for our marriage to be the organisation and I didn't want to be proposed to like that ... I was young and romantic and under the influence of stupid bourgeois literature.'

On a foggy and freezing February night, at one o'clock in the morning and despite all the danger they had talked about, Mehdi quietly crept into the house. I had just fallen asleep when I was jolted awake by the sound of the front door. Hamid was relaxed and reading his book.

'Hamid! Did you hear that? It was the front door. Someone has opened it!'

'Go to sleep, it isn't any of our business.'

'What do you mean? Are you expecting someone?'

'Yes, it's Mehdi. I gave him the key.'

'Didn't you say it was too dangerous?'

'They lost track of him some time ago. And we have taken every precaution. He needs to talk to Shahrzad; they're at odds over a few issues and need to make certain decisions. I couldn't

204

be their go-between any more and we were forced to arrange a meeting.'

I wanted to laugh. What a strange couple! A husband and wife who used any excuse other than love and missing each other to be together.

Mehdi was supposed to leave early in the morning, but he didn't. Hamid said they still hadn't come to an agreement. I laughed and went about my work. Late in the afternoon when Hamid came home, the three of them talked and argued for hours behind closed doors. Shahrzad's cheeks were rosy and she seemed more lively than usual, but she was avoiding my eyes and, just like a shy schoolgirl whose secret has been exposed, she was trying to act as if nothing had happened.

Mehdi stayed for three nights and in the middle of the fourth night he left as quietly as he had come. I don't know if they ever saw each other again, but I am certain that those few days were the sweetest days of their lives. Massoud shared their seclusion and went from Mehdi's arms to Shahrzad's embrace, making them laugh with his sweet-talk and all the games and tricks he knew. From behind the honeycomb glass, I even saw Mehdi's shadow going around the living room on all fours with Massoud riding on his back. It was so strange. I never thought a man who was so serious that he hardly ever smiled could develop such a close relationship with a child. Behind those doors, Mehdi and Shahrzad were themselves; their true selves.

After Mehdi left, Shahrzad was depressed and irritable for several days and kept herself busy reading. By then she had read almost all our books. She used to sleep with a volume of Forough's poetry under her pillow.

Towards the end of February, she asked me to buy for her a few shirts and trousers and a large handbag with a strong shoulder strap. Every handbag I bought, she said it was too small. Finally, I gave up and said, 'Then you want a duffel bag, not a handbag!'

'Bravo, yes! And it shouldn't be too big, it shouldn't attract attention, it should be easy to carry, it should be just large enough to hold everything I have.'

I thought to myself, Including your gun? From the first day she

205

arrived, I knew she had a gun and I was always terrified that the children might find it.

Shahrzad was getting ready to leave. She was just waiting for an order or a piece of news, which arrived in the middle of March and before the new year. She set aside her old clothes and bag and asked me to get rid of them. She packed her new clothes and other belongings in her new duffel bag and carefully arranged Massoud's drawings at the very bottom, next to her gun. She was in a strange mood. She had grown tired of living in secret, staying indoors and being immobile; she craved fresh air, being on the street and among people, but now that the time had come for her to leave, she seemed sad and depressed. She kept hugging Massoud and saying, 'How can I tear myself away from him?' She would hold him tight and hide her tearful eyes in his hair.

Massoud had sensed that Shahrzad was preparing to leave. Every night before going to bed and every day before leaving the house with me, he would make her promise not to leave while he was gone, and at every opportunity he would tell her, 'You want to leave? Why? Have I been bad? I promise not to come in your bed in the morning and wake you up any more ... If you are going away, take me with you, otherwise you will get lost; you don't know the streets around here.' And with all this, he was making Shahrzad even more unhappy and uncertain, and he was not only making her heart ache, but mine as well.

On her last night with us, Shahrzad slept next to Massoud and told him stories, but she couldn't hold back her tears. Massoud, who like all children saw and understood things through his heart's eyes, held Shahrzad's face in his small hands and said, 'I know when I wake up in the morning you will be gone.'

At half past midnight, Shahrzad left the house as planned. From that very moment, I missed her and felt the void she had left behind.

Before leaving, she held me in her arms and said, 'Thank you for everything. I leave my Massoud in your care. Watch over him. He is very sensitive. I am worried about his future.' And then she turned to Hamid and said, 'You are a fortunate man; value your life. You have a wonderful family. I don't want anything to disrupt the peace and serenity of this home.'

Hamid looked at her with surprise and said, 'Do you know what you are saying? Come on! Let's go, it is getting late.'

The next day, when I went to clean and tidy up the living room, I took the volume of Forough's poetry from under her pillow. There was a pencil tucked in it. I opened the book to that page and saw she had underlined these verses:

Which summit, which peak?
Give me refuge you flickering lights,
you bright mistrusting homes
on whose sunny rooftops laundered clothes
sway in the arms of scented soot.
Give me refuge you simple wholesome women
whose soft fingertips trace
the exhilarating movements of a fetus beneath your skin,
and in your open collars
the air forever mingles with the smell of fresh milk.

A tear rolled down my cheek. Massoud was standing in the doorway. With sorrow in his eyes he asked, 'She's gone?'

'Good morning, my dear. Well, sooner or later she had to go back to her own home.'

He ran into my arms, put his head on my shoulder and cried. He never forgot his darling Auntie Sheri. Even years later, when he had turned into a vigorous young man, he would say, 'I still dream of the house I have built for her and we live in it together.'

After Shahrzad left, I got busy preparing for the new year – spring cleaning, new clothes for the children, sewing new bed sheets, changing the living room curtains. I wanted the new year celebration to be a fun and exciting experience for the children. I tried to observe all the traditional customs and rituals and hoped that it would all be etched in their minds as a sweet memory of their childhood. Siamak was responsible for watering the seed sprouts

207

we were growing on plates, Massoud was painting eggs, and Hamid would laugh and say, 'I can't believe you are doing all this. What are you wasting all this energy for?'

But I knew that, deep in his heart, he too was excited and happy about the new year. Ever since he had started spending most of his free time with us, he could no longer avoid being involved in our daily lives and unconsciously expressed his pleasure.

I hired someone to help me clean the house from the rooftop all the way down to the cellar. The scent of a new year wafted through the house.

For the first time, we went on the new year social calls as a complete family. We participated in new year events and even spent the traditional thirteenth-day celebrations on a picnic outside of town with Hamid's family. After the holidays, happier and more energetic, I again became busy with my own and Siamak's studies and the end of the school year exams.

Hamid was spending even more time at home, waiting for a telephone call that wouldn't come. He was restless and impatient, but there was nothing he could do. I didn't mind; I was pleased to have him home. With the end of the exams and the start of the summer, I planned various entertainments for the children. I wanted us to spend the entire summer together. Now that I had a driver's licence, I had promised them that in the afternoons I would take them to the cinema, or the park, or to a party, or an amusement park. They were happy and content and I felt a strong sense of fulfilment.

One afternoon, on the way home from the park, I bought a newspaper, some bread and a few other groceries. Hamid had still not come home. I put everything away and started cutting the bread, which I had laid on top of the newspaper. As I cut the bread, the newspaper headline gradually emerged. I shoved the bread aside. The words stabbed into my eyes like daggers. I couldn't fully grasp their meaning. As if struck by a bolt of electricity, I was frozen to the spot and trembling. I couldn't take my eyes off the newspaper. There was a storm in my mind and a riot in my stomach. The children noticed my strange state and came over to me, but I couldn't understand what they were saying. Just then, the door opened and Hamid rushed in, looking distraught. Our eyes met; so it was true, there was no need to say anything.

Hamid fell to his knees, pounded his fists on his thighs and hollered, 'No!' Then he keeled over and put his forehead on the floor.

He was in such a state that I forgot my own horror. The children were staring at us with fear and confusion. I collected myself, pushed them out and told them to go play in the yard. Looking back at us, they walked out without protest and I hurried over to Hamid. He put his head on my chest and wept like a child. I don't know how long we sat there and cried. Hamid kept repeating, 'Why? Why didn't they tell me? Why didn't they let me know?'

After a while, his rage and grief sparked him into action. He washed his face and ran out of the house like a madman. There was nothing I could do to stop him. All I said was, 'Be careful, you may all be under surveillance. Be alert.'

I read the newspaper article. In the course of a military operation, Shahrzad and a few others had been trapped. To avoid falling into the hands of the SAVAK, they had all committed suicide by holding exploding grenades. I read the article over and over again, thinking that looking at it from different angles I might discover the truth, but the rest of the article was all the usual insults and the damning of traitors and saboteurs. I hid the newspaper so that Siamak wouldn't see it. In the middle of the night, Hamid returned home exhausted and desperate. He threw himself on the bed still fully dressed and said, 'Everything is in chaos. All the lines of communication have been severed.'

'But they have your telephone number. They will call if it becomes necessary.'

'Then why haven't they called all this time? It has been more than a month since any of them contacted me. I knew about the operation; I was supposed to be part of it, I had been trained for it. I don't understand why they put me aside. If I had been there, this would have never happened.'

'You mean you would have single-handedly fought that massive military force and saved everyone? If you had been there, you would have been dead, too.'

And I thought to myself, Why did they not include him or contact him? Was it Shahrzad's doing? Was she protecting Hamid's family by excluding him?

Two or three weeks went by. Hamid was nervous and chain-smoking. He was waiting for news, jumping every time the telephone rang. He went to extreme lengths to track down Mehdi and the other key players, but he couldn't find the slightest lead. Every day, there was news of more arrests. Hamid again checked the various escape routes. The printing house was purged and certain employees were dismissed. The days were fraught with events and incidents; danger floated in the air. We spent every second expecting a disaster or news of one.

'Everyone is in hiding,' I said. 'Maybe they have all left. Go on a trip for a while and come back when everything has calmed down. You still haven't been identified; you can leave the country.'

'I will not leave the country under any circumstance.'

'Then at least go to a small village, to one of the provinces, go somewhere far away and stay there until all this unrest quietens down.'

'I will not be away from the home or office telephones. They may need me at any moment.'

I did my best to resume our normal routines, but nothing was normal. My soul was grieving and I was terrified for Hamid's life. Shahrzad's face and the memories of the few months we had spent together did not leave me for one instant.

The day after the news broke about the military operation, Siamak found the newspaper, took it to the rooftop and read the article. I was in the kitchen when he walked in looking pale and clutching the newspaper.

'Did you read it?' I asked.

He laid his head on my lap and cried.

'Don't let Massoud find out,' I said.

But Massoud had figured it all out. He grew sad and quiet and often just sat in a corner. He stopped making things and drawing pictures for his Auntie Sheri. He stopped asking about her and was obsessively careful never to mention her name. A short time later, I noticed that his drawings now featured dark colours and strange scenes; colours and images that I had never seen in his pictures. I would ask him about them, but he wouldn't tell a story or offer any explanation. I was afraid that the sadness that he neither spoke about nor forgot would permanently affect his gentle and cheerful soul. He was made to laugh, love and comfort others, not to grieve and suffer.

There was little I could do to shield my children from life's painful experiences and the bitter realities that they would have to face. This, too, was part of their growing up.

Hamid was in an even worse condition than the boys. He aimlessly wandered around, sometimes he would disappear for a few days, but he would return no less distraught and I would know that he had not found what he was searching for. The last time he left, we had no news of him for more than a week. He didn't even call to see if anyone had tried to contact him.

I was constantly anxious. Ever since Shahrzad's death I no longer liked to buy the newspaper, but now every day, earlier than the day before, I would hurry to the news-stand and wait until the daily newspapers were delivered. I would stand on the street and leaf through each issue with trepidation and when I was certain there was no bad news, I would calm down and walk back home. In reality, I didn't read the newspaper to learn the news, I wanted to make certain there was no news.

Towards the end of July, I finally read the news that I had dreaded. The twine that held the bundle of newspapers together had still not been cut when the large, black headline made me freeze. My knees started to shake and I gasped for air. I have no memory of how I paid for the newspaper and how I made my way back home. The boys were playing in the yard. I quickly went upstairs and closed the door behind me. Right there behind the door, I sat down and spread the newspaper on the floor. I felt as though my heart was about to leap out of my throat. The article stated that the leadership of a terrorist organisation had been decimated and that our beloved country had been cleansed of those traitors. The list of names marched before my eyes. There were ten of them. Mehdi's name was among them. I read the list again. No, Hamid's name wasn't there.

I felt faint; I didn't know what emotion I was experiencing. I mourned those who had lost their lives, but there was a spark of hope gleaming in my heart. Hamid's name wasn't there. I thought, Then he is still alive, perhaps he is on the run, perhaps he has not even been identified and can come home. Thank God. But, what if he has been arrested? I was dazed and confused. Without much hope, I called the printing house; there was still an hour left of the work day, but there was no answer. I felt I was going to lose my mind. I wished there was someone I could talk to, someone I could consult with, someone to console me. I told myself that I had to be strong, that one single word of what was inside me could destroy us.

I spent the next two days in darkness and fear. Hoping to distract myself, I worked like a madwoman. On the second night, what I had subconsciously expected happened.

It was past midnight, I was about to fall asleep. I don't know how they suddenly appeared in the middle of the house. Siamak ran to me, someone tossed Massoud who was screaming into my arms, a soldier was aiming a rifle at the three of us huddled on my bed. I don't know how many they were, but they were all over the house, grabbing and throwing everything they could get their hands on into the middle of the rooms. I could hear Bibi's terrified voice downstairs and it added to my panic. They threw the contents of every dresser, cabinet, closet, shelf and suitcase in a heap; with knives they tore through sheets, mattresses and pillows. I didn't know what they were looking for. I kept thinking, This is good news, Hamid must still be alive, he has not been arrested, that is why they are here ... But what if he has been caught and they are gathering all these books and documents and letters as evidence ... and who gave them our address?

All these thoughts and a thousand other vague ones were rushing through my mind. Massoud clung to me and stared at the soldiers, Siamak sat quietly on the bed. I took his hand; it was ice cold and trembling faintly. I looked at his face. He was all eyes; he was monitoring their every move. I saw something on his face other than fear and it made me shudder. I will forever remember the flames of rage and hatred that blazed in the eyes of that nine-year-old boy. I thought of Bibi and realised that I hadn't heard her voice for some time. I wondered what had happened to her. I wondered if she was dead. The soldiers told us to get off the bed. They tore through the mattress, then again told us to get back on the bed and to stay there.

The sun had risen by the time they left our home, carrying documents, papers and books. Massoud had been asleep for about half an hour, but Siamak still sat there, pale and silent. It took me a while to muster the courage to climb down from the bed. I kept thinking one of them must be hiding somewhere, watching us. I searched the rooms. Siamak followed me everywhere. I opened the door and walked outside. No, there was no one there. I ran down the stairs. The door to Bibi's bedroom was wide open and she lay sprawled sideways on her bed. I thought, My God, she is dead. But when I reached her, I heard her rasping and trying to breathe. I propped her up on a couple of pillows, poured a glass of water and tried to trickle some in her mouth. There was no longer any need to try to conceal anything. There was no secret left for me to be afraid of divulging. I picked up the telephone and called Hamid's father. He tried to remain calm and I sensed that the news wasn't all that startling to him; it was as if he expected it.

I went through the house. Everything was in such disarray that I thought I could never put things back in order again. My house was in ruins. It looked like a ravaged country after the enemy has left. I wondered, Do I now have to sit and wait for casualties?

There were such huge piles of odds and ends in Bibi's few rooms that I wondered how she had fitted in so many useless things. Old

213

curtains, hand-stitched tablecloths with stains that had not come out after multiple washes, old decorative pieces of cloth, small and large pieces of leftover fabric from clothes that had been sewn, worn and thrown away many years ago, warped and yellowed old forks, chipped and broken plates and bowls waiting for a china repair man who never came ... Really, why did Bibi keep all those things? What part of her life was she searching for in them?

There was true mayhem down in the cellar – broken chairs and tables, empty bottles of milk and soda scattered around in the dirt, mounds of rice that had poured out of slashed burlap sacks ...

Hamid's parents walked into the house and looked around in disbelief. Seeing the state everything was in, his mother screamed and burst into tears. She kept crying, 'What has become of my child? Where is my Hamid?'

I looked at her with surprise. Yes, one could cry, but I was as cold and hard as ice. My brain would not cooperate with me. It refused to grasp the magnitude of the disaster.

Hamid's father quickly carried Bibi to the car and forced Hamid's mother to follow them. I had no will or energy to help or console anyone or to answer any questions. I was void of emotion. All I knew was that I couldn't sit still and I kept walking from room to room. I don't know how long it took for Hamid's father to come back. He took Siamak in his arms and broke into tears. I watched him with indifference. He seemed to be miles away from me.

Massoud's unrelenting and terrified screams finally brought me back. I ran towards the stairs and picked him up. He was drenched in sweat and trembling.

'It's all right, son,' I said. 'Don't be afraid. It's all right.'

'Gather your things,' Hamid's father said. 'You will stay with us for a few days.'

'No, thank you,' I replied. 'I am more comfortable here.'

'You can't stay here. It's not wise.'

'No, I'm going to stay. Hamid may try to contact me. He may need me.'

He shook his head and firmly said, 'No, my dear. There is no need. Collect your things. If you are more comfortable at your father's house, I will take you there. I guess our house isn't all that safe either.'

I realised he knew more than he was saying, but I didn't have the courage to ask. I didn't want to know. Amid all that chaos and confusion, I managed to find a large duffel bag. I grabbed any piece of the boys' clothing that I could see and stuffed them in the bag, then gathered a few things for myself as well. I didn't have the energy to change my clothes; I just threw on a chador over my nightgown and walked down the stairs with the boys. Hamid's father locked the doors behind us.

I didn't speak a word during the entire drive. Hamid's father talked to the boys and tried to distract them. As soon as we arrived at Father's house, the boys jumped out of the car and ran inside. I looked at them. They were still wearing their pyjamas. They seemed so small and defenceless.

'Look, my girl,' Hamid's father said, 'I know you are scared, you are in shock, it has been a terrible blow, but you have to be strong, you have to face reality. How long are you going to sit there dazed and silent and in a world of your own? Your children need you. You have to take care of them.'

At last, my tears started to flow. I wept and asked, 'What has happened to Hamid?'

He leaned his forehead on the steering wheel and remained silent.

'He is dead! Isn't he? He has been killed, just like the others. Hasn't he?'

'No, my dear, he is alive. That much we know.'

'Have you heard from him? Tell me! I swear I won't tell anyone. He is hiding in the printing house, isn't he?'

'No. They raided the printing house two days ago. They turned it inside out and shut it down.'

'Then why didn't you tell me? Was Hamid there?'

'Almost ... he was near by.'

'Well?'

215

'He is under arrest.'

'No!'

For a while, I couldn't say anything. And then I impulsively said, 'So in fact, he too is dead. He was more afraid of being arrested than of being killed.'

'Don't think like this. Have hope. I will do whatever I can. I have called on a thousand people since yesterday. I have met with a few well-connected officials and lined up a whole lot of acquaintances, and I have an appointment with a lawyer later today. Everyone says we should be hopeful. I am optimistic. And you have to help me by staying in constant contact with us. For now, we should thank God he is alive.'

I spent the next three days in bed. I wasn't sick, but I was so drained and exhausted that I couldn't do anything. It was as if the fears and anxieties of the past several months, together with that final blow, had sapped me of all energy and strength. Massoud would sit next to me and stroke my hair. He would try to force me to eat and watched over me like a nurse. All the while, Siamak walked around the reflecting pool in total silence. He didn't talk to anyone, didn't fight, didn't break things and didn't play. There was a disquieting glint in his deep, dark gaze that scared me more than his temper tantrums and aggressions. Overnight, he seemed fifteen years older and had the temperament of a tense and bitter man.

On the third day, I finally got out of bed. I had no choice. I had to carry on with my life. Mahmoud, who had just learned what had happened, came to Father's house with his wife and children. Ehteram-Sadat was talking incessantly but I had no patience for any of it. Mahmoud was in the kitchen, talking to Mother. I knew he had come hoping to gather more information. Faati came into the room, put the tea tray on the floor and sat down next to me. Just then, I heard Siamak's thunderous and hysterical screams come from the yard. I ran to the window. With hatred in his voice, he was shouting obscenities at Mahmoud and hurling rocks at him. Then he suddenly swung around and with surprising force pushed poor Gholam-Ali into the pool, then picked up a flowerpot and flung it to the ground, shattering it. I didn't know what had made him that furious, but I knew it wasn't without cause. I actually felt relieved. After three days, he was finally releasing his emotions.

Ali ran over to Siamak, yelled at him to shut up and raised his hand to strike him in the mouth. The world turned dark before my eyes. 'Put your hand down!' I screamed. Then I jumped into the yard through the window and lunged at Ali like a tigress protecting her cub. 'If you ever raise a hand to my child again I will tear you to pieces!' I shouted.

I held Siamak in my arms. He was shaking with rage. Everyone was staring at me in silence and surprise. Ali took a step back and said, 'I just wanted to shut him up. Look at the havoc he has raised. Look at what he did to this poor boy.' And he pointed to Gholam-Ali who was standing next to his mother like a drenched mouse, sniffling.

'Didn't you hear the horrible things he said to his uncle?' Ali said.

'His uncle must have said something to make him this angry,' I retorted. 'He hasn't made a sound in this house for three days.'

'This urchin isn't even worthy of me talking to him,' Mahmoud scowled. 'Aren't you ashamed of yourself for selling out your brother for an imp of a child? You will never learn, will you?'

By the time Father came home, the house was again quiet. It was the calm after a storm that gives everyone a chance to take a measure of the damage. Mahmoud and his wife and children had left; Ali was in his room upstairs; Mother was crying and didn't know whether she should side with me or with her sons; Faati was hovering over me and helping me pack the children's clothes.

'What are you doing?' Father asked.

'I have to go,' I said. 'My children shouldn't grow up being mistreated and castigated, especially not by their kin.'

'What happened?' Father snapped.

'What can I say?' Mother lamented. 'Poor Mahmoud was only showing his concern. He was talking to me in the kitchen and the

217

boy overheard us. You won't believe the hell he raised. And then the sister and brothers got into a fight.'

Father turned to me and said, 'No matter what has happened, I will not let you go back to that house tonight.'

'No, Father, I have to go. I haven't enrolled the children in school and classes start next week. I haven't taken care of anything yet.'

'Fine, go, but not tonight and not alone.'

'Faati will come with me.'

'Wonderful! What a great protector! I mean there should be a man with you. The house may be raided again. Two women and two young boys shouldn't be there alone. Tomorrow, we will go together.'

He was right; we had to wait another night. After dinner, Father asked Siamak to sit with him and he started talking to him the way he used to do when Siamak was younger.

'Well, my son, now tell me what happened that made you so angry,' Father quietly said.

And just like a tape recording, and unaware that he was imitating Mahmoud, Siamak said, 'I heard him tell Grandmother, "The louse is a subversive. Sooner or later, they will execute him. I never liked him or his family. I knew they were up to no good. I guess we shouldn't have expected any better from a suitor that Mrs Parvin introduced. How many times did I tell you to marry her off to Haji Agha ..."' Siamak paused for a few seconds. 'Haji Agha something or other.'

'Probably Haji Agha Abouzari,' Father said.

'Yes, that's it. And then Uncle Mahmoud said, "But you said he was too old, that he had been married before, and you ignored the fact that he was a pious man and had a shop in the bazaar stocked with merchandise. Instead, you gave her to a faithless two-bit communist. That filth, he deserves what he gets. He should be executed."'

Father held Siamak's head against his chest and kissed his hair.

'Don't listen to any of this,' he said gently. 'They are not smart enough to understand. Your father is a good man. Rest assured that they will not execute him. I talked to your grandfather today. He said he has hired a lawyer. God willing, everything will work out.'

I spent the entire night thinking about how we were supposed to live without Hamid. What was I to do with the children? What were my responsibilities? How was I going to protect them from what people said?

The next morning we returned to our war-torn house with Father, Mrs Parvin and Faati. Father was shocked to see the state of my home. As he was leaving he said, 'I will send the boys from the shop to come and help. This is more work than you three women can handle.' Then he took some money from his pocket and said, 'Take this for now and let me know if you need more.'

'No, thank you,' I said. 'I don't need any money right now.'

But his offer made me think about our financial situation. How was I going to cover our expenses? Would I have to be forever dependent on my father or on Hamid's father or on others? I was again overwhelmed with anxiety. I tried to comfort myself; the printing house would reopen and resume work, and Hamid was a shareholder.

For three entire days, Faati, Mrs Parvin, Siamak, Massoud, Father's employees and occasionally Mother worked with me until we finally restored some order in the house. Hamid's mother and sisters came to tidy up Bibi's rooms downstairs. By then, Bibi had been released from the hospital and was convalescing at their house.

In the process, I went down to the cellar and threw away all the odds and ends.

'God bless the SAVAK,' Faati laughed. 'They made you finally discover what's in this house and forced you to do a major spring clean!'

The next day, I enrolled the boys in school. Poor Massoud started year one in such poor spirits and, unlike Siamak, he tried so hard not to give me any trouble. On the first day of school, I could read in his eyes his fear of that unknown environment, but he said nothing. When I was saying goodbye to him, I said, 'You are a good boy and you will quickly find friends. I am sure your teacher will like you very much.'

'Will you come to pick me up?' he asked.

'Of course I will. Do you think I will forget my kind and darling son?'

'No,' he said. 'I'm just afraid you will get lost.'

'Me? Get lost? No, my dear, adults don't get lost.'

'Yes, they do. And we can't find them again; just like Daddy and Shahrzad.'

It was the first time since Shahrzad's death that he had spoken her name, and her full name, not Auntie Sheri, which is what he used to call her. I didn't know what to say. I wondered how he had interpreted their disappearance in his young mind. I took him in my arms and said, 'No, my son. Mothers don't get lost. They know the scent of their children and they follow it and find their children wherever they may be.'

'Then, don't you cry while I'm not there!' he said.

'No, son, I won't cry. When did I ever cry?'

'You always cry when you are alone in the kitchen.'

There was nothing I could hide from that child. With a lump in my throat, I said, 'Crying isn't a bad thing. Sometimes we need to cry. It makes our heart feel lighter. But I won't cry any more.'

As time went on, Massoud proved to be just as trouble free at school. He did his homework on time and was careful to never upset me. The one effect of that night that remained in him and which he couldn't hide from me were his terrified screams that would wake us up in the middle of the night.

Two months passed. The universities opened. But the last thing on my mind was going to classes. Every day, Hamid's father and I went to see different people, made requests, pleaded and begged, lined up contacts and connections; we even wrote to the office of Queen Farah pleading that Hamid not be tortured and executed and asking to have him transferred to an ordinary prison. Several influential people made promises, but we were not sure to what extent

220

our efforts were effective and what Hamid's circumstances really were.

Sometime later, a trial was held and it was determined that Hamid had not participated in armed activities. He was saved from being executed and was instead sentenced to fifteen years in prison. Eventually, we were given permission to take him clothes, food and letters. Every Monday I would stand at the prison gates, holding a large bag of food, clothes, books and writing materials. Much of it was usually returned to me on the spot and of those items the prison guards did accept, I didn't know what was in fact delivered to him.

The first time they gave me his dirty clothes to wash, I was startled by their strange smell. They smelled of stale blood, of infection, of misery. Terrified, I inspected every piece. The sight of blood and pus stains drove me insane. I closed the bathroom door, turned the taps on full and wept to the roaring sound of water pouring in the bath. What was he suffering in prison? Would it not have been better if he had died the way Shahrzad and Mehdi died? Was he spending every second praying for death? Over time, by carefully examining his clothes I learned about his injuries and their severity. I knew which ones were more serious and which ones were healing.

Time was passing and there was no indication that the printing house would be allowed to reopen. Every month, Hamid's father gave me some money for us to live on, but how long could that go on? I had to make a decision. I had to find a job. I was neither a child, nor incapable. I was a woman responsible for two children and I didn't want to raise them on the charity of others. Sitting still, whining and holding my hand out in front of this and that person was beneath me, beneath my children, and especially beneath Hamid. We had to live with honour and pride; we had to stand on our own two feet. But how? What work could I do?

The first thought that occurred to me was to become a seamstress and to work for Mrs Parvin, with Faati's assistance. Although I wasted no time getting started, I hated the work, especially because I had to go to Mother's and Mrs Parvin's houses every day where I had to face Ali and occasionally Mahmoud, and I had to tolerate Mother's reprimands.

'Didn't I tell you sewing is the most important thing for a girl?' she would say. 'But you didn't listen and wasted your time going to school.'

Every night I read the employment classifieds in the newspapers and every day I went to different firms and companies to apply for a job. Most of the private companies were looking for secretaries. Hamid's father cautioned me about work environments and certain issues that working women faced. His warnings were valid. In some offices I was leered at and appraised from head to toe as if they were selecting a lover, not an employee. It was in the course of these interviews that I realised having a school diploma was not enough. I needed other skills. I went to two sessions of a typing class and after I learned the basic rules I stopped going because I had neither the time nor the money to pay for the tuition. Hamid's father gave me an old typewriter and I spent the nights practising. Then he introduced me to an acquaintance who worked in a government agency. The day I went for my interview, I found myself face to face with a man aged thirty-one or thirty-two with piercing, intelligent eyes who looked at me with curiosity and in the course of the interview tried to discover the information I was not volunteering.

'You have written here that you are married. What does your husband do?'

I hesitated. I thought because Hamid's father had made the introductions, he might know about my circumstances. I mumbled that my husband was a freelancer and unaffiliated with a company. I could tell by his look and his sarcastic grin that he didn't believe me.

Weary and tense, I said, 'I am the one looking for a job, so why is my husband any of your business?'

'I was told you have no other source of income.'

'Who told you?'

'Mr Motamedi, the vice-president who recommended you.'

222

'Would you not hire me if I did have another source of income? Aren't you looking for a secretary?'

'Yes, madam, we are. But there are many applicants who are better educated and more qualified than you. In fact, I don't understand why Mr Motamedi recommended you, and so strongly!'

I didn't know what to say. Hamid's father had told me that when I went to job interviews I should never mention that my husband was in prison. Yet, I couldn't lie, because sooner or later I would be found out. Besides, I needed a job and that position was well suited to me. I was desperate and losing hope. With tears rolling down my cheeks and in a voice that was barely audible, I said, 'My husband is in prison.'

'For what?' he asked with a frown.

'He is a political prisoner.'

He grew quiet. I didn't dare speak and he didn't ask any more questions. He started to write something and after a few seconds he looked up. He seemed upset. He handed me a note and said, 'Don't discuss your husband with anyone. Take this note to the office next door and give it to Mrs Tabrizi. She will explain your responsibilities to you. You start tomorrow.'

The news of my taking a job exploded like a bomb.

With eyes that seemed to be popping out of their sockets, Mother asked, 'You mean in an office? Like men?'

'Yes. There is no difference between men and women any more.'

'May God take my life! The things you say! It's the day of reckoning! I don't think your father and brothers will allow it.'

'It is none of their business,' I snapped. 'No one has the right to interfere in my life and the lives of my children. Everything they did to me in the past was enough. Now I am a married woman. It's not as if my husband is dead. He and I have power over my life. Therefore, it is best that they don't belittle themselves.'

This simple ultimatum closed everyone's mouth. Although I didn't think Father was too opposed to my working, as he had on several occasions expressed his pleasure that I was standing on my own two feet and not relying on my brothers.

The job proved effective in boosting my morale. I started feeling a certain sense of self and security. Although I was often exhausted, I was proud of not needing anyone.

At the agency, I was an assistant and an office manager. I did everything; I typed, answered the telephones, did the filing, oversaw certain accounts and sometimes even translated letters and documents. At first everything was difficult. I found every one of my duties confusing and overwhelming. But barely two weeks later, I had a better understanding of my responsibilities. Mr Zargar, who was now my supervisor, patiently explained everything to me and monitored my work. But he never again asked me about my private life or expressed any curiosity about Hamid. Gradually, I started correcting grammatical and stylistic mistakes in the texts I was given to type. After all, I had been studying Persian literature at the university and had spent half my time during the past decade reading books. My supervisor's attention and encouragement gave me more confidence. Eventually, he would simply tell me what he wanted to express in a letter or a report and I would write it for him.

I enjoyed my work, but I was facing a problem that I had not thought of before. I could no longer go to the prison every week and it had been three weeks since I had had any news of Hamid. I was worried. I told myself, No matter how, I must go there this week.

The day before, I prepared everything. I cooked a few dishes and packed some fruit, pastries and cigarettes. Early the next morning, I went to the prison. The guard at the front gate rudely and sarcastically asked, 'What's the matter? You couldn't sleep last night so you showed up at the crack of dawn? I'm not going to accept any deliveries this early.'

'Please,' I said. 'I have to be at work by eight o'clock.'

He started mocking and insulting me.

'You should be ashamed of yourself,' I said. 'What kind of language is this?'

It was as if he was waiting for me to object so that he would have an excuse to make every vulgar comment about me and my husband. Even though over time I had faced every insult and disrespect, until then no one had cursed us in that manner and shouted obscenities at me. I was shaking with rage. I wanted to tear him to pieces, but I didn't dare utter a single word. I was afraid Hamid would no longer receive my letters and at least a small portion of the food I brought.

With trembling lips and swallowing my tears, insulted and broken, I went to work, still carrying the bag. With his sharp eyes, Mr Zargar noticed how distraught I was and called me to his office. While handing me a letter to type, he asked, 'What is the matter, Mrs Sadeghi? You don't seem well today.' I wiped away my tears with the back of my hand and I explained what had happened. He shook his head angrily and after a brief silence he said, 'You should have told me sooner. Don't you know what emotional state your husband will be in if he doesn't hear from you this week either? Go quickly and don't come back until you have delivered everything to him. And from now on, you will come to work on Mondays after you have dropped off his things at the prison. Do you understand?'

'Yes, but sometimes I have to wait until noon. What can I do about my absenteeism? I can't lose this job.'

'Don't worry about your job,' he said. 'I will write it down as you being away on office business. This is the least I can do for these selfless men and women.'

How kind and understanding he was. I saw similarities between him and Massoud and I thought my son would grow up to be like him.

Over time, the children and I adapted to the new routine of life. The boys consciously did their best to not create any new problems for me. We ate breakfast together every morning and got ready for the day. Even though their school wasn't too far away, I drove them there in the same Citroën 2CV that had been a true saviour during this time. At lunchtime they walked home, bought bread on the way, warmed up the food I had prepared ahead, ate and took some downstairs for Bibi, too. The poor woman had been ailing terribly ever since her hospital stay, but she didn't want to live anywhere other than in her own home, which meant we had to take care of her as well. Every day after work, I would do our shopping and then stop by to see her. I would clear away her dishes, tidy her room and chat with her for a while before going upstairs. And then the housework would start. Washing, cleaning, cooking for the next day, giving the boys their dinner, helping them with their homework and a thousand other chores that would take until eleven or twelve o'clock to finish. Finally, I would collapse like a corpse and sleep. Given all that, I no longer thought I could continue my education. I had already lost one year and it seemed I would have to lose many more.

That year, another event distracted us for a while. After many family fights and arguments, Faati got married. Mahmoud, who felt he had learned a lesson from my marriage, was determined to have Faati marry a devout bazaar merchant like himself. Faati, who unlike me was meek and easily bullied, did not dare object to the suitor Mahmoud recommended, even though she despised the man. Apparently, the punishments I had suffered had left such an impression on her that she seemed to have forever lost her self-confidence and the ability to voice her opinion. As a result, the responsibility of defending her rights fell on my shoulders, which once and for all confirmed my title as the family's fighting cock.

This time, however, I acted with greater wisdom. Without engaging in any discussions with Mahmoud or Mother, I privately talked to Father. I shared with him Faati's point of view and asked him to not bring about the misery of yet another daughter by consenting to a forced marriage. Although my footprints were later detected in Father's decision and made Mahmoud loathe me more than ever before, still, the marriage did not take place. Instead, Faati married another suitor whom Uncle Abbas had introduced and whom Faati had taken a liking to.

Sadegh Khan, Faati's husband, was a kind, handsome and educated young man who came from a cultured middle-class family and worked as an accountant in a government agency. Although he was not wealthy and Mahmoud contemptuously described him as a wage-earner, Faati was happy, and the boys and I liked him. Understanding my sons' need for a father, Sadegh Khan developed a friendly relationship with them, often arranging entertainments for them and taking them on outings.

Our life had almost settled into a regular routine. I liked my job and I had found good friends who filled the lunch hours and idle times with jokes, laughter and gossip. Often our discussions were about Mr Shirzadi, one of the departmental directors, who disliked me and always found fault with everything I did. Everyone said he was a sensitive man and an excellent poet, but I saw nothing in him other than hostility and a foul temper, so I was careful not to cross paths with him or give him any excuse to criticise me. Yet he constantly made wisecracks and snide remarks, insinuating that I had been hired through internal connections and that I was not qualified for my job. My friends told me not to worry, that it was just his disposition, but I felt he was more ill-tempered with me than with anyone else. I knew that behind my back he called me Mr Zargar's belle. Over time, I too developed a strong dislike of him.

'The only thing he doesn't look like is a poet,' I would tell my friends. 'He looks more like a Mafioso. Poetry requires a delicate soul, not all this arrogance, aggression and spite. The poems are probably not even his. Perhaps he threw a miserable poet in prison and now holds a knife to the guy's throat to write poetry under his name.' And everyone would laugh.

I think all this talk finally reached his ears. One day he used the excuse of a few small typographical errors to tear up a ten-page report that I had worked hard to prepare and he tossed the pieces on my desk. I lost my temper and I screamed, 'Do you even know what is bothering you? You are constantly looking for excuses to criticise my work. What wrong have I ever done to you?'

'Huh! Madam, you can't do any wrong to me,' he growled. 'I have read your hand. Do you think I am like Zargar and Motamedi and you can wrap me around your little finger? I know the likes of you very well.'

I was shaking with anger and was about to answer him when Mr Zargar walked in and asked, 'What is going on? Mr Shirzadi, what is the matter?'

'What is the matter?' he snarled. 'She doesn't know how to do her job. She is two days late and she hands me a report full of mistakes. This is what happens when you hire an illiterate woman just because she is pretty and has the right connections. Now you have to live with the consequences.'

'Watch what you are saying,' Mr Zargar snapped. 'Control yourself. Please come into my office, I would like to have a word with you.' And he put his hand on Mr Shirzadi's back and practically pushed him into his office.

I was holding my head between my hands and trying hard not to cry. My friends gathered around me and tried to comfort me. Abbas-Ali, the janitor on our floor who always looked out for me, brought me a glass of hot water and candied sugar and I busied myself with work.

An hour later, Mr Shirzadi walked into my office, stood in front of my desk and while trying to avoid looking into my eyes, he begrudgingly said, 'I am sorry. Please forgive me.' And he quickly walked out.

Stunned, I looked at Mr Zargar who was standing in the doorway and I asked, 'What happened?'

'Nothing. Forget what happened. This is how he is. He is a good man with a kind heart, but he is also tense and sensitive about certain things.'

'About me, for instance?'

'Not you exactly, but anyone who he thinks has usurped someone else's rights.'

'Whose rights have I usurped?'

'Don't take it seriously,' Mr Zargar said. 'Before we hired you, he recommended we promote one of his assistants who had just earned his university degree. We had almost finished the process when you were referred to me for the position. Before I interviewed you, I promised Shirzadi that I would not be influenced by Motamedi's request, but I hired you and he considers this unfair and prejudicial. Naturally, being as sensitive as he is, he can't tolerate what he calls an "injustice". Ever since then, he has become my adversary and yours. He already disliked Motamedi because he has an inherent animosity towards executives and superiors.'

'It seems he is right,' I said. 'I really have taken someone else's rights. But knowing all this, why did you hire me?'

'Come on! Have I now ended up owing you something? I thought with his qualifications, the other candidate could find another job. As a matter of fact, he was hired a week later. But given your circumstances, you would have had a difficult time finding work. In any case, with my profound apologies, I had to tell Shirzadi about your husband. But don't worry, he is a trustworthy man. Between you and me, he has been tangled up in politics all his life.'

The next day, Mr Shirzadi came to my office. He looked pale and sad and his eyes were red and swollen. For a while he stood there looking uncomfortable, but finally he said, 'You know, I can't help it. My anger runs too deep.' And he went on to recite one of his poems about how rage has taken root in his soul and turned him into a rabid wolf. 'I have mistreated you,' he said. 'To be honest, your work is actually quite good. I had a tough time finding errors in it, when the two-sentence letters these bosses and executives write are filled with a thousand mistakes.'

Mr Shirzadi became one of my best supporters and friends. Unlike Mr Zargar, he was very curious about Hamid's political activities, the group he belonged to and the circumstances under which he was arrested. His passion and excitement to hear what I had to say made me open up when in fact I had no interest in talking about any of this. At the same time, his compassion was laced with such anger and hatred towards the regime that it frightened me. Once as I was talking, I noticed that his face had turned almost blue.

'Are you well?' I asked, concerned.

'No, I am not,' he said. 'But don't worry, I often feel this way. You have no idea what goes on inside me.'

'What?' I asked. 'Perhaps I feel the same way but I just can't verbalise it.'

As usual, he started to recite a poem. This one was about a city mourning the massacre of the masses while he remained as thirsty for revenge as a fasting man thirsts for water on a scorching-hot noon.

No! I who had suffered the greatest blows had never experienced anger and sorrow this profound. One day he asked me about the night our home was raided. I told him a little about what had happened. Suddenly he lost control and fearlessly shouted in verse that the tribe of aggressors had turned the city into a city of wild dogs and the lions were nowhere to be found but in the pastures.

Terrified, I leaped up and closed the door. 'For the love of God, people will hear you,' I pleaded. 'That SAVAK agent is on this floor.' In those days, we believed that half our colleagues were SAVAK agents and we treated them with dread and caution.

From then on, Mr Shirzadi started reading his poems to me, just one of which would have been enough to result in the execution of whoever composed it or recited it. I understood and grasped their meaning with my flesh and blood and committed them to memory. Shirzadi was one of the survivors of the political defeats of the 1950s, which had left his young and sensitive spirit crushed and had led him into a life of bitterness. I observed him and wondered whether the harsh experiences of childhood and youth were always this ever-lasting. And I found my answer in one of his poems about the failed 1953 coup d'état, in which he wrote that, from that moment on, his eyes always perceived the sky as floating in a sea of blood and saw the sun and the moon only through the glint of a dagger.

The more I got to know Mr Shirzadi, the more I worried about Siamak. I often recalled the rage and hatred I had seen in his eyes on the night our house was raided and I asked myself, Will he become like Shirzadi? Will he, too, surrender to loathing and loneliness instead of embracing hope, joy and the beauties of life? Do social and political issues leave such permanent scars on susceptible souls? My son! I had to find a solution.

*

Summer had come to an end. It was almost a year since Hamid's arrest. Given the court's sentence, we had to live another fourteen years without him. We had no choice but to get used to our circumstances. Waiting had become the main objective of our lives.

The time for registering for classes at the university was getting close. I had to decide to either give up for ever on continuing my education and take that old wish to my grave, or sign up for classes and accept the hardship it would place on myself and on my children. I knew the courses would become more difficult each term. I also knew that with the limited time I had, I would not be able to coordinate my classes so that they would not interfere with my work. Even if my superiors didn't complain, I felt I didn't have the right to take advantage of their kindness and consideration.

Yet, my job had proven to me the value of higher education. Each time others bossed me around and felt that they could blame me for their mistakes simply because they were better educated than me, I felt sorry for myself and the desire to go to university rekindled in my heart. Also, for years to come I would have to single-handedly manage and support our lives, and I had been thinking about finding a means to earn a higher salary that would meet the future needs of my children. Clearly, having a university degree would make a big difference in my situation.

As I expected, everyone in my family believed that I should give up the idea of going back to university. But what I found surprising was that Hamid's family felt the same way.

'You are under a lot of pressure,' Hamid's father said sympathetically. 'Don't you think managing both a job and the university will be too much for you?'

With her usual anxiety, Hamid's mother interrupted him and said, 'You are at work from morning until late afternoon, and I guess you will then want to go to the university. But what about these boys? Why don't you think about these innocent children who will be left all alone?'

Manijeh, who was in the last months of her pregnancy and who had for years failed the university entrance exams and had finally given up and got married, turned to her parents and said with her

231

usual smugness, 'Don't you understand? It's all about rivalry! After all, our Mansoureh went to university.'

I tried to control myself, but I had become less tolerant. I was no longer an awkward and clumsy girl from the provinces to put up with snide remarks and to have my needs and desires dismissed as unimportant. The anger that simmered inside me washed away my doubts and fears.

'Now that I have to be both mother and father to my children and to financially support them,' I said, 'I have to think about earning a higher salary. My current income is not enough to pay for their future needs and their expenses are increasing from one day to the next. And please don't worry; your grandchildren will not suffer from any lack of love and attention. I have thought of everything.'

In truth, I had thought of nothing. That night I sat with the boys and tried to explain everything to them. They listened carefully as I listed the pros and cons of my going back to university. When I said that the biggest problem was that I would have to come home later than I already did, Siamak pretended he was no longer listening to me and started playing with his toy car that made a hideous noise. I realised he was not willing to accept spending any more time alone than he already did. I stopped talking and looked at Massoud. With innocent eyes, he was observing the expression on my face. Then he got up, walked over to me, stroked my hair and said, 'Mummy, do you really want to go to university?'

'Look, my dear, if I go back, we will all benefit. It will be a little difficult, but it will end soon. And in return, I will be able to earn more money and we will have a better life.'

'No ... I mean do you really like going to university?'

'Well, yes,' I said. 'I worked hard to be able to go to university.'

'Then go. If you like to, go. We will do our own chores and when it gets dark we will go downstairs and stay with Bibi so we don't get scared. Maybe Dad will come back by then and we won't be alone.'

Siamak threw his toy car across the room and said, 'What a

stupid child! It's not like Dad is some place where he can come back whenever he wants to. He can't!'

'Look, my dear,' I said gently. 'We have to be optimistic and hopeful. Just the fact that Daddy is alive is reason enough for us to be grateful. And he will eventually come back home.'

'What are you saying?' Siamak snapped. 'You want to fool a kid? Grandfather said Dad has to stay in prison for fifteen years.'

'But a lot can happen in fifteen years. As a matter of fact, every year their sentence is reduced for good behaviour.'

'Yes, then it will be ten years. What's the use? By then I will be twenty, what would I need a father for? I want my dad now, right now!'

Again, I wallowed in doubt. At the office my friends believed I should not lose the opportunity to finish studying for my degree. Mr Zargar encouraged me, saying he would arrange for me to take classes during the day on the condition that I finish my work after office hours.

Coincidentally, it was during those days that the authorities finally agreed to my repeated requests for us to be granted permission to visit Hamid. I was both happy and nervous. I called Hamid's father and he quickly came over to the house. 'I won't tell his mother and you shouldn't tell the children,' he said. 'We don't know what shape Hamid is in. If we see that he is presentable, we will take them next time.'

His words added to my anxiety. All night, I dreamed that Hamid was brought to me, broken and bloody, just so that he could spend the last moments of his life in my arms. Tired and nervous, we set out early the next morning. I don't know whether the visiting room and its windows were all dusty or I was seeing everything from behind a veil of tears. Finally, they brought Hamid. Contrary to our expectations, he was clean and neat, his hair was combed and his face was shaven. But he was unbelievably thin and gaunt. Even his voice sounded different. For a few minutes none of us could speak. His father regained his composure before we did and asked him about the conditions in prison. Hamid gave him a sharp look that suggested he had asked an inappropriate question and

233

said, 'Well, it's prison. I have got through the tough times. Tell me about yourselves. How are the children? How is Mother?'

Evidently, he had not received most of my letters. I told him that the boys were well and growing up fast, that they were both among the top students in their class, that Siamak had started year five and Massoud was in year one. He asked about my job. I told him that because of him everyone was good to me and watched over me. Suddenly, there was a gleam in his eyes and I realised that I shouldn't talk about such things. Finally, he asked me about university and I told him about my doubts. He laughed and said, 'Do you remember how you dreamed about getting your school diploma? Even a university degree isn't enough for you. You are talented and hard working. You have to advance. You will even go for a doctorate degree.'

There was no time for me to explain what a heavy burden continuing my education would put on my shoulders and how much of my time it would devour. All I said was, 'It will be difficult to study and work, and take care of the children, too.'

'You will manage it all,' he said. 'You are no longer the clumsy girl you were ten or eleven years ago. You are a capable woman who can make the impossible possible. I am so proud of you.'

'Do you really mean it?' I said with tears in my eyes. 'You are no longer ashamed of having a wife like me?'

'When was I ever ashamed? You have been a dear wife and you have grown and become more complete with every day that has passed. Now, you are every man's dream. I'm just sad that I and my children have tied you down.'

'Don't say that! You and my children are the dearest things in my life.'

I so desperately wanted to hold him in my arms, put my head on his shoulder and cry. Now I felt filled with energy. I felt I could do anything.

I registered for a few courses that were being held at times that were convenient for me. I talked to Mrs Parvin and Faati, and they agreed to help with the boys. Mrs Parvin's husband was ill, but she

234

said she could spend one or two afternoons with the boys, and Faati and Sadegh Khan agreed to take care of them three nights a week. Faati was in the last months of her pregnancy and it was difficult for her to come and go. So I gave our car to Sadegh Khan so that he could bring Faati to our home or take the boys to their house, and occasionally take everyone to the cinema or on outings. Meanwhile, I took advantage of every opportunity to study; during my free time at the office, early in the morning, and at night before I went to bed. I often fell asleep at my books. The chronic headaches I had suffered since my youth were getting worse and more frequent, but I didn't care. I took painkillers and went on with my work.

My responsibilities now included those of a mother, a house-keeper, an office worker, a university student and the wife of a prisoner. And I tended to the last with the greatest care. The food and other necessities that I wanted to take to prison for Hamid were prepared by every member of the family with great ceremony, almost in a religious ritual.

Over time, I learned how to manage my workload and grew accustomed to it. It was then that I realised we are capable of far more than we believe. After a while, we adapt to life and our rhythm adjusts to the volume of our tasks. I was like a runner on the track of life and Hamid's voice saying 'I am proud of you' echoed in my ears like the applause of spectators in a huge sta-dium, intensifying my strength and agility.

One day I was sifting through the previous day's newspapers when my gaze fell on the funeral notices. I rarely paid any attention to these, but that day my eyes suddenly froze on a name. The notice was for the funeral of Mr Ebrahim Ahmadi, Parvaneh's father. My heart ached. I remembered his decency and kind face. Tears welled in my eyes and memories of Parvaneh filled my mind. Time and distance could not erase my love for her and my desire to see her again. After the telephone conversation I had had with her mother several years earlier, I had never heard from them, and I was so overwhelmed with life that I didn't try to contact her mother again.

I had to go to the funeral. It was perhaps the only opportunity I had to find Parvaneh. No matter where she was, she would certainly go to her father's funeral.

Walking into the mosque, I was nervous and my palms were sweaty. I searched for Parvaneh in the row where the bereaved were sitting, but I didn't see her. Could it be that she hadn't come? Just then a rather fat lady whose blonde hair had escaped her black lace headscarf looked up and our eyes met. It was Parvaneh. How could she have changed so much in twelve or thirteen years? She threw herself in my arms and we spent almost the entire ceremony crying without speaking a word. She was mourning her father's passing and I was pouring out all that I had suffered over the years. After the ceremony, she insisted that I go to their house. Once most of the visitors had left, we sat facing each other. We didn't know where to start. Now that I looked at her, I saw that she was still the same Parvaneh, except that she had gained weight and dyed her hair lighter. The circles under her eyes and the puffiness of her face were because of all the crying she had done in recent days.

'Massoum,' she finally said, 'are you happy?'

I was stunned, I didn't know what to say. I was always confused when asked this question. As my silence grew longer, she shook her head and said, 'Oh dear! It seems there is no end to your troubles.'

'I am not ungrateful,' I said. 'I just don't know what happiness means! But I have many blessings in life. I have my children; two healthy boys. And my husband is a good man, even though he is not with us. I work, I study ... remember my undying dream?'

'You are still not going to give up,' she said, laughing. 'This diploma isn't all that valuable. What do you think I have done with mine?'

'I received my diploma a long time ago. I am now studying Persian literature at Tehran University.'

'Are you serious? That is excellent! You really do have perseverance. Of course, you were always a smart student, but I didn't think you would still be studying with a husband and children. It's good that your husband doesn't object.'

'No, he has always encouraged me.'

236

'That's wonderful! Then he must be a wise man. I should meet him.'

'Yes, God willing, in ten or fifteen years!'

'What do you mean? Why? Where is he?'

'He is in prison.'

'May God take my life! What did he do?'

'He is a political prisoner.'

'Are you serious? In Germany I often hear Iranians, the guys who are members of the Confederation and others who oppose the government, talk about the political prisoners. So your husband is one of them! People say they torture them in prison. Is it true?'

'He hasn't said anything to me, but I have often washed blood off his clothes. Recently our permission to visit him was again revoked, so I don't know what condition he is in now.'

'Then who supports you financially?'

'I told you, I work.'

'You mean you have to single-handedly manage your lives?'

'Managing life isn't that difficult, it's the loneliness that is tough. Oh, Parvaneh, you can't imagine how lonely I am. Even though I am constantly busy and don't have a moment to rest, I always feel lonely. I am so happy I have finally found you. I really needed you ... But now you tell me. Are you happy? How many children do you have?'

'Life is all right,' she said. 'I have two daughters. Lili is eight and Laleh is four. My husband isn't bad. He's a man like all other men. And I have got used to life over there. But with Father gone, I can't leave my mother alone any more; especially now that my sister Farzaneh has two young children and is busy with her own life. And you can't count on the sons. I think we will have to come back and live here. Besides, my husband, Khosrow, had already been thinking about us moving back.'

Parvaneh and I had more to share than we could manage in one day. We needed many long days and nights. We planned for me and the boys to go to their house on Friday and spend the day with her. It was a wonderful day. I talked more than I had ever talked in my life. Fortunately time and distance had not severed our friendship. We could still talk to each other more freely and comfortably than with anyone else. Opening up to others had always been difficult for me and the need to keep Hamid's life a secret had made me even less at ease with people. But now I could reveal the most secret corners of my heart to Parvaneh. I had again found my friend and I would never lose her again.

Fortunately, Parvaneh's move back to Iran was quickly arranged and after a short trip to Germany her family relocated to Tehran. Her husband started to work and she found a part-time position at the Iran-Germany Society. I now had another person I could lean on. Parvaneh had shared my life story with her husband and having been moved by it, he somehow felt responsible for me and my sons. Our children grew to like each other and became good playmates. Parvaneh was constantly planning events for them and took them to the cinema, to the swimming pool, or to the park. The presence of Parvaneh's family brought a different nuance to our lives and I started to see new joy and excitement in my dispirited sons whose days had become even lonelier and more unstructured after Faati gave birth and could no longer spend as much time with them.

Another year passed. We could again visit Hamid regularly and once a month I took the boys to see him. But after each visit they were out of sorts and it would take a week for them to return to their normal selves. Massoud would grow quieter and sadder, and Siamak would become wilder and more highly strung. Hamid looked visibly older each time we saw him.

I continued to go to university and took a few credits each term. I was now an official employee at the agency and although I still didn't have a bachelor's degree, I was doing more specialised and advanced work. Mr Zargar still watched over me and confidently gave me assignments. Mr Shirzadi and I had remained close friends. He was still disagreeable and bad-tempered, occasionally starting fights and arguments that made him more miserable than anyone else. I tried to lessen his deep sense of pessimism towards everything, assuring him that he had no enemies and that there was no hidden motive behind what people did and said. And to all this he would reply, 'Fear banished trust from my mind, my only beloved is suspicion.'

He was not comfortable in any gathering, he would not join any group, he detected the footprints of traitor politicos in every action, and he believed everyone was a mercenary and a paid minion of the regime. His colleagues did not mind his company, but he always kept himself on the sidelines.

I once asked him, 'Don't you get tired of being alone?'

In response he recited one of his poems about being sorrow's friend and loneliness's beloved, his hopelessness being as eternal as the sun and as vast as the ocean.

One day Mr Zargar jokingly said, 'Come on! Why do you take everything so hard? Things are not as bad as you think. These problems exist in every society. The rest of us are not satisfied either, but we don't make a mountain out of a pile of hay and we don't grieve all the time.'

Mr Shirzadi replied with one of his typical poems about how no one understands him.

After he started a heated argument with the director-general of the agency, stormed out of the man's office and slammed the door behind him, everyone gathered around to mediate. 'Give in a little,' someone said. 'After all, this is a government agency, not your auntie's house, and we have to tolerate some things.'

Mr Shirzadi yelled in verse that he would never bend and bow his head.

I intervened. 'Mr Shirzadi, please try to stay calm. You can't just walk out of this company. You have to be able to hold on to some job.'

'I cannot do it,' he said.

'So what are you going to do now?' I asked.

'I will leave. I must leave this place . . .'

He not only left the agency, but soon he left the country. The day he came to collect the last of his belongings, he said goodbye to me and added, 'Give my regards to your hero husband.' And he asked me to recite a poem to Hamid: that they take to the gallows those who speak the truth.

With Mr Shirzadi's departure, calm was restored at the agency. Even Mr Zargar, who apparently did not have a problem with Mr Shirzadi, had towards the end seemed unable to tolerate him. Still, his memory, his profound sorrow and the torment he suffered stayed with me for ever and drove me to do all that I could so that my children would not turn out to be as bitter and as disheartened as he was.

At home, I tried to create an environment in which my boys would not forget laughter. I started a joke-telling contest. Anyone who could tell a first-hand joke would receive a prize. We would mimic and imitate each other; I wanted them to learn to laugh at themselves and at their problems and shortcomings. We tried speaking with different accents. I encouraged them to sing, to turn up the volume when they played music on the stereo or the radio, to listen to upbeat music to which we would dance. At night, despite being so tired I could barely move, I would play games with them and tickle them until they were faint with laughter, and we would have pillow fights until they would agree to go to bed.

It was exhausting, but I had to do it. I had to keep that gloomy environment lively, I had to make up for my hours of absence, I had to inject joy into them so that they would never look at the world through Mr Shirzadi's eyes.

Soon after her marriage, Faati gave birth to a beautiful girl with sky-blue eyes. She named her Firouzeh (turquoise). The boys adored her, especially Massoud who was always eager to play with her.

Mrs Parvin's husband passed away and she found peace and freedom; especially because she had managed to transfer ownership of their house to herself prior to his death. Still, she never spoke well of him and never forgave him for what he had done to her. After his death, she started spending much of her time with us. She stayed with the children if I had to work late and did most of the housework so that I would have more time to rest and to spend with the boys. In a way she felt responsible for my fate and my loneliness, and tried to make up for it.

On Mahmoud's recommendation, Ali asked for the hand of a

reputable bazaar merchant's daughter. They became formally betrothed and plans were made for an elaborate wedding to be held that autumn in a hall that served men and women guests separately. The match was to Mahmoud's liking and he promised all sorts of cooperation and assistance, agreeing to all the idiotic conditions the bride's family laid down; all of which were more like ancient trade practices than arrangements for a marriage.

When Father complained, 'We cannot spend this much money ... what is all this nonsense?' Mahmoud simply replied, 'The investment will soon pay off. Wait and see the dowry she will bring and the deals we will make side by side with her father.'

Ahmad had completely left the family circle. No one liked to talk about him and everyone tried as far as possible to not even speak his name. It had been some time since Father had thrown him out of the house. 'Thank God, he doesn't know where you live,' Father said. 'Otherwise, he would create more scandals for you and come to you for money.'

Ahmad had crashed at such great speed that everyone had given up on him. Mrs Parvin was the only one who still saw him and she would secretly tell me about him.

'I have never seen anyone so determined to destroy their own life,' she said. 'What a shame. He was such a handsome man. If you saw him now, there is no way you would recognise him. One of these days, they will find his corpse in a street gutter somewhere in the south part of town. The only reason he is still alive is because of your mother. Don't tell anyone; if your father finds out he will really give her a hard time. But the poor woman is a mother and he is her beloved son. In the morning when your father leaves the house, Ahmad comes over and your mother feeds him, cooks kebab for him, washes his clothes, and if she can, she puts some money in his pocket. To this day, if anyone tells her Ahmad is a heroin addict, she will rip out their guts. The poor woman is still hoping he will recover.'

Mrs Parvin's prediction soon came true. But along with himself, Ahmad destroyed Father, too. In his last stages of decline, Ahmad did anything for money. In a desperate moment of need and poverty, he went to Father's house and was busy rolling up a carpet so that he could take it and sell it when Father arrived and got into a tussle with him. It was more than Father's weary heart could take. He was taken to the hospital and we spent several days behind the doors of the intensive care unit. Father's condition improved and he was transferred to an ordinary ward.

I took the children to the hospital every day. Siamak had grown taller and he could pass himself off as older than he was so he easily got a visitor's pass, but even with a thousand tricks and plenty of begging, Massoud saw Father only twice. During his visits, Siamak would just hold his grandfather's hand and sit next to him without speaking a word.

We were hopeful that Father would recover, but unfortunately he suffered another massive heart attack. He was returned to the intensive care unit where twenty-four hours later he surrendered his life to his life giver. And I lost my only support and refuge. After Hamid was sent to prison, I felt lonely and isolated. After Father's death, I realised that his presence, even from a distance, had cast a cover of safety over me and that in my darkest moments the glow of his presence had brightened my heart. With Father gone, the bonds that had tied me to his house grew weak.

For a week, I could not stop my tears. But my instincts soon urged me to become aware of those around me and I realised that my tears were insignificant compared to Siamak's profound sadness and silence. That child had not shed a single tear and was ready to explode like a balloon that did not have room for even one more puff of air. But Mother groused, 'What a shame! With all the love Mostafa Khan gave this child, he didn't cry a single tear when they put that man in his grave. The boy didn't care at all.'

I knew Siamak's emotional state was far worse than it appeared. One day I left Massoud with Parvaneh and I took Siamak to visit Father's grave. I kneeled down beside the grave. Siamak stood over me like a dark and gloomy cloud. He was trying to look away and remain detached from the time and space he was in. I started to talk about Father, about my memories of him, about his kindness and the void his death had left in our lives. Slowly, I made Siamak sit down next to me and I continued to talk until he suddenly started to cry and poured out all the tears he had kept inside him. He cried until night fell. When Massoud came home and saw Siamak crying, he too burst into tears. I let them pour everything out. They had to rid themselves of all the pain that had piled up inside their small hearts. Then I sat them down and asked, 'What do you think we should do to honour Grandfather's memory? What does he expect of us and how should we live for him to be pleased with us?' And in the course of all this, I, too, realised that I had to try to go on with my normal life while forever holding on to my memories of him.

Three months after Father's death, Ahmad, too, rushed to the world beyond in the same wretched manner as Mrs Parvin had predicted. A street sweeper found his body on a road in the south section of the city. Ali went to identify the body. No funeral was held and other than Mother, whose back was bent with grief, no one cried. Hard as I tried to recall a fond memory of Ahmad, I couldn't. I felt guilty for not being sorry that he had died. I did not mourn him, but for a long time whenever I thought of him a vague sorrow would press against my heart.

Given the circumstances, Ali could not hold a marriage celebration. Instead, he quietly took his wife to the family house, which Father had several years earlier legally transferred to Mother. Depressed and alone, Mother all but retired from life and relinquished the running of the household to the new bride. And thus, the door to the house that in hard times had been my only refuge was forever closed to me.

CHAPTER FOUR

It was mid-1977. I was sensing political unrest in the country. The way people talked and behaved had palpably changed. In offices, on the streets and especially at the university, people spoke more daringly. The conditions at the prison had improved and Hamid and the other prisoners were to receive more amenities. There were also fewer restrictions for delivering clothes and food to them. But in my broken heart I found no glimmer of hope and I could not imagine the magnitude of the events that were taking shape.

It was a few days before the new year, and the air smelled of spring. Lost in my thoughts, I returned home and came face to face with a strange scene. In the middle of the hall there were a few sacks of rice, large tins of cooking lard, bags of tea and legumes, and several other foodstuffs. I was surprised. Hamid's father occasionally brought rice for us, but not all these other things. Ever since the printing house was shut down, they too were under financial pressure.

When Siamak saw the surprised look on my face, he laughed and said, 'Wait until you see the best part.' And he held out an envelope towards me. It was open and I could see a stack of one-hundred tuman bills in it.

'What is all this?' I asked. 'Where did it come from?'
'Guess!'

244

'Yes, Mum, it's a contest,' Massoud added cheerfully. 'You have to guess.'

'Did your grandfather go to all this trouble?'

'No!' Siamak said.

And they both started to laugh.

'Did Parvaneh bring them?'

'No.'

More laughter.

'Mrs Parvin? Faati?'

'No way!' Siamak said. 'You will never guess . . . Shall I tell you?'

'Yes! Who brought these things?'

'Uncle Ali! But he said I should tell you they came from Uncle Mahmoud.'

I was stunned.

'Why? What for?' I asked. 'Did he see a prophecy in a dream?'

I picked up the telephone and called Mother's house. She didn't know anything.

'Then let me talk to Ali,' I said. 'I want to know what is going on.'

When Ali came to the phone, I said, 'What is going on, Ali Agha? Are you feeding the poor?'

'Please, sister. It was my duty.'

'What duty? I have never asked for anything.'

'Well, that's because you are gracious and noble, but I have to live up to my obligations.'

'Thank you, dear Ali,' I said. 'But my children and I don't need anything. Please come right now and take all these things away.'

'Take them and do what with them?' Ali asked.

'I don't know. Do whatever you want. Give them to the needy.'

'You know, sister, this has nothing to do with me. Brother Mahmoud sent them. Talk to him. And it wasn't just you; he did the same for a lot of people. I just delivered everything.'

'Really!' I said. 'So it is alms from the gentleman? Of all the unimaginable . . . ! Don't tell me he has gone mad!'

'What sort of talk is this, sister? And here we were, thinking we were doing a good deed!'

'You have done enough good deeds for me. Thank you. Just come and take this stuff away as soon as possible.'

'I will, but only if brother Mahmoud asks me to. You should talk to him yourself.'

'Certainly,' I said. 'I will do just that!'

I called Mahmoud's house. The number of times I had called that house were fewer than the fingers on one hand. Gholam-Ali answered and after a warm hello he handed the telephone to his father.

'Hello, sister! What a surprise. What made you finally think of us?'

'As a matter of fact,' I said dryly, 'that is exactly what I wanted to ask you. What made you finally think of us? You have sent alms!'

'Please, sister. It's not alms, it's your right. Your husband is in prison because he fought for freedom and against these godless people. We who don't have the strength to fight and to endure prison and torture are obliged to at least watch over the families of the brave.'

'But my dear brother, Hamid has been in prison for four years. Just as I have so far managed without needing anyone, with the grace of God, I shall continue to do the same in the future.'

'You are right, sister,' he said. 'Shame on us, we were fast asleep and clueless, we were oblivious. You must forgive us.'

'Please, brother. All I mean is that I can manage my own life. I don't want my children to grow up on charity. Please send someone to take these things . . .'

'Sister, it is my duty. You are our beloved and Hamid is our pride.'

'But, brother, Hamid is that same insurgent who deserved to be executed.'

'Don't make snide remarks, sister. You really hold a grudge, don't you? . . . I have already confessed that I was ignorant. To me, any man who fights this system of tyranny is praiseworthy, be he a Muslim or an infidel.'

'Thank you very much, brother,' I said sternly. 'Still, I have no need for the food. Please send someone to take it away.'

'Give it to your neighbours,' he snapped indignantly. 'I don't have anyone to send over there.'

And he hung up the telephone.

During the months that followed, the changes became more palpable. No one at the office was supposed to know that my husband was a political prisoner, but almost everyone knew and until then they had all treated me guardedly and took care not to frequent my office too often. But now all those cautions and constraints had disappeared. People did not seem to be afraid of associating with me and my circle of acquaintances was rapidly growing. And my co-workers no longer complained about my excessive absences and the hours I spent studying.

Soon, the transformation became even more pronounced. My family members, my friends at the university, and my colleagues at work started talking openly about my life and my circumstances. They enquired about Hamid's well-being, expressed sympathy and concern, and praised him. At social gatherings, I was often invited to sit at the head of the room and found myself the centre of attention. As uncomfortable as I was with all this, for Siamak it was a source of pride. Elated, he talked openly and proudly about his father and answered people's questions about how Hamid had been arrested and the night our home was raided. Needless to say, given his young, imaginative mind, he often embellished his recollections.

Barely two weeks after the start of the school year, I was summoned to Siamak's school. I was worried, thinking he had again started a fight and beaten up a classmate. But when I walked into the school administration office, I realised I was there for a different reason. A group of teachers and supervisors greeted me and closed the door to make sure the principal and other administrators wouldn't become aware of my presence. Obviously, they didn't trust them. And then they started to ask me about Hamid, about the political situation in the country, the changes that were under way, and the revolution. I was stunned. They acted as if I was the source of secret plans for an insurrection. I answered their questions about Hamid and his arrest, but in response to all other

247

questions, I kept repeating, 'I don't know. I am not involved in any way.' In the end, it became clear that Siamak had talked about his father, the movement for a revolution, and our involvement in it, with such exaggeration that enthusiasts and supporters had thought to not only verify his claims, but to establish direct contact with key players.

'Of course, from a father like that, we should expect a son like Siamak,' a teary-eyed teacher proclaimed. 'You can't imagine how beautifully and passionately he talks.'

'What has he told you?' I asked, curious to know what Siamak told strangers about his father.

'Like an adult, like an orator, he fearlessly stood in front of all of us and said, "My father is fighting for the freedom of the oppressed. Many of his friends have died for the cause and he has been in prison for years. He has persevered under torture and not uttered a single word."'

On my way back home, conflicting emotions simmered in me. I was happy that Siamak was asserting himself, gaining attention and feeling proud. But I was troubled by his hero-building and hero-worshipping personality. He had been a difficult child all his life and now he was in the confusing and delicate stages of early youth. I worried how after being subjected to all those insults and humiliations he was now going to digest the praise and approval. Would his undeveloped personality be able to withstand such highs and lows? And I wondered why he needed so much attention, approval and love. I had tried as far as possible to give him all that.

The respect and admiration of those around us was intensifying from one day to the next. It all seemed exaggerated and far-fetched and I wondered if it was rooted in mere curiosity. Regardless, it was gradually becoming difficult and annoying for me. At times, I felt insincere, hypocritical and guilty. I would ask myself, What if I am taking advantage of my circumstances and deceiving people? I constantly explained to everyone that I didn't know much about my husband's beliefs and ideals and that I had never collaborated

248

with him. But people didn't want to hear the reality. At work and at the university, during every political discussion people pointed to me and in every election chose me to represent them. Each time I said that I didn't know much and that I had no connections, they interpreted it as my being inherently modest. The only person who did not change his behaviour towards me was Mr Zargar who carefully monitored the changes taking place around me.

The day the employees decided to elect a Revolution Committee and announced their support for the roaring swell of the masses, one of the staff members, who until recently had only warily said hello and goodbye to me, made an eloquent speech in praise of my revolutionary, humanitarian and freedom-loving character and nominated me as a candidate. I stood up and, with a confidence that I had gained from a difficult social life, I thanked the speaker but objected to his claims, saying earnestly, 'I have never been a revolutionary. Life put me in the path of a man who had a particular view of politics and I fainted the first time I had to face a small part of the foundation and framework of his beliefs.'

Everyone laughed and a few people applauded.

'Believe me,' I said. 'I am telling the truth. This is why my husband never involved me in his activities. With all my being, I pray for his release, but when it comes to political ideologies and political clout, I am of no use to anyone.'

The man who had nominated me shouted in protest, 'But you have suffered, your husband has spent years in prison, and you have single-handedly managed your life and raised your children. Is all this not a reflection of your sharing his ideologies and beliefs?'

'No! I would have done the same if my husband had been thrown in prison for theft. This is a reflection of the fact that as a woman and a mother, I have a duty to manage my life and my children's lives.'

There was uproar, but from the approving look on Mr Zargar's face I knew I had done the right thing. But this time, the employees made a heroine of me because of my humility and sincerity, and elected me.

*

The excitement of the revolution was growing and with its scope broadening, every day there was a new blossom of hope in my heart. Was it possible that what Shahrzad and the others had given their lives for, and Hamid had suffered years of prison and torture for, could become a reality?

For the first time, my brothers and I were on the same side, we wanted the same thing, we understood each other and we felt close. They behaved like brothers and were supportive of me and my sons. Mahmoud's kindness had extended to the point that whatever he bought for his children, he bought for my sons, too.

With tears in her eyes, Mother would thank God and say, 'What a shame that your father isn't here to see all this love. He always worried and said, "If I die, these children won't see each other from one year to the next, and more alone than all of them will be this daughter of mine whom her brothers will not lend a helping hand to." I wish he were here to see how these same brothers would now give their lives for their sister.'

Mahmoud's connections allowed him access to the latest news and communiqués. He brought flyers and tape recordings, Ali reproduced them, and I distributed them at work and at the university. Meanwhile, Siamak and his friends were on the streets shouting slogans and Massoud was drawing pictures of the demonstrations and writing 'Freedom' across them. Since summer, we had been participating in meetings, lectures and protests against the Shah's regime. Not once did I consider which group or party was organising the events. What difference did it make? We were together and we all wanted the same thing.

With every day that passed, I felt one step closer to Hamid. I was starting to believe that having a complete family and a father for my children was no longer an unattainable dream. With all my being I was happy that Hamid was alive. Seeing his tormented face no longer made me wonder whether it would have been better if he had died with his friends instead of enduring years of torture. I was starting to believe that all he had suffered had not been futile and that soon he would reap the rewards of his struggles. This was their dream that was becoming reality; the people had risen and were shouting in the streets, 'I will not live under the burden of tyranny.' When Hamid and his friends talked about such days, it had all seemed too far-fetched, idealistic and unreal.

With the revolution gaining strength, I found that I had less and less control over my children. They had grown very close to their uncle. With a devotion that was truly strange and new to me, Mahmoud would come and take the boys to speeches and debates. Siamak delighted in these events and happily followed his uncle. But soon Massoud started to distance himself and used different excuses to not join them. When I asked him why, he simply said, 'I don't like it.' I pressed for a more convincing answer and he replied, 'I get embarrassed.' I couldn't understand what he was embarrassed about, but I decided to not push him any further.

Siamak, on the other hand, was becoming more enthusiastic every day. He was in high spirits and had stopped causing trouble at home. It seemed as if he was letting out all his anger and frustration by shouting slogans. Gradually, he developed a particular discipline in observing religious practices. He had always had a difficult time waking up in the morning, but now he was making sure he did not miss his early morning prayers. I didn't know whether I should be happy or concerned about the changes in him. Some of the things he did, such as turning off the radio when music was being played or refusing to watch television, took me back many years and reminded me of Mahmoud's fanatical behaviour.

Towards the middle of September, Mahmoud announced that he wanted to hold an elaborate memorial for Father. Although it was already a month after the one-year anniversary of his passing, no one objected. Honouring the memory of that dear man and offering alms in commemoration of his pure soul were always welcome. Given that martial law and strict curfews were in force, we decided it was best to hold the ceremony at noon on a Friday and we all got busy, eagerly cooking and preparing for the event. The number of guests was increasing every minute and I was privately praising

Mahmoud for his courage in arranging the ceremony during those volatile times.

On the day of the memorial, we were all busy working at Mahmoud's house from early in the morning. Ehteram-Sadat who was getting fatter every day was panting and rushing back and forth. I was peeling potatoes when she finally dropped down next to me. 'You have gone to a lot of trouble,' I said. 'Thank you. We are all grateful to you.'

'Oh, don't mention it,' she said. 'After all, it was about time for us to hold a proper prayer service for Father, God rest his soul. Besides, given the circumstances, it is a good excuse to gather people together.'

'By the way, dear Ehteram, how is brother these days? Knock on wood; it seems you two no longer have problems with each other.'

'Please! We are beyond all that. I hardly ever see Mahmoud to want to fight with him. By the time he comes home he is so tired and preoccupied that he leaves me and the children alone and doesn't complain about anything.'

'Is he still as obsessive?' I asked. 'When he performs his ablutions, does he still say, "That wasn't good enough, that wasn't good enough, I have to do it again"?'

'May the devil's ear be deaf; he is a lot better. He is so busy that he doesn't have time to keep washing his hands and feet and repeating his ablutions. You know, this revolution has completely changed him. It is as if this was the cure to his pains. He says, "According to the Ayatollah, I am in the forefront of the revolution, which is no different than a jihad in the name of God, and I will merit God's greatest blessings." In fact, much of his obsession is now over the revolution.'

The speeches started after lunch. We were in the back room and couldn't hear very well. Fearing that voices could be heard out on the street, no one was using a loudspeaker. The living room and dining room were packed with people and there were others in the front yard standing outside the windows. After a couple of speeches about the revolution, the tyranny of the government and our duty to overthrow the current regime, Ehteram-Sadat's uncle spoke. By then he was a well-known mullah who because of his outspokenness had spent a few months in prison and was considered a hero. He first spoke a little about Father's virtues and then he said, 'This honourable family has for years fought for faith and country and they have suffered the wounds. In 1963, after the events of 5 June and the arrest of Ayatollah Khomeini, they were forced to leave their home and they migrated from Qum because their lives were in danger. They suffered fatalities, their son was killed, their son-in-law is still in prison and only God knows what tortures he has had to endure ...'

For a few seconds, I was confused. I couldn't understand who he was talking about. I nudged Ehteram-Sadat and asked, 'Who is he talking about?'

'About your husband, of course!'

'I mean the young man who was killed ...'

'Well, he's talking about Ahmad.'

'Our Ahmad?' I exclaimed.

'Of course! Haven't you ever wondered that he died under mysterious circumstances? In the middle of the street ... and they informed us three days after the fact. And when Ali went to the coroner's office to identify his body he saw signs of assault and battery on his corpse.'

'He probably got into a fight over drugs with another addict.'

'Don't say such things about the dead!'

'And who told your uncle all that rubbish about our move from Qum?'

'Don't you know? It was after the events of 5 June that your family left Qum. Father and Mahmoud were in terrible danger. You were probably too young to remember.'

'As a matter of fact, I remember very well,' I said irately. 'We moved to Tehran in 1961. How could Mahmoud allow himself to say such lies to your uncle and to take advantage of people's passion and excitement?'

Now the speech was about Mahmoud, saying that from a father like that a son like him was expected: a son who had dedicated his life and wealth to the revolution and who had not turned aside from any toil or sacrifice ... He financially supported the families of tens of political prisoners and watched over them like a father, the most important among them being his own sister and her family for whom he had shouldered the burden of life and had never let them feel needy or alone.

At this point, Ehteram-Sadat's uncle motioned to Siamak who suddenly stood up from among the crowd and walked over to him. It seemed as if Siamak had been trained and knew exactly when to get up and play his part. The mullah stroked Siamak's head and said, 'This innocent child is the son of one of Islam's crusaders who has been in prison for years. The criminal hand of the regime has orphaned this boy and hundreds of others like him. Thank God that this boy has a kind and self-sacrificing uncle, Mr Mahmoud Sadeghi, who has filled the empty place of his father. Otherwise, God only knows what would have become of this beleaguered family ...'

I felt nauseous. I felt as if my shirt collar was choking me. I reflexively clawed at it and the top button tore off and flew to the floor. I stood up with such fury on my face that Mother and Ehteram-Sadat became alarmed. Ehteram tugged at my chador and said, 'Massoum, sit down. For the love of your father's spirit, sit down. It's improper.'

Mahmoud, who was sitting behind the mullah and facing the crowd, looked at me with apprehension. I wanted to scream, but I couldn't make a sound. Looking scared and surprised, Siamak who had been standing next to the mullah made his way towards me. I grabbed his arm and snapped, 'Aren't you ashamed of yourself?'

Mother was smacking herself on the cheek and saying, 'May God take my life! Girl, don't shame us.'

I looked at Mahmoud with loathing. There were so many things I wanted to say to him, but suddenly the reciting of elegies started and everyone stood up and began beating their chests. I made my way through the crowd and, still clutching Siamak's arm, I walked out of the house. Massoud was holding on to the hem of my chador and running behind us. I wanted to beat Siamak until he was black and blue. I opened the car door and shoved him inside. He kept asking, 'What is the matter with you? What happened?'

'Just shut up!'

I sounded so harsh and angry that the boys did not utter a single word all the way home. Their silence gave me time to think. I asked myself, What has this poor boy done? What is he guilty of in all this?

When we arrived home, I cursed the earth and the sky, and Mahmoud, Ali and Ehteram, and then sat down and burst into tears. Siamak was sitting in front of me, looking ashamed. Massoud brought a glass of water for me and with tears in his eyes asked me to drink it so that I would perhaps feel better. Slowly, I quietened down.

'I don't know why you are so upset,' Siamak said. 'Whatever it is, I am sorry.'

'You mean you don't know? How could you not know? Tell me, is this what you do at all the events Mahmoud takes you to? Do they parade you in front of people?'

'Yes!' he said, proudly. 'And everyone praises Dad a lot.'

I heaved a sigh of anguish. I didn't know what to say to my son. I tried to remain calm and not frighten him.

'Look, Siamak, we have lived without your father for four years and we have never needed anyone, especially not your uncle Mahmoud. I have struggled so that you could grow up with integrity and not with people's pity and charity, so that no one will ever look on you as needy orphans. And so far, we have always stood on our own two feet. We may have suffered some hardship, but we kept our pride and honour and your father's pride and honour. But now this freak, Mahmoud, has for his own benefit put you on display like a puppet and he is taking advantage of you. He wants people to feel sorry for you and to say, Bravo, what an excellent uncle he is. Have you ever asked yourself why in the past seven or eight months Mahmoud has suddenly taken an interest in us when in all these years he never once asked how we were faring? Look, my son, you have to be much wiser than this and not let anyone take advantage of you and your emotions. If your father

255

finds out that Mahmoud is using you and him in this manner, he will be very upset. He doesn't agree with Mahmoud on even one single issue and he would never want himself and his family to become tools in the hands of Mahmoud and others like him.'

At the time, I didn't know what Mahmoud's real motives were, but I no longer allowed the boys to accompany him anywhere and I stopped returning his telephone calls.

It was mid-October. Schools and universities were often closed. I had only one term left to finish my seemingly unending studies for a bachelor's degree, but there was always a strike or a demonstration at the university and classes were not being held.

I went to different political gatherings and listened to everything that was being said, weighing it all to see whether there was any hope of saving Hamid or not. At times, I was optimistic and everything seemed bright and beautiful, and at other times, I was so disheartened that I felt as if I was plunging down a well.

Wherever a voice was being raised in defence of political prisoners I was there on the front lines, with the boys' fists waving like two small flags on either side of me. With all the pain, anger and misery I had suffered, I would shout, 'Political prisoners must be freed.' Tears would well up in my eyes, but my heart felt lighter. Seeing the crowds alongside me, I was overwhelmed with excitement. I wanted to hold every person in my arms and kiss them. It was perhaps the first and the last time I experienced such emotions for my fellow countrymen. I felt they were all my children, my father, my mother, my brothers and my sisters.

Soon there were rumours that the political prisoners were going to be released. People said some of them would be freed on 26 October to coincide with the Shah's birthday. Hope was again taking root in my heart, but I tried not to believe any of the reports. I could not bear another disappointment. Hamid's father increased his efforts to secure Hamid's release. He gathered more and more letters of recommendation and sent them to the authorities. We worked hand in hand and kept each other informed of the progress we were making. I shouldered the responsibilities he assigned to me with passion and devotion.

Through our contacts we eventually learned that one thousand political prisoners were to be pardoned. Now we had to make sure that Hamid's name would be included on the list.

'Isn't this another political game to appease the masses?' I hesitantly asked Hamid's father.

'No!' he said. 'Given the volatile situation, the government can't afford to do that. They have to at least release a group of the well-known prisoners so that the people see them with their own eyes and perhaps quieten down. Otherwise, the situation will get worse. Be hopeful, my girl. Be hopeful.'

But I was terrified of feeling hopeful. If Hamid was not among those released, I would be devastated. I was even more worried about the children. I was afraid that after all this hope and anticipation, they might not be able to bear the shock of defeat and disappointment. I tried hard to keep information from them, but out on the streets rumours flooded every corner like a surging torrent. Flushed with excitement, Siamak would come home with the latest news and I would coolly respond, 'No, my son, this is all propaganda meant to pacify the people. For now, they are not likely to do any of this. God willing, when the revolution succeeds, we will open the prison gates ourselves and bring your father home.'

Hamid's father approved of my approach and adopted the same tactic with Hamid's mother.

The closer we got to 26 October, the stronger my anticipation. I impulsively kept buying things for Hamid. I could no longer curb my fantasies and thought about the plans we could make after his release. But a few days before 26 October, after a lot of running around and many meetings, Hamid's father came to the house looking dejected and exhausted. He waited until a suitable time when the boys were busy and then said, 'The list is almost complete. Apparently they have not added Hamid's name to it. Of course, I have been assured that if the situation continues like this, he will be released, too. But chances are slim that it would be this time around; the list is mostly made up of religionists.'

257

Swallowing the lump in my throat, I said, 'I knew it. If I were that lucky, my life wouldn't have turned out like this.'

In the blink of an eye, all my hopes turned into despair and with tears in my eyes I again closed the windows that had opened up in my heart. Hamid's father left. Hiding my deep sorrow and disappointment from the children was difficult.

Massoud kept hovering over me and asking, 'What is the matter? Do you have a headache?'

And Siamak asked, 'Has something new happened?'

I told myself, Be strong, you have to wait a little longer. But I felt as if the walls of that house were closing in on me and crushing me. I couldn't stand being in that sad and lonely home. I took the children by the hand and walked out of the house. There was a large crowd shouting slogans in front of the mosque. I was drawn towards them. The mosque's yard was swarming with people. We made our way into their midst. I didn't know what had happened and I couldn't understand what they were shouting. It made no difference; I had my own slogan. Raging and close to tears, I screamed, 'Political prisoners must be freed.' I don't know what there was in my voice, but a few moments later, my slogan was everyone's slogan.

A few days later there was an official holiday. Dawn had not yet broken and I was tired of tossing and turning in bed. I knew security measures would be tight and I should not leave the house. I didn't know how to calm my restless nerves. I had to keep busy. As always, I took refuge in work. I wanted to purge all my energy and anxiety through hard, mindless labour. I stripped the sheets off the beds, took down the curtains and put them in the washing machine. I washed the windows and swept the rooms. I had no patience with the children and told them to go and play in the yard. But I quickly realised that Siamak was brewing a scheme to leave the house. I yelled at them, called them back in and sent them to take a bath. I cleaned the kitchen. I didn't feel like cooking. The leftovers from the day before were enough for us, and Bibi had become so weak and ate so little that no matter what I cooked, she still ate only a bowl of yogurt and a piece of bread. In ill humour, I fed the children and washed the dishes. There was nothing left to do. I wanted to sweep and clean the yard, but I was about to collapse with exhaustion. It was exactly what I had wanted. I dragged myself into the shower, turned on the water and started to weep. This was the only place where I could comfortably cry.

By the time I left the bathroom it was close to four in the afternoon. My hair was still wet, but I didn't care. I put a pillow on the floor in front of the television and lay down. The boys were playing next to me. I was about to fall asleep when I saw the door open and Hamid walk in. I closed my eyes tight for that sweet dream to continue, but there were voices around me. Carefully, I opened my eyes a little. The boys were gaping at a thin man with white hair and moustache. I froze. Was I dreaming? My father-in-law's jubilant, yet cracked voice brought all three of us out of our daze.

'Here you are!' he said. 'I present to you your husband. Boys, what is the matter with you? Come here. Your dad is home.'

When I took Hamid in my arms, I realised he was not much bigger than Siamak. Of course, I had seen him many times in recent years, but he had never seemed as emaciated and gaunt. Perhaps it was the clothes that sagged on his thin frame that made him seem so frail. He looked like a boy dressed in his father's clothes; everything was at least two sizes too big for him. His trousers were pleated around his waist and held up by a belt. The shoulders of his jacket were drooping so much that the sleeves came down to his fingertips. He kneeled down and took the boys in his arms. Trying to embrace all three of my loved ones, I draped myself over them. We were all crying and sharing the pain we had each suffered.

Wiping away his tears, Hamid's father said, 'Enough! Get up. Hamid is very tired and very sick. I picked him up at the prison infirmary. He needs to rest. And I will go bring his mother.'

I walked over to him, hugged and kissed him and laid my head on his shoulder. I wept and said over and over again, 'Thank you, thank you . . .'

259

How kind, wise and considerate that old man was to have single-handedly borne the struggles and anxieties of those few days.

Hamid had a fever.

'Let me help you take your clothes off and go to bed,' I said.

'No,' he said. 'Let me first take a bath.'

'Yes, you are right. You should wash off all the filth and misery of prison and then sleep peacefully. Fortunately, we had oil today and the water heater has been on since this morning.'

I helped him undress. He was very weak and could barely stand. With each piece of clothing that I took off of him, he looked smaller and smaller. In the end, I was horrified at the sight of the scrawny figure that was no more than skin sagging on bones, covered with scars. I sat him down on a chair and took off his socks. Seeing the thin, raw skin and the abnormal condition of his feet pushed me over the edge. I wrapped my arms around his legs, laid my head on his knees and wept. What had they done to him? Would he ever again be a healthy, normal human being?

I gave him a bath and helped him put on the new undershirt, shorts and pyjamas that I had bought at the peak of my hopefulness. Although they were too big for him, still they didn't sag on him as much as his suit did.

Slowly, he lay down on the bed. It was as if he wanted to savour every second. I pulled the sheet and blanket over him; he put his head on the pillow, closed his eyes and said with a deep sigh, 'Am I really sleeping in my own bed? All these years, I have spent every day and every second wishing for this bed, this house and this moment. I can't believe it has come true. What utter pleasure!'

The boys were watching him and taking in his every move with love, admiration and a little reluctance and reserve. He called them over. They sat down next to the bed and the three of them started talking. I brewed tea and sent Siamak to the pastry shop at the corner to buy some pastries and toasted bread. I prepared some fresh orange juice and warmed up the leftover soup. I kept taking him something to eat. Finally he laughed and said, 'My dear, wait. I can't eat too much. I am not used to it. I have to eat a little at a time.'

An hour later, Hamid's mother and sisters arrived. His mother was half crazed with joy. She was fluttering around him like a butterfly and speaking to him tenderly while constantly crying. Hamid didn't even have the energy to wipe away his tears and kept saying, 'Mother, stop. For the love of God, calm down.' But she continued kissing him from head to toe until her incoherent words turned into sobs. Then she leaned against the wall and sank down to the floor. Her eyes were dazed and her hair was tousled. She looked terribly pale and was having difficulty breathing.

Manijeh suddenly threw her arms around her mother and screamed, 'Bring some hot water and sugar. Quickly!' I ran to the kitchen and fetched a glass of hot water and candied sugar and spooned it into her mouth, and Mansoureh splashed some cold water on her face. Hamid's mother shuddered and burst into tears. I looked around for the boys. They were standing behind the door, their tearful eyes moving back and forth between their father and grandmother.

Slowly, the excitement subsided. Hamid's mother refused to leave the bedroom, but she promised to stop crying. She put a chair at the foot of the bed and sat with her eyes glued to Hamid. All she did was occasionally wipe away a tear that quietly rolled down her cheek.

Hamid's father went out into the hall and sat with Bibi who was saying prayers under her breath. He stretched out his legs and leaned his tired head against a floor cushion. I was certain he had spent the entire day frantically rushing around. I took him some tea, put my hand on his hand and said, 'Thank you. You have done a lot today; you must be exhausted.'

'If only all effort and exhaustion reaped such results,' he said.

I could hear Mansoureh comforting her mother. 'For the love of God, Mother, stop it. You should be happy. Why are you sitting there grief-stricken and weeping?'

'I am happy, my girl. You cannot imagine how happy I am. I never thought I would live long enough to see my only son at home again.'

'Then why are you sitting there crying and breaking his heart?'

'Just look at what those villains have done to my child,' Hamid's mother moaned. 'Look how weak and frail he is. Look how old he has become.' And then she said to Hamid, 'May God allow me to give my life for you. Did they hurt you a lot? Did they beat you?'

'No, Mother,' Hamid said sounding uneasy. 'I just didn't like the food. And then I caught a cold and got sick. That's all.'

Amid the chaos, Mother who had not heard from me in a few days called to see how we were. She was shocked when I told her Hamid was home. Barely half an hour later, everyone showed up bearing flowers and pastries. Mother and Faati broke into tears when they saw Hamid. And Mahmoud, ignoring everything that had happened between us, kissed Hamid on the cheeks, hugged the boys, cheerfully congratulated everyone and took control.

'Ehteram-Sadat, get the tea tray ready and brew a good amount of tea,' he said. 'They are going to have a lot of guests. Ali, open the door to the living room and arrange the chairs and side tables around the room. And someone should prepare the fruit and pastry platters.'

'But we are not expecting anyone,' I said with surprise. 'We haven't told anyone yet.'

'No need for you to tell anyone,' Mahmoud said. 'The list of the prisoners who have been released has been published. People will know and they will come.'

I immediately realised he was planning something and I angrily said, 'Listen, brother, Hamid is not well and he needs to rest. You can see for yourself that he has a high fever and has difficulty breathing. Don't you dare ask anyone to come here.'

'I won't, but they will come.'

'I will not let anyone in this house,' I snapped. 'I am telling you now so no one gets upset later.'

Mahmoud suddenly looked like the air had been let out of him. He just stood there gaping at me. And then as if he had remembered something he said, 'You mean you don't even want to call a doctor to come see this poor man?'

'Yes, I do. But it is a holiday. Where am I going to find a doctor?'

'I know a doctor,' he said. 'I will call him and ask him to come.'

He started making telephone calls and an hour later a doctor, accompanied by two men, one of whom was carrying a large camera, arrived at the house. I cast a scolding look at Mahmoud. The doctor asked everyone to leave the bedroom and started examining Hamid, while the photographer took pictures of his scars.

In the end, the doctor diagnosed Hamid's illness as chronic pneumonia. He wrote numerous prescriptions and told Hamid to make sure he took his medications and got his injections on time. About Hamid's diet, the doctor told me I should very gradually increase the amount of food he ate. Before he left, he gave Hamid two injections and some pills to take that night until we could buy everything we needed the next day. Mahmoud gave the prescriptions to Ali and told him to buy everything first thing in the morning and to bring them over.

It was only then that everyone suddenly remembered that martial law was in force and there was a curfew. They all quickly gathered their things and left. Hamid's mother didn't want to go, but his father took her away by force with the promise that he would bring her back early the next morning.

After everyone left, with much begging and pleading I convinced Hamid to drink a glass of milk and gave the boys a light supper. I was so exhausted that I didn't have the energy to gather up the dishes scattered around the house. I just dragged myself to bed and lay down next to Hamid. The doctor had given him a sedative and he was already fast asleep. I looked at his thin face for a while and cherished his being there. Then I turned and looked at the sky outside the window, thanking God with my entire being and vowing to return Hamid to his former self. I fell asleep before I could finish my prayer.

CHAPTER FIVE

A week later, Hamid's condition had improved. He no longer had a fever and was able to eat more, but he was still far from healthy. He had a cough that became worse during the night and suffered from a general weakness that was the result of four years of mal-nutrition and untreated illnesses. However, I slowly began to realise that these were not Hamid's real problem. More than being physically sick, he was mentally unwell. He wallowed in depression, didn't want to talk, showed no interest even in the news, which in those days was critical and grave, didn't want to see his old friends, and refused to answer any questions.

'Do you think his depression and lack of interest in what goes on around him is normal?' I asked the doctor. 'Is everyone who is released from prison like this?'

'To a certain extent yes, but not this severely,' the doctor said. 'Of course, in varying degrees, they all experience intolerance for crowds, a sense of alienation and difficulty readapting to a normal family life. But Hamid's unexpected release, this revolution, which has always been his dream and his goal, and being in the bosom of a family that has so warmly welcomed him should excite him and give him a new passion for life. These days, the problem I have with people like Hamid is how to keep them calm so that their emotional state is more in tune with their physical condition.'

'But in Hamid's case, I have to prod and provoke him to simply go through normal daily routines.'

I couldn't understand the reason for his depression. At first, I attributed his silence to his illness, but he wasn't all that unwell any more. I thought perhaps our families were not giving him the space and the time he needed to readapt to life. There were so many people around us all the time that we couldn't even find half an hour to talk to each other. Our house was like a caravanserai with a constant flow of people coming and going. To make matters worse, on Hamid's second night at home, his mother had brought her things over and had stayed with us. And then Monir, Hamid's oldest sister, had arrived with her children from Tabriz. Although everyone helped around the house, neither Hamid nor I could stand the throng.

I knew Mahmoud was to blame for much of the mayhem. As if he had discovered a creature that was a freak of nature, he showed up every day with a new group of spectators. To stop me from complaining, he had made himself responsible for meals and constantly had food delivered to the house, saying that I should give the excess to the needy. I was surprised by all that generosity and splurging. I didn't know exactly what lies he had concocted, but he was somehow pretending that Hamid had been released from prison as a result of his efforts. If he had dared, I am sure he would have loved to strip Hamid naked every day so that he could show his scars to the audience.

Politics was always a hot topic at the house. Eventually, some of Hamid's old friends and new fellow believers started coming to see him. They brought with them eager young disciples to see the great hero up close and to listen to him talk about the history of the organisation and about their comrades who had sacrificed their lives. But Hamid didn't want to see any of them and would come up with different excuses to avoid them. In their company, he was always quieter and more depressed. I was surprised, because he did not react that way to Mahmoud's friends and others who came to see him.

One day when the doctor came to examine Hamid, he asked

me, 'Why is your house always so crowded? Didn't I tell you my patient needs to rest?' And before leaving, when everyone could hear him, he said, 'I told you on that first day that this patient requires calm, clean air, silence and rest to recover and to return to his normal self. But this house is always like a sports stadium. It's no surprise that he is in a worse emotional state than he was on the first day. If you continue like this, I will no longer accept any responsibility for his health.'

Everyone gaped at him.

'What should we do, Doctor?' Hamid's mother asked.

'If you can't keep the doors to this house closed, then I suggest you take him some place else.'

'Yes, my dear doctor, from the very beginning I wanted to take him to my house,' she said. 'It is larger and not so jam-packed.'

'No, madam,' the doctor said. 'I mean a quiet place where he can be alone with his wife and children.'

I was elated. He was saying what I had been wishing for in my heart. Everyone offered a suggestion and they all left earlier than usual. Mansoureh waited for everyone to leave and then said, 'The doctor is right. Even I am going crazy here, never mind this poor man who has spent four years in isolation and silence. You know, the only solution is for you to go to the Caspian coast and for Hamid to convalesce there. Our villa is sitting there useless and empty, and we won't tell anyone where you are.'

I was beside myself with joy. This was the best thing we could do. And the Caspian coast was the land of my dreams. Given that by order of the government the schools were closed and because of unrest at the university classes were not being held, we could easily spend some time in the north.

The beautiful and vibrant seaside autumn welcomed us with a pleasant sun, a blue sky and a sea that changed colour every second. A cool breeze brought the salty smell of the sea to the shore and the sunshine provided a sweet excuse to sit on the beach.

The four of us stood on the terrace of the villa. I asked the children to take a deep breath and told them that air could breathe new life into anyone. I turned and looked at Hamid. But he didn't see that beauty, didn't hear my words, didn't smell the sea and didn't feel the breeze on his face. Doleful and indifferent, he went back inside. I told myself, Don't give up! And I thought, I have the right setting and the necessary time; if I can't help him, then I don't deserve to be called a wife and I don't deserve this blessing that God has given me.

I planned a regular schedule for us. On sunny days, and there was no shortage of them that year, I came up with different excuses to take Hamid for a walk on the beautiful sandy beach or in the woods. Sometimes we walked as far as the main road to do our shopping and strolled back. Drowned in his thoughts, he would follow me without speaking. He either didn't hear my questions or answered them with a nod or a simple yes or no. Still, I took no notice and talked about things that had happened in his absence, about beauty and nature, and about our lives. I played with the children, sang songs and laughed. At times, I sat mesmerised by the scenery that like a painting on canvas was so beautiful it seemed unreal. Euphoric, I would praise all that splendour. On these occasions, Hamid's only reaction was to look at me with surprise. He was moody and listless. I stopped buying the newspaper and turned off the radio and television. Every piece of news seemed to agitate him even more. Having lived for so long with anxiety and stress, living without the news was pleasant and relaxing for me, too.

The children were not cheerful and happy either. 'We robbed them of their childhood too soon,' I said to Hamid. 'They suffered terribly. But it is not too late. We can make it up to them.' Hamid shrugged and looked the other way.

He observed his surroundings with such indifference that I even thought he might have become colour-blind. I created a colours game with the children. Each of us had to name a colour that we could not see in our surroundings. We often had differences of opinion and appointed Hamid as the referee. He would listlessly take a quick look around and offer an opinion. I kept telling myself, I am more stubborn than he is, and I wondered how long he would resist and ward us off. I extended our daily walks. He was no longer short of breath after a long stroll. He was stronger and had gained some weight. I kept talking without sounding frustrated or disappointed until he slowly started to open up. At times when I felt he wanted to talk, I would become all ears and I would not disturb the setting.

We had been on the coast for a week when, one bright and sunny day in October, I prepared for us to go on a picnic. After walking for some time, we spread our blankets on a hill with a stunning view. On one side, the sea and the sky had displayed every shade of blue and merged together at some faraway point. And on the other side, the lush forest was reaching for the sky with every colour present in nature. The cool autumn breeze was making the colourful branches dance and its chill on our cheeks was pleasant and revitalising.

The children were playing. Hamid was sitting on the blanket, looking out at the horizon. His face had taken on some colour. I handed him a cup of freshly brewed tea and I turned and stared at some distant point.

'Is something wrong?' he asked.

'No,' I said. 'I'm just thinking.'

'Thinking about what?'

'Forget it. They weren't pleasant thoughts.'

'Tell me!'

'Will you promise not to get upset?'

'Yes! Why?'

I was happy that he was curious to know what was on my mind.

'I used to think that it would have been better if you, too, had died,' I said.

His eyes gleamed.

'Really?' he said. 'So we think alike.'

'No! Back then, I thought you would never return to your life and you would die a slow and agonising death. If you had died with the others, it would have been instantaneous and you would have suffered less.'

'I always think about this, too,' he said. 'It torments me that I wasn't worthy of such an honourable death.'

'But now I am happy you didn't die. These days, I often think about Shahrzad and I am grateful to her for having kept you alive for us.'

He turned away and again stared out at the horizon.

'For four years, I have been thinking about what they did to me,' he said pensively. 'How had I betrayed them? Why didn't they keep me informed? Didn't I deserve at least a message? Towards the end, they even cut off my lines of communication. I had been trained for that mission. Perhaps if they hadn't lost their trust in me . . .'

His tears didn't allow him to go on.

I was afraid that the slightest move I made would close the small window that had opened. I let him cry for a while. When he quietened down, I said, 'They didn't consider you an outsider. You were their constant friend and dear to them.'

'Yes,' he said. 'They were the only friends I ever had. They were everything to me. I would have sacrificed everything for them; even my family. I never denied them anything. But they rejected me. They threw me away like a traitor, a lowlife, and they did it right when they most needed me. How can I ever hold my head up again? Won't people ask, How come you didn't die with them? Perhaps people think I was a snitch and betrayed them. Ever since I have come home, everyone looks at me with suspicion and doubt.'

'No! No, my dear, you are wrong. They loved you more than they loved anyone else, even more than they loved themselves. Even though they needed you, they put themselves in greater danger than ever before just to spare your life.'

'That's rubbish. We had no such agreement between us. Our principal concern was our goal. We were trained to fight and to die for it. There was no room for this sort of drivel. Among us, only the traitors and those who could not be trusted were rejected. And that is exactly what they did to me.'

'Oh, Hamid, that is not what happened,' I pleaded. 'My dear, you are wrong. I know things that you don't. Shahrzad did this for us.

269

Before all else, she was a woman and she longed for a quiet family life with a husband and children. Do you remember the love she showed Massoud? He filled the empty place of a child in her heart. As a woman, as a mother, she could not deprive Massoud of a father and make an orphan of him. Even though she believed in the fight for freedom, even though her goal was the welfare of all children, once she experienced maternal feelings, like all mothers she made an exception for her own child. Like all mothers, the well-being of her child and the dreams she had for him became a greater priority. A tangible priority that was different from the abstract slogan of happiness for all the children in the world. It is an instinctive bias that even the purest souls experience when they become a parent. It is impossible for a woman to feel as much compassion for a child dying of hunger in Biafra as she would for her own child. Shahrzad became a mother during the four or five months she lived with us, and she did not want to deprive her son of anything in life.'

Astonished, Hamid looked at me for a while and then he said, 'You are wrong. Shahrzad was strong, she was a fighter. She had great ideals. You cannot compare her to an average woman, not even to yourself.'

'My dear, being strong and being a fighter is not incompatible with or an impediment to being a woman.'

We sat quietly until Hamid said, 'Shahrzad had great goals. She—'

'Yes, but she was a woman. She talked to me movingly about the emotions and the hidden aspects of a woman who suffers because of what she has been deprived of in life. She talked about things she had been unable to talk about until then. Let me put it this way, one day she said she was jealous of me. Can you believe it? She was jealous of me! I thought she was joking. I told her I was the one who should be jealous. I told her she was a perfect woman when I, like women a hundred years ago, had to spend my life slaving in the house, and that according to my husband, I was a symbol of oppression. Do you know what her response was?'

Hamid shook his head.

'She recited a poem by Forough.'

'Which poem? Do you remember it?'
I recited it:

Which summit, which peak?

What have you given me,
you simple deceptive words,
you who renounce bodies and desires?
If I had put a flower in my hair,
would it not have been more seductive
than this hoax,
than this reeking paper crown on my head?

Which summit, which peak?
Give me refuge you flickering lights,
you bright mistrusting homes
on whose sunny rooftops laundered clothes
sway in the arms of scented soot.
Give me refuge you simple wholesome women
whose soft fingertips trace
the exhilarating movements of a fetus beneath your skin,
and in your open collars
the air forever mingles with the smell of fresh milk.

I went on: 'Do you remember the night she left? She was clutching Massoud to her chest, kissing him, smelling him, crying. As she was leaving, she said, "No matter how, you must protect your family and raise your children in a safe and happy environment. Massoud is very sensitive. He needs a mother and a father. He is fragile." At the time, I didn't grasp the true meaning of her words. It was only later that I realised her constant insistence that I protect my family was not her giving me advice, she was actually struggling with herself.'

'It is hard to believe,' Hamid said. 'The person you are describing isn't like Shahrzad at all. Do you mean to say she followed that path against her will? That she didn't believe in our cause? But no one forced her into it. She could have walked away from it and no one would have reproached her.'

'Hamid, how could you not understand? It was another part of her. A hidden part that until then she didn't even know existed. The one thing she did for this side of her that showed only fleetingly was to save you from death. Not including you in the mission was to protect you. And keeping you uninformed was to protect themselves; in case you were arrested. I don't know how she managed to convince the others, but she did.'

There was a certain expression of doubt, surprise and hope on Hamid's face. Although he hadn't completely accepted everything I had said, after four years he was considering other reasons for his having been excluded. The greatest change this vague hope made in him was that it broke his silence. From that day on, we constantly talked. We examined our relationship and circumstances, and analysed our personalities and behaviour after having lived a secret life. One after the other, the snags were unravelling and with each one a small window was opening on to freedom, happiness and relief from unspoken frustrations. And the self-confidence he had long considered dead was beginning to grow again.

Sometimes in the middle of a discussion he would look at me with surprise and say, 'You have changed so much! You seem so mature and well-read. You sound like a philosopher, a psychologist. Did a few years of university change you this much?' 'No!' I would say with a pride I did not want to conceal. 'Life's hardships forced me to change. I had to; I had to understand so that I could choose the right paths. I was responsible for my children's lives. There was no room for mistakes. Luckily, your books, the university and my job made it possible.'

After two weeks, Hamid was more energetic and in better spirits. He was starting to resemble his old self. Just as his mental and emotional gloom was lifting, his body was gaining strength. With their perceptive eyes, the boys noticed the changes in their father and allowed themselves to grow closer to him. Captivated and excited, they watched his every move, followed his orders and laughed when he laughed; and hearing them brightened my life. With his return to health and the rekindling of his hunger for life, Hamid's needs and desires reawakened, and after all that darkness and deprivation our amorous nights brought us intense passion.

Hamid's parents and Mansoureh came to stay with us for a two-day holiday. They were surprised and thrilled to see the dramatic change in Hamid.

'Didn't I tell you this was the solution?' Mansoureh said.

Hamid's mother was ecstatic. She constantly hovered over him, gushed with affection and thanked me for his return to health. Her behaviour was so touching that even at the height of our joy it made me want to cry.

It was cold and rainy the entire two days, but we sat around the fireplace and talked. Bahman, Mansoureh's husband, would tell us the latest jokes about the Shah and then Prime Minister Azhari, and Hamid would laugh from the bottom of his heart. Although everyone was convinced that he had fully recovered, I decided to extend our stay by another week or two, especially because Hamid's mother had privately told me that Bibi was not faring too well and that a few of Hamid's activist friends were searching high and low for him. Bahman suggested they leave their car behind for us and return home by a car service so that we could travel to different towns along the coast. Though in those days there was a shortage of petrol and it was hard to come by.

We spent another beautiful two weeks in the north. We had bought a volleyball for the boys and Hamid played with them every day. He ran with them and exercised, and the boys who had never experienced such a relationship with their father were grateful to him and to God. They worshipped Hamid as if he were an idol. Massoud's drawings often depicted a four-member family picnicking, playing, or walking amid flowers and gardens with a bright sun shining in the sky, smiling down at the happy family. All the reserve and formality between the boys and their father had melted away. They talked to him about their friends, their school and their teachers. Siamak boasted about his pro-revolution activities, telling Hamid about the places his uncle Mahmoud had taken him to and the things he had heard. Hamid was surprised and pensive.

One day, tired from playing with the boys, he dropped down on the blanket next to me and asked for a cup of tea. 'These kids have so much energy,' he said. 'They just don't get tired.'

'What do you think of them?' I asked.

'They are delightful. I never thought I would love them this much. I see my entire childhood and youth in them.'

'Do you remember how much you hated children? Do you remember what you did when I told you I was pregnant with Massoud?'

'No, what did I do?'

I wanted to laugh. He didn't even remember how he had abandoned me. But that wasn't the time to air grievances and relive bitter memories.

'Forget it,' I said.

'No, tell me,' Hamid insisted.

'You relinquished all responsibility.'

'You know very well that my problem wasn't children, I just wasn't sure of my own life and future. I always thought I would live only another year. In those circumstances, having children was very foolish for both of us. Be honest, don't you think you wouldn't have suffered as much during these past years if you hadn't had children and all this responsibility?'

'If it weren't for the boys I wouldn't have had a reason to live and to fight,' I said. 'Their existence forced me into action and made everything tolerable.'

'You are a strange woman,' he said. 'At any rate, now I am very happy that I have them and I am grateful to you. The situation has changed. A good future awaits them and I am not worried any more.'

Hearing Hamid speak those words was a blessing. I smiled and said, 'Really? So having children now is not a problem and it doesn't frighten you?'

He leaped up and said, 'Oh, no! For the love of God, Massoum, what are you saying?'

'Don't worry,' I said, laughing. 'It's not like one would know this early. But it's not unlikely. I am still in my childbearing years and as you know I didn't have any contraceptive pills here. But all jokes aside, if we were to have another child, would you be as frightened and as troubled as you were before?'

He thought for a while and then said, 'No. Of course, I don't want any more children, but I am not as opposed to it as I used to be.'

When we were done discussing and sorting out our personal issues, we started talking about political and social matters. He still didn't fully understand what had happened during the years he had been in prison, what had led to his release and why people had changed so much. I talked to him about the university students, about my colleagues and about everything that had come to pass. I talked about my experiences, about people's reaction towards me and the palpable change in their attitude recently. I spoke about Mr Zargar who had hired me solely because Hamid was a political prisoner, about Mr Shirzadi who was an objector by nature and because of political and social suppression had turned into a creature of hatred and suspicion. And finally, I talked about Mahmoud who according to himself would give his life and all his worldly goods to the revolution.

'Mahmoud is a real phenomenon!' Hamid said. 'I never thought he and I would ever take two steps in the same direction.'

By the time we arrived back in Tehran, the seventh-day ceremony for Bibi's death had already been held. Hamid's parents had not found it necessary to let us know she had passed away. In reality, they were afraid that the crowds and the traffic of family and friends would be too stressful and trying for Hamid.

Poor Bibi, her death did not affect anyone's life and it did not make anyone's heart tremble. In reality, she had died years earlier. Her passing was void of even the sadness that one feels over the death of a stranger. It paled in comparison to the death of the youth and of the activists who in those days were being killed by the dozen.

The doors and windows of the downstairs rooms were shut and the book of Bibi's life, which must have once been sweet and exciting, came to an end.

Our return to Tehran took Hamid back to a period years earlier. Books and pamphlets started arriving from here and there and with every day that passed there was a larger crowd around him. Those who knew him from the old days built him into a hero for the younger generation: a former political prisoner and a survivor of the self-sacrificing founders of their movement. They chanted slogans for him, lauded his superiority and welcomed him as a leader. And all the while, Hamid was not only regaining his confidence, but growing prouder every day. He talked to them like a leader and lectured them on the ways and means of resistance.

A week after our return, he went to the printing house with a group of his devoted followers. They broke through the seals and locks and used the equipment that still remained to start a modest print shop. Although it was quite basic, it met their needs for reproducing bulletins, pamphlets and newsletters.

Like a faithful dog, Siamak was always at his father's heels, obeying his instructions. He was proud of being Hamid's son and wanted to be next to him at any gathering. In contrast, Massoud, who hated being the centre of attention, started to distance himself from them, staying with me and spending his time drawing images of street protests in which there was never any violence. In his illustrations no one was ever injured and there was never any blood.

On the ninth and tenth days of Muharram, commemorating the martyrdom of Imam Hossein, a large crowd came to our house and we all went and joined the demonstrations that had been planned for that day. Surrounded by his friends, Hamid was separated from us, and his parents returned home early. Hamid's sisters, Faati, her husband, Sadegh Agha, and I were careful not to lose each other in the crowd and shouted slogans for so long that we all lost our voices. I was excited and thrilled to see people vent their anger and frustration, but I still couldn't push away the fear and apprehension that was clawing at me. It was the first time Hamid had witnessed the tidal wave of popular feeling about the revolution.

As I had suspected, it deeply affected him and he threw himself with abandon into the fray.

Several weeks later, I started to notice changes in myself. I was getting tired more easily and I felt a little nauseous in the mornings. Deep in my heart, I was happy. I told myself, We are now a real family. This child will be born under different circumstances. A pretty little girl can bring even more warmth to our family. Hamid has not experienced the joys of nurturing an infant.

Still, at first I didn't have the courage to tell him. When I finally did, he laughed and said, 'I knew you would get us into trouble again. But it isn't so bad. This child, too, is the product of the revolution. We need more manpower.'

The exciting days of the revolution were bursting with events. We were all busy. Our house was as crowded and as bustling as Mahmoud's. But gradually, our home became the meeting place for political activists. Although it was still dangerous and gathering in groups was prohibited, Hamid went about his business and simply said, 'They wouldn't dare interfere with us. If they arrest me again, I will become a legend. They won't take that risk.'

Every night, we stood on the roof and, together with all the other people standing on rooftops across the city, we chanted, 'God is great.' We used the escape route Hamid had devised years earlier to go to neighbours' homes, talk and exchange ideas late into the night. Everyone, young and old, considered themselves political pundits. The Shah's departure from the country escalated the excitement.

Mahmoud had arranged it so that whenever necessary we could gather at his house to receive the latest news and information about various events. Hamid and Mahmoud's cooperation was friendly. They didn't engage in political debates, but they exchanged information about their activities, offered each other suggestions, and Hamid shared his knowledge of armed resistance and guerilla warfare with Mahmoud and his friends. At times, their discussions continued until dawn.

As the date of Ayatollah Khomeini's return to Iran grew closer, collaboration between different political factions and groups became more intense and coordinated. And among the people, many old enmities were forgotten and many severed relationships were re-established. For instance, we were reunited with our maternal uncle who had been living in Germany for twenty-five years. Like all Iranians living abroad, he was excited and tried to keep abreast of the events by staying in regular telephone contact with Mahmoud. And Mahmoud was now talking to my cousin Mahboubeh's husband and they were exchanging news about the events in Tehran and Qum. At times, I felt I no longer knew Mahmoud. He had become generous with his wealth and spared no expense for the revolution. I often asked myself, Is this the same Mahmoud?

My thirteen-year-old Siamak was growing up fast and performing his duties like a man alongside his father. I rarely saw him and often didn't know what he had to eat for lunch and dinner, but I knew he was happier than ever before. Massoud's responsibility was to write slogans on walls. With his fine penmanship, he sometimes wrote them on large sheets of paper and if he had time he even adorned them with various designs. Every day, he went running through the streets with a group of other children. Despite the danger, I couldn't stop them. In the end, I had to join his group as a lookout. I would stand guard at the corner so that they could safely write their slogans and then I would correct their spelling mistakes. This way, I could keep an eye on my son and share his support of the revolution. Massoud took great, innocent pleasure in having done something illegal with his mother as his accomplice.

The only sadness that weighed on my heart was my renewed separation from Parvaneh. This time it wasn't physical distance that separated us, it was the difference in our political beliefs that kept us apart. Although during Hamid's imprisonment she had been very supportive, had taken care of my children and was one of the few people who frequented our house, not long after Hamid's release, she severed her relationship with us.

Parvaneh and her family were supporters of the Shah and considered the revolutionaries to be rogues and ruffians. Each time we saw each other, our discussions and arguments intensified our differences. Oftentimes, we unintentionally slighted each other and parted on the verge of getting into yet another fight. Gradually, we lost interest in seeing each other, to the degree that I didn't know when they packed their belonging and again left the country. My avid support for the revolution was at odds with my sorrow over losing Parvaneh again, and couldn't blot it out.

The sweet and exhilarating early days of the revolution passed like the wind. Joy and excitement climaxed on the afternoon of 11 February with the collapse of the provisional government. The revolutionaries took over government buildings and television and radio stations. The national anthem was broadcast on the television and the host of a children's programme recited Forough's poem that starts with verse, 'I dreamed that someone is coming ...' I was ecstatic. Singing our anthem, we went from house to house, embraced each other, offered sweets to one another and congratulated everyone. We felt free. We felt light. We felt as if a heavy weight had been lifted from our shoulders.

The schools quickly reopened and businesses and companies resumed trading, but life was chaotic and far from normal. I returned to work. But at the agency, everyone spent the day arguing. Some believed we should all register in the newly founded party of the Islamic Republic as a show of support for the revolution, while others argued there was no need. After all, they said, these were no longer the days when everyone was forced to join the Shah's Rastakhiz Party.

Amid all this, I became the centre of attention. Everyone was congratulating me, as if I had single-handedly carried out the revolution, and they all wanted to meet Hamid. Finally, one day when on his way from the printing house Hamid came to pick me up at work, my colleagues dragged him inside and greeted him as they would greet a hero. Hamid, who despite his activities was a shy man and got flustered when taken by surprise, spoke only a few words, distributed the publication his organisation had just printed, and answered a few questions.

My co-workers and friends described Hamid as a handsome, caring and charming man and they congratulated me. I was intoxicated with pride.

CHAPTER SIX

We were living triumphantly and savouring our newly gained gift of freedom. The sidewalks were crammed with vendors selling all the books and pamphlets that not too long ago could cost you your life if you were found in possession of them. All sorts of magazines and newspapers were available; we talked freely about everything; we were not afraid of the SAVAK nor of anyone else.

But the oppression we had lived under had not allowed us to learn how to properly profit from freedom. We didn't know how to debate, we were not accustomed to hearing opposing points of view, we were not trained to accept different thoughts and opinions. Consequently, the revolution's honeymoon did not last even a month and ended far sooner than we thought.

Differences of opinion and personal inclinations, which until then had been veiled by the solidarity of having a common enemy, revealed themselves more harshly and forcefully as time passed. Battles over beliefs quickly resulted in people taking sides, each accusing the other of being an enemy of the people, the nation and religion. Every day a new political group came into existence and challenged the others. That year, all the customary new year's social visits and gatherings passed with heated political arguments and even fights.

My own fateful encounter took place at Mahmoud's house when

we went to visit his family for the new year. An argument between Hamid and Mahmoud escalated into a row.

'The only thing people want and which they started this revolution for is Islam,' Mahmoud said. 'Therefore, the government should be an Islamic government.'

'I see!' Hamid retorted. 'Would you please explain to me what an Islamic government actually means?'

'It means the implementation of all the tenets of Islam.'

'Meaning a return to fourteen hundred years ago!?' Hamid exclaimed.

'The rules of Islam are the rules of God,' Mahmoud countered. 'They do not get old and are always relevant.'

'Then would you please explain what the laws of Islam are with respect to the country's economy? And what about the laws pertaining to civil rights?' Hamid asked. 'I guess you want to bring back harems, travelling on camels and cutting off hands and feet!'

'This, too, is God's rule,' Mahmoud snapped. 'If they had punished thieves by cutting off their hands, there wouldn't be so many of them, and there wouldn't be so many traitors and swindlers. What would a faithless man like you know about God's rules? There is wisdom to it all.'

The argument led to Hamid and Mahmoud exchanging insults. Neither could tolerate the other. Hamid talked about human rights, freedom, the repossession of property, the division of wealth, and government by committee, and Mahmoud called him faithless, godless and an infidel whose death was requisite. He even accused Hamid of being a traitor and a foreign spy. And in return, Hamid labelled Mahmoud dogmatic, dry-minded and a traditionalist.

Ehteram-Sadat, her children, and Ali and his wife sided with Mahmoud. And I, saddened by Hamid's isolation, felt obliged to support him and rushed to his aid. Faati and her husband were indecisive and didn't know which side to take. All the while, Mother looked desperate, understood nothing of what was being said and simply wanted peace to be restored.

Worst of all, Siamak was stuck in the middle, dazed and confused, not knowing who was right. He still had fresh in his mind

Mahmoud's religious teachings of several months earlier and yet he was living in his father's intellectual and political environment. Until that day, Siamak had not truly grasped the profound conflict between the two. During the time his uncle and his father were cooperating with each other, their opposite standpoints had melded together in his mind. But now the two men were at odds, leaving him lost and disillusioned.

Siamak was no longer committed or partial to either man; he again became tense and quarrelsome. And finally one day, after a long argument he put his head on my chest and wept as he used to do when he was a child. I comforted him and asked him what was troubling him. 'Everything!' he said, still sobbing. 'Is it true that Dad doesn't believe in God? That he is Mr Khomeini's enemy? Does Uncle Mahmoud really believe Dad and his friends should be executed?'

I didn't know what to say.

Our daily life returned to the way it had been years ago. Again, Hamid forgot his home and family. He was constantly travelling around the country and spent the rest of his time writing articles and speeches, and publishing newspapers, magazines and newsletters. Although he saw no reason why Siamak shouldn't be at his side, Siamak was no longer eager to be with him.

The schools, universities and businesses had reopened and people were busy with their lives. But there were scenes of arguments and fights over ideas and beliefs everywhere. At the university, any group that got to a room first occupied it, hung their name on the door and started distributing newsletters and leaflets. This behaviour wasn't exclusive to the students; even the professors were divided into factions and fought with each other. The walls and doors were covered with conflicting slogans and leaks and disclosures such as photographs of students or professors receiving awards from the Shah or Queen Farah.

I don't remember how we studied that year and how we managed to take our final exams. Everything was overshadowed by ideological wars. Yesterday's friends now beat each other almost to death and when the opponent was defeated, or even lost his life, they would celebrate and consider it a great victory for their group.

I was happy it was my last term at the university.

Hamid laughed and said, 'What an ardent student! You love studying so much that it seems you have no intention of finishing.'

'You are shameless!' I said. 'I could have finished in three and a half years, but because of you, I had to drop out of university and when I went back I took only a few credits each term so that I could work and take care of the kids, too. And despite all this, I have a very high expected grade. You can be sure I will be accepted in the post-graduate programme as well.'

Unfortunately, the turmoil at the university, the dismissal of many professors and the regular cancellation of classes meant that again I could not finish and a few credits were outstanding for the following term.

At work, it was the same situation. Every day a few people were labelled as former SAVAK agents, and shocking accusations and rumours were rampant. The purging of anti-revolution elements had become part of every political group's mandate and each faction accused the other of being anti-revolutionary.

The scene was different at our house. Siamak was bringing the Mujahedin's newspaper home from school.

In mid-September 1979, I gave birth to my daughter. This time, Hamid was there. After the delivery, when I was transferred to the maternity ward, he laughed and said, 'This one resembles you more than the others!'

'Really? Why? I thought she was a little olive-skinned.'

'For now she is more red than olive-skinned, but she has dimples in her cheeks. She is very cute. We are going to name her Shahrzad, aren't we?'

'No!' I said. 'We decided that unlike Shahrzad she should have a long and happy life and that we would give her a name that suits her.'

'What would you say suits this tiny little girl?'

'Shirin.'

284

Given that Shirin was going to be my last child, I wanted to enjoy every minute of her infancy, which I knew would pass all too quickly. Siamak didn't pay much attention to our newcomer, but Massoud, who showed no signs of jealousy, would gaze at that little miracle and say, 'She is so tiny, but she has everything! Look at the size of her fingers! Her nostrils look like two tiny zeros.' And he would laugh at Shirin's ears and the little tuft of hair on the crown of her head. Every day after school, Massoud would sit and talk to her or play with her. Shirin seemed to love him, too. The moment she saw him she would start giggling and flailing her arms and legs. When she was older, apart from my own, she would leap only into Massoud's arms.

Shirin was a healthy girl. Emotionally, she was a combination of Siamak and Massoud. She was pleasant and cheerful like Massoud, and mischievous and restless like Siamak. Her lips and cheeks resembled mine, but she had inherited Hamid's wheat-coloured skin and large black eyes. I was so busy with her that I wasn't bothered by Hamid's long absences and I didn't want to take part in his work and activities. I was even neglecting Siamak. As always, he was doing well in school and his grades were good, but I didn't know what else he was involved in.

After my three-month maternity leave from work, I decided to take another year off without pay. I wanted to raise my daughter in peace and pleasure, earn my bachelor's degree and possibly prepare for the graduate school entrance exams.

Other than family members, Shirin had another ardent fan in Mrs Parvin who by then was not working and very alone. It seemed people no longer ordered custom-made clothes and she had hardly any clients left. She rented out the two rooms at the far end of the yard and started earning a small income, which stopped her from worrying about the lack of customers. Mrs Parvin was spending much of her free time with me and when I registered for the winter term at the university, she happily agreed to take care of Shirin on the days I had classes.

The university was still in turmoil. I was distraught the day a group of students threw a time-honoured and highly respected professor out of the university gates with a kick in the pants because his book had received a royal award from the Shah. What made it worse was that a few other professors stood by and watched with a smile on their lips, nodding in approval. When I told Hamid about it, he shook his head and said, 'In a revolution, there is no room for futile sympathies. Eradication is one of the pillars of any revolt, but unfortunately these people don't know how to conduct it properly and are behaving irresponsibly. After every revolution, rivers of blood have flowed and the masses have avenged hundreds of years of tyranny. But here, nothing is happening.'

'What do you mean nothing is happening?' I exclaimed. 'Only recently the newspapers published the photographs of former government officials who have been executed.'

'That handful of people? If the powers that be hadn't executed even those few, they themselves would have come under suspicion.'

'Don't say that, Hamid. You frighten me. I think even this is too much.'

'You are too emotional,' he said. 'The problem is that our people don't have a culture of revolution.'

Over time, the unrest and the political and social conflicts escalated to the point that the university was officially closed. The country was far from peace and stability. There were rumours circulating about a civil war and the secession of several provinces, particularly Kurdistan.

Hamid was often travelling. This time, he had been away for more than a month and we had no news of him. Again, my worries and anxieties started, but I no longer had the patience and tolerance I used to have. I decided to have a serious conversation with him when he returned.

After six weeks, he came home exhausted and unkempt. He went straight to bed and slept for twelve hours. The next day the noise the children were making finally woke him up. He took a bath, ate a proper meal and, healthy and well rested, sat at the kitchen table and started joking around with the boys. I was washing the dishes when, sounding surprised, he asked, 'Have you gained weight?'

'As a matter of fact, no. I have actually lost a lot of weight in the past few months.'

'Then you had gained weight before?'

I wanted to throw something at him. He had forgotten that seven months earlier I had given birth; that was why he hadn't asked about our daughter. Just then, Shirin started to cry. I turned to Hamid and angrily said, 'Do you remember now? You, sir, have another child!'

He would not admit that he had forgotten Shirin existed. He took her in his arms and said, 'Wow, she has grown so much! She is so chubby and cute!'

Massoud started listing his sister's talents and traits: how she smiled at him, grabbed his finger tightly, recognised everyone in the family, had two teeth and had begun crawling.

'I haven't been away that long,' Hamid said. 'Did she change so much in this short a time?'

'As a matter of fact,' I said, 'she had already teethed before you left and she could do a lot of things, but you weren't around to see any of it.'

Hamid didn't go out that night. Around ten o'clock the doorbell rang. He leaped up, grabbed his jacket and ran towards the rooftop. And I was suddenly transported back to years earlier. Nothing had changed. I felt sick.

I don't remember who was at the door. Whoever it was, they did not pose any danger, but Hamid and I were both badly shaken. I looked at him with bitterness. Shirin was sleeping. The boys were excited to see their father at home and didn't want to go to bed, but I ordered them to go to their room. Hamid took a small book from his pocket and went to the bedroom.

'Hamid, sit down,' I said sternly. 'I have to talk to you.'

'Ugh!' he said impatiently. 'Does it have to be tonight?'

'Yes, it has to be tonight. I am afraid there may be no tomorrow.'

'Oh, how grave and poetic!'

'You can say whatever you want and make fun as much as you want, but I will say what I have to say. Look, Hamid, all these years I have put up with all sorts of misery and I have never demanded anything from you. I have respected your ideas and ideals even though I do not believe in them. I have tolerated loneliness, fear, anxiety and your absences. I have always put your needs first. I have suffered middle-of-the-night raids, my life being turned upside down, and years of insults and humiliation behind the prison gates. I have single-handedly shouldered the burden of our life and raised the children.'

'So, what's your point? You have kept me awake so that I can say thank you? Fine, thank you. Madam, you are remarkable.'

'Don't act like a spoiled child,' I snapped. 'I don't want your thanks. I want to say that I am no longer a seventeen-year-old girl to worship your heroisms and be content with them. And you are no longer a strong and healthy thirty-year-old man who can fight and struggle the way you used to. You said if the Shah's regime falls, if the revolution triumphs, and if the people get what they want, you will go back to a normal life and we will quietly and happily raise our children together. Think about them. They need you. Stop all this. I don't have the patience and the strength for it any more. Your main goal has been achieved and you have performed your duty towards your ideals and your country; leave the rest for those who are younger.

'For once in your life, put your children first. The boys need a father. I can't fill your place in their lives any more. Do you remember the month we spent on the Caspian coast? Do you remember how happy and lively they were? Do you remember how they talked and shared everything with you? Now, I have no idea what Siamak is up to and who his friends are. He is in his adolescent years; it is a dangerous and difficult age. You have to spend time with him and keep an eye on him. Besides, we have to plan for their future. Their expenses are increasing every day and with this inflation I cannot shoulder the responsibility alone. Do you even know how we have managed to live this past year with me on leave without pay? Believe me, even the pittance I had saved for a rainy day is gone. How long does your old father have to support us?'

'The money he gives to you every month is my salary,' Hamid retorted.

'What salary? Why are you fooling yourself? How much do you think the printing house makes for it to want to pay an idle guy who never shows up at work?'

'So what is your problem?' he asked. 'You need more money? I will tell them to increase my salary. Then will you be satisfied?'

'Why can't you understand what I'm saying? Of everything I've said, you heard only the bit about money?'

'The rest was all nonsense,' he said. 'Your problem is that you don't have any ideals in life. Doesn't serving the people have any place in your materialistic mind?'

'Don't start with your slogans,' I said. 'If you are really concerned for the nation and the needy people, then let's go to the far-flung corners of the country and become teachers, work for the people and teach them something; let's buy a piece of land and become farmers and grow food, or do anything else that you consider to be service to the people. Even if we have no income, I will never complain. I just want us to be together. I want my children to have a father. I swear I will live wherever you want. I just want us to get away from this battle of nerves, this constant fear and anxiety. Please, for once in your life make a decision for the sake of your family and your children.'

'Are you done?' he said angrily. 'Are you really that simple-minded and fanciful? Do you really think that after all the training, all the suffering, all the years in prison, just now that we are so close to our goal I will hand everything over to these people and move to some godforsaken corner of the country and plant beans with four and half peasants? My mission is to institute a democratic government. Who said the revolution has triumphed? We still have a long way to go. My duty is for all nations to be free. When are you going to understand this?'

'Tell me, what is a democratic government?' I asked. 'Isn't it a government elected by the people? Well, the people have done just that; except that you, sir, will not accept the fact that the people, the ones you have been beating your chest for, have voted for an Islamic government. Now, who exactly do you want to go to war with?'

'Come on ... what vote? They took the votes from uninformed, revolution-crazy people who didn't know what trap they were falling into.'

'Whether they knew or not, they elected this government and they have not withdrawn their vote or their support. You are neither their advocate nor their representative and you must respect their choice even if it is contrary to your beliefs.'

'Meaning I should sit idly by and wait for everything to be destroyed?' he said. 'I am a political thinker, I know the correct way to govern, and now that the foundation is ready, we must finish what we started. And to this end, I will not turn away from any fight or struggle.'

'Fight? Fight with whom? There is no Shah. You want to fight against the republican government? Fine, do it. Announce your plans and four years from now put them to the vote. If your way is the right way, the people will certainly vote for you.'

'Come on, don't fool yourself. It's not as if the Islamists would allow it. And exactly what people are you referring to? The people who are predominantly illiterate and in fear of God and the Prophet offer everything they own to the religious fanatics?'

'Literate or illiterate, these are the people and this is what they have voted for,' I repeated. 'But you want to impose your own style of government on them.'

'Yes! If necessary, I will do that, too. And when the people realise what is to their benefit and who is working for their greater good, they will side with us.'

'And what about those who don't side with you, those who have different beliefs?' I asked. 'Right now, there are hundreds of political groups and factions in this country and they all believe they are right and they are not likely to accept your style of government. What will you do with them?'

'It is only the malevolent and the traitors who do not think

290

about the good of the people and oppose it. They must be removed.'

'Meaning, you would execute them?'

'Yes, if necessary.'

'Well, the Shah did that. Why did you all shout that it was tyranny? What a fool I was to think so highly of you and to have such high hopes for you! Little did I know that after all that fighting for the people and love of the nation and preaching about human rights, the gentleman wants to become an executioner! You are so mired in your own fantasies that you actually believe the religious fanatics will sit quietly by and wait for you to take up arms, start another revolution and mass-murder all of them. Of all empty dreams! They will kill you! They will not repeat the Shah's mistake. And with what you have in mind, they would actually be in the right.'

'This itself exemplifies their fascist tendencies,' Hamid argued. 'And that is why we must be armed and strong.'

'You are not short of fascist tendencies yourself,' I snapped. 'Even if the impossible happens and your organisation takes over the government, if you don't massacre more people than them, you certainly won't massacre any fewer.'

'That's enough!' he shouted. 'You never had the brains for revolution.'

'No, I didn't and I don't. All I want is to protect my family.'

'You are utterly self-absorbed and egotistical.'

Arguing with Hamid was useless. We had come full circle and returned to where we were years earlier. Everything was starting all over again, but this time I was tired and fed up, and he was more brash and fearless. I struggled with myself for several days. When I thought about my life and my future, I concluded that pinning my hopes on him was stupid and futile. I had to count only on myself; otherwise, I would not be able to manage our lives.

I decided to forgo the remainder of my leave from work and Mrs Parvin agreed to come to the house every day and take care of Shirin.

*

Mr Zargar was surprised to see me back at work.

'Would it not have been better if you had stayed with your daughter until the end of your leave and until things calmed down a little?' he asked.

'Don't you need me any more? Or has something happened that I am not aware of?' I said.

'No, nothing special has happened and we always need you. It's just that the issue of women having to wear headscarves and the purges have created some unrest.'

'That is not important for me. I have lived most of my life wearing headscarves and chadors.'

The day had not yet ended when I fully grasped the meaning of Mr Zargar's words. The free and open atmosphere of the early days of the revolution had disappeared. Like everywhere else, the employees had formed different groups and every group was in conflict with another one. Some of my co-workers tried to distance themselves from me. Every time I entered a room, conversations would abruptly end or for no apparent reason someone would make a snide remark. In contrast, others would try to secretly engage me in conversation and, as if I were the leader of all leftist factions, requested all sorts of information. The Revolution Committee of which I was the first elected member had been dismantled and other committees had formed. The most important of these was the Eradication Committee, which apparently held everyone's destiny in its hands.

'Didn't they identify and dismiss the SAVAK agents last year?' I asked Mr Zargar. 'Then why are they holding so many meetings and spreading so many rumours?'

Mr Zargar laughed bitterly and said, 'After you have been here a few days, you will understand. People we have known for years have overnight become ardent Muslims. They have grown beards, carry their prayer beads all day, constantly recite prayers and are out to settle a few scores, dismiss a few people and profit from what they can take. You can no longer tell apart these opportunists from the revolutionaries. I think they are far more dangerous for the revolution than people who openly object and stand in opposition. By the way, make sure to go to the noon prayers, otherwise you'll be done for.'

'You know I am a religious person and I have never stopped praying,' I said. 'But praying in this agency, where even its premises have been unlawfully expropriated, and praying in front of these people just to prove that I am pious is something I won't do. I have never been able to worship in a crowd and in front of others.'

'Put all this talk aside,' Mr Zargar warned. 'You must go to noon prayers. A whole lot of people are waiting to see you pray.'

Every day the list of people who were to be purged from the agency was posted on the bulletin board. And daily, with dread in our hearts, we stared at that board that would determine our destinies and sighed with relief when we didn't see our name on it, considering that to be a good day.

The day war broke out between Iran and Iraq, we heard the noise of the bombing and ran to the rooftop. No one knew what had happened. Some said it was an attack by the anti-revolutionaries, others believed it was a *coup d'état*. I was worried about the children and hurried home.

From that day on, the conflict became yet another complication of life. The nightly blackouts, the various shortages, the scarcity of oil and other fuels just as the weather was turning cold and when I had an infant at home, and, worse yet, the nightmarish images of war I had in my head, all weakened my morale.

I covered the window in the children's room with black fabric and at night, when the electricity was cut and there were sporadic air raids, we sat by candlelight and listened with horror to the sounds coming from outside. Hamid's presence would have been a great comfort, but just as he had never been with us at critical times, this time too he was absent. I didn't know where he was, but I no longer had the energy to fear for him.

The shortage and rationing of petrol completely disrupted public transportation. Oftentimes, Mrs Parvin had difficulty finding a taxi or a bus to come to our house in the morning and had to walk part of the way.

One day she was late and I arrived at work later than usual. As soon as I walked into the building, I realised something unusual had happened. The guard at the door turned away from me. He not only didn't greet me, he didn't answer when I said hello to him. A few of the agency's drivers who were sitting in the guard-room peeked out and stared at me. As I walked down the hallway, everyone who passed by me quickly looked away and pretended they hadn't seen me. I walked into my office and froze. The room had been ransacked. The contents of all the drawers had been emptied out on my desk and there was paper scattered everywhere. My knees started to shake. Fear, anger and humiliation were burning my insides.

Mr Zargar's voice brought me back to reality. 'Excuse me, Mrs Sadeghi,' he said. 'Would you please come to my office?'

Silent and stunned, I followed him like a robot. He invited me to sit. I fell into a chair. He spoke for a while, but I didn't hear a word he said. Then he handed me a letter. I took it from him and asked what it was.

'It is from the central office's Eradication Committee,' he said. 'I thought . . . it says you have been dismissed . . .'

I stared at him. Unshed tears were burning my eyes and a thousand thoughts were rushing through my mind.

'Why?' I asked in a choked voice.

'You have been accused of having communist leanings and of promoting and being affiliated with anti-revolution groups.'

'But I have no political leanings and I have not promoted any group! I was on leave for almost a year.'

'Well, because of your husband . . .'

'But what do his actions have to do with me? I have said a thousand times that I don't share his beliefs. I should not be blamed for his offences.'

'That is true,' Mr Zargar said. 'Of course, you can always dispute the charges. But they claim to have proof and several people have testified.'

'What proof? What have people testified to? What have I done?'

'They say in February 1979 you brought your husband to the

office to publicise his communist ideology, that you organised a question and answer session, and distributed anti-revolution newspapers.'

'But he had only come to pick me up. The guys dragged him in by force!'

'I know, I know. I remember. I am just informing you of their claims and you can officially challenge their decision. But to be honest, I think both you and your husband are in danger. Where is he anyway?'

'I don't know. He has been gone for a week and I have not heard from him.'

Tired and weak, I went back to my office to gather my belongings. Tears were welling up in my eyes, but I would not allow them to flow. I didn't want my adversaries to witness my desolation. Abbas-Ali, the janitor on our floor, slid into my office with a tea tray. He acted as if he had stepped into forbidden territory. He gazed sadly at me and at the room for a few seconds and then whispered, 'Mrs Sadeghi, you don't know how upset I am. I swear on my children's lives, I said nothing against you. I never saw anything other than goodness and kindness from you. Everyone is so upset.'

I laughed bitterly and said, 'Yes, I can tell from their behaviour and from their false testimonies. People with whom I have spent seven years have conspired against me so expertly that now no one will even look at me.'

'No, Mrs Sadeghi, that's not how it is. They are all terrified. You won't believe the trumped-up charges they have come up with against your friends Mrs Sadati and Mrs Kanani. There is talk that they will be dismissed, too.'

'I don't think it's as bad as that,' I said. 'You are exaggerating. And even if they are dismissed, it won't be because of their friendship with me. This is all about old grudges and jealousies.'

I picked up my handbag, which was bulging with my things, took the folder that contained my personal papers and made to leave.

'Missus, for the love of God, don't blame me,' Abbas-Ali pleaded. 'Absolve me.'

I wandered around the streets until noon. Gradually, anxiety replaced my humiliation and anger: anxiety about the future, anxiety for Hamid and the children, and anxiety over money. With inflation continuing to rise alarmingly, what was I going to do without a salary? For the past two months the printing house had made no money and Hamid's father had not been able to scrape together an income for Hamid.

I had a splitting headache and struggled to make my way home.

'What are you doing home so early?' Mrs Parvin asked with surprise. 'And you went to work late this morning. If you continue like this, they will fire you.'

'They just did!'

'What? Are you serious? May God take my life! It is my fault for having been late this morning.'

'No,' I said. 'They don't fire people for showing up late, for not working, for harassing others, for being incompetent, for theft, for lechery, for promiscuity, for dishonesty, or for stupidity. They fire the likes of me; someone who has worked like a mule, someone who knows her job, someone who has to pay for her children's expenses. I was tainted and they had to fire me so that the agency would be purged and purified.'

I did not feel well for several days. I had a severe headache and slept only a few hours with the help of the Novalgin Mrs Parvin gave me. Hamid had returned from a trip to Kurdistan, but he stopped by the house only a couple of times. He said they had a lot of work to do and he was spending the nights at the printing house. I didn't even have the chance to tell him I had been dismissed from work.

The news I was hearing about Hamid and his organisation was becoming more troubling and my fears were deepening by the day. And then, the nightmare I had experienced once before happened again.

In the middle of the night, government forces stormed the house. From their exchanges I realised that the printing house had been raided at the same time, and that Hamid and others who were there with him had been arrested.

The same insults, the same horror, the same hatred; it was as if I was being forced to watch an old, horrible movie for a second time. Those probing hands and eyes, whose memory still made me shudder with disgust, were again going through the most private corners of my life and I was feeling the same chill and nakedness I had experienced years ago. But this time, Siamak's rage was not just in his eyes. He was now a quick-tempered fifteen-year-old, writhing with anger, and I was terrified that he would suddenly give voice to his loathing, verbally or physically. I was clutching his hand and begging him under my breath to stay calm, to say nothing and to not make the situation any worse than it was. And all the while, with the colour drained from his face, Massoud watched the scene while holding Shirin in his arms and making no effort to keep her quiet.

Everything started all over again. Early the next morning, I called Mansoureh and asked her to tell her father very calmly what had happened. Did Hamid's parents have the strength to live through such a bitter ordeal a second time? An hour later, his father called. Hearing his pained voice made my heart ache.

'Father,' I said. 'We have to start all over again, but I don't know from where. Do you know anyone who could find a trace of him?'

'I don't know,' he said. 'Let me see if I can find someone.'

The house was in complete disarray and we were all overwrought and on edge. Siamak was roaring like a lion, punching and kicking walls and doors, cursing the earth and the sky. Massoud was behind the sofa, pretending to be asleep. I knew he was crying and didn't want anyone to intrude on his privacy. Shirin, who was generally a pleasant child, had picked up on the tension and would not stop crying. And I, shaken and confused, was fighting away horrifying thoughts.

On the one hand, I was cursing Hamid and blaming him for having again shattered our lives, and on the other, I was asking myself, Is torturing prisoners still a common practice? I wondered what condition he was in. He used to say that the first forty-eight hours was when they inflict the worst pain on prisoners. Could he survive it? His feet had only recently started to look normal again.

What exactly was he accused of? Would he have to stand trial in the Revolutionary Court?

I wanted to scream. Needing to be alone, I went to my bedroom and closed the door. I put my hands over my ears to not hear the children and I let my tears flow. I saw my reflection in the mirror. I looked pale, horror-struck, helpless and disoriented. What was I to do? What could I do? I wanted to run away. If it weren't for the children, I would have headed for the mountains and deserts and I would have disappeared. But what was I going to do with them? I was like a captain whose ship was sinking and whose passengers were looking at him with hope in their eyes. But I was more broken than my ship. I needed a lifeboat to help me escape, to take me some place far away. I no longer had the strength to carry that heavy burden of responsibility.

The sound of the baby crying had grown louder and it was slowly turning into agonising screams. I instinctively got up and wiped away my tears. I had no choice. The children needed me. That ship caught in a storm had no captain but me.

I picked up the telephone and called Mrs Parvin. I quickly explained what had happened, asked her to stay home and wait for me to take Shirin there. Mrs Parvin was still screaming desperately when I hung up. Shirin had finally calmed down in Massoud's arms. I knew he couldn't bear to see his sister cry and would stop pretending to be asleep. Siamak was sitting at the kitchen table. His face was flushed, he had clenched his jaw and his fists and I could see the swollen veins on his forehead throbbing.

I sat next to him and said, 'Look, my son, yell if you want to yell. Yell as much as you want to and let it all out.'

'They came and turned our life upside down, they arrested Dad, and we sat here like idiots and watched them do whatever they wanted,' he shouted.

'What exactly did you want us to do? What could we do? Could we have stopped them?'

He pounded his fists on the table. There was blood on the edge of his hands. I took them in mine and held them tight. He started yelling obscenities. I waited until he calmed down.

'You know, Siamak,' I said, 'when you were a boy you got into fights with everyone and became very agitated. I used to hold you in my arms and you would punch me and kick me until you got rid of all your anger. If it still calms you down, then come here.'

And I took him in my arms. He was considerably taller and stronger than me and could easily have pulled away. But he didn't. He put his head on my shoulder and cried. A few minutes later, he said, 'Mum, you are so lucky, you are so calm and strong!'

I laughed and thought, Let him have this impression of me . . .

Massoud was watching us with tears in his eyes. Shirin had fallen asleep in his arms. I motioned to him and he gently put Shirin down and came to me. I put my arms around him, too, and the three of us cried tears that united us and gave us strength. A few minutes later, I pulled myself away and said, 'Well, boys, we shouldn't waste any time. Crying isn't going to help your father. We have to come up with a plan. Are you ready?'

'Of course!' they both replied.

'Well then, hurry up and pack a few things. You will stay with Mother for a few days and Mrs Parvin will take care of Shirin.'

'What will you do?' Massoud asked.

'I have to go to your grandfather's house so that we can find out where your father is. Perhaps we can get some news of him. We have to go to many different places; there are hundreds of government committees and military departments.'

'I will come with you,' Siamak said.

'No, you have to take care of your brother and sister,' I said. 'After your father, you are responsible for the family.'

'First of all, I won't go to Grandmother's house because Uncle Ali's wife will be upset; she wants to cover herself in front of me and she will constantly nag and complain. Second, Mrs Parvin will be taking care of Shirin, and Massoud is a big boy who doesn't need me to watch over him.'

He was right, but I didn't know what our true situation was and I worried that his young and quick-tempered spirit might not be able to handle some of what we would encounter.

'Look, son,' I said. 'You have other duties, too. You have to find help. Tell your uncle Ali what has happened and see if he knows anyone in any of the committees. I have heard that his brother-in-law has joined the Revolutionary Guards. If necessary, go talk to him. But make sure you don't say anything that would make your father's situation any worse than it is.'

'Of course, I won't,' Siamak said. 'I'm not a child. I know what to say.'

'Fine. Then I want you to go to your aunt Faati's house and tell Sadegh Agha everything that has happened. Perhaps he knows people who can help. And if you want, you can stay with them. For now, we have to find out where your father is. I will tell you the rest of what you need to do later.'

'Don't you want me to tell Uncle Mahmoud?' Siamak asked. 'You know he can help. They say he is the head of one of the committees.'

'No. After the fight he and your father had, I don't think he will do anything to help. We'll leave that for later. I will come and see you as soon as I can. And you don't need to go to school tomorrow. Hopefully, everything will be much clearer by Saturday.'

Not only did nothing become clearer, everything became more vague and complicated. Hamid's father and I spent the next two days going to see every one of his friends and acquaintances, but it was useless. Those who had previously held a position of influence had mostly left the country and the others had either lost their jobs or were on the run.

'Things have changed,' Hamid's father said. 'We don't know anyone any more.'

We had no choice; we had to start searching for Hamid ourselves. The heads of police departments and divisions denied any involvement, claimed they had no information, and referred us to various government committees. At the committees we were asked what crime Hamid was charged with. We didn't know what to say and with fear and trepidation I would mumble that I thought he was accused of being a communist. No one felt a responsibility to give us an answer. Or perhaps it was because of security issues that they would not tell us where Hamid was being held.

Two days later, more exhausted than before and hoping to find help and support, I went to Mother's house. Faati and the children were there, waiting and worried.

'Couldn't you have at least called?' Siamak said irately.

'No, my dear, I couldn't. You have no idea what it has been like. We have been to a thousand places and only returned to your grandfather's house late last night. And I had to stay there because we had another appointment at seven-thirty this morning. But you have talked to your grandmother, haven't you?'

'Yes, but I want to know what you and Grandfather have managed to find out.'

'You can be sure that whenever I have good news, you will be the first person to hear it. Now go and gather your things; we have to go back home.'

Then I turned to Ali and said, 'Ali, you and Mahmoud know so many people at different committees. Can't you find out where they have taken Hamid?'

'To be honest, sister, forget about Mahmoud. He refuses to even hear Hamid's name. As for me, I can't openly ask around and investigate. After all, your husband is a communist and before you know it, I will be labelled and accused of a thousand things. But I will inquire indirectly.'

I was disappointed and wanted to say something to him, but I controlled myself. In spite of everything, I needed him.

'Sadegh will contact a few people he knows,' Faati said. 'Don't torture yourself like this. There is nothing you can do. And why do you want to go back home?'

'I have to go,' I said. 'You won't believe the condition the house is in. I have to tidy it up. And the boys have to go back to school on Saturday.'

'Then leave Shirin with us,' she said. 'You want to go here and there and she will be in the way and hold you back. You know how much Firouzeh loves her and plays with her as if she were a doll.'

Firouzeh was five years old and as beautiful and adorable as a flower, but Faati was four months' pregnant with her second child.

'No, my dear,' I said. 'In your condition, you can't take care of a baby and I am more comfortable having the kids with me. If only Mrs Parvin could . . .'

Mrs Parvin, who had lovingly taken care of Shirin those two days and now was ruefully listening to me talk about taking her back home, jumped up and said, 'Of course I will come with you!'

'Don't you have any work you need to do?' I asked. 'I don't want to impose.'

'What work? Thank God, I have no husband and no tag-alongs, and these days no one wants custom-made dresses. I'll come and stay with you for a week, until things get more organised.'

'Mrs Parvin, I love you! What would I do without you? And how can I ever make up for all your kindness?'

We spent all day Friday tidying up the house.

'The first time they ransacked the house, Father, God rest his soul, sent a few people to help me out,' I said to Mrs Parvin. 'Now look how alone and abandoned I am. I miss Father so much and need him so desperately.'

My voice broke and Massoud, who I didn't know was watching us, ran to me, took my hand and said, 'But you have us! We will help you. For the love of God, don't be sad!'

I ruffled his beautiful hair, looked into his kind eyes and said, 'I know, my dear. As long as I have you, I have no sorrow.'

This time, the raiders had left untouched Bibi's rooms and the cellar, which was almost empty. Therefore, our work was limited to the upstairs rooms, which by late afternoon were almost organised and the house at least appeared tidy. I sent the boys to take a bath, forced them to do the homework they had fallen behind with, and asked them to get ready to go to school the next day. But Siamak was restless. He didn't want to do his homework and kept agitating me. I knew he had every right to feel unsettled, but I could tolerate only so much.

Finally, I sat the boys down and sternly said, 'You can see how much I have to do and deal with, you know how many headaches and worries I have, and you know how many things I have to manage at the same time. Now, how much energy do you think I have? If you don't help me and only add to my problems, I will collapse. And the best way you can help is to do your homework so that I will have one less thing to worry about. Will you help me or not?'

Massoud wholeheartedly promised and Siamak hesitantly promised ...

On Saturday, I again went to several government committees. Hamid's father looked as if he had aged several years and was visibly breaking under the weight of his anguish. I felt sorry for him and didn't want him to accompany me everywhere.

All my running around that day was to no avail. No one would give me a straight answer. I realised I had no choice but to turn to Mahmoud for help. I would have been more comfortable talking to him on the telephone, but I knew every member of his family had been told that if I ever called they should tell me he was not home. Reluctantly, I went to his street and waited at the corner until I saw him come home and go inside. I rang the doorbell and walked in. Ehteram-Sadat greeted me coldly. Gholam-Ali saw me in the yard and cheerfully said, 'Hello, Aunt!' But suddenly remembering that he was not to exchange pleasantries with me, he frowned and walked away.

'Well, I'm sure you are not here to inquire about my health,' Ehteram-Sadat said. 'If you came to see Mahmoud, he isn't home and I'm not sure if he will be back tonight.'

'Go and tell him to come here,' I said. 'I know he is home and I want to talk to him. I saw him come in.'

'What?' she said, feigning surprise. 'When did he come in? I didn't see him.'

'Clearly, you never see what goes on in your house,' I said. 'Tell him I just need two minutes of his time.'

Ehteram-Sadat sulked, wrapped her chador around her round figure and walked away grumbling. I wasn't angry with her; I knew she was just obeying Mahmoud's orders. A few minutes later, she came back and said, 'He is saying his prayers and you know how long his prayers take.'

'That's all right,' I said. 'I will wait. I will wait until tomorrow morning if I have to.'

After some time, Mahmoud finally came and with a foul-tempered look mumbled a hello. Every cell in my body detested being in that house. In a choked voice I said, 'Mahmoud, you are my older brother. I have no one but you. Father left me in your care. For the love of your children, don't let my children become orphans. Help me.'

'It's none of my business,' he grumbled. 'It's not as if it's up to me.'

'Ehteram-Sadat's uncle has a lot of influence in the Revolutionary Court and the government committees. Just arrange for a meeting. All I want is to find out where Hamid is and what condition he is in. Just take me to Ehteram's uncle.'

'Really! You want me to go and say this godless atheist is my relative? Please exonerate him? No, my dear, I didn't find my honour and respect on the side of the road to give it up like this.'

'You don't need to say anything,' I implored. 'I will talk to him myself. I'm not even going to ask them to release him or to pardon him. They can even sentence him to life in prison. I just don't want torture … execution … ' And I burst into tears.

With a triumphant look in his eyes and a smirk on his lips, Mahmoud shook his head and said, 'It's great the way you remember us when you are in trouble. Until now mullahs were bad, conservatives were bad, there was no God, there was no Prophet. Right?'

'Stop it, brother. When did I ever say there is no God and no Prophet? To this day, I have never missed a single prayer. And most of the mullahs are far more open-minded and enlightened than the likes of you. Wasn't it you who boasted everywhere you went that your brother-in-law was a revolutionary, a political prisoner and had been tortured in prison? No matter what, he is the father of my children; don't I have the right to know where he is and in what condition? For the love of your children, help me.'

'Get up, sister. Get up and get a hold of yourself,' he said. 'Do you think it's that simple? Your husband has led a revolt against God and Islam, he is an atheist, and Your Highness wants every-

304

one to leave him alone so that he can wreak any havoc he wants and destroy the country and our faith?

'Let's be fair, if he were in power, would he have left a single one of us alive? If you love your children, you will tell the truth ... huh? Why are you suddenly quiet? No, my dear, you have read this all wrong. God sanctions the spilling of that man's blood. I have spent all my life devoted to Islam, and now you expect me to go to Haji Agha and force him to commit a sin for the sake of a faithless man who has turned his back on God? No, I will never do such a thing, nor would Haji Agha agree to let the enemy of God and Islam go without punishment. Even if the whole world begged him, he would still do what is right.

'Did you think it is still the Shah's era and you can save that man by pulling a few strings? No, my dear, now it is all about truth and righteousness, it is about faith and who has the power to forgive.'

I felt as if I was being beaten over the head with a sledgehammer; my eyes burned and I was seething with rage. I cursed myself for having gone to see Mahmoud. Why did I ask that hypocrite who knew nothing about God for help? Clenching my jaw, I wrapped my chador around me, stood facing him and I screamed, 'Say it! Say, "I used him as much as I needed to and now I have no use for him any more, I don't need a partner any more, I want to stuff my stomach alone." You imbecile! It torments God to see servants like you.'

And I ran cursing out of that house. Every fibre in my body was trembling.

It took us two weeks to find out Hamid was in Evin Prison. Every day, I put on my chador and, with his parents or alone, I went there trying to find prison officials or others who could provide reliable information. Hamid's crime was indisputable. They had so many photographs and speeches and articles he had written that there was no way to deny anything. I don't know if he was ever put on trial and, if so, when.

Barely a month and a half after his arrest, during one of our visits to the prison, Hamid's father and I were ushered into a room.

'I think they have finally granted us a visit,' I whispered to him. Excited, we both stood there and waited. A few minutes later, a prison guard walked in holding a package. He put it on the table and said, 'These are his personal effects.'

I stared at him. I couldn't understand what he meant. Then he snapped, 'Aren't you Hamid Soltani's family? He was executed the day before yesterday and these are his things.'

I felt as if a live wire had been attached to me. My entire body was shaking. I looked at Hamid's father. With his face as white as chalk and his hands squeezing his chest, he crumpled and fell into a chair. I wanted to go to him, but my legs wouldn't cooperate. I felt dizzy and then I felt nothing at all.

The blare of the ambulance siren made me come to. I opened my eyes.

They took Hamid's father to the intensive care unit and I was taken to the emergency room. I had to let my family know. I could remember Faati's and Mansoureh's telephone numbers and I gave them to the nurse.

Hamid's father remained hospitalised, but I was released and went home that night. I couldn't look my children in the eye. I didn't know how much they knew and I didn't know what to tell them. I had no energy to talk or even to cry. I had been injected with so many sedatives that soon I fell into a dark and bitter sleep.

It took three days for me to come out of that state of shock and delirium, and it took three days for Hamid's father to finally lose his battle against death and to reach eternal peace and freedom. The only thing I managed to say was, 'How fortunate he is. Now, he is at peace.'

I envied him more than anyone in the world.

The funeral services for the father and son were held together and we could mourn Hamid without fear and foreboding. Seeing my sons' sad faces, puffy eyes and slight figures dressed in black broke my heart. I spent much of the ceremony reliving the memories of my life with Hamid, which was now condensed into the one month we had spent on the Caspian coast. From my own family, only Mother and Faati attended the funeral.

We stayed at my mother-in-law's house until the seventh-day ceremony. I couldn't even remember where Shirin was. Every so often, I would ask Faati, but I wouldn't hear her answer and an hour later I would ask her again.

Hamid's mother was in a grave condition. Faati said she would not survive the heartbreak. She talked constantly and every single word she uttered reduced everyone to tears. I was surprised she could talk so much. When faced with a tragedy, I always grew quiet and drowned in dark thoughts as I sat and stared at some point. Sometimes, she held my sons and said they smelled like their father. Other times, she pushed them away and screamed, 'Without Hamid, what do I want them for?' Every now and then, she cried for her husband and moaned, 'If Agha Morteza was here, I could bear it,' and later she thanked God that he was dead and not there to witness that tragedy.

I knew the boys were suffering and that environment would soon break them. I asked Faati's husband, Sadegh Agha, to take them away. Siamak was ready to escape that house, but Massoud clung to me and said, 'I'm afraid if we leave you will cry a lot and something bad will happen to you.' I promised him I would take care of myself and make sure nothing happened to me. With the children gone, I felt the lid was lifted off my heart. My tears, which were not allowed to flow in their presence, poured out and my breath burst out of my chest with my sobs.

When I returned home, I knew I could not mourn any more and I could not waste any more time. My problems were too great to allow me a prolonged bereavement. My life was a mess; the children were behind in school and their final exams were drawing close; and, most important of all, I had no work and no source of income. We had lived through the past few months with the help of Hamid's father and now he was gone. I had to think of something. I had to find a job.

My mind was in a muddle over other problems as well. One day at my mother-in-law's house, I had overheard Hamid's aunt and his uncle's wife quietly talking in the room where I was resting. It was then that I learned Hamid's grandfather had bequeathed the house we were living in to all his children. Out of respect for their mother and for Hamid's father, who paid her expenses and took care of her, Hamid's uncles and aunts had never brought up the subject of their share. But with Bibi and their brother gone, they no longer had any reason not to claim their inheritance. And a few days later, I was there when Hamid's brothers-in-law were talking with each other. Monir's husband said, 'According to the law, because the son died before the father, his family is not entitled to any inheritance. You can ask anyone . . .' It was strange how in all that commotion I heard conversations that had to do with my life.

Regardless, the danger I sensed made me come out of mourning sooner than expected and it muted my grief over Hamid's loss. My dark and lonely nights were filled with excruciating anxiety. I couldn't sleep and I couldn't sit still. I paced around the house thinking and sometimes I spoke to myself like a madwoman. All the doors had closed on me. Without a job, without Hamid, without his father, without a home, without any inheritance, and with the stamp on my forehead identifying me as the widow of an executed communist, how was I going to save my children from that stormy sea and deliver them to safety?

'Father, where are you? Can you see that your prediction came true? Your daughter is alone and abandoned in the world. Oh, how desperately I need you!'

Late one night when I was again drifting around the house like a sleepwalker, the sound of the telephone ringing made me jump. Surprised by a call at that hour, I answered the telephone. A voice coming from far away said, 'Massoum, is that you? Oh, my dear. Is it true that Hamid . . . that Hamid has passed away?'

'Parvaneh? Where are you? How did you find out?' I said as tears started to stream down my face.

'Then it's true? I heard it on one of the Iranian radio stations tonight.'

'Yes, it's true,' I said. 'Both Hamid and his father.'

'What? Why his father?'

'He had a heart attack,' I explained. 'He died of sorrow.'

'Oh, my dear, you must be so alone. Will your brothers help you?'

'Please! They won't take a single step for me. They didn't come to the funeral and they didn't even bother with a simple condolence.'

'Well, at least you have your job and you don't need anyone to support you.'

'What job? I was purged.'

'What do you mean? What does being purged mean?'

'It means they fired me.'

'Why? And with two kids ... what are you going to do?'

'Three.'

'Three? When? How long has it been since we last spoke?'

'A long time ... two and a half years. My daughter is eighteen months old.'

'May God make them pay,' Parvaneh said. 'Do you remember how you supported them? You said we were conceited and immoral, that we swindled the people, that we were traitors, that the country had to be turned upside down and people had to take back their rights and what was rightfully theirs ... Look at you now! If you need money, if you need help, please tell me. All right?'

Sadness and tears were choking me.

'What is it?' she said. 'Why are you silent? Say something.'

I suddenly remembered a line of poetry and I said, 'I have no fear of the enemy's taunts, but do not make me worthy of a friend's pity.'

Parvaneh was quiet for a few seconds. Then she said, 'I am sorry, Massoum. Forgive me. I swear I can't help it. You know me; I can't keep anything inside. I am terribly sad for you and I just don't know what to say. I thought you had reached what you wanted, that you were living a happy life. I never imagined this. You know how much I love you. You are closer to me than my sister. If we

309

don't take care of each other then who will? Swear on your children's lives that you will tell me if you ever need anything.'

'Thank you, I will,' I said. 'Just hearing your voice is a big help. For now, I need self-confidence more than anything else and your voice gives that to me. All I need is for us to stay in touch.'

I thought about different kinds of work and again considered sewing, which I had always hated but which seemed to have been etched into my destiny. Mrs Parvin promised to help, but she had hardly any clients left. I knew that no government agency would hire me and the selection committees at private companies and organisations that worked with or for the government would never consider me as a potential employee. I started looking for work at small private businesses, but that, too, was useless. The economy was bad and no one was hiring new employees. I even thought about making pickles and preserves and selling them to grocery stores, or taking orders for cakes, pastries, or other foods. But how? I had no experience.

Around that time, one day Mr Zargar called. Contrary to his usual manner, he sounded flustered. He had just heard about Hamid's death. He offered his condolences and asked if he and a few of my old colleagues could come to extend their sympathy. The following day, he came to the house with five of my former office friends. Seeing them renewed my pain and I started to cry. The women cried with me. Mr Zargar was flushed, his lips were quivering and he was trying not to look at us. When we calmed down, he said, 'Do you know who called me yesterday to express his sorrow over what has happened?'

'No! Who?'

'Mr Shirzadi; from America. In fact, I heard the news from him.'

'So he is still living there?' I asked. 'I thought after the revolution he would come back.'

'He did. You won't believe what state he was in. I had never seen anyone that excited and happy. He looked years younger.'

'Then why did he leave again?'

'I don't know. I asked him, "Why are you going? Your dream has come true." All he said was, "Life's dream was nothing more than this: the death of hope or the hope for death.'"

'You should have kept him at the agency,' I said.

'Forget it!' Mr Zargar said. 'They are even trying to get rid of me!'

'Haven't you heard?' Mrs Molavi said. 'They have built a case against Mr Zargar.'

'What case?' I asked. 'What did you do?'

'I did what you did,' Mr Zargar explained.

'But they can't pin any of that on you!'

Mr Mohammadi said, 'Why not? They consider Mr Zargar to be head to toe one of those who prospered under the old regime; an arrogant, corrupt swindler!'

Everyone laughed.

'You are too kind!' Mr Zargar said.

I wanted to laugh. The accusation of being among the wealthy who had thrived under the Shah's government was gradually becoming a compliment.

'They harassed me for a while because my uncle was a successful lawyer and I had studied abroad and have a foreign wife,' Mr Zargar explained. 'You must remember how the director of the agency couldn't stand the sight of me. Well, he tried to use this opportunity to get rid of me. But his plan didn't work.' Then he said, 'But tell me, what are you doing these days?'

'Nothing! I have no money and I am desperately looking for a job.'

Later that night, Mr Zargar called and said, 'I didn't want to mention this in front of the others, but if you really need work, I may be able to arrange something temporary.'

'Of course I need to work! You cannot imagine my circumstances.' And I went on to briefly tell him about my desperate situation.

'For now, we have a few articles and a book that need to be edited and typed,' he said. 'If you can find a typewriter, you can start working on these at home. The money may not be much, but it won't be too little either.'

311

'I think God has appointed you my saviour angel! But how can I work for the agency? If they find out, it will be terrible for you.'

'They don't need to know,' he said. 'We will draw up the contract under a different name and I will deliver the work to you myself. You don't need to go there.'

'I really don't know what to say and how to thank you.'

'There is no need for thanks. You do excellent work and few have your grasp of the Persian language. Just try to find a typewriter. I will bring the documents tomorrow afternoon.'

I was beside myself with joy, but where was I going to find a typewriter? The one Hamid's father had given me years ago to practise on was very old. Just then, Mansoureh called. Among Hamid's sisters, she was the kindest and the most sensible. I told her about Mr Zargar's offer.

'Let me ask Bahman,' she said. 'They probably have an extra one at the company that they can lend to you.'

When I hung up, I felt relieved and happy. I thanked God that it had been a good day.

I started working from home. I typed, edited and occasionally sewed. Mrs Parvin was my companion, assistant and partner. She came to the house almost every day to either take care of Shirin or for us to sew together. Whatever money she made, she carefully calculated my share. But I was sure she was giving me more than was rightfully mine.

She was still beautiful and energetic. I couldn't believe that after Ahmad's death she had never had any other companion. Her eyes still filled with tears every time she talked about him. People's opinion of her was worth nothing to me. She was a noble and delightful woman who had helped me more than my own family. She was so kind and generous that she willingly sacrificed her own comfort and profit for the well-being of others.

Faati, too, tried to do whatever she could to help me. But with two small children and her husband earning a modest salary, she had a thousand problems of her own. In those days, everyone was grappling with one difficulty or another. The only people around me whose lives were improving were Mahmoud and Ali who continued to accumulate wealth. Apparently they were using Father's shop, which now belonged to Mother, to receive subsidised goods from the government and they were selling them in the open market at several times the cost.

By then, Mother was old and tired and dealing with her own problems. I saw her less often and when I did go to visit her at her house, I would do my best not to run into my brothers. I had also stopped going to social events and family gatherings, until one day when Mother called and joyfully broke the news that, after trying for several years, Ali's wife was finally pregnant. To celebrate and give thanks for that blessing, she was hosting a dinner in commemoration of Imam Abbas and she invited me to join them.

'Well, congratulations!' I said. 'Please extend my best wishes to Ali's wife, but you know I will not come to the dinner.'

'Don't say that,' she said. 'You have to come. This is in commemoration of Imam Abbas, how can you refuse? You know it will be a bad omen. Do you want more misery in your life?'

'No, Mother. I just don't want to see them.'

'Then ignore them, just come to the dinner and pray. God will help you.'

'To be honest,' I said, 'I really do feel the need to go to a religious commemoration or a pilgrimage to have a good cry and empty my heart, but I don't want to lay eyes on my contemptible brothers.'

'For the love of God, stop saying such things,' she scolded. 'No matter what, they are your brothers. And besides, what wrong has Ali done? I saw myself how much time he spent calling this place and that place to help you.' And she went on to argue, 'Then come for my sake. Do you have any idea how long it has been since I saw you? You go to Mrs Parvin's house, but you don't stop by to see me. Don't you ever think your mother is going to be here for only a very short time?'

And she burst into tears and continued to cry until I finally agreed to go.

At the commemoration ceremony I cried non-stop, asked God to give me the strength to bear the heavy burden of my life, and prayed for my children and their future. Mrs Parvin and Faati cried and prayed next to me. Ehteram-Sadat, dripping gold jewellery, was sitting at the head of the room and avoided looking at me. Mother was reciting prayers under her breath and counting her prayer beads. Ali's wife, proud and jubilant, was sitting next to her mother and wouldn't make a move for fear that she would miscarry. She constantly asked for different foods that were immediately put in front of her.

After the guests left, we started cleaning up until Sadegh Agha who had taken the children out came to fetch Faati and me. Mother kissed the children, sat them down in the yard and brought them some soup. Just then, Mahmoud arrived and Ehteram-Sadat rolled into the yard like a big ball. But Mother didn't let them leave. She took some soup for Mahmoud and they started whispering together. I could tell I was the subject of their conversation, but I was so hurt and angry at Mahmoud that I didn't want anyone to mediate, even though I knew I would some day need him. What's more, I didn't want my sons to witness or be part of any conversation or argument between me and my brother.

I called Siamak and Massoud and said, 'Siamak, come and take the baby's bag to the car and wait for me there. And Massoud, you take Shirin.'

'Where are you off to?' Mother said. 'The kids just got here and they still haven't finished their soup.'

'Mother, I have to leave, I have a lot of work to do.'

I called Siamak again and he came running to the window to take the bag from me.

'Mum, did you know Uncle Mahmoud has bought a new car?' he said. 'We're going to take a look at it until you come.' And he called Gholam-Ali to go with him.

Massoud said, 'Mum, bring Shirin yourself, I am going to go with them.' And the boys all ran out to the street.

Mother had planned the reconciliation very well and it seemed Mahmoud had come prepared.

'You tell me to not do wrong, to not be disloyal,' he said to

314

Mother. 'But I have sacrificed my right, I have overlooked all the insults because the Prophet said a Muslim should be forgiving. But I cannot ignore fairness and justice for faith, for the Prophet and for God.'

I was agitated, but knowing Mahmoud, I could also interpret his comments as some sort of apology. Mother called out to me and said, 'My girl, come here for a minute.'

I put on my sweater; the early March weather was cool and pleasant. I picked up Shirin and reluctantly walked out into the yard. Just then we heard the boys shouting out on the street and Mahmoud's youngest son, Gholam-Hossein, came running into the yard, yelling, 'Come quickly, Siamak and Gholam-Ali have got into a fight.'

Then Mahmoud's daughter ran in crying and screaming, 'Dad, hurry! He's killing Gholam-Ali.'

Ali, Mahmoud and Sadegh Agha tore out of the yard. I put Shirin down, grabbed the chador hanging on the railings, pulled it over my head and ran out after them. I pushed my way through the crowd of neighbourhood kids who had gathered around. Ali had pinned Siamak against the wall and was cursing him, and Mahmoud was slapping him hard in the face. I knew how heavy Mahmoud's hand was and I could feel the sting of each blow with my entire being.

Wild and insane, I screamed, 'Let him go!' And I leaped towards them. My chador fell to the ground as I threw myself between Siamak and Mahmoud and hurled my fists at Mahmoud's face, but they only landed on his shoulders. I wanted to tear him to pieces. This was the second time he had abused my children. Just because they had no father to protect them, Mahmoud and Ali thought they could do whatever they wanted to them.

Sadegh Agha pulled my brothers away, but with my fists clenched I continued to shield Siamak like a sentinel. It was only then that I caught sight of Gholam-Ali sitting on the edge of the street gutter, crying. His mother was rubbing his back and hissing insults. The poor boy still couldn't breathe comfortably. Siamak had hurled him to the ground and he had hit his back on the cement edge of the gutter. I was terribly concerned and instinctively said, 'My dear, are you all right?'

'Leave me alone!' Gholam-Ali yelled furiously. 'You and that vicious nutcase!'

Mahmoud stuck his face into mine and with an expression distorted by rage, he growled, 'Mark my words, they will hang this one, too. These boys are the seed and spawn of that faithless miscreant. They will end up just like him. Do you think you will still clench your fists at his hanging?'

Screaming with rage, I shoved the children into my dilapidated car and cried and cursed all the way home. I cursed myself for having gone there, I cursed the boys for attacking everyone like fighting cocks, I cursed Mother, Mahmoud and Ali. I drove recklessly, constantly wiping away my tears with the back of my hand. At home, I angrily paced the rooms. The children watched me with fear in their eyes.

After I had calmed down a little, I turned to Siamak and said, 'Are you really not ashamed of yourself? How long do you want to continue attacking people like a rabid dog? You turned sixteen last month. When are you going to start acting like a human being? What if something had happened to him? What if he had hit his head on the edge of the kerb? What the heck would we have done? They would put you in prison for the rest of your life or hang you!'

I burst into tears.

'I'm sorry, Mum,' Siamak said. 'I'm really sorry. I swear to God I didn't want to start a fight. But you don't know the things they were saying. First they kept boasting about their car and making fun of ours, and then they said we should be even poorer and more miserable than we are because we're not Muslims and don't believe in God. I didn't say anything. I ignored them. Didn't I, Massoud? ... But they wouldn't stop and started saying nasty things about Dad. And then they imitated him being hanged. Gholam-Hossein stuck out his tongue and leaned his head to one side and everyone laughed. And then he said they didn't bury Dad in the Muslims' cemetery, they threw his body in front of the dogs because he was filth ... I don't know what happened; I couldn't

316

stop myself. I slapped him. Gholam-Ali came to stop me and I shoved him and he just flopped down and hit his back … Mum, are you saying that no matter what anyone says I have to stand there like a coward and do nothing? If I hadn't hit him, the anger would have killed me tonight. You don't know how they were making fun of Dad.'

He started to cry. I looked at him for a while. I wanted to slap Gholam-Hossein a couple of times myself. The thought made me laugh.

'Between you and me, you gave him one heck of a beating!' I said. 'But the poor boy couldn't breathe. I think he may have broken a rib.'

The boys realised that I understood the situation they were in and to some extent didn't hold them responsible. Siamak dried his eyes and chuckled, 'And the way you leaped right in!'

'They were hitting you!'

'I didn't care. I was willing to take ten more slaps in exchange for hitting Gholam-Hossein just one more time!'

We laughed. Massoud jumped in the middle of the room and started imitating me. 'The way Mum tore into the street with her chador, I thought she was Zorro! Short as she is, she put her guards up just like Muhammad Ali! If Uncle Mahmoud had so much as blown on her she would have gone flying up to the neighbour's rooftop. But the funny thing is they were all scared. They stood there with their jaws hanging!'

Massoud was describing the scene so comically that we fell to the floor laughing.

It was wonderful. We hadn't forgotten how to laugh.

The new year was close, but I was in no mood to prepare anything. I was just happy that damned year was finally ending. In response to a letter from Parvaneh, I wrote, 'You cannot imagine the year I have had. Every day brought a new disaster.'

On Mrs Parvin's insistence, I made new clothes for the children. But our humble new year celebration didn't include spring cleaning and I didn't prepare the traditional table setting of *Haft Seen*.

Hamid's mother insisted that we bring in the new year at her house. She said it was the first new year after Hamid's and his father's passing and everyone was going to her house. But I didn't have the patience for it.

I realised the new year had started only when I heard the neighbours cheering. Hamid's empty place in our home was painfully palpable. I had spent seven new years with him. Even if he wasn't there with me, I always felt his presence. But now, there was nothing but loneliness and vulnerability.

Massoud was holding a photograph of his father and looking at it. Siamak was in his room with the door closed and wouldn't come out. Shirin was wandering around the house.

I closed the door to my bedroom and cried.

Faati, Sadegh Agha and their children walked in, dressed in new clothes and making a racket. Faati was taken aback by our sombre celebration. She followed me to the kitchen and said, 'Sister, I am surprised at you! For the sake of the children, you should have at least set the *Haft Seen* table. When you said you weren't going to your mother-in-law's house, I thought it was because everyone would automatically start grieving again and you didn't want the children to get upset. But now I see you are worse than them. Go and get dressed. Whatever it was, that year is over. I hope the new year will be a happy one for you and make up for all the suffering.'

'I doubt it,' I sighed.

Discussions about vacating the house and selling it started after the new year holidays. Hamid's mother and Mahboubeh argued and fought against it, but the aunts and uncles were in agreement that it was time to sell. The real estate market, which had suffered after the revolution because of all the talk about confiscating and redistributing properties, had recently improved and prices were slightly higher. They wanted to sell the house as quickly as possible in case prices plunged again or the government decided to confiscate it.

When I received formal notice of their decision, I sent back a message saying that I would not move until the end of the school

318

year and only then would I start looking into other options. But what other options? I was struggling just to keep the children clothed and fed; how was I going to pay rent as well?

Hamid's mother and sisters were worried, too. At first they suggested we live with Hamid's mother. But I knew she could not tolerate noisy children running around the house and I didn't want to stifle the children and make them miserable in their own home. Finally, Hamid's uncle suggested that they renovate the two rooms and the dilapidated garage at the far end of the garden for me and the children to live in. That way we and Hamid's mother would remain independent and at the same time her daughters would no longer worry about her living alone.

Given that I and my children had no rights to an inheritance from Hamid's father, I was very grateful for their offer.

By the end of the school year, the renovations at my mother-in-law's house were almost complete. But Siamak's suspicious behaviour was distracting me from planning our move. He had rekindled my old anxieties. He was coming home later in the afternoon than usual, arguing constantly about politics and seemed to be leaning towards the ideologies of certain political groups. I could not tolerate any of it. To protect my children from greater harm, I had tried hard to keep politics out of our lives. Perhaps that was exactly why Siamak was becoming more and more curious and interested in it.

I had met a few of his new friends at Hamid's funeral; they came to lend a hand. Although they all seemed to be good, healthy young men, I didn't like the fact that they were constantly whispering to each other. It was as if they always had secrets. Over time, they started coming to our house more often. I wanted Siamak to have good friends and to come out of his shell, but I had an uneasy feeling. The voice of my mother-in-law, who always said, 'Hamid's friends destroyed him,' kept ringing in my ears.

Soon I learned that Siamak had become an ardent member of the Mujahedin. In every gathering he would stand with clenched fists and defend them. He brought their newspapers and bulletins to the house, driving me to the brink of insanity. Our discussions about politics always ended in a fight and they not only didn't create any understanding between us, they drove Siamak farther away from me. One day I sat down and, trying hard to remain calm, I talked to him about his father and the devastation politics had brought to our life. I talked about the hardships Hamid and his friends endured, about the miseries they suffered and about how in the end it had all been futile. And I asked him to promise me that he would not take that same path.

In a voice that was now that of a man, Siamak said, 'What are you saying, Mum! It is impossible. Everyone is immersed in politics. There isn't a single student in class who doesn't belong to one group or another. Most are Mujaheds and they are all really good guys. They believe in God and pray and they fight for people's freedom.'

'In other words,' I said, 'they are halfway between your father and your uncle and they are repeating the mistakes both of them made.'

'Not at all! They are very different. I like them. They are good friends and they support me. You don't understand, if I am not one of them, I will be all alone.'

'I don't understand why you always have to latch on to others,' I snapped.

He bristled and looked at me with anger. I knew I had made a mistake. I lowered my voice, allowed my tears to stream down my face and said, 'I am sorry. I didn't mean it. I just can't stomach another political game in this house.' And I begged him to end his involvement.

The result was that Siamak promised to never formally join a political group or organisation, but he said he would not stop being a supporter, or as he put it 'a sympathiser', of the Mujahedin.

I asked Sadegh Agha, who had a friendly relationship with Siamak, to talk to him and keep an eye on him. But the situation was getting worse. I discovered that Siamak was selling the Mujahedin's newspaper out on the streets. At school his grades were suffering and he barely made it through the final exams. Even before the grades were announced, I knew he had failed a few classes.

One day Sadegh Agha called to warn me that the Mujahedin were organising a large demonstration for the next day. From early the next morning I watched Siamak like a hawk. He put on his jeans and sneakers and wanted to go out with the excuse of buying something at the store. I sent Massoud instead. As the morning wore on, he became more and more restless. He went to the yard and fiddled with the plants for a while, then he picked up the hose and started watering the garden patch while watching the house from the corner of his eyes. I pretended I was busy doing something in the cellar, but I was watching him from behind the wicker shade. He slowly put down the hose and started tiptoeing towards the front door. I ran up the cellar stairs and reached the door ahead of him. Standing with my arms out, I grabbed hold of the door frame.

'That's enough!' he yelled. 'I want to go out. Stop treating me like a child. I am sick of it!'

'The only way you can go out of this house today is over my dead body!' I screamed.

Siamak took a step towards me. Massoud, with an indomitable look on his face, came to my rescue and stood between us. The anger that Siamak could not take out on me, he took out on Massoud. He started beating and kicking him, all the while hissing from between his clenched teeth, 'Get lost, you chicken. Who do you think you are? Don't meddle, you scrawny carcass.'

Massoud tried to reason with him, but Siamak yelled, 'Shut up! It is none of your business.' And then he struck Massoud in the face so hard that he lost his balance.

I cried and said, 'I thought my eldest son was my support. I thought he would fill his father's empty place. But now I see that he is happy to trade me for a bunch of strangers, even when I beg him to not go out this one day.'

'Why shouldn't I go?' he snapped.

'Because I love you, because I don't want to lose you the way I lost your father.'

321

'Why didn't you stop my father who was a communist?'

'Because I was no match for him. I did everything I could, but he was stronger than me. You are my child. If I am not strong enough to stop you, then I might as well die.'

Siamak pointed to Massoud and yelled, 'If you don't let me go, I will kill him.'

'No, kill me instead. I will die if anything happens to you, so you might as well do it yourself.'

There were tears of rage in his eyes. He glowered at me for a while and then turned and walked towards the house. He kicked off his shoes and sat with his legs crossed on the wooden bed on the terrace in front of Bibi's rooms.

Fifteen minutes later, I told Shirin, 'Go to your brother and give him a kiss; he is upset.'

Shirin ran, struggled to pull herself up on the bed and started caressing Siamak. He slapped her hand away and growled, 'Leave me alone!'

I went and took Shirin, put her down on the ground and said, 'My son, I understand how exciting it is to be a member of a political group and to want to do heroic things. Dreaming of saving the people and humanity is very gratifying. But do you know what lies behind it and where it will end? What is it that you want to change? What is it that you are willing to risk your life for? Do you want to sacrifice yourself so that a bunch of people kill a bunch of other people and gain power and wealth? Is that what you want?'

'No!' he said. 'You don't understand. You don't know anything about this organisation. They want to bring justice to the people.'

'My dear heart, they all say this. Have you ever heard anyone who wants to seize power say he doesn't want to bring justice to the people? But for all of them justice is achieved only when their group comes to power, and if anyone stands in their way they will not waste any time sending him to hell.'

'Mum, have you even read a single book they have written?' Siamak asked. 'Have you even heard a single speech they have given?'

'No, my dear, I haven't. It's enough that you have read their books and listened to their speeches. Do you think they are right in what they say?'

'Yes, of course! And if you had, too, you would understand.'

'And what about the other groups and organisations? Have you read their books, too? Have you listened to their speeches, too?'

'No, I don't need to. I know what they say.'

'But wait, that's not right,' I reasoned. 'You can't this easily claim that you have found the right path and are willing to sacrifice your life for it. Perhaps other groups are saying something better. How many opinions and ideologies have you looked into and studied without prejudgment before making your decision? Have you read a single one of your father's books?'

'No, his way wasn't the right way. They were atheists; perhaps even anti-religion.'

'Nonetheless, he also believed he had found the right way to save humanity and to bring about justice. And he made his choice after years of studying and learning. But, you, who don't have one hundredth his knowledge, claim that he was wrong his entire life and that he lost his life following the wrong path. Perhaps you are right; I believe this, too. But think about it. If with all his experience he made such a costly mistake, why wouldn't you? You don't even know the names of the various schools of political philosophy and thought. Think, my son. Life is the most precious thing you have. You cannot risk it over a mistake, because you will not be able to take it back.'

'You know nothing about this organisation and you question it for no good reason,' Siamak stubbornly argued. 'You think they want to deceive us.'

'You are right; I don't know anything about them. But I do know that someone who uses the emotions of innocent, inexperienced youth for his own gain is not an honest and decent person. I did not find you on a street corner to now simply give you up so that some guy can seize power.'

I am still proud of the perseverance and determination I showed that day. By late afternoon, news of the arrests and killings spread and turmoil followed. Every day, Siamak heard about more friends

323

who had been arrested. The Mujahedin's leaders were in hiding and on the run, but the youth were being killed by the dozen. Every afternoon the names and ages of those executed were broadcast on television and Siamak and I would listen with horror to the never-ending lists. Each time Siamak heard the name of someone he knew, he roared like a tiger trapped in a cage. I wondered what the parents of those young boys and girls felt when they heard their child's name on the television. And selfishly, I thanked God that I had stopped Siamak from going out that day.

People reacted differently to the incident. Some were in shock, others were either indifferent or nervous, and there were those who were happy. Such contrasting reactions in a society that not too long ago had seemed so united was hard to believe.

One day I ran into a former colleague who was deeply involved in politics. He looked at me and said, 'What is the matter, Mrs Sadeghi? You look like your ships have sunk.'

'Aren't you worried about the situation and the news we hear every day?' I asked with surprise.

'No! I think everything is exactly as it should be.'

At the start of the summer, we moved to our rooms at my mother-in-law's house. Leaving my home after seventeen years was not easy. Every brick in that building held a story and brought a memory back to life for me. With the passage of time, even the harshest recollections seemed sweet. We still called the living room 'Shahrzad's room', we still called the ground floor 'Bibi's home'. Hamid's scent still lingered in every corner and I was still finding his things in the nooks and crannies of every room. I had lived the best days of my life in that house.

I chided myself to be logical. I had no other choice. I started packing our belongings. I sold some things, threw some away and donated others. Faati said, 'Keep the good furniture. Perhaps you will move to a bigger house. Isn't it a shame to get rid of your sofas? You bought them in the first year of the revolution, remember?'

'Oh, I was so hopeful then. I thought I was going to have a wonderful life. But I have no use for these sofas now. I will never have a bigger house, or at least not any time soon, and our new rooms are so small. Besides, how many parties do you think I will be giving? I've decided to take only our basic needs.'

Our new home was made up of two connecting rooms and a garage that had been converted into a living room and a kitchen. The bathroom and toilet were attached to the building, but had to be accessed from the outside. I put the boys in one room and Shirin and I shared the other one. We put the boys' desks, my desk, the typewriter and the sewing machine in the bedrooms, and arranged a couple of small sofas, a coffee table and the television in the living room. All three rooms had access to the garden, which was large with a round reflecting pool at its centre. My mother-in-law's house was at the opposite end of the garden.

After everything had been moved out of our old house, I walked through the rooms, ran my hands over the walls that had witnessed my life, and said goodbye to them. I went up on the rooftop and retraced Hamid's escape route as far as the neighbouring house, I watered the old trees in the yard, and through the dusty windows I looked into Bibi's rooms. There had once been so much commotion in that silent house. I dried my tears and with a heavy heart I locked the doors, saying goodbye to that part of my life, happiness and youth. And I left.

CHAPTER SEVEN

The children were very sad about the move and unsettled by the chaos and confusion. And they expressed their unhappiness by stubbornly refusing to help and cooperate. With his arm over his eyes, Siamak was sprawled out on a bed with its mattress askew and Massoud was outside, squatting next to the wall with his chin on his knees, drawing lines on the brick paving with pieces of plaster left over from the construction. Fortunately, Shirin was with Mrs Parvin and I didn't have to worry about her, too.

I didn't have the strength to do everything by myself, but I couldn't force the boys to help me. I knew from their silence that the slightest provocation would ignite tantrums and start a fight. I went to one of the rooms, took a deep breath, swallowed the lump in my throat and tried to calm myself down and find the energy to deal with them. Then I brewed some tea and went to the corner bakery that had just started baking for the afternoon. I bought two Persian flatbreads and quietly went back to the house. I spread a carpet outside in the garden, laid out tea, bread, butter, cheese and a bowl of fruit, and called the boys over to eat. I knew they were hungry. All they had eaten that day was a sandwich at eleven o'clock before we left our old home. They kept me waiting for a while, but the smell of fresh bread and the scent of the cucumbers I was peeling whetted their appetite and like a pair of wary cats they inched their way over to the spread and started to eat.

When I was certain that their ill humour had given way to the satisfaction of having eaten a tasty meal, I said, 'Look, boys, leaving that house where I had spent my youth and the best days of my life was more difficult for me than it was for you. But what could we do? We've left that house, but life goes on. You are both young and just starting out. One day you will build homes for yourselves that will be much bigger and far more beautiful than that house.'

'They didn't have the right to take our home away from us,' Siamak said angrily. 'They didn't have the right!'

'Yes, they did,' I said calmly. 'They had agreed to keep the house as long as their mother was alive. But after she died, they had to divide their inheritance.'

'But they never even came to see Bibi! We were the ones who took care of her.'

'Well, that was because we were living in that house and using it. It was our duty to help her.'

'And we don't have a share of Grandfather's house either,' Siamak added crossly. 'Everyone inherited a share except us.'

'Well, that is the law. When a son dies before his father, his family does not inherit anything.'

'Why is the law always against us?' Massoud asked.

'Why do you care so much about the inheritance?' I asked. 'And who told you all this?'

'Do you think we are stupid?' Siamak said. 'We have heard it a thousand times, starting at Dad's funeral.'

'We don't need any of it,' I said. 'For now, we are living in your grandfather's house and they have spent all this money renovating these rooms for us. What difference does it make if it is in our name or not? We are not paying rent and that itself is very good. You two will grow up and build your own houses. I don't like my children to think about money and inheritances like vultures.'

'They took what was rightfully ours,' Siamak said.

'You mean you want to live in that old house?' I said pointing across the garden. 'I have much bigger dreams for you. Soon you will both go to university and start working. You will become doctors or engineers. And what a house you will build! New, modern, with the best furniture. You won't even take a second look at that ancient ruin. And like old-fashioned women, I will go from house to house searching for wonderful wives for you. Oh, what beautiful girls I will find for you. I will go everywhere and boast that my sons are doctors or engineers, that they are tall and handsome, have beautiful cars and houses that look like palaces. Girls will faint left and right.'

The boys were grinning from ear to ear and wanted to laugh at me and my exaggerated affectations.

'Well, Siamak Agha, do you prefer blondes or brunettes?' I continued.

'Brunettes.'

'How about you, Massoud, do you prefer girls who are fair or olive-skinned?'

'I want her to have blue eyes, the rest doesn't matter.'

'Blue like Firouzeh's eyes?' I asked.

Siamak laughed and said, 'You rascal, you just showed your hand!'

'Why? What did I say? Mum's eyes are sometimes blue, too.'

'Rubbish! Mum's eyes are green.'

'Besides, Firouzeh is like my sister,' Massoud said coyly.

'He is right,' I quipped. 'She's like his sister now, but may be like his wife when she grows up.'

'Mum! Don't say these things! And you, Siamak, stop laughing over nothing.'

I hugged him and said, 'Oh, what a wedding I will have for you!' All that talk put me in better spirits, too.

'Well, boys, how do you think we should arrange the house?'

'House?' Siamak quipped. 'The way you say it one would think it really is a house.'

'Of course it is. It's not important how big a house is, what's important is how you decorate it. Some people move into a shack or a dank basement and fix it up so well that it looks more beautiful and comfortable than a hundred palaces. Everyone's home reflects their style, taste and personality.'

'But this place is so small.'

'No, it's not. We have two bedrooms and a living room and this beautiful, sprawling garden that half the year adds to our living space. Let's fill the garden with flowers and plants and paint the reflecting pool and put goldfish in it. Every afternoon, we will turn on the fountain and sit here and enjoy it. How about that?'

The children's attitude had changed. Instead of the sadness and disappointment of an hour ago, there was excitement in their eyes. I had to take advantage of the opportunity.

'Well, gentlemen, get up. The larger bedroom is yours. Go and arrange it and decorate it for yourselves. The new paint looks nice, doesn't it? The smaller bedroom will be mine and Shirin's. You move the heavy furniture and I'll take care of the rest. The round table and chairs belong in the garden. Massoud, the garden is in your hands. Once we have settled in, survey it and see what you need and which plants and flowers we should buy. And Siamak Khan, you need to instal the aerial on the roof and run a telephone wire over from Grandmother's house. Also, you and Massoud should put up the curtain rods. By the way, let's not forget to clean the wooden bed in Bibi's home and bring it here. It's good to have it out in the garden. We'll throw a carpet over it and if we want we can sleep outside. It will be fun, won't it?'

The children were excited and started making suggestions. Massoud said, 'We should have different curtains for our bedroom. The ones from the other house were too dark and thick.'

'You are right. We will go together and pick a fabric with a floral pattern and I will make matching bedcovers. I promise you will have a bright and elegant room.'

And so the children grew to accept that house and we adapted to our new life. A week later we were almost settled in and after a month we had a thriving garden full of flowers, a beautiful and glistening reflecting pool, and rooms with cheerful curtains and decoration.

Mrs Parvin was pleased that we had moved. She said our new home was easier to get to. The children's grandmother was also happy that we were there and, according to her, she was less scared. Every time the air-raid sirens went off and the power was cut we would rush over to her house so that she wouldn't be alone. The children had somehow adapted to the wartime conditions and considered it part of their daily lives. During the bombings and missile attacks when we had to live in the dark, Shirin sang for us and we accompanied her. It took everyone's mind off the bombardment, except for Grandmother who always sat and stared at the ceiling with horror.

Mr Zargar regularly came to see us and brought work for me. We had become good friends. We often confided in each other and I sought his advice about the boys. He, too, was now alone. At the start of the war, his wife and daughter had moved back to France.

One day he said, 'By the way, I received a letter from Mr Shirzadi.'

'What has he written?' I asked. 'Is he well?'

'Actually, I don't think so. He seems very lonely and depressed. I'm afraid being away from his homeland is going to break him. Lately his poems are more like letters from exile that tug at your heart. I simply wrote: "You are lucky to be there and living a comfortable life." You won't believe what he wrote back.'

'What did he write?'

'Unlike you, I can never remember poetry. He wrote a very long and painful poem that reflects his feelings about living in a foreign land.'

'You are right,' I said. 'He is not going to survive the loneliness and depression.'

My prediction came true too soon and our heartbroken friend found eternal peace; a peace that he had perhaps never experienced in his life on earth. I attended the memorial service his family held for him. He was praised and honoured, but the silence about his poetry, which had reigned while he was alive, still continued.

Mr Zargar introduced me to a few publishing companies and I started working for them from home. Eventually, he found a regular job for me at a magazine that offered a steady and secure salary. It wasn't much, but I made up for the shortfall with the freelance projects I continued to do.

I enrolled the children in the school near our home. At first, they went there moping and unhappy, sad to be separated from their friends. But a month later, they hardly ever mentioned their old school. Siamak made a lot of new friends and Massoud who was kind and pleasant soon gained everyone's affection. Shirin who had turned three was cheerful and charming. She danced, talked incessantly and played with her brothers. I wanted to send her to a nearby daycare centre, but Mrs Parvin wouldn't hear of it.

'Do you have too much money on your hands?' she chided. 'You are either at the magazine offices or sitting at home typing, reading, writing, or sewing. And then you want to pour that hard-earned money in these people's pockets? No, I won't let you. It's not as if I'm dead.'

I was getting used to the new rhythm of life. Although the war was still raging and the news was horrifying, I was so engrossed in life that the only time I truly felt the war was when the air-raid sirens went off. And even then, if we were all together, I wasn't too apprehensive. I always thought the best death would be for us to die together, in one place.

Fortunately, the boys had still not reached the age when they would have to serve in the military and I was certain that by then the conflict would be over. After all, how many years could we continue fighting? And luckily my boys weren't among those who dreamed of going to the front.

I was starting to believe that my hardships were behind me and that I could live a normal life, raising my children in relative calm.

Several months passed. The government continued to lash back at dissenters and opposition groups. Murders and assassinations were rampant. Political activists went underground, the leaders of various organisations escaped, the war continued and I again started to worry about my sons and their future, keeping a close eye on them.

It seemed that my talks, together with recent events, had been effective and Siamak didn't have much contact with his Mujahedin friends, or at least so I thought. As spring approached, my worries lessened. The boys were busy studying for their final exams and I started hinting that they needed to start preparing for the university entrance exams as well. I wanted them to be so immersed in school and studying that they wouldn't have time to think about anything else.

One spring night, I was busy typing a document I had edited, Shirin was sleeping and the light in the boys' room was still on, when the sound of the doorbell, followed by someone pounding on the door, made me freeze. Siamak hurried out of his room and we stared at each other in shock. Massoud walked out looking sleepy. The sound of the doorbell wouldn't stop. The three of us went towards the door. I pushed the boys back and carefully opened the door a crack. Someone shoved the door open, held a piece of paper up in front of my face, then pushed me aside and several Revolutionary Guards stormed in. Siamak tore out of the house and started running towards his grandmother's house. Two guards chased after him, grabbed him and threw him down on the ground in the middle of the garden.

'Leave him alone!' I screamed.

I started to run to him but a hand pulled me back into the house. I kept screaming, 'What is going on? What has he done?'

One of the Revolutionary Guards who looked older than the others turned to Massoud and said, 'Put your mother's chador over her.'

I couldn't stay calm. I could see Siamak's shadow as he sat in the garden. Dear God, what were they going to do to my dear heart? I imagined Siamak being tortured and I screamed and fainted. When I came to, Massoud was splashing water on my face and the men were taking Siamak away.

'I won't let you take my child!' I screamed.

I ran after them.

'Where are you taking him? Tell me!'

The older Revolutionary Guard looked at me sympathetically and when the others were out of earshot he whispered, 'We are taking him to Evin Prison. Don't worry, they won't hurt him. Come next week and ask for Ezatollah Haj-Hosseini. I will give you his news myself.'

'Take my life, but please don't harm my child,' I pleaded. 'For the love of God, for the love of your children!'

He shook his head compassionately and left. Massoud and I ran after them to the end of the street. The neighbours were watching from the corner of their drawn curtains. When the Revolutionary Guards' car turned the corner, I collapsed in the middle of the street. Massoud dragged me back to the house. All I could see was Siamak's pale face and terrified eyes, and I could hear his trembling voice as he shouted, 'Mum! Mum, for the love of God, do something!' I had convulsions all night. This was something I could not survive. He was only seventeen years old. His greatest crime was perhaps selling the Mujahedin's newspaper at some street corner. He had not been in regular contact with them for some time. Why had they come after him?

The next morning I somehow managed to drag myself out of bed. There was no one I could turn to for help but I couldn't sit idly by and watch my child be destroyed. My life was like reruns on television, except that each time the events were slightly different and each time I could bear it less. I got dressed. Massoud had fallen asleep on the sofa fully dressed. I gently woke him up and said, 'I don't want you to go to school today. Wait here until Mrs Parvin comes and give Shirin to her. And call your Aunt Faati and tell her what has happened.'

Still groggy, he said, 'Where are you going this early? What time is it?'

'It's five o'clock. I'm going to Mahmoud's house to see him before he leaves for work.'

'No, Mum! Don't go there.'

'I have no choice. My child's life is in danger and Mahmoud knows a lot of people. No matter how, I have to make him take me to Ehteram-Sadat's uncle.'

'No, Mum. For the love of God, don't go there. He won't help you. Have you forgotten?'

'No, my dear, I haven't forgotten. But this time it's different. Hamid was a stranger to him, but Siamak is his blood, his nephew.'

'Mum, you don't know.'

'Know what? What don't I know?'

'I didn't want to tell you, but yesterday afternoon I saw one of those Revolutionary Guards at the corner.'

'So?'

'He wasn't alone. He was talking with Uncle Mahmoud and they were looking at our house.'

I felt the world spinning around me. Had Mahmoud betrayed Siamak? His own nephew? It was impossible. I ran out of the house. I don't know how I drove to Mahmoud's house. I pounded on the door like a madwoman. Gholam-Hossein and Mahmoud opened the door in a panic. Gholam-Ali had enlisted in the army and had been at the front for some time. Mahmoud was still wearing house clothes.

'You, you scoundrel, brought the Revolutionary Guards to my home?' I screamed. 'You brought agents to arrest my son?'

He looked at me coldly. I was waiting for him to deny it, to get angry, to be insulted by my accusation. But with that same coldness he said, 'Well, your son is a Mujahed, isn't he?'

'No! My son is too young to pick sides. He has never been a member of any organisation.'

'That's what you think, sister ... you've stuck your head in the snow. I myself saw him selling newspapers on the street.'

'That's it? You sent him to prison for that?'

'It was my religious responsibility,' he said. 'Don't you know what treason and murders they are committing? I am not going to trade my faith and the afterlife for your son. I would have done the same if he was my own son.'

'But Siamak is innocent. He isn't a member of the Mujahedin!'

'That is none of my business. It was my duty to inform the authorities. The rest is up to the Islamic Court of Justice. If he is innocent, they will release him.'

'Just like that? What if they make a mistake? What if my child perishes for a mistake? Could you live with that on your conscience?'

'Why would that be any of my concern? If they make a mistake, they are to blame. Even then, it won't be too bad. He will be considered a martyr, he will go to heaven and his spirit will forever be grateful to me for having saved him from a fate like his father's. These people are traitors to our country and religion.'

The only thing keeping me on my feet was rage.

'No one is as big a traitor to his religion and country as you are,' I screamed. 'The likes of you are destroying Islam. When did the Ayatollah ever give such fatwas? You would do any dirty deed for your own gain and chalk it up to faith and religion.'

I spat on his face and walked out. I had a splitting headache. Twice I pulled over to the kerb and vomited bitter bile. I went to Mother's house. Ali was about to leave for work. I grabbed his arms and begged him to help me, to find an acquaintance who had some influence, to ask his father-in-law for help. He shook his head and said, 'Sister, I swear I am devastated. Siamak grew up in my arms. I loved him . . .'

'Loved?' I shouted. 'You talk as if he is already dead!'

'No, that's not what I meant. All I want to say is that no one will do anything, no one can do anything. Now that he has been labelled as a Mujahed, everyone will turn aside. It's because those miscreants have killed so many people. Do you understand?'

I went to Mother's room, dropped down on the floor and beat my head against the wall, moaning, 'Here you are, these are your beloved sons, ready to kill their nephew, a seventeen-year-old boy. And you tell me not to take things to heart, that we are all of the same blood.'

Just then Faati arrived with Sadegh Agha and their baby. They picked me up off the floor and helped me go back home. Faati couldn't stop crying and Sadegh Agha was gnawing at his moustache.

'To be honest, I am worried for Sadegh,' Faati whispered. 'What if they accuse him of being a Mujahed, too? He has got into a few political arguments with Mahmoud and Ali.'

Tears were streaming down my face.

'Sadegh Agha, let's go to Evin,' I begged. 'Perhaps they will give us some information.'

We went to Evin Prison, but it was a wasted effort. I asked for Ezatollah Haj-Hosseini, but I was told he would not be in that day.

Dazed and confused, we returned home. Faati and Mrs Parvin tried to force me to eat something, but I couldn't. I kept thinking, What will Siamak have to eat? I wept and wondered what I should do and whom I should turn to.

Faati suddenly said, 'Mahboubeh!'

'Mahboubeh?!'

'Yes! Our cousin Mahboubeh. Her father-in-law is a cleric. They say he is an important man and Auntie used to say he is very decent and kind.'

'Yes, you are right!'

I was like a drowning woman grabbing driftwood, a glimmer of hope in my heart. I got up.

'Where are you going?' Faati asked.

'I have to go to Qum.'

'Wait. Sadegh and I will go with you. We will go together, tomorrow.'

'Tomorrow will be too late! I will go by myself.'

'You can't!' she exclaimed.

'Why can't I? I know where my aunt's house is. Her address hasn't changed, has it?'

'No, but you can't go alone.'

Massoud started getting dressed and said, 'She won't be alone. I will go with her.'

'But you have school . . . and you didn't go today.'

'Who cares about school under these circumstances? I won't let you go alone and that's that. Now I am the man of the house.'

Leaving Shirin with Mrs Parvin, we left. Massoud took care of me as he would a child. On the bus, he tried to sit up straight so that I could rest my head on his shoulder and sleep. He made me eat a few biscuits and forced me to drink water. When we arrived, he pulled me along and found a taxi. It was dark by the time we reached my aunt's house.

Stunned to see us there and at that hour, my aunt stared at my face and said, 'May God have mercy! What has happened?'

I burst into tears and said, 'Aunt, help me. I am about to lose my son, too.'

Half an hour later, my cousin Mahboubeh and her husband Mohsen arrived. Mahboubeh was still a cheerful woman, just a little plumper and more mature looking. Her husband was a handsome man and seemed to be intelligent and caring. Their love and affection for each other was apparent. I wept uncontrollably and explained everything that had happened. Mahboubeh's husband comforted me and spoke reassuringly.

'It is impossible that they would arrest him based on such weak evidence,' he said. And he promised to take me to see his father the next day and to help in any way he could. Eventually, I calmed down a little. My aunt forced me to eat a light dinner, Mahboubeh gave me a sedative, and after twenty-four hours I went into a deep and bitter sleep.

Mahboubeh's father-in-law was an endearing and compassionate man. He was touched by my grief and tried to comfort me. He made a few calls, wrote down several names and a few notes, which he gave to Mohsen, and asked him to accompany me back to Tehran. On the way, I ceaselessly prayed and pleaded with God. As soon as we arrived home, Mohsen started contacting different people until he finally managed to arrange a meeting at Evin Prison for the following day.

At Evin, the warden exchanged pleasantries with Mohsen and then said, 'It is certain that he is a Mujahedin sympathiser, but to date they have found no reliable and binding evidence against him. We will release him as soon as the usual legal procedures are complete.' And he asked Mohsen to extend his greetings to his father.

The warden's words kept me on my feet for ten months. Ten dark and painful months. Every night I dreamed that they had tied Siamak's legs and were flogging the soles of his feet. His flesh was sticking to the whip and shredding off. And every night I woke up screaming.

I think it was a week after Siamak's arrest when one day I caught sight of myself in the mirror. I looked old, wretched, thin and sallow. Strangest of all was the cluster of white hair that had suddenly appeared on the right side of my head. After Hamid's execution, I had started to see a few strands of white in my hair, but this was new.

I was constantly in touch with Mahboubeh and, through her, with her husband and father-in-law. I went to a meeting at Evin Prison that had been arranged for the parents of inmates. I asked about Siamak. The prison official knew him well and said, 'There is no need to worry, he will be released.'

I was overjoyed, but then I remembered what one of the mothers at the meeting had said. 'When they say, "He will be released," they mean released from life.'

Horror and hope were killing me. I tried to work as much as I could just to have less time to think.

Reports of universities reopening became reality. I went to register for the few credits I still had to complete so that I could finally reach the goal for which I had worked so hard. With a frown on his face and with the utmost cool, the administrator said, 'You are not eligible to register.'

'But I have been attending the university!' I said. 'I just need these few credits to get my degree. Actually, I have already taken the courses; I just have to take the final exams.'

'No,' he said. 'You have been subject to eradication and dismissal.'

'Why?'

'You mean you don't know?' he said with a sneer. 'You are the widow of a communist who was executed and the mother of a traitor and dissenter.'

'And I am proud of both of them,' I retorted angrily.

'You can be as proud as you want, but you cannot attend classes and receive a degree from this Islamic university.'

'Do you know how hard I have worked for this degree? If the universities hadn't been closed I would have received my degree several years ago.'

He shrugged.

I spoke with several other administrators, but it was useless. Defeated, I walked out of the university. All my efforts lay in waste.

*

338

The gentle sun of late February was shining. The winter's biting cold had gone and the cool scent of spring was wafting in the air. Sadegh Khan had taken my car to the garage to be repaired. I walked to work. I was terribly depressed and tried to keep myself busy. Around two in the afternoon, Faati called and said, 'Come here after work. Sadegh has picked up the car from the garage and will fetch the kids ...'

'I'm not in the mood,' I said. 'I'll just go home.'

'No, you have to come,' Faati insisted. 'I need to talk to you.'

'Has something happened?'

'No. Mahboubeh called; they are in Tehran. I asked them to come here. They may have some news.'

When I hung up, I wondered. Faati had sounded different. I started to worry. A last-minute project landed on my desk and I went back to work, but I couldn't concentrate. I called home and told Mrs Parvin, 'Get Shirin ready. Sadegh Agha will come to pick her up.'

She laughed and said, 'He is already here. He was waiting for Massoud who just walked in. They are going to Faati's house. When are you going?'

'As soon as I finish work,' I said. And then I added, 'Tell me the truth, has something happened?'

'I don't know! If something had happened, Sadegh Agha would have told me. My dear, don't worry so much over nothing. You are wasting away.'

As soon as I handed in my assignment, I left the office and took a taxi to Faati's house. She opened the door. I looked at her probingly.

'Hello, sister,' she said. 'Why are you looking at me like that?'

'Tell me the truth, Faati. What has happened?'

'What? Does something have to happen for you to visit us?'

Firouzeh half ran, half danced over and leaped into my arms. Shirin came running, too. I looked at Massoud. He was standing there looking calm and pensive. I walked in and quietly asked him, 'What is going on?'

'I don't know,' he said. 'We just got here. They are acting strange; constantly whispering to each other.'

339

'Faati!' I screamed. 'What has happened? Tell me. I am losing my mind!'

'For the love of God, stay calm,' she said. 'Whatever it is, it is good news.'

'Is it about Siamak?'

'Yes, I have heard they are going to release him before the new year.'

'Perhaps even sooner,' Sadegh Agha added.

'Who said this? Where did you hear it?'

'Calm down,' Faati said. 'Sit and I will bring some tea.'

Massoud grabbed hold of my hand. Sadegh Agha was laughing and playing with the children.

'Sadegh Agha, for the love of God, tell me exactly what you know.'

'To be honest, I don't know much. Faati knows more than I do.'

'Who did she hear it from? From Mahboubeh?'

'Yes, I think she spoke with Mahboubeh.'

Faati walked in with the tea tray and Firouzeh skipped over with a plate of pastries.

'Faati, for the love of your children, sit down and tell me exactly what Mahboubeh said.'

'She said, it's all done, Siamak will be released very soon.'

'Like when?' I asked.

'Perhaps this week.'

'Oh my God!' I exclaimed. 'Is it really possible?'

I leaned back on the sofa. Faati was well prepared. She quickly handed me a bottle of nitroglycerine drops and a glass of water. I took the medication and waited until I felt calmer. Then I stood up to leave.

'Where are you going?' Faati asked.

'I have to go tidy up his room. If my son is coming home tomorrow, everything has to be neat and ready. There are a thousand things I have to do.'

'Sit down,' she said quietly. 'Why can't you ever sit still? To be honest, Mahboubeh said he might be coming home tonight.'

I fell back on the sofa. 'What do you mean?'

340

'Mahboubeh and Mohsen have gone to Evin, just in case they release him today. You have to control your nerves. They may show up any minute. You must stay calm.'

Restless and impatient, every few minutes I asked, 'What happened? When are they going to get here?'

And then I heard Massoud shout, 'Siamak!' And I saw my son walk in.

My heart couldn't take all that joy and excitement. I thought it was going to burst out of my chest. I clutched Siamak in my arms. He was thinner and taller than before. I was short of breath. Someone splashed water on my face. Again, I held my son. I touched his face, his eyes, his hands. Was it really my darling Siamak?

Massoud hugged Siamak and cried for an hour. How had this kind and gentle boy, who had bravely shouldered the responsibilities of life and given me hope, kept all those tears inside him for so long?

Laughing and excited by the commotion, Shirin, who was at first a bit reticent, leaped into Siamak's arms.

The night passed with indescribable joy, exhilaration and delirium.

'I have to see your feet,' I said.

'Come on, Mum.' Siamak laughed. 'Don't be ridiculous!'

The first person I called was Mahboubeh's father-in-law. I cried and thanked him and showered him with every term of endearment.

'I didn't do much,' he said.

'Yes, you did. You gave me back my son.'

Two days passed in a frenzy of family visits. Mansoureh and Manijeh kept a close eye on their mother who was becoming more fragile, forgetful and confused. She believed Siamak was Hamid.

I had made so many pledges and promises to God that I didn't know where to begin. I dropped everything I had to do and the four of us went on a pilgrimage to Imam Reza's shrine in Mashad. From there we went to Qum to thank my aunt, Mahboubeh, her husband and my saviour angel her father-in-law.

What sweet, happy days. I felt alive again. With my children at my side, nothing could bring me sorrow.

Siamak would soon turn eighteen. He had missed one year of school, but because I had entered him in school a year sooner than usual, he was not behind agewise. He had to enrol in school, but given his prison record, they would not accept him. I had always hoped my children would reach the highest levels of education, but now I had to accept the fact that my son would be deprived of even a school diploma.

Not being allowed to finish school was a heavy blow to Siamak. He was agitated and restless. Being idle, staying at home and living an unstructured life was not prudent. Especially since a few of his old friends had started coming around again. Although Siamak didn't seem too interested in them, their presence made me nervous.

Siamak decided to find a job. He saw how hard I worked and how frugally I managed our lives and he wanted to help. But what sort of work could he do? He had no capital to start a small business and no education. At the same time, the war with Iraq was still raging and moving closer to us. I was grappling with these thoughts and worries when one day Mansoureh came to see me and I shared my concerns with her.

'As a matter of fact, that is exactly why I came to see you,' she said. 'Siamak has to continue his education. Among the new generation of our family, everyone has gone to university. It is unacceptable for Siamak to not even have a school diploma.'

'I have looked into it,' I said. 'He can go to night school and take the general education exams. But he says he wants to work. He says if he can't go to university, a school diploma serves no purpose. With or without it he will have to work and he might as well start now.'

'Well, Massoum,' she said, 'I have another plan in mind. I don't know how you will react to it, but please keep it between us.'

'Of course!' I said, surprised. 'What is it?'

'You know that my Ardeshir finished secondary school last

342

year. He has to go for his military service and this war doesn't seem to be ending. Under no circumstances will I let them send my son to the front. Besides, as you know, he has always been somewhat cowardly. He is so terrified that if a bullet doesn't kill him, his fear will. We have decided to send him out of the country.'

'Send him out? How? Everyone who has to serve in the military is banned from leaving the country.'

'That's the problem,' Mansoureh said. 'He has to cross the border illegally. We have found someone who charges a quarter of a million tumans and takes kids across the border. I was thinking of sending the two of them together. They can look after each other. What do you think?'

'Well, it sounds like a good idea,' I said. 'But I have to come up with the money.'

'Don't worry about that,' she said. 'If you are short of some, we will help. But it is very important that they go together. Siamak can take care of himself, but Ardeshir will need help. If he knows he will not be alone, he will agree to go more easily. And we will be less worried.'

'But where would they go?' I asked.

'There are many places they can go to. Every country accepts refugees. They will receive a stipend for a while and they can continue their education,' she said. 'But tell me, what are you really concerned about? The money?'

'No. If it is to my child's benefit, I will sell everything I have and I will borrow. But I have to be sure it is to his advantage. Give me a week to think about it and to discuss it with him.'

I spent two days deliberating about what I should do. Was it wise to leave a boy Siamak's age in the care of a smuggler? How dangerous was it to cross the border illegally? He would have to live all alone somewhere on the other side of the world. If he ever needed help, whom could he turn to? I had to seek advice. Privately, I explained the situation to Sadegh Agha.

'Honestly, I don't know,' he said. 'Everything has its own risks and this is going to be dangerous. I have no notion of life in the

343

West, but I know of many people who have recently sought asylum in different countries; a few of them were actually returned.'

The next day, Mr Zargar was delivering some work assignments to me. He had gone to university in the West and could offer me reliable advice.

'Of course, I have no experience of crossing the border illegally and I don't know how dangerous it is,' he said. 'But more and more people are taking the risk. If Siamak is accepted as a refugee, which as a former political prisoner he certainly will be, he won't have any financial difficulties and, if he has the will, he can get the best education. The only problem is loneliness and life in exile. Many youths his age become depressed and develop serious emotional problems and not only do they fail to study, but they can't lead a normal life. I don't want to frighten you, but the rate of suicide is high among them. Send him only if you know a truly caring person over there who can to a certain extent fill your place and keep an eye on him.'

The only person I knew and trusted overseas was Parvaneh. I went to Mansoureh's house and called her from there. I was afraid our telephone at home was tapped. After I explained the situation, Parvaneh said, 'Definitely do it. You cannot imagine how worried I have been for him. Send him by any means you can and I promise you I will take care of him as if he were my own son.'

Her sincerity and eagerness lessened my worries and I decided it was time to talk to Siamak. I had no idea how he would react.

Shirin was sleeping. I quietly opened the door to the boys' bedroom and walked in. Siamak was lying on his bed, staring at the ceiling. Massoud was sitting at his desk, studying. I sat down on Massoud's bed and said, 'I want to talk to you two.'

Siamak jolted up and Massoud swung towards me and said, 'What has happened?'

'Nothing! I have been thinking about Siamak's future and we need to make a decision.'

'What decision?' Siamak said sarcastically. 'Do we have the right to make decisions? All we can do is say yes to whatever they tell us.'

'No, my dear, it's not always like that. All this week, I have been thinking about sending you to Europe.'

'Huh! You are dreaming!' he said. 'Where would we get the money from? Do you know how much it will cost? At least two hundred thousand tumans for the smuggler and just as much to live on until the request for asylum is processed.'

'Bravo! And how accurate!' I said. 'How do you know all this?'

'Oh, I've looked into it extensively. Do you have any idea how many of my friends have already left the country?'

'No! Why didn't you tell me?'

'Tell you what? I knew you couldn't afford it and it would just make you sad.'

'The money isn't important,' I said. 'If it is for your good, I will find it. Just tell me if you want to go or not.'

'Of course I want to go!'

'And what do you want to do over there?'

'I want to study. Here, they will not let me go to university. I have no future in this country.'

'Don't you think you will miss us?' I asked.

'I will, a lot, but how long can I sit here and watch you type and sew?'

'You will have to leave the country illegally,' I said. 'It is very dangerous. Are you willing to accept the risk?'

'The risk is no greater than military service and being sent to the front, is it?'

He was right. In another year, Siamak would be drafted and the war didn't seem to be ending.

'But there are a few conditions and you have to promise you will do them and you cannot ever break your promise.'

'All right. But what are the conditions?' he asked.

'First, you have to promise me that you will not go anywhere near the Iranian political groups and organisations. You cannot get involved with them. Second, you will study as far as the highest degree possible and you will become a well-educated and respectable man. Third, you will not forget us and, whenever you can, you will help your brother and sister.'

'You don't need to ask me to make these promises,' Siamak said. 'They are exactly what I intend to do.'

'Everyone says that, but then they forget,' I said.

'How could I possibly forget you three? You are my entire life. I hope that one day I can make up for all your love and hard work. You can be sure I will study well and I will stay away from politics. To be honest, I am sick of every single political group and faction.'

We spent hours talking about how Siamak would leave the country and how we could come up with the money. He was alive again; excited and hopeful and at the same time worried and nervous. I sold two of our carpets and the few pieces of gold jewellery I had left. I even sold my wedding ring and Shirin's small gold bangle, and I borrowed some money from Mrs Parvin. But I still didn't have enough. Mr Zargar, who always kept an eye on me and understood my problems even before I spoke of them, showed up one day with fifty thousand tumans and said it was my back pay.

'But I didn't have this much money due to me!' I said.

'I added a little to it.'

'How much? I need to know how much I owe you.'

'It's not much,' he said. 'And I will keep account of it and take it out of your future pay.'

In exactly one week, I gave Mansoureh two hundred and fifty thousand tumans and confidently announced that we were ready. She looked at me with surprise and said, 'Where did you get all this money? I had put aside a hundred thousand tumans for you.'

'Many thanks, but I managed it myself.'

'What about the money they will need for the few months they will be in Pakistan? Can you cover that, too?'

'No, but I will come up with it.'

'Don't,' she said. 'This money is here and it's ready.'

'All right,' I said. 'But I will pay you back over time.'

'You don't need to,' Mansoureh said. 'This is your money, it is your children's share. If Hamid had died a week later, half this house and everything else would have been yours.'

'If Hamid hadn't died,' I said, 'your father would still be alive.'

Contacting the smuggler, a young, skinny, dark-skinned man

dressed in the traditional clothes of his province, was another story in itself. His secret name was Mrs Mahin and he would talk on the telephone only if the caller asked for her. He said the boys should be ready to leave for Zahedan, a city in south-eastern Iran, at a moment's notice. He promised that with the help of a few friends he would safely take them across the border into Pakistan and deliver them to the United Nations' offices in Islamabad. He said he would dress them in sheepskin and they would move across the border among a herd of sheep.

I was terrified, but I tried to hide it from Siamak. He was a fear-less adventurer and found all this more exciting than frightening.

The night we received the order from the smuggler, the boys left for Zahedan with Bahman, Mansoureh's husband. Saying goodbye to Siamak, I felt as though one of my limbs was being severed from my body. I didn't know if I was doing the right thing or not. I vac-illated between sadness over our separation and horror over the danger he faced. That night, I did not leave my prayer rug. I prayed and cried and put my son in God's hands.

Three days passed with fear and anxiety until we received word that the boys had safely crossed the border. Ten days later, I spoke to Siamak. He had arrived in Islamabad. He sounded so sad and so far away.

And then for me there was the pain of separation. Massoud missed Siamak terribly and my crying every night upset him even more. Mansoureh was in far worse condition. She had never been separated from her son for even a day and was now inconsolable. I kept telling her, and myself, 'We must be strong! In these times, to save our children and for the sake of their future, we mothers must bear the sorrow of their absence. This is the price we have to pay; otherwise we will not be good mothers.'

Four months later, Parvaneh called from Germany and handed the telephone to Siamak. I screamed with joy. He had arrived. Parvaneh assured me that she would take care of him, but he had to spend a few months in a refugee camp. Unlike others who idled away the days, Siamak spent the time learning German and was quickly accepted in school and eventually to the university. He studied mechanical engineering and never forgot his promises.

Parvaneh had arranged for him to spend his holidays with her family and she diligently kept me informed of his progress. I was happy and proud. I felt I had accomplished one-third of my responsibility. I worked with great energy and gradually repaid my debts. Massoud took meticulous care of me and our lives. While studying, he also played the role of the family's father and with his unfailing love engulfed me in happiness and hope. And Shirin, with her playfulness, her antics and her sweet-talk brought spirit and joy to our home. I had found peace, albeit a temporary one. There were still problems and worries circling us and the ruinous war with Iraq seemed eternal.

In the days when I had again learned to laugh, Mr Zargar, gravely and with his eyes glued to the coffee table, proposed to me. Although I knew his daughter and his French wife had left Iran several years earlier, I didn't know he was divorced. He was a wise and learned man and suitable in every way. Life with him could solve many of my emotional as well as material needs. And I was not indifferent to him. I had always liked and admired him as a man and a dear friend and companion, and I could easily open my heart to him. Perhaps he could give me the love and affection that Hamid had never completely given me.

After Hamid's death, Mr Zargar was the third man to propose to me. In the case of the first two, I had said no without a moment's hesitation. But in Mr Zargar's case, I wasn't sure what to do. From both a logical and an emotional point of view, marrying him seemed the right thing to do, but for some time I had noticed how Massoud was carefully observing me, seeming restless and on edge. One day, without any overture, he said, 'Mum, we don't need anyone, do we? Whatever you need, just tell me and I will provide it. And tell Mr Zargar not to come around so often. I can't stand him any more.'

And so I realised I should not disrupt the newly gained peace in our lives nor divert my attention away from my children. I believed it was my duty to be at their service with my entire being and that I should be the one filling their father's empty place, not a stranger. Mr Zargar's presence might have been welcome in my life, but it was very clear that it would make my children, especially my sons, uncomfortable and unhappy.

A few days later, with profound apologies I said no to Mr Zargar, but asked him to never deprive me of his friendship.

CHAPTER EIGHT

The events in my life unfolded in such a way that I always had a chance to breathe and fortify myself in the interim, and the longer the period of calm, the worse the shock of the next incident. Believing this, I was plagued by hidden anxieties even in the best of times.

With Siamak safely gone, it seemed my gravest concern had been resolved. Although I missed him terribly and at times my longing to see him seemed unbearable, I never regretted sending him away and never wished that he would return. I talked to his photograph and wrote long letters to him about everything that was going on in our lives. Meanwhile, Massoud was so gentle and kind that he not only didn't create any problems for me, but was often my problem solver. He went through the difficult and turbulent years of adolescence with patience and poise. He felt a deep sense of responsibility towards Shirin and me, shouldering much of what needed to be done in our daily lives. I had to be careful not to take advantage of all that kindness and self-sacrifice and not to expect more from that young man than he was capable of.

Massoud would stand behind me, massage my neck and say, 'I'm afraid you will get sick working so hard. Go to bed and rest.'

And I would say, 'Don't worry, my dear. No one gets sick from hard work. The fatigue goes away with a good night's sleep and two days' rest each week. What makes you sick is idleness and useless thoughts and anxieties. Work is the essence of life.'

More than being my son, Massoud was my partner, my friend and my adviser. We talked about everything and we made decisions together. He was right, we didn't need anyone else. My only concern was that later in life, people would take advantage of his goodness and his willingness to give way; just as his sister could make him do anything she wanted with a kiss, a tear, or a plea.

Massoud acted like a responsible father towards Shirin. He went to enrol her in school, talked to her teachers, walked her to school every day and bought whatever she needed. During the air raids he would pick her up and hide her under the stairs. I delighted in their loving relationship, but unlike most mothers, I was not happy that they were growing up. In fact, it frightened me and my fear deepened as the war dragged on.

Every year, I told myself the war would end by next year and before Massoud would have to serve in the military, but the war wasn't ending. News of our neighbours' or friends' children having been martyred terrified me even more and learning that Gholam-Ali, Mahmoud's son, had been killed at the front made me lose heart. I will never forget the last time I saw him. I was shocked to see him standing at the front door. I had not seen him in many years. I don't know whether it was the army uniform or the strange glint deep in his eyes that made him look much older than he was. He was not the old Gholam-Ali.

I greeted him with surprise and said, 'Has something happened?'

'Does something have to happen for me to come and see you?' he asked reproachfully.

'No, my dear, you are always welcome. I was just surprised because this is the first time you have ever come here. Please come in.'

Gholam-Ali seemed uncomfortable. I poured him a cup of tea and started casually to ask about the family, but I said nothing about the uniform he was wearing or the fact that he had voluntarily enlisted in the army and had been at the front. I think I was afraid of talking about it. The war was steeped in blood, pain and death. When I finally stopped talking, he said, 'Aunt, I have come to ask for your forgiveness.'

'For what? What have you done, or what are you about to do?'

'You know I have been at the front,' he said. 'I am on leave and I will be going back. Well, it's war and, God willing, I may become a martyr. And if I am to be so fortunate, I need you to forgive me for the way my family and I have treated you and your sons.'

'God forbid! Don't say such things. You are just starting life. May God never bring the day that something bad happens to you.'

'But it won't be bad, it will be a blessing. It is my greatest wish.'

'Don't say these things,' I chided. 'Think about your poor mother. If she ever hears you talk like this she will be devastated . . . I really don't understand how she could let you go to war. Don't you know that the consent and approval of your parents is more important than anything else?'

'Yes, I know. But I have her approval. At first she kept crying and weeping. Then I took her to the hotel where some of the victims of war are housed and I said, "Look how the enemy has destroyed people's lives. It is my duty to defend Islam, my country and our people. Do you really want to stand in the way of my religious obligation?" Mother is really a woman of faith. I think her belief is far stronger than my father's. She said, "Who am I to challenge God? I am satisfied with his satisfaction."'

'Fine, my dear; but wait until you have finished school. God willing, the war will be over by then and you will be able to build a comfortable life for yourself.'

He snickered and said, 'Yes, just like my father. That's what you mean, isn't it?'

'Well, yes. What is wrong with that?'

'If no one else knows, you certainly do. No, that is not what I want! The front is something else. It is the only place where I feel close to God. You have no idea what it's like. Everyone willing to give his life, everyone sharing the same goal. No one talks about money and status, no one boasts, no one is after greater profit. It is a contest of devotion and self-sacrifice. You cannot imagine how the guys try to overtake each other to be on the front line. True faith is there, without hypocrisy, without deceit. It was there that I met true Muslims who put no value on worldly goods and material things. I am at peace when I am with them. I am close to God.'

I was looking down and thinking about the words of deep belief coming from that young man who had found his truth. Gholam-Ali's sad voice broke the silence.

'When I started going to Father's shop in the afternoons, the things he did troubled me. I was starting to question everything. You haven't seen the new house, have you?'

'No, I haven't. But I have heard it is very large and beautiful.'

'Yes, it's big,' he said. 'It's as big as you can imagine. You can get lost in it. But, Aunt, it is expropriated property, stolen, do you understand? With all his talk about faith and devoutness, I don't know how Father can live there. I keep telling him, "Father, this house is not religiously sanctioned; its rightful owner has not given his consent." And Father says, "The hell with its owner, he was a swindler and a thief and he ran away after the revolution. You are worried that Mr Thief doesn't approve?" The things he says and does confuse me. I want to run away. I don't want to be like him. I want to be a real Muslim.'

I kept him there for dinner. When he said his evening prayer, the purity of his faith and belief made me shiver. As we were saying goodbye, he whispered to me, 'Pray that I become a martyr.'

Gholam-Ali's wish came true and I grieved for a long time. But I could not bring myself to go to Mahmoud's house to extend my condolences. Mother was angry with me, saying that I had a heart of stone and harboured a grudge as stubbornly as a camel. But I just could not step into that house.

A few months later, I saw Ehteram-Sadat at Mother's house. She looked old and broken and her skin sagged on her face and neck. Seeing her, I started to cry. I hugged her, but I didn't know what to say to a mother who had lost her child and I muttered a customary condolence. She gently pushed me away and said, 'There is no need for condolences! You should congratulate me. My son has been martyred.'

I was stunned. I looked at her with disbelief and wiped away my tears with the back of my hand. How does one congratulate a mother who has lost her son?

When she left, I asked Mother, 'Is she really not pained by her son's death?'

'Don't say that!' Mother said. 'You have no idea how she is suffering. This is how she consoles herself. Her faith is so strong that it helps her tolerate the pain.'

'You are probably right about Ehteram, but I am sure Mahmoud has taken every advantage of his son's martyrdom to make a profit—'

'May God take my life! What are you saying, girl?' Mother scolded. 'They have lost their son and you are making wisecracks behind their back?'

'I know Mahmoud,' I said. 'Don't tell me he hasn't benefited from his son's death? It is impossible. Where do you think he gets all his money from?'

'He is a merchant. Why are you so jealous of him? Everyone has their share in life.'

'Come on, you know very well that honest and clean money doesn't pour in like this. Isn't Uncle Abbas a merchant, too? And he got started in business thirty years before Mahmoud. How come he still has that one shop and Ali who just got started is shovelling money in? I hear he has signed for a house worth several million tumans.'

'Now you're going after Ali? God be praised, some people are like my sons, clever and devout, and God helps them. Others are unlucky like you. That is how God wants it and you shouldn't be so resentful.'

I didn't go to see Mother for a long time. I often went to Mrs Parvin's house, but I never knocked on Mother's door. Perhaps she was right and I was jealous. But I could not accept that at a time when people were suffering from war and hardship, my brothers were increasing their wealth from one day to the next. No! It was not moral or humane. It was sinful.

*

I passed this quiet period in relative poverty, with hard work, and concern for the future.

A year after Siamak left, Hamid's mother passed away from a cancer that spread quickly. Her desire to die was palpable and I believed she herself was hastening the spread of her illness. Despite her critical condition, she did not forget us in her will and she made her daughters promise that they would not allow us to lose our home. I knew that Mansoureh had been instrumental in this, and later, she did everything she could to stay true to her mother's wish, standing firm against her sisters.

Mansoureh's husband was an engineer and he quickly demolished the old house, replacing it with a four-storey apartment building. During construction, he made every effort to circumvent our side of the garden so that we would not have to move. For two years we lived with dirt, dust and noise until that beautiful building was complete. There were two apartments, each one hundred metres square, on each floor, except for the third floor that was one large apartment where Mansoureh and her family lived. They gave us one of the apartments on the ground floor and Mansoureh's husband turned the other one into his office. Manijeh had the apartments on the first floor. She lived in one and rented the other one.

When Siamak found out that we had an apartment, he irritably said, 'They should have given us a second apartment so that you could rent it and have some income from it. Even that would have been half what is rightfully ours.'

'My dear boy,' I said laughing. 'You are still not giving up? It is very kind and caring of them to have given us this apartment. They certainly didn't have to do it. Think of it this way: we now have a beautiful new home and it did not cost us anything. We should be happy and grateful.'

Our apartment was finished before the others so that we could move into it and the other side of the garden could also be renovated. We were happy that we each had our own bedroom. Shirin was a bad room-mate and I was pleased to be free of her fun and games and messiness, while Shirin was delighted to be free of my tidiness and constant complaints. Massoud was thrilled with his bright and beautiful bedroom and still considered Siamak to be his room-mate.

The years were flashing by. Massoud was in the last year of school and the war still continued. Every year that he passed his final exams with excellent grades, my anxiety increased.

'What is your rush?' I griped. 'You can go slower and get your diploma a year or two later.'

'Are you suggesting that I fail?' he said.

'What is wrong with that? I want you to stay in school until the war ends.'

'God, no! I have to finish quickly and take some of the responsibility off your shoulders. I want to work. And don't worry about military service. I promise you I will be accepted at the university and I will have several more years before I have to serve.'

How could I tell him that he would not pass the universities' selection process?

Massoud graduated from school with excellent grades and studied day and night for the university entrance exams. By then he knew that given our family's past, there was little chance of his being admitted to a university. To console me and perhaps to boost his own morale he would say, 'I have no political record and everyone at school was pleased with me, they will support me.'

But it was useless. His application was rejected because of his family's past political involvements. When he heard the news, he pounded his fist on the table, hurled his books out of the window and wept. And I, who saw all my hopes for his future disappear, cried with him.

All I could think of was how to protect him from the war. In a few months he would have to report for military service. Siamak and Parvaneh called and said that I had to send Massoud to Germany by any means possible. But I could not convince him.

'I can't leave you and Shirin alone,' he argued. 'Besides, how would we come up with the money? You have only recently finished paying back what you borrowed for Siamak.'

'Money is not important. I will find a way. The important thing is to find someone trustworthy.'

And that was not a simple matter. The only lead I had was a telephone number and the code name 'Mrs Mahin'. I called, a man answered and said he was Mrs Mahin, but he did not have the same accent as the young man I had spoken to a few years earlier. Then he started asking strange questions and I suddenly realised that I was falling into a trap so I quickly hung up.

I asked Mansoureh's husband for help. A few days later, he told me the smugglers who had taken Siamak and Ardeshir across the border had all been arrested and severe border controls were now in force. And from others I heard about boys who had been arrested while trying to leave the country and about smugglers who had taken the money and abandoned the boys in the mountains or the desert.

'What's all the grieving for?' Ali said maliciously. 'Is your kid any better than other kids? Just like Gholam-Ali, they all have a duty to fight for their country.'

'The likes of you should fight because you benefit from the blessings of this country,' I retorted. 'We are strangers here, we have no rights. You have all the money, status and comfort, but my son, with all his talent, does not have the right to get an education and to work. He is rejected by every selection committee because of his relatives' beliefs, which he does not share. Now, tell me, in deference to which religion does he have to die for this country?'

At the time, my only logic was that of protecting my child and I was at a loss. I could not find a safe and reliable means of sending him out of the country. And Massoud would not cooperate at all and constantly argued with me.

'Why are you so panicked?' he asked. 'Two years of military service is not that long. Everyone has a duty to serve and I will serve, too. Afterwards, I can get a passport and leave the country legally.'

But I could not accept that.

'The country is at war! It's not a joke. What will I do if something happens to you?'

357

'Who says everyone who goes to war will be killed?' he said. 'There are all these kids coming back healthy and in one piece. In the end, there is a risk in whatever we do. Do you think escaping the country illegally is any less dangerous?'

'But many boys also die. Have you forgotten Gholam-Ali?'

'Come on, Mother. Don't make things so difficult. What happened to Gholam-Ali has terrified you, but I promise to come back alive. Besides, by the time I am called to serve and have finished my training period the war may have ended. And since when have you become such a coward? You are the only woman I know who is not afraid of the sirens and the air raids. You used to say, "The chance that our house will be hit is as great as us getting into a car accident, but we don't spend every day worrying about car accidents."'

'When you and Shirin are with me, I am not afraid of anything,' I explained. 'But you don't know the horror I feel when the sirens go off and I am not with you. And now, if they send me to the front with you, I will have no worries and no fears.'

'Really! What nonsense. Do you expect me to tell them I won't go anywhere without my mother? I want my mummy?'

It was always like this. Our arguments would end with jokes and laughter and a kiss on the cheek.

Finally, the day arrived when together with thousands of other young men Massoud left for military training. I tried to remain optimistic. My days and nights were like an open prayer rug before God and my hands were raised in supplication for the war to end soon so that my son could return home.

The conflict had been a part of our lives for seven years, but I had never so profoundly felt its horror. Every day, I witnessed the funeral processions for the martyrs and I wondered whether the number of casualties and wounded soldiers had suddenly increased, or whether there had always been that many. Wherever I went I now came across mothers in the same circumstances as me. It was as if I could instinctively identify them. Having surrendered to fate, we consoled each other in choked voices and with fear in our eyes, all knowing we were terrible liars.

Massoud completed his training period, but there was no sign of a miracle and the war didn't end. My efforts to have him assigned to a less dangerous location were useless, so one day I took Shirin's small hand and we went to see him off to the front. Dressed in his uniform, Massoud looked older and his kind eyes were filled with apprehension. I could not hold back my tears.

'Mum, please,' he said. 'You have to control yourself, you have to take care of Shirin. See how strong Faramarz's mother is, see how calmly the rest of the parents are saying goodbye to their sons?'

I turned and looked. To my eyes, the mothers were all weeping, even though they shed no tears.

'Don't worry, my dear,' I said. 'I will be fine. I will calm down in an hour and in a few days I will get used to you being away.'

He kissed Shirin and tried to make her laugh. Then he whispered to me, 'Promise me you will be as beautiful, healthy and strong by the time I come back.'

'And you promise me that you will come back unharmed.'

I kept my eyes on his face until the last possible moment and impulsively ran alongside the train as it moved out. I wanted to etch the lines of his image in my memory.

It took a week for me to accept the fact that Massoud was gone, but I did not get used to it. I not only missed him and worried about the danger he was in, but I felt his absence daily. With him gone, I suddenly realised how much of a partner he had been and what a heavy load he had lifted from my shoulders. I thought about how after a short time we selfishly deem someone's help to be their obligation and we forget their generosity. Now that I had to do everything on my own, I appreciated everything Massoud had done for me and my heart ached each time I did a task that used to be his.

'I was devastated when Hamid was executed,' I told Faati. 'But the truth is that his death had no effect on my everyday life, because he had never accepted any responsibilities at home. We mourned the passing of a loved one and a few days later returned to our normal routine. The absence of a man who helps and

359

participates in family life is far more tangible and to the same degree much harder to get used to.'

It took three months for us to learn how to live without Massoud. Shirin who had always been a cheerful girl didn't laugh as much and at least once a night she would find an excuse to sit and cry. I found my only peace in praying. I would sit at my prayer rug for hours, forgetting myself and everyone around me. I would even forget that Shirin had not had any dinner and I would not notice that she had fallen asleep on her schoolbooks or in front of the television.

Massoud called us whenever he could. Every time I talked to him my mind was at ease for twenty-four hours, but then anxiety would set in again and, like a stone rolling downhill, gain strength and speed with every minute that passed.

When two weeks had gone by with no news of him, I was beside myself with worry and I started calling the parents of his friends who had been sent to the front with him.

'My dear lady, it is too soon to be worried,' Faramarz's mother said matter-of-factly. 'I think the boy has spoiled you. It is not as if they are at their auntie's house and can call home whenever they want. Sometimes they are posted in areas where for weeks they don't have access to a bath, much less a telephone. Wait at least a month.'

A month with no news from a loved one who is under a shower of bullets and shells is difficult, but I waited. I tried to fill my days with work, but my mind would not cooperate and I could not concentrate.

Two months went by and I finally decided to make inquiries at the military department responsible. I should have done it sooner, but I was afraid of the answer I might have received. With trembling legs, I stood in front of the building. I had no choice; I had to walk in. I was directed to a large, crowded room. Men and women with pale faces and bloodshot eyes were standing in line for their turn to be told where and how their children had perished.

When I sat in front of the administrator's desk, my knees were shaking and the sound of my heart pounding was echoing so loudly in my ears that I could hardly hear anything else. For what seemed like an eternity, he leafed through his notebooks and then asked, 'What is your relationship with Private Massoud Soltani?' My mouth opened and closed several times before I was able to tell him I was his mother. He didn't seem to like my answer. He frowned, looked down and again leafed through his notebooks. Then, with feigned kindness and reverence, he asked, 'Are you alone? Is his father not with you?'

My heart was about to leap out of my throat. I swallowed hard, tried to hold back my tears and in a voice that sounded unfamiliar to me, I said, 'No! He has no father. Whatever it is, tell me!' And I half screamed, 'What is it? Tell me what has happened!'

'Nothing, ma'am, don't worry. Stay calm.'

'Where is my son? Why haven't I heard from him?'

'I don't know.'

'You don't know?' I cried. 'What does that mean? You sent him there and now you tell me you don't know where he is?'

'Look, dear mother, the truth is that there has been heavy military action in the region and parts of the border have exchanged hands. We still don't have accurate information about our troops, but we are investigating.'

'I don't understand. If you have taken back the territory, then you have found things there.'

I could not bring myself to say 'bodies', but he understood what I meant.

'No, dear mother, so far no body has been found with your son's identification tags. I have no further information.'

'When will you know more?'

'I don't know. They are inspecting the area. It is too soon to comment.'

A few people helped me get up from the chair, men and women who were waiting to hear similar news. A woman asked the person ahead of her to keep her place in the line and helped me as far as the door. The queue was just like the ones people stood in for subsidised food and supplies.

361

I don't know how I made my way back home. Shirin had still not returned from school. I paced the empty rooms and called out my sons' names. My voice reverberated through the apartment. Siamak! Massoud! And I repeated their names louder and louder as if they were hiding somewhere and calling them would make them answer me. I opened their closet. I smelled their old clothes and clutched them to my chest. I don't remember much else.

Shirin found me and called her aunts. They brought a doctor who gave me an injection of sedatives. Restless sleep and dark nightmares followed.

Sadegh Khan and Bahman continued to investigate. A week later, they said Massoud's name was on the list of soldiers missing in action. I couldn't understand what it meant. Had he turned to smoke and disappeared? Had my brave son perished in such a way that nothing remained of him? As if he never existed? No, it was not logical. I had to do something.

I remembered one of my colleagues saying that one month after his nephew disappeared in the war they found him in a hospital. I couldn't sit and wait for the bureaucrats. I wrangled with my thoughts all night long and in the morning I got out of bed having made a decision. I stood under the shower for half an hour to get rid of the effects of the sedatives and sleeping pills, got dressed and looked at myself in the mirror. So much of my hair had turned white. Mrs Parvin, who had stayed with me during those dark days, looked at me with surprise and said, 'What is going on? Where are you going?'

'I am going to search for Massoud.'

'You can't go alone! They will not let a lone woman go to a war zone.'

'But I can search the nearby hospitals.'

'Wait!' she said. 'Let me call Faati. Perhaps Sadegh Agha can arrange his work and go with you.'

'No. Why should that poor man neglect his life and work just because he is my brother-in-law?'

'Then ask Ali, or even Mahmoud,' she insisted. 'No matter what, they are your brothers. They won't leave you all alone.'

362

I laughed bitterly and said, 'You know that is rubbish. In the most difficult moments of my life they abandoned me more than any stranger would have done. Besides, I need to go alone. This way, I can take my time and search for my innocent child. If there is someone with me, I will end up having to come home, leaving my search unfinished.'

I took a train to Ahvaz. Most of the passengers were soldiers. I shared a compartment with a couple who were also searching for their son. The difference was that they knew he had been wounded and was in a hospital in Ahvaz.

Spring in Ahvaz was more like a scorching summer and it was there that after almost eight years I finally grasped the true meaning of war. The tragedy, the suffering, the devastation, the chaos. I saw no smiling face. There was commotion everywhere with people bustling about, but just like gravediggers and mourners at a burial, their movements and expressions were devoid of any joy or spirit, and a constant fear and veiled anxiety hovered deep in their eyes. Everyone I talked to was somehow bereaved.

I went from one hospital to another with Mr and Mrs Farahani whom I had met on the train. They found their son. He had been wounded in the face. The scene of the father and mother reuniting with their son was heart wrenching. I told myself, If Massoud has lost his face, I will recognise him by his little toenail. It wasn't important if I found him crippled and missing an arm or a leg. I just wanted him to be alive so that I could hold him in my arms again.

Seeing so many wounded, disabled and maimed young men shouting in pain drove me mad. My heart broke for their mothers and I wondered, Who is accountable? How could we have been so unaware, thinking that those air raids alone constituted the war? We had never understood the depth of the calamity.

I searched everywhere, going to different military offices and departments until I finally found a soldier who had seen Massoud on the night of the military operation. The young man's wounds were healing and he was about to be transferred to Tehran. Trying to smile reassuringly, he said, 'I could see Massoud, we were advancing together. He was a few steps in front of me when the explosions started. I was knocked unconscious. I don't know what happened to the others, but I have heard that most of the casualties and martyrs from our squadron have already been found and identified.'

It was useless. No one knew what had happened to my son. The phrase 'missing in action' was like a sledgehammer that kept pounding on my head. On my way back to Tehran, the load of pain I was carrying seemed a thousand times heavier. I went home in a daze and walked straight into Massoud's room as if I had forgotten to do something. I went through his clothes. I thought a few of his shirts needed ironing. Oh, my child's shirts were wrinkled! I started ironing as if it was the most important task I had. My entire focus was on the invisible wrinkles on his clothes. Each time I held them up to the light they still looked creased and I had to iron them again ...

Mansoureh was talking non-stop, but only a small part of my brain was aware of her presence. And then I overheard her say, 'Faati, it is worse like this. She is really losing her mind. She has been ironing the same shirt for two hours. It would have been better if they had told her he was martyred. Then she could at least mourn for him.'

I tore out of the room like a wild dog and screamed, 'No! If they tell me he is dead, I will kill myself. I am only alive with the hope that he is alive.'

But I, too, felt that I was not far from losing my sanity. I often found myself talking out loud to God. My relationship with him had severed; no, it had transformed into the hostile relationship between a merciless power and someone who had been beaten and had given up on life. A defeated person who had no hope of being saved and in her final moments had found the courage to say whatever was in her heart. I spoke with irreverence. I saw God as an idol that demanded sacrifice and I had to carry one of my children to the altar. I had to choose between them. I sometimes delivered Siamak or Shirin to be sacrificed instead of Massoud and then, with a guilty conscience and deep hatred for myself, I would again

364

grieve and ask myself, What would they think of me if they ever found out that I would sacrifice one of them for the other?

I was incapable of doing anything. Mrs Parvin had to bathe me by force. Mother and Ehteram-Sadat offered advice and talked about the honour and eminence of martyrs. Mother tried to instil a fear of God in me. 'You have to be content with his pleasure,' she said. 'Everyone has a fate. If this is his will, you have to accept it.'

But I went mad and screamed, 'Why should he give me this fate? I don't want it! Haven't I suffered enough? How long did I go from prison to prison, wash blood from my loved ones' clothes, mourn, work day and night, and raise my children despite a thousand miseries? All for what? For this?'

'Don't speak evil!' Ehteram-Sadat cried. 'God is testing you.'

'How long do I have to pass his tests? God, why do you keep testing me? Do you want to prove your power to someone as wretched as me? I don't want to pass your tests. I just want my child. Give me back my child and give me a fail grade!'

'May God spare you!' Ehteram-Sadat scolded. 'Don't raise God's wrath. Do you think you are the only one? All these mothers, every woman who has a son the same age as yours is in the same situation. Some have had four or five children martyred. Think about them and stop being so ungrateful.'

'Do you think I thank God when I see other people's misery?' I screamed. 'My heart breaks for them. My heart breaks for you. My heart breaks for myself for having lost my nineteen-year-old son and for not having even a corpse to hold in my arms ...'

I was starting to accept Massoud's death. That was the first time I mentioned his corpse. But those fights and arguments were making me feel much worse. I lost count of the days and months; I took sedatives by the fistful and thrashed about in a world between sleep and wakefulness.

One morning I woke up with my throat so dry that I thought I would choke. I made my way to the kitchen and saw Shirin washing dishes. I was surprised. I didn't like her to do housework with those tiny hands.

'Shirin, why aren't you in school?' I asked.

She stared at me with a reproachful smile and said, 'Mum, schools closed for the summer a month ago!'

I stood there aghast. Where had I been?

'What about your exams? Did you take the final exams?'

'Yes!' she said grudgingly. 'That was a long time ago. Don't you remember?'

No, I didn't remember and I didn't remember how thin, sallow and sad she had become. I had been so selfish. In all those months wallowing in my own sorrow, I had forgotten she existed; I had forgotten the little girl who was perhaps grieving as much as I was. I held her in my arms. It was as if she had long wished for that moment. She was trying to bury herself deeper in my embrace. We were both crying.

'Forgive me, my dear,' I said. 'Forgive me. I had no right to forget you.'

Seeing Shirin so unhappy, so thirsty for love and so helpless, pulled me out of my apathy and stupor. I had another child for whom I had to live.

Heartbroken and alone, I resumed my daily life. I tried to stay at work longer and drove myself harder. I could not concentrate on anything at home. I decided never to cry in front of Shirin. She needed a normal life, she needed fun and joy. That nine-year-old girl had been harmed enough. I asked Mansoureh to take her with them when they went to their villa on the Caspian coast. But Shirin didn't want to leave me alone and so I went with them.

The villa was the same as it had been ten years earlier and the northern coast, with the same beauty as before, was waiting to transport me back to the best days of my life. The sound of the boys playing together echoed in my ears. I felt Hamid's eager gaze following me. I sat for hours and watched him play with the children. Once I even picked up their ball and threw it back to them. These beautiful images would suddenly end with an intrusive sound. God, how quickly it had all passed. Those few days had been my share of a sweet family life. The rest had all been filled with pain and suffering.

Everywhere I looked brought back a memory. Sometimes I would instinctively open my arms to embrace my loved ones and I would suddenly come to, look around me with shock and wonder if anyone had seen me do that. One night, when I sat on the beach drowned in my thoughts, I felt Hamid's hand on my shoulder. His presence seemed so natural. I murmured, 'Oh, Hamid, I am so tired.' He squeezed my shoulder, I laid my cheek on his hand, and he gently stroked my hair.

Mansoureh's voice made me jump.

'Where have you been? I've been looking for you for an hour!'

I could still feel the warmth of Hamid's hand on my shoulder. I wondered, What sort of fantasy is it that seems this real? If madness means breaking with reality, I had reached it. It was so pleasant. I could surrender to it and live the rest of my life in sweet illusions, in the freedom of insanity. The temptation drove me to the edge of the cliff. It was only Shirin and my responsibility for her that forced me to resist taking the plunge.

I knew I had to go back home. I was suddenly afraid the fantasies would defeat me. On the third day, I packed my things and returned to Tehran.

One warm August day, at two in the afternoon, everyone at the office suddenly started running and shouting with joy. They were all congratulating each other. Alipour opened the door to my office and yelled, 'The war is over!' I didn't move from my chair. What would I have done if they had given me this news a year ago?

I had not gone to make enquiries at any military department in a long time. Even though as the mother of a soldier missing in action I was extended every courtesy, the officials' expressions of respect were as painful to hear as the insults I had endured behind the prison gates as the mother of a Mujahed and the wife of a communist. I could not tolerate them.

*

367

More than a month had passed since the end of the war. The schools had not yet reopened. At eleven in the morning, the door to my office flew open and Shirin and Mansoureh burst in. I leaped up in horror, afraid to ask what had happened. Shirin threw herself in my arms and started to cry. Mansoureh stood there staring at me with tears streaming down her face.

'Massoum!' she said. 'He is alive! He is alive!'

I fell in my chair, leaned my head back and closed my eyes. If I was dreaming, I wanted never to wake up. Shirin was slapping me with her small hands. 'Mum, wake up,' she pleaded. 'For the love of God, wake up.' I opened my eyes. She laughed and said, 'They called from headquarters. I talked to them myself. They said Massoud's name is on the list of prisoners of war; on the United Nations' list.'

'Are you sure?' I asked. 'You may have misunderstood. I have to go there myself.'

'No, you don't have to,' Mansoureh said. 'When Shirin came to my apartment in a state, I called them myself. Massoud's name and all his information is on the list. They said he will soon be exchanged.'

I don't know what I did. Perhaps I danced like a lunatic and genuflected in prayer on the floor. Fortunately, Mansoureh was there and pushed everyone out of my office so that they wouldn't see me behaving like a madwoman. I had to go somewhere holy. I needed to ask God's forgiveness for all my blasphemy; otherwise, I was afraid that happiness would run through my fingers like water. The closest place Mansoureh could think of was the Saleh Shrine.

At the shrine, I clung to the enclosure around the tomb and repeated over and over again, 'God, I was wrong, forgive me. God, you are great, you are merciful, you must forgive me. I promise to make up for all the prayers I have missed, I will give alms to the poor ...'

Now that I look back at those days, I realise I had really gone insane. I talked to God as a child talks to her playmate. I defined the rules of the game and I watched carefully to make sure neither one of us broke those rules. Every day I begged him not to turn away from me. Like a lover who had made up with her beloved after a long separation, I was both eager and scared. I constantly pleaded with him in the hope that he would forget my past ingratitude and understand my circumstances.

I was alive again. Joy had returned to my home. The sound of Shirin's laughter was once more ringing through the rooms. She would run and play, throw her arms around my neck and kiss me.

I knew that being a prisoner of war was harsh and gruelling, I knew Massoud was suffering, but I also knew that it would pass. All that mattered was that he was alive. I spent every day waiting for his freedom. I kept cleaning and tidying the house and rearranging his clothes. Months passed, each month becoming more difficult than the one before, but the hope of seeing him again kept me on my feet.

At last one summer night they brought my son home. For many days beforehand, the neighbourhood streets were decorated with lights and banners, congratulating him on his return, and flowers, sweets and syrups bathed our home with the scent of life. The apartment was crowded with people. I didn't know many of them. I was thrilled to see my cousin Mahboubeh and her husband. When I saw her father-in-law had also come, I wanted to kiss his hand. To me he was the personification of piety and love.

Mrs Parvin was in charge of the reception. Mansoureh, Faati, Manijeh and Firouzeh, who was now a beautiful young girl, had been busy for several days preparing everything. The day before, Faati had looked at me and said, 'Sister, colour your hair. If that boy sees you looking like this he will faint!'

I agreed. I would have agreed to anything. Faati coloured my hair and plucked my eyebrows. Firouzeh laughed and said, 'It's as if Auntie is getting married! She looks as beautiful as a bride.'

'Yes, my dear, it's as if it is my wedding. But it's much better than that. I wasn't as happy as this the day I got married.'

I put on a beautiful green dress. It was Massoud's favorite colour. And Shirin wore the pink dress I had just bought for her. By early afternoon we were both ready and waiting. Mother came with Ali and his family. Ehteram-Sadat also came. She looked shattered. Her repressed grief was growing deeper with time. I tried to avoid looking into her eyes. I was somehow ashamed that my child was alive and hers had died.

'Why did you bring Ehteram?' I asked Mother.

'She wanted to come. Is something wrong?'

'The envy in her eyes makes me uncomfortable.'

'What nonsense! She is not envious at all. She is a martyr's mother; her status is much higher than yours. God holds her in the highest esteem. Do you really think she would be jealous of you? No, my dear, she is actually very happy and you don't need to worry about her.'

Perhaps Mother was right, perhaps Ehteram-Sadat's faith was so strong that it kept her going. I tried to not think about her any more, but I continued to avoid her eyes.

Shirin kept lighting the small brazier for burning wild rue, but it kept going out.

It was past nine o'clock and I was running out of patience when the caravan arrived. With all the sedatives I had taken and all the time I had had to prepare for that moment, I started shaking violently and I fainted. How beautiful that moment was when I opened my eyes and found myself in Massoud's arms.

Massoud was taller but very thin and pale. The expression in his eyes had changed. What he had endured had matured him. He had a limp and was often in pain. From his behaviour, his insomnia and the nightmares he had when he did manage to sleep I realised how much he had suffered. But he did not like to talk about it.

Wounded and barely alive, he had been captured by the Iraqi army and treated at several hospitals. He still had wounds that had not healed. At times he suffered excruciating pain and broke into a fever. The doctor said his limp could be corrected by complicated surgery. After he had regained his strength he underwent the procedure and fortunately it was successful. I took care of him and fussed over him like a child. Every moment with him was precious to me. I would sit and watch him sleep. His handsome face looked like that of a child when he slept. I gave him the nickname God-given. God had really given him back to me.

Massoud slowly regained his physical health, but emotionally he was not the energetic and lively young man he used to be. He didn't draw or sketch any more. He had no plans for the future. Sometimes his friends, fellow soldiers and former cellmates came to see him and he would be distracted for a while. But again he would grow quiet and withdrawn. I asked his friends not to leave him alone. Among them there were men of every age.

I decided to discuss Massoud's depression with Mr Maghsoudi, who in time would come to play a pivotal role in my son's life. He was about fifty years old, had a kind face and seemed worldly; Massoud had a lot of respect for him. 'Don't worry,' he said. 'All of us were more or less the same way. And this poor boy was badly wounded, too. He will gradually recover. He has to start working.'

'But he is very talented and smart,' I said. 'I want him to study.'

'Of course he should. As a war veteran, he can go to university.'

I was ecstatic. I gathered his books and said, 'Well, recuperation time is over. You have to start planning for your future and finish everything that has been left unfinished. And the most important of these is your education. You have to start this very day.'

'No, Mum, it's too late for me,' Massoud said quietly. 'My brain doesn't work any more and I don't have the patience to study and prepare for the entrance exams. There is no way I would be admitted.'

'No, my dear. You can use the quotas and benefits that allow veterans to go to university.'

'What do you mean?' he asked. 'If I don't qualify academically, it doesn't make any difference whether I am a veteran or not. I will not be admitted.'

'If you study, you will be more qualified than anyone else,' I argued. 'And being able to get a university degree is a right they have given to all veterans.'

'In other words they have given me the right to take away some-one else's right. No, I don't want it.'

'You will be taking what is yours by right; a right that was unjustly taken away from you four years ago.'

'Just because they took my right from me back then, now I should do the same to someone else?' he contended.

'Right or wrong it is the law. Don't tell me you have got used to the law always being against you? My dear, sometimes it is for you. You have fought and suffered for these people and this country. Now these people and this country want to reward you. It's not right that you should reject.'

Our seemingly endless arguments finally ended with me as the victor. Of course, Firouzeh was very instrumental in this. She was in her last years of school and came over to the apartment every day with her books so that Massoud would help her with her homework, forcing him to study as well. Her kind and beautiful face brought the joy of life into Massoud's face. They studied, talked and laughed together. Occasionally, I would insist that they leave their books and go out for some fun.

Massoud applied to the Department of Architecture at the university. He was accepted. I kissed him and congratulated him. 'Between you and me, it wasn't my right,' he said, laughing, 'but I am very happy!'

Massoud's next problem was to find a job.

'It is embarrassing for a guy my age to still be a burden to his mother,' he often said. And a few times he even mumbled something about dropping out of university. I again turned to Mr Maghsoudi who had a relatively senior position at a ministry.

'Of course there is work for him,' he said with confidence. 'And it doesn't have to interfere with his studies.'

Massoud easily passed the required exams, the selection process and the interviews, which were mostly a formality, and he was hired. The stigma we had been branded with seemed to have been suddenly erased. Now, he was a precious gem. And as the mother of a war veteran, I was extended every respect and offered jobs and resources that at times I had to reject.

That drastic change was comical. What a strange world it was. Neither its ire nor its kindness had any substance.

CHAPTER NINE

My days were quiet and had a normal routine. My children were
all healthy, successful and busy with their work and education.
And we had no financial difficulties. I had a relatively good
income and Massoud was earning a higher than standard salary. As
he was a veteran, there was also financial aid available to him to
buy a car and a house. Siamak, who had finished his studies and
was working, constantly offered to help us financially.

After the war ended, Parvaneh started travelling to Iran regularly. Each time we saw each other, the distance of years vanished
and we returned to our youth. She was still funny and playful and
made me feel faint with laughter. I could never forget my debt to
her. For ten years, she had taken care of my son like a loving
mother. And Siamak still spent all his holidays with her family.
Parvaneh regularly filled me in on the details of his life and I would
close my eyes, trying to build in my mind the time I had lost with
my son. My longing to see him was the only sadness that occasionally darkened my horizon.

For two years, Siamak had been insisting that I go to Germany
to see him. But my concerns for Massoud and worries over Shirin,
who was still quite young, had stopped me. Finally, I could no
longer bear not seeing him and I decided to go. I was terribly nervous. The closer I got to the date of my departure the more restless
I became. I was surprised that I had endured ten years of being

away from him, becoming so immersed in the difficulties of life that days would pass without my even looking at his photograph.

Hamid used to say, 'Groundless stress and melancholy are characteristics of the bourgeoisie ... When your stomach is full, when you don't care about the misery of others, you dredge up these wishy-washy emotions.' Perhaps he was right, but I had always felt the pain of being separated from Siamak and because there was nothing I could do about it, I had stifled those emotions, not even admitting to myself how desperately I needed to see him. Now that there was relative calm in my life, I had the right to miss my son and long to see him.

When I was saying my goodbyes, Shirin looked troubled and with utter cheekiness said, 'I am not upset that you are leaving; I'm just upset that they didn't give me a visa.' She was a fourteen-year-old know-it-all who, confident of the love she received, impetuously said whatever came into her head. Despite her objections, I left her in the care of Massoud, Faati, Mansoureh and Firouzeh, and I flew to Germany.

I walked out of the customs section at Frankfurt airport and looked around with breathless anticipation. A handsome young man walked over to me. I stared at his face. Only his eyes and his smile looked familiar. The tousled locks of hair on his forehead reminded me of Hamid. Despite all the photographs of Siamak I had put on display around the house, I still expected to see an immature young boy with a thin neck. But he was now a tall, dignified man standing there with his arms wide open. I put my head on his chest and he held me tight. What profound pleasure it is to hide like a child in the arms of your offspring. My head barely reached his shoulder. I inhaled his scent and wept with joy.

It took a while for me to notice the beautiful young girl who was rapidly taking photographs of us. Siamak introduced her. I couldn't believe she was Lili, Parvaneh's daughter. I took her in my arms and said, 'You have grown up so much and you are so beautiful. I had seen your photographs, but they don't do you justice.' She laughed from the bottom of her heart.

We got into Siamak's small car and he said, 'We will first go to Lili's house. Aunt Parvaneh has prepared lunch and she is waiting for us. Tonight, or if you want tomorrow, we will go to the town where I live. It is two hours away.'

'Bravo!' I said. 'You haven't forgotten your Persian and you don't speak with an accent.'

'Of course I haven't forgotten. There are plenty of Iranians here. And Aunt Parvaneh refuses to talk to me if I speak in any language other than Persian. She is even more unrelenting with her own kids. Isn't she, Lili?'

On the way to Parvaneh's house I realised there was an attraction between Lili and Siamak that went beyond friendship and family ties.

Parvaneh's home was beautiful and cosy. She greeted us with great joy. Khosrow, her husband, had aged more than I expected. I said to myself, It's normal. It has been fourteen or fifteen years since I last saw him. He probably thinks the same about me. Their children had all grown up. Laleh spoke Persian with a thick accent and Ardalan who had been born in Germany could understand us, but would not reply in Persian.

Parvaneh insisted that we spend the night at their house, but we decided to drive to Siamak's home and visit Parvaneh again the following weekend. I wanted at least a week to become reacquainted with my son. God only knew how much we both had to talk about, but when we were finally alone I didn't know what to say, where to start and how to bridge the gap that years of separation had created. For a while, Siamak asked me about different family members and I would say they were well and send their love. And then I would ask, 'Is the weather always this nice here? You won't believe how hot it is in Tehran . . .'

It took twenty-four hours for the ice of unfamiliarity to melt and for us to start talking more intimately. Fortunately, it was the weekend and we had plenty of time. Siamak spoke about the hardships he had experienced after he left us, about the dangers he had faced when crossing the border, about his life in the

375

refugee camp, about starting university and finally about his job. I told him about Massoud, about what he had suffered, about the days when I thought he was dead and about his return. I talked about Shirin, her mischiefs and her feistiness that reminded me more of him than of Massoud. There was no end to our conversations.

On Monday, Siamak went to work and I went for a stroll around the neighbourhood. I was amazed at how big and beautiful the world was and I wanted to laugh at how trivially we think of ourselves as the centre of the universe.

I learned how to shop. Every day I cooked dinner and waited for him to come home, and every evening he took me out to show me a different sight. We never stopped talking, but we did stop discussing politics. He had been away for so long that he no longer had a clear understanding of the new environment and the real issues in Iran. Even the vocabulary and the expressions he used were outdated and reminded me of the early days of the revolution. The things he said sometimes made me laugh.

One day he got upset and said, 'Why are you laughing at me?'

'My dear, I am not laughing at you. It's just that some of the things you say are a bit odd.'

'What do you mean, odd?'

'They sound like things one hears on foreign radio stations,' I explained.

'Foreign radio stations?'

'Yes, the radio stations that transmit from outside the country; especially those that are owned by opposition groups. Just like you, they get the real and the false news all mixed up and use expressions that were common years ago. Any kid would know in a split second that they are transmitting from abroad. Sometimes the things they say are comical and, of course, annoying. By the way, are you still a Mujahedin sympathiser?'

'No!' he said. 'To be honest, I cannot accept or comprehend some of the things they do.'

'Such as?'

'Joining forces with the Iraqi army and attacking Iran; fighting against Iranian troops. Sometimes I wonder what would have happened if I had stayed with them and come face to face with Massoud on the battlefield. It is a recurring nightmare that jolts me awake in the middle of the night.'

'Thank God you came to your senses,' I said.

'Not all that much. These days, I think a lot about Dad. He was a great man, wasn't he? We should be proud of him. There are a lot of people here who share his beliefs. They say things about him that I never knew. They really want to meet you and hear you talk about him.'

I looked at him warily. That old dilemma was still plaguing his soul. I didn't want to distort the image he had of his father and rob him of the pride he felt, but I saw that need and dependence as a reflection of his immaturity.

'Look, Siamak, I have no patience for that sort of theatre,' I said. 'You know I did not share your father's beliefs. He was a kind and decent man, but he had faults and shortcomings, too. The biggest was his one-sided point of view. To him and those who shared his politics, the world was divided in two. Everyone was either with them or against them, and everything that had to do with the opposing group was bad. Even in the arts, they considered only artists who shared their perspective to be true artists; everyone else was an idiot. If I said I liked some singer or thought someone was a good poet, your father would argue that the singer or poet supported the Shah or was anti-communist, therefore his work was rubbish. He would actually make me feel guilty for enjoying a song or a poem!

'They had no personal opinions and individual preferences. Do you remember the day Ayatollah Taleghani died? Our neighbours, Mr and Mrs Dehghani, who were supporters of a leftist faction, kept coming to our house and calling because they didn't know what to do. Before his death the Ayatollah had spoken against the people who had rioted in Kurdistan and they didn't know how to react to his death. All day long they chased after the leftist leaders to learn whether they should mourn or not. Finally orders came that the Ayatollah had been a supporter of the people and his death should be mourned. Mrs Dehghani suddenly burst into tears and went into deep mourning! Remember?'

'No!' Siamak said.

'But I do. I want you to rely on your own thoughts and beliefs, to weigh the good and bad of everything by reading and learning, and then make decisions and draw conclusions. Sheer ideology will trap you, it will make you prejudiced, it will obstruct individual thought and opinion, and create bias. And ultimately, it will turn you into a one-dimensional fanatic. Now, I would be happy to say all this to your friends as well, and I will list their and your father's mistakes for them.'

'Mum, what are you saying?' Siamak said crossly. 'We have to keep his memory alive. He was a hero!'

'I am tired of heroisms,' I said. 'And my memories of the past are so bitter that I don't want to relive them. Besides, you should forget all this and instead think about your future. Your life is ahead of you, why do you want to drown yourself in the past?'

I don't know to what extent Siamak accepted what I said or if it had any effect on him, but neither one of us ever expressed any interest in talking about politics again.

I asked him about Parvaneh and her family so that I could find out more about the secret he was harbouring in his heart. And he finally opened up to me.

'You can't imagine how kind and smart Lili is,' he said. 'She is studying business management. She will finish this year and start working.'

'Are you in love with her?' I asked.

'Yes! How did you know?'

I laughed and said, 'I found out at the airport. Mothers are quick to pick up on these things.'

'We want to get engaged, but there are problems.'

'What problems?'

'Her family. Of course, Aunt Parvaneh is wonderful. She has been like a mother to me and I know she loves me. But in this case, she is taking her husband's side.'

'What does Khosrow say?'

'I don't know. He doesn't approve and puts strange constraints and conditions on us. He thinks the same way Iranian men thought a hundred years ago. You would never know he had studied and lived here for so many years.'

'What does he say?' I asked.

'We want to get engaged and he says, "No, you can't!"'

'Is that it? Don't worry, I will talk to them and see what the problem is.'

Parvaneh had no objections. In fact she was happy about Siamak's relationship with Lili.

'Siamak is like my own son,' she said. 'He is Iranian, he speaks our language and we understand each other. I am always afraid that my children will marry a German with whom I cannot develop any sort of a relationship. I know everything about Siamak; I even know who his ancestors were. He is smart, has studied well, is now successful and has a bright future ahead of him. Most important of all, he and Lili love each other.'

'Then what is the problem?' I asked. 'It seems Khosrow Khan doesn't agree with you.'

'Yes, he does. The problem is that we and the children think differently. We are still Iranian and cannot accept certain things, but our children grew up here and cannot understand our point of view. And these two keep talking about a long engagement.'

'Parvaneh, I am surprised at you! Even if they want to stay engaged for a year, what is wrong with that? It is now common in Iran. Maybe they want to get to know each other better, maybe they want to save some money before they get married, or maybe they just want to give themselves more time.'

'You are so simple!' she exclaimed. 'Do you know what they mean by a long engagement? They mean an informal marriage. Like some of the kids around them, they want to live together. And their definition of "long" is at least five years, after which they will decide whether they still want to be together or not. If they do, they will make the marriage official; otherwise, they will separate. And they don't mind if they end up having a child. If they separate, one of them will take the kid!'

My eyes were wide with disbelief. 'No!' I said, stunned. 'I don't think this is what they mean by a long engagement.'

'Yes, my dear, it is. Every single night, Lili and Khosrow get into a fight over it. To be honest, Khosrow will never be able to accept this. And I don't think you would expect him to.'

'Of course not!' I said, flabbergasted. 'How dare they? If Mahmoud and the others only knew! Now I understand why Khosrow Khan has been so cold and distant. The poor man! I am surprised at Siamak. He seems to have forgotten where he comes from. Has he really become that much of a Westerner? In Iran a simple conversation between a boy and a girl can still lead to bloodshed and this gentleman wants to live with someone's daughter for five years without marrying her? Of all impossible things!'

That night we sat and talked into the early hours of the morning. Siamak and Lili argued about the value of getting to know each other before marrying and the worthlessness of a piece of paper, and we argued about the value of a properly-structured family, the necessity for an official marriage and respect for the ties of kinship. Finally, we came to the conclusion that, for our sake, the children should go through with the 'irrelevant and idiotic' process of marriage and if ever they felt they no longer suited each other they could void that piece of paper and get a divorce. We also decided that they should get married while I was there and as soon as they had set up their home and were ready to start their life together.

'I am truly grateful!' Khosrow said. 'You can't imagine what a weight you have lifted from my shoulders.'

'It really is a strange world,' I replied. 'I still cannot digest any of this.'

The beauty and sweetness of my trip was made complete with Lili and Siamak's wedding. I was delighted to have a daughter-in-law who was kind, intelligent, charming and Parvaneh's daughter. I was enjoying myself so much that I didn't want to go back home.

The wonderful memories of that time will stay with me for ever.

My best souvenirs were all the photographs that later adorned the walls, shelves and tables in my home.

The good years pass quickly. In the blink of an eye, Shirin was in the last year of school and Massoud was finishing his last term at the university. He was terribly busy preparing his final project and thesis, and his responsibilities at work had increased. But his recent silence had nothing to do with any of this. There was something weighing on his mind and I could tell he wanted to talk to me but was hesitating. I was surprised; we had always been open and comfortable with each other. Still, I let him wrestle with his doubts. Finally one night when Shirin had gone to a friend's birthday party he came and sat next to me and said, 'Mum, would you be very upset if I decide to leave you and Shirin and live in a separate house?'

My heart sank. What had happened for him to want to leave us? Trying to remain calm, I said, 'Every child will one day leave his parents, but it all depends on the reason why.'

'For example, marriage.'

'Marriage? You want to get married?' I asked, surprised. 'Oh my dear, that is wonderful! It is my dream.'

The truth was that I had thought a lot about Massoud getting married. For years I had dreamed of the day he would marry Firouzeh. They had liked each other and had been close ever since they were children.

'Thank God,' Massoud said. 'I was afraid you wouldn't approve.'

'Why wouldn't I? Congratulations! Now tell me, when should we have the wedding ceremony?'

'Slow down, Mum! First I have to ask for her hand and see if she will agree to become my wife.'

'Nonsense!' I exclaimed. 'Of course, she will agree. Who better than you? They have loved you ever since you were a little boy. And on several occasions they even made veiled comments about why you were not stepping forward. Poor Firouzeh was worse than all of them. She never managed to hide her secret from me. It is always there in her eyes. Oh that dear girl! She will make a beautiful bride.'

Massoud stared at me and said, 'Firouzeh? What are you talking about? Firouzeh is like a sister to me, like Shirin.'

I was shocked. How could I have been so wrong? That close relationship, those meaningful looks, those long hours of sharing confidences: were they all rooted in fraternal affection? I cursed myself for having spoken so rashly.

'Then, who is she?' I asked, trying hard to regain my composure. But still, there was a coldness rippling in my voice.

'Mina's cousin, Ladan,' Massoud said. 'She is twenty-four; she is beautiful. She is from a well-respected family. Her father has retired from the Ministry of Transportation.'

'Of course I know who they are. How long has this been going on, you rascal? How come you never peeped a word?'

I started to laugh. I wanted to make up for my initial coldness. Just like a child, my laughter cheered him up and he started to talk.

'I met her three months ago and it has only been a month since we expressed our feelings for each other.'

'You have known her for only three months and you have already decided to marry her? It must be a high fever!'

'Mum, why would you say such a thing? Some men ask for a girl's hand in marriage without having even seen her.'

'Yes. But, my son, we have two kinds of marriage. One is based on logic and particular conditions, and the other one is based on love. A traditional marriage, when someone makes introductions and there is a formal request for a girl's hand, is the first kind. In that case, the circumstances of both sides are looked into, both families articulate their expectations, the elders weigh the conditions, compromises are made, and only when they are certain that there is potential, they involve the young couple and they see each other a few times. If they like each other, they will get married with the hope that they will grow to love one another.

'But in a marriage based on love, two people develop deep feelings for each other and don't pay much attention to anything else. Because of their love, they turn a blind eye to things that may be missing in their relationship and they adjust. If they face objections, they accept the responsibility and stand up to others, and regardless of any logical and rational arguments, they get married. It seems your plan fits this second model. In which case, the couple should get to know each other very well and make certain that their love is strong and enduring enough to make up for any lack of compatibility and withstand the disapproval of others. Now, don't you think three months is not enough time to develop such a deep bond and to achieve true love?'

'I'm sorry, Mum, but you are philosophising again,' Massoud said impatiently. 'I want my marriage to be a mix of the two kinds you described. Why can't we be in love and have the right conditions, too? I think the problem is that you don't know anything about love. According to you, even two or three days after your wedding, you still hadn't had a chance to take a good look at your husband. Therefore, I don't think you can be a fair judge of love. Ladan says, "Love is like an apple that falls in your lap. It happens in a split second." See how beautiful her interpretation of love is? She is so sensitive and stunning. You must meet her.'

My heart ached. I wanted to tell him there was a time when I would have given my life for the one I loved. But I checked myself and instead said, 'What do I know about love? What do you know about me? As Forough wrote, "All my wounds are from love."'

'But you never said anything.'

'And I haven't said anything now. Just know that you are not the only one here who is familiar with love.'

'Well, what are you suggesting we do?'

'I am not suggesting you do anything. You have to give yourselves time, test your love and let it temper.'

'We don't have time,' Massoud argued. 'She has a suitor. They have asked for her hand and her parents might marry her off any day. We will lose each other for ever!'

'This itself is a test,' I said. 'If she really loves you, she will not be goaded into marriage.'

'You don't know her circumstances; her family is pressuring her. You of all people should understand.'

'My son, she is an educated and intelligent girl, and from what you have told me, her parents are sensible people. They are very different from your grandparents thirty years ago. If she tells them she does not want to get married straight away, they will understand and they will not force her into it. Things are very different now.'

'What is different?' Massoud argued. 'Our culture is still the same culture. Families still think a girl's only objective in life is to get married and they can force her into it. In fact, her parents wanted to marry her off when she was eighteen, but she resisted.'

'Then she can resist again for one more year,' I said patiently.

'Mum! Why are you taking sides? Why don't you just say you don't want me to marry her?'

'I won't say that. I haven't even met this girl. She may be a wonderful person. All I am saying is wait.'

'We don't have time to wait!'

'Fine,' I said, irately. 'Then would you please tell me what it is I am supposed to do?'

He jumped up and put a piece of paper in front of me.

'This is their telephone number. Call them right away and arrange to go there the day after tomorrow.'

I was confused. On the one hand, I scolded myself not to do as he asked. On the other hand, I wondered if I was taking sides against a girl I had never met. I remembered how Mother had dragged her heels and delayed everything when Mahmoud said he wanted to marry Mahboubeh. Besides, this was the first time my son had so passionately asked me for something. I shouldn't say no. And still, the image of Firouzeh, Faati and Sadegh Khan's disappointed faces would not fade away from my mind. What a blow this would be to them!

'Are you sure you don't want to think about this a little longer?' I asked.

'No, Mum, her father said if there is someone else, he should step forward by the end of the week, otherwise Ladan will marry the suitor they have selected for her.'

I had no choice. I picked up the telephone and called. They immediately knew who I was. Obviously, they had been waiting for my call.

Massoud was happy. It was as if a weight had been lifted off his shoulders. He kept hovering over me.

'Come on, let's go buy pastries for tomorrow,' he said. 'It's getting late!'

I wasn't in the mood and I hadn't finished my work, but I thought if I said no, he would interpret it as another sign of my disapproval. I didn't want to take his happiness away from him. In the car, he talked non-stop, but all I could think about was Firouzeh and Faati. Wasn't it Firouzeh's presence that had brought him back to life and reawakened his interest in his education? Then, what had happened? I who claim to know my son so well, was I so terribly wrong?

With her usual perceptiveness and mischief, Shirin quickly picked up on Massoud's unusual mood.

'What is going on?' she asked. 'The gentleman is jumping with joy!'

'Nothing is going on,' I said. 'Tell me about the birthday party. Did you have fun?'

'It was excellent. We played plenty of music and danced. By the way, I have to invite everyone over. I must have a birthday party. I have gone to everyone's house, but I have never thrown a party. How about next month?'

'But your birthday is in the summer!' I said.

'It doesn't matter. I just need an excuse. Nothing ever happens here anyway, I might as well invite my friends.'

'Perhaps something will happen and you will be able to invite your friends to a wedding,' I said.

With her eyes wide, Shirin turned and stared at Massoud. 'A wedding? Whose wedding?'

'My wedding,' Massoud said. 'Your brother's wedding. Would you like it if I got married?'

'You? Get married? No, to be honest, I wouldn't like it,' Shirin said bluntly. 'But I guess it depends on who she is.'

'We don't know her,' I said. 'They met and took a liking to each other.'

'Don't tell me it's that cheeky girl who calls here all the time,' Shirin snapped. 'It's her, isn't it? I knew something was going on. Mum, you know, she's the pest who calls and hangs up.'

Massoud blushed and retorted, 'What do you mean by "pest"? She is shy. When she calls and someone else answers the telephone, she gets embarrassed and hangs up.'

'Shy?' Shirin scoffed. 'Sometimes she does talk. She shamelessly asks, "Is Massoud Khan home?" And when I ask for her name she coyly says she will call back later. She sounds so conceited!'

'That's enough!' Massoud chided. And then he turned to me and said, 'By the way, we should order flowers for tomorrow. And remember to wear something elegant ...'

I looked at him with surprise and said, 'You sound like you have done this a hundred times! You know the routine very well.'

'Not really,' he said. 'Ladan told me what we need to do to please her parents.'

'I'm coming, too!' Shirin announced.

'No,' I said. 'You can come the next time we go to see them.'

'Why? I have to see her. I am the sister-in-law and I have to approve of her!'

'Not when the sister-in-law is still a kid,' Massoud replied.

'I am not a kid! I am eighteen years old. Mum, would you please say something?'

'Massoud,' I said, 'what is wrong with her coming along? Usually, it's the suitor's mother and sister who go to ask for the girl's hand. And stop calling her a kid. I was already a mother when I was her age.'

'No, Mum, not now, it's not prudent. She can come next time.'

Shirin sulked and cried but none of it made Massoud change his mind. Apparently, he had received orders from above and non-compliance was not an option.

The basket of flowers was so large that it wouldn't fit in the car. We finally managed to put it in the boot, but we had to leave the door open.

'Did you have to buy such a huge basket of flowers?' I asked.

'Ladan said, "You have to bring as large a bouquet as possible so that it will stand out among the ones others have brought."'

'What a stupid thing to say!'

Their house was old and sprawling. The rooms were all furnished with antiques and there was one of every china vase I had ever seen in stores or elsewhere. The sofas and chairs were in the classical style, with high legs, gold-leafed armrests, and red, yellow and orange upholstery. There were replicas of old paintings in heavy, ornate gold-coloured frames and red curtains with tassels and gold-coloured lining ... The house looked more like a hotel or a restaurant than a cosy and comfortable home.

Ladan's mother was about the same age as me, with bleached-blonde hair and full make-up. She was wearing high-heeled sandals and no stockings, and she smoked one cigarette after the other. Her father was dignified-looking with salt and pepper hair and a pipe in the corner of his mouth. He constantly talked about his family, their former prestige and status, their important relatives and their trips overseas.

I mostly listened and the night passed with simple introductions and casual conversation. I could tell they were waiting for me to bring up the more important topic that had brought us together, but I felt it was too soon. When I asked to use the bathroom, Ladan's mother insisted that she take me to one of the bathrooms in the section of the house where their private rooms and bedrooms were. She wanted me to see the rest of their home. But even in the family room, all the seats were gaudily upholstered and I didn't see a single comfortable chair. To be polite, I said, 'You have a beautiful home.'

'Would you like to see the rest of the rooms?' she asked eagerly.

'No, no thank you. I won't intrude.'

'Oh, please! Come with me.'

And with her hand on my back she half pushed me towards the bedrooms. Although I hated this, a mix of curiosity and wickedness made me go along with her. The curtains in all the rooms were heavy and expensive, adorned with ribbons and tassels. The rest of the furnishings were equally ornate and in the same style.

'Why didn't you say anything?' Massoud complained on the way home.

'Say what? It was just our first meeting.'

He turned away from me and didn't speak another word.

At home, Shirin was still not talking to Massoud. Instead, she addressed me and said, 'Well, tell me all about it! What went on in the stone castle?'

'Nothing special,' I said.

Already angry at having been excluded, she griped, 'Fine, don't tell me! I'm an outsider, a stranger; I'm not even a human being. You think I'm a child, a spy, you hide everything from me.'

'No, my dear. That is not true,' I said consolingly. 'Let me get changed and I will tell you all about it.'

She followed me to my bedroom and sat on the bed with her legs crossed.

'So, tell me!'

'You ask and I will answer,' I said while taking off my dress.

'What is the girl like?'

As hard as I tried to think of a striking characteristic in her, nothing came to my mind. I hesitated and said, 'She is a little short. A little shorter than me, but a lot heavier.'

'You mean she is fat?'

'No, just plump. Well, I'm skinny; someone who is heavier than me isn't necessarily fat.'

'And what about the rest?'

'I think she has fair skin. But she was wearing a lot of make-up and the room wasn't very bright so I couldn't really tell. I think she has brown eyes. She has dyed her hair light brown, closer to blonde.'

'Oh! What was she wearing?'

'A tight black skirt, above the knees, with a black, pink and purple patterned jacket.'

'Straight hair?'

'I don't think so. She had curled it, but there were a few too many curls.'

'Great!' she exclaimed. 'What an enchantress! And what about Mummy and Daddy?'

'Don't talk like that, it's not nice. They seem quite respectable. Her mother is about the same age as me; well, she was wearing a lot of make-up, too. But she was dressed very elegantly. And their house is filled with fine china, antiques, tasselled curtains and classic gold-coloured furniture.'

'This gentleman, who had turned into such a fanatic after the war that he got upset if I wore a tiny bit of make-up and constantly complained about my headscarf being too far back on my head, now wants to marry that kind of girl? And with his Hezbollahi friends?'

'To be honest, I don't understand it at all,' I said. 'Everything seems to have turned upside down.'

'Well, despite all this, did you like her?'

'What can I say?'

Just then I turned and saw Massoud leaning against the door, watching me with eyes full of reproach and hurt. He shook his head and without saying a word he went to his room.

With every meeting, the profound differences between our two families became more evident and I saw how incompatible Massoud and Ladan were. But Massoud saw none of it. He was so infatuated that he was blind to everything around him. He was wary of talking to me and I kept silent. The only words we exchanged on the subject were about our back and forth visits. With no comment or discussion, I went with him and listened to the conversations.

I learned that for their older daughter, Ladan's parents had requested a marriage portion of a hundred gold coins, but their son-in-law had promised them double that. I learned where the family had purchased the wedding ring for Ladan's maternal cousin who had recently married, how much they had paid for the wedding dress, and which gem was used in the jewellery set her paternal cousin wore at the ceremony.

Of course, I knew it wasn't all true; sometimes the stories were contradictory. 'Oh, you are so lucky,' I once said in utter meanness. 'In the past few weeks you have gone to at least ten weddings!' They grew quiet and looked at each other. I could tell they were getting bored. But then they started arguing about whether it was better to have a wedding in the summer or the autumn.

I didn't know what to do. The more I tried, the harder it was for me to warm to that girl and the more impossible it seemed to establish a normal relationship with those superficial people who were completely preoccupied with money, clothes, hairstyles and make-up. Still, I didn't want to have a talk with Massoud. I was afraid that any comment or observation I made would be construed as my taking a defensive position. He had to discover the incompatibilities on his own.

Finally, under pressure from Ladan, Massoud broached the subject and, with a resentment and coldness that I had never heard in his voice, said, 'Well, Mum, how long do you want to drag out this game?'

'Which game?'

'Your refusal to talk about me and Ladan and our plans.'

'What would you like me to say?'

'Your opinion!'

'But I am more interested in your opinion,' I said. 'I think you have got to know Ladan's family a little. What do you think of them?'

'What do I care about her family?' he said. 'It is her I love.'

'Everyone grows up in a family and shares the same background and upbringing.'

'And what is wrong with their background? They have a lot of class.'

I paused. That word didn't exist in Massoud's vocabulary.

'What do you mean when you say, "They have class"? In your opinion, what sort of people have class?'

'I don't know!' he said irritably. 'What kind of question is that? They are respectable people.'

'Why do you think they are respectable people? Because they have a lot of antiques? Because instead of thinking about comfort and beauty, they surround themselves with things that are just expensive? Because they constantly talk about clothes and hair

390

colour? Or because they always talk behind each other's backs and are obsessed with their rivalries?'

'But you love beautiful things, too,' Massoud argued. 'You always complain that my shirt and trousers don't match and for every piece of furniture you go to a hundred different stores.'

'My dear, appreciating beauty and wanting your home to be handsomely furnished is a reflection of a passion for life and I have nothing against it at all. Everyone's life is a mirror image of their taste, their thinking and their culture.'

'So seeing their house you realised that there is something wrong with their thinking and culture?'

'Didn't you?'

'No!'

'Have you ever seen even a small bookshelf in that house? Have you ever seen one of them read a book? Have they ever talked about a scholarly work or a piece of art or an antique without mentioning its monetary value?'

'That is nonsense! Not everyone puts their books on display. And why would you even go looking for their books?'

'Because I want to see what their intellectual leanings are.'

'Come on! We have books from every order, sect and side. Who would know what our intellectual leanings are?'

'Someone who is a thinker and an intellectual.'

'How?'

'On a communist's bookshelf there are books on that ideology, from the basic to the advanced. His novels are mostly by Maxim Gorky and other Russian writers. And he has the works of Romain Rolland and the like. He has very few books on other philosophies and ideologies. A non-communist intellectual's shelves include a couple of basic books on communist theory, which have been abandoned half read. The rest of the books would be what the communists describe as "bourgeois books" ...

'Having Ali Shariati's books in your library doesn't mean you have strong leanings towards Islam, because after the revolution everyone bought his books. But the libraries of ardent Muslims are packed with prayer books, books on Islamic theory and philosophy, books on religious guidance and the like. In contrast, the book-shelves of nationalists are filled with biographies of politicians and an assortment of books on Iranian history. In addition, every well-educated person has a few books on their field of study and area of expertise.'

'But why do you care so much about their intellectual and political leanings?'

'Because my entire life has been affected by various political groups and their beliefs, and I want to know who I am dealing with this time.'

'But you are against politics and you keep making us promise not get involved in it,' Massoud argued.

'Yes, but have I ever told you not to read and learn? Like every intelligent person, you have to understand different schools of thought so that you can tell right from wrong and not become a tool in the hands of those seeking power. Has Ladan ever talked to you about something she has read or any ideas or points of view she has? You are a talented artist. Do you two share any likes or dis-likes when it comes to the arts? And most important of all, with the religious beliefs you developed after being a prisoner of war, how do you want to come to terms with a family whose only notion of Islam is a commemoration dinner in honour of Imam Abolfazl, which they host as if it were a wedding? They are sup-porters of the Shah, waiting for the Crown Prince to return. Not because of their political beliefs, but because drinking alcohol was allowed and they could wear bikinis on the beach. With our back-ground, what do you think we would have to talk about? My dear Massoud, this girl has nothing in common with you. She will never even dress the way you would like her to. You will have a fight every time you want to go out.'

'Don't worry,' he countered, 'she said she would even wear a chador if I asked her to.'

'And you believed her? But even that wouldn't be right. A person who has a solid character and her own thoughts and prin-ciples shouldn't be so irresolute.'

'So the poor girl is now irresolute, too?' he snapped. 'And she only said it because of her love for me. No, Mother, you are looking for excuses. You think everyone is bad except us.'

'No, my dear, I never said that. I am sure they are very good people; perhaps even better than us. But they are very different.'

'No, that is just an excuse.'

'You asked for my opinion and I gave it to you. This is about your life, your future and you know that is what matters most to me.'

'Mum, I love her. Something happens to me when she talks, when she laughs. I have never met a woman as feminine as her. She is different.'

I was astounded. Yes, he was right. How could I have not seen it? Massoud was fascinated by that girl because she was different from all the other women in his life. She flaunted the femininity that the women around him had always tried to conceal. To be fair, there was a certain coquettishness in her manner, in every move she made, even in her voice over the telephone. She was seductive and alluring. Simply put, she was a temptress. It was only natural that my inexperienced son who had hardly ever seen such feminine qualities was so affected by them. But how could I make him understand that the attraction he felt was far from love and not the right foundation to build a life on? Under those circumstances, no amount of words or logic would work and they would only make him more stubborn and defensive.

'My greatest wish is my children's happiness,' I said. 'And I believe that happiness is hinged on a marriage filled with love and understanding. I respect your love and I will do whatever you ask, even if it is against my wish. My only condition is that you stay engaged for one year. You will get to know each other better because you will be freer to spend time together. In the meantime, we can save and prepare for a wedding that would suit them; as you can see, they have high expectations.'

Despite their initial objections, Ladan's family finally gave in to my determination and agreed to a long engagement. I was certain their concerns were not because of any religious beliefs; they simply wanted to make certain the marriage would take place. They decided to have an elaborate engagement party so that everyone in their large family could meet the future groom and they set the date for the following week. I couldn't hide the issue any more. I had to let everyone know. But how was I going to tell Faati, Firouzeh and Sadegh Agha?

One morning, I went to see Faati and started talking about fate, destiny and God's will. She listened for a while, then looked at me with suspicion and asked, 'Sister, what is going on? What are you trying to tell me?'

'You know, I always dreamed of coming here one day to talk about Firouzeh and to ask for her hand for Massoud. But God doesn't seem to want that to happen.'

Faati's face darkened and she said, 'I've had a feeling that something is going on. Now tell me, is it God that doesn't want it or is it you?'

'How can you say such a thing? I love Firouzeh more than I love Shirin. This was my greatest wish and I always considered it a done deal. But I don't know why this boy has suddenly lost his mind and fallen in love. He stubbornly says, "I want her," and he forced me to go ask for the girl's hand. And now they are getting engaged.'

I saw Firouzeh's shadow. She was standing frozen in the doorway, holding the tea tray. Faati ran and took the tray from her. Firouzeh stared at me with eyes that silently asked, Why? Her face was filled with disappointment and sorrow, but slowly, shades of anger and insult appeared as well. Then she turned around and ran to her room.

'Ever since she was a child, you went around saying Firouzeh belongs to Massoud,' Faati said angrily. 'And they always had such a wonderful relationship with each other. You cannot tell me Massoud did not like her.'

'He did, very much, and he still does. But he says his feelings for her are fraternal.'

Faati laughed and walked out of the living room. I knew there was a lot she wanted to say, but she was holding her tongue out of respect for me. I followed her to the kitchen.

'My dear, you have every right to be angry,' I said. 'I am losing my mind over this. All I have managed to do is to delay the ridiculous wedding. They are supposed to stay engaged for a year and I am hoping this boy's eyes will open.'

'Well, he has fallen in love and hopefully they will have a happy life. And you shouldn't be like a nasty mother-in-law and hope for their separation even before they have got engaged.'

'But, Faati, you don't know,' I sighed. 'If they had just one thing in common, I wouldn't feel so terrible. You cannot imagine how different they are. I am not saying she is a bad girl, but she is not for us. You will come and see for yourself. As a matter of fact, I would appreciate your opinion. Perhaps I have misjudged her because I was against it from the start. But I am very good; I don't say anything. Shirin, on the other hand, refuses to even look at the girl. If Massoud ever hears the things she says about her, he will never speak our names again and I will lose him for ever.'

'Well, she must have some good qualities for Massoud to want her so much,' Faati said. 'And after all, he is the one who has to like her.'

'Do you want me to talk to Firouzeh?' I asked her. 'You can't imagine how terrible I feel for her.'

Faati shrugged and said, 'She may not be in the mood to talk.'

'At worst, she will throw me out of her room. It doesn't matter.'

I knocked softly and opened the door a little. Firouzeh was lying on her bed. Her blue eyes were red and her face was wet with tears. She turned her back to me so that I wouldn't see her face. My heart ached. I couldn't stand to see that sweet girl cry. I sat on the edge of the bed and caressed her.

'Massoud doesn't deserve you,' I said. 'Mark my words, he will regret this. The only loser here is him. I don't know why after all the pain and hardship he has suffered, God doesn't want him to have a quiet and happy life. All I hoped for was for you to be the one to create that life for him. Too bad he didn't deserve it.'

Her delicate shoulders were shaking, but she didn't speak. I knew the pain of being defeated in love. I got up and went home feeling tired and broken.

From our family, Mother, Faati, Sadegh Khan, Massoud's aunts and Mrs Parvin attended the engagement party. Massoud, handsome as ever and dressed in an elegant suit and tie, was standing next to Ladan who had just come from the hair salon. She was wearing a lace dress and had lace flowers in her hair.

'Fabulous!' Shirin scoffed. 'Look at the groom. Didn't he used to say he hates ties because they are like a leash? What happened? She put the leash on him this easily? Oh, if only his colleagues at the ministry could see him now!'

I tried to look happy and excited, but the truth was that I wasn't feeling at all well. I thought, What dreams I had for Massoud's wedding. I always imagined it would be one of the best nights of my life. And now . . . Shirin was being very surly and complained about everything. Every time someone congratulated the young couple and wished them happiness, she turned away and said, 'Yuck!' I kept telling her she was being rude and for Massoud's sake she should stop, but she ignored me. When Ladan's family insisted that the groom's sister perform what they called the 'knife dance' and deliver the cake knife to Ladan while dancing, Shirin refused and indignantly said, 'I hate these antics.'

Massoud was glaring at us. I didn't know what to do.

Barely three months after the engagement party, Firouzeh married. Apparently I was the last person to be told about her impending wedding. I knew she had many suitors, but I didn't think she would get married that soon. I went to see her.

'My dear, why so fast?' I asked. 'Give yourself some time to grow to like someone in peace and with an open mind, someone who will value a precious gem like you.'

'No, Auntie,' she said with a bitter laugh. 'I will never again fall in love like that. I gave my parents the authority to select whomever they thought suitable. Of course, I don't dislike Sohrab. He is a good and sensible man. I think over time I will forget the past and grow to like him a lot.'

'Yes, of course,' I said. And I thought, But this flame in your heart will never extinguish. 'Still, I wish you had waited a year or so. I don't think that engagement will last. There are already signs of discord.'

'No, Auntie. Even if Massoud comes right now, falls at my feet, ends his engagement and asks for my hand, I will turn him down. Something in my heart and the idol I had built of him are both broken. It would never be like before.'

'You are right and I am sorry for what I said. I really didn't mean anything by it. But you don't know how I wished you would be my daughter-in-law.'

'Please, Auntie. Enough! I wish you had never said these things to me. They are the reason I am so unhappy. From the day I opened my eyes in this world I saw myself as your daughter-in-law and Massoud's wife. And now I feel like a wife whose husband has cheated on her in front of her eyes, when in fact poor Massoud hasn't done anything wrong. We had no commitments to each other and he has the right to decide his own future and choose the woman he loves. It was all your talk that created a false illusion in me.'

Fortunately, Sohrab was a kind, wise, well-educated and handsome man. He came from a cultured family and was studying in France. A month after their wedding, the young couple left for Paris. Together with Faati and the rest of the family, I bade them farewell with a heavy heart and tearful eyes and wished them everlasting happiness.

Ladan and Massoud's engagement lasted only seven months. Massoud was like someone who had suddenly woken up from a deep sleep.

'We had nothing to talk about!' he said. 'I would talk for hours about architecture, art, religion and culture but Ladan, who had expressed so much interest in the beginning, wasn't interested in any of it. All she thought about was clothes and hair and make-up. She wasn't even interested in any sports. And you can't imagine how shallow her thoughts and ideas were. The only time she paid any attention was when there was talk about money. They were strange people. They were willing to forgo food on the table, accept any disgrace and go into debt, as long as they could show up at some party wearing a dress no one had seen them in before. Their notion of respectability and reputation was worlds apart from what we are accustomed to.'

I finally breathed a sigh of relief, but I was terribly sorry that we had lost precious Firouzeh, especially since I could already sense Massoud's regret. I think Firouzeh's marriage was the first of several blows that finally woke him up, but it was too late.

Massoud again drowned himself in work, his relationship with Shirin was restored, and our home regained its former peace and warmth. But Massoud still blamed himself for having hurt me and wanted to somehow make up for it.

One day he came home and excitedly said, 'Good news! Your problem is resolved.'

'My problem? I don't have a problem!' I said.

'I mean your problem with the university. I know how much you always dreamed of finishing your bachelor's degree and continuing your studies. I will never forget the look on your face the day they expelled you. I talked to a few people, including the head of the Department of Literature; we served in the army together. He has agreed for you to take the few credits you need to receive your degree. Then you can apply for the master's degree programme. And knowing you, you will probably get your doctorate degree, too.'

Conflicting thoughts rushed through my mind. I certainly had no hunger left for that piece of paper.

'I used to have a classmate named Mahnaz,' I said. 'She had a favourite saying that she wrote in fine handwriting on a sheet of paper and pinned it to the wall. "All I ever desired I reached when I no longer desired it."'

'What? You mean you don't want your degree?'

'No, my dear, I'm sorry you wasted your time.'

'But why?'

'For years they denied me my right. The least of the losses I suffered because of them was not being able to receive the increase in salary that I so desperately needed during those difficult years.

And now, with a thousand pleas and by pulling strings, they have agreed to do me a favour! ... No. I don't want it. Today, I am known for my knowledge and expertise, and for my editing work I get paid the same amount that someone with a PhD would receive. No one asks to see my degrees any more. Even the mention of it makes me laugh.

'Besides, the way these people give away degrees and titles, they have lost their value for me. I wanted to achieve something on my own merit, not through charity.'

That year, Shirin was accepted in the university. She wanted to study sociology. I was happy and proud that all three of my children had got a university education. Shirin quickly found new friends. And I, wanting to keep an eye on her associations from a distance, encouraged her to have their gatherings at our home. I felt safer that way. Over time, I got to know her friends and our apartment turned into a regular hang-out for them. Although their presence interfered with my work, broke my concentration and quiet, and I had to do more cooking and cleaning, I was pleased and did it all willingly.

Two years later, in early winter Parvaneh's and my first grandchild was born. I went to Germany to be there for the birth of the beautiful and charming baby girl that Siamak and Lili named Dorna. Parvaneh and I fussed over her and constantly argued about whom she most resembled. Although I was now a grandmother, the happiness and joy I experienced made me feel younger and livelier than I had felt for the previous ten years.

Dorna was two months old and tearing myself away from her was difficult, but I wanted to return to Iran for the new year. I didn't want to leave Shirin and Massoud alone for much longer.

Back home, I quickly noticed that something had changed. Among Shirin's friends there was a young man I had not seen before. Shirin introduced him as Faramarz Abdollahi and said he was a post-graduate student at the university. I greeted him and said, 'Welcome to the fold of these great sociologists, but can you put up with them?'

He laughed and said, 'With great difficulty!'

I looked at him with curiosity.

'Oh, Faramarz, are you making fun of us?' Shirin chided him coyly.

'Of course not, my lady! You are the crown we wear with pride.'

Shirin giggled and I said to myself, I see!

After everyone left, Shirin asked me what I thought about her friends.

'I already know most of them and they haven't changed since the last time I saw them,' I said.

'But what did you think about the ones you had not met before?'

'The tall girl who was sitting on the sofa; she is new, isn't she?'

'Yes. Her name is Negin and the guy who was sitting next to her is her fiancé. They are really good kids. They are getting married next month; we are all invited.'

'That's wonderful, they suit each other.'

'Well, what about the other ones?' Shirin persisted.

'What other ones? Who else was new to your group?'

I knew all those questions were her roundabout way of finding out what I thought about Faramarz, but I enjoyed teasing her.

Finally, she got fed up and snapped, 'You mean you didn't notice a man that big?'

'They are all big. Which one are you referring to?'

'I mean Faramarz!' she said, exasperated. 'He was admiring you. He said, "Your mother is so beautiful. She must have been a knockout when she was young."'

I laughed and said, 'What a lovely young man!'

'That's it? That's all you have to say about him?'

'How could I possibly have an opinion about someone I barely exchanged two words with? Why don't you tell me about him and I will see if his character matches his appearance.'

'What do you want me to say?'

'Whatever you know about him; even things you may think are irrelevant.'

'He is the second of three children, he is twenty-seven and he is very well educated. His mother is a teacher and his father is a civil engineer and travels most of the time. He works for his father's firm.'

'But that doesn't match what he is studying,' I said. 'Isn't he in the Department of Sociology?'

'No! I told you, he is in the Department of Technology.'

'Then what is he doing in your group? Where did you meet him?'

'He is best friends with Soroush, Negin's fiancé. They were always together and we used to see him often. He officially joined our group around the time you went to Germany.'

'All right. Tell me more.'

'What else can I tell you?'

'You only gave me some general information. Now tell me about his character.'

'How would I know?'

'What do you mean?' I asked. 'Did you become his friend because he is the second of three children, his mother is a teacher, his father is an engineer and he's in the Department of Technology?'

'Mum, it's impossible to talk to you! You make it sound as if he is my boyfriend.'

'Well, he may be, but I'm not concerned about that. For now, I am more interested in knowing what kind of a person he is.'

'You are not concerned?' Shirin asked surprised. 'You mean it would be all right with you if we are very close?'

'Look, soon you will be twenty-one and an adult. I trust you and I trust the way I raised you. I know you don't lack any love in your life to blindly fall for the first gesture of affection. You know what your rights are and you will not let anyone violate them, you respect religious and social norms, you are smart and sensible, and you have foresight. I know you will not give in to whim and impulse.'

'Really? Is that how you see me?' she asked.

'Of course! Sometimes, you think and make decisions more rationally than I do, and you can control your emotions better than I can.'

'Are you serious?'

'Why do you doubt yourself? Maybe your feelings are so strong that you worry they may affect your judgment,' I said.

'Oh, yes! You have no idea how scared I am.'

'That's good. It shows that your brain is still working.'

'Honestly, I don't know what to do.'

'Do you have to do anything?'

'Don't I?'

'No. The only thing you have to do is study, plan your future and get to know yourself and him much better.'

'But I can't stop thinking about him,' Shirin said. 'I want to see him more, to spend more time with him . . .'

'Well, you see him at the university and you can invite him here whenever you want. Of course, only when I am home. I want to get to know him, too.'

'Aren't you worried that I . . . I don't know . . . that I may go too far?'

'No,' I said. 'I trust you more than I trust my eyes. Besides, if a girl wants to go too far, she will do it even if she is shackled and chained. We must have internal restraints, and you do.'

'Thanks, Mum, I feel so much better. And you can be sure I will keep a grip on everything.'

After the new year holidays, one day when Shirin was not at home, Massoud came and sat next to me and said, 'Mum, I need to make a serious decision about my future.'

'As a matter of fact,' I said, 'I have been meaning to talk to you about that. But I must say, I really don't believe in the traditional approach to choosing a wife. I want you to find a girl you like, someone who is compatible with you, someone you know well. I was actually hoping you would meet someone at the university or at work.'

'To be honest, I made such a big mistake last time that I am now very scared. And I don't think I will ever fall in love like that again. However, there is an opportunity that is sensible and practical in every respect. And if you think it is appropriate, I will pursue it. Frankly, almost all my friends are now married and I'm very much alone.'

The memory of Firouzeh tugged at my heart. I sighed and said, 'Well, tell me about this opportunity.'

'Mr Maghsoudi has a twenty-five-year-old daughter who is studying chemistry at the university. And he has been dropping hints that he wouldn't mind having me as a son-in-law.'

'Mr Maghsoudi is a wonderful man and I am sure he has a fine family,' I said. 'But there is one problem.'

'What problem?'

'He is the deputy director of the ministry; it is a politically appointed position.'

'Come on, Mum! You are really going too far. Don't tell me you are afraid he will be thrown in prison and executed!'

'Why wouldn't I be afraid? I am terrified of politics and political games. That is exactly why I was worried when you started working there and made you promise that you would never accept a sensitive position or a political appointment.'

'If everyone thought like you, who would run the country?' Massoud asked. 'I'm sorry, but I think you need to see a psychologist!'

Regardless, Massoud decided to ask for that young woman's hand in marriage. Shirin and I were ready to leave for Mr Maghsoudi's house when Massoud said, 'Could I ask you for a favour? Out of respect for Mr Maghsoudi, would you please wear a chador?'

I lost my temper and snapped, 'Look, my dear, did you forget that we are human? That we think for ourselves and have our own principles and beliefs, and we cannot constantly transform ourselves into people we are not? Do you know how many times I have had to change how I cover myself because of what men saw fit? I wore a chador in Qum, I wore a headscarf in Tehran, I married your father and he didn't want me to wear any hijab at all, then came the revolution and I had to wear a long manteau and a headscarf, and when you wanted to marry Miss Ladan you wanted me to be elegant and fashionable. Back then you wouldn't

403

have even minded if I wore a low-cut dress, but now that you want to marry your boss's daughter, you want me to wear a chador! No, son. I may not have been able to stand up to many people in my life, but I can certainly stand up to my son. And I want to tell you that as a middle-aged woman who has experienced the good and the bad in life, I can think for myself and I can choose what I wear. We will go there dressed the way we normally dress and we will not act falsely just to please them.'

Atefeh was a devout, dignified and, most important, a sensible girl. She was fair and had large hazel eyes. Her mother, who maintained full hijab even in front of Shirin and me, was a ceremonious hostess. And Mr Maghsoudi, to whom I still felt indebted, was as usual kind and courteous. He had gained some weight, his hair had turned white and he played constantly with his prayer beads. From the moment we arrived, he and Massoud started discussing work and completely ignored the fact that we were there for a very different reason.

Although the atmosphere in their home somehow reminded me of Mahmoud's house, I did not have any negative feelings. Their air of faith and piety somehow instilled peace and calm in me. There was no hint of the fear of wrongdoing and the angels of hell. Instead I sensed the angels of love and affection fluttering around. Unlike Mahmoud's house, laughter and joy was a not a sin here. So much so that Shirin, who because of her uncles' attitudes did not have much regard for very religious families, quickly warmed up to Atefeh and they started chatting together.

Everything proceeded quickly and easily, and we celebrated Massoud and Atefeh's wedding in the middle of spring. Although Massoud had a few years earlier used the benefits available through the ministry to buy a nice apartment, Mr Maghsoudi insisted that they live on the first floor of his house, which was vacant and which he had set aside for Atefeh.

I tried hard to appear cheerful the day Massoud packed his things. I gave him a hand and playfully teased him. But when he left, I sat on the bed in his empty room and stared at the walls. I suddenly felt the apartment had lost its spirit and my heart was heavy with sadness. I said to myself, The chicks are flying away and the nest will soon be empty. For the first time, I was afraid of the future and the loneliness that lay ahead of me.

Shirin, who had just arrived home, opened the door a little and said, 'He is gone? It's so empty here.'

'Yes, the children all leave,' I said. 'But this is the best kind of parting. Thank God he is alive and well and I finally saw him get married.'

'Mum, between you and me, we are really alone now,' Shirin said.

'Yes, but we still have each other and it will be a few years before you leave, too.'

'A few years!' she exclaimed.

'You are not going to think about getting married until you finish your studies. Right?'

She pursed her lips and shrugged. 'Who knows? Maybe I will get married in a couple of months.'

'What? I will not let you!' I said firmly. 'What is your hurry? You shouldn't even think about it until you have finished university.'

'But there may be circumstances—'

'What circumstances? Don't let anyone talk you into anything. Study with peace of mind, start working, and stand on your own two feet so that you don't end up browbeaten, with your hands tied, and forced to accept any humiliation. And only then start thinking about marriage. There is always time to get married. But once you do, you will forever be responsible for home and family. It is only now when you are young and single that you can be carefree. These years are short and they will never come back. Why would you want to make the best stage of your life even shorter?'

Massoud came to see me regularly and kept saying, 'It's enough, you should stop working. You're at the age when you should rest a little.'

405

'But, son, I like my work,' I would argue. 'For me it is now more of a hobby. Without it I will feel useless.'

Still, he wouldn't give up. I don't know how he managed to record all my work history and arranged for me to receive a pension. Of course, I was pleased to have a regular income, but I could not stop working and kept myself busy with a few projects. Massoud, too, was regularly giving me more money than I needed.

He was earning a generous salary, but he wasn't happy with his work. And I didn't want him to continue with a government job. I kept nagging, 'You are an artist, an architect, why have you got yourself all tangled up in a complicated and tedious government position? Promotions in this sort of post are deceiving. The moment your crowd leaves, you will fall flat on your face. You should only accept appointments that you know you are truly qualified for. All of you who are so pious and such strong believers, why is it that when it comes to status and position you become so irresponsible and phoney and believe you deserve any job?'

'Mum, do you know what your problem is? You have been burned too many times. But don't worry, I really don't have the patience for all that bureaucracy. With a few of my friends we are planning to start our own firm. I will stay here until I have fulfilled my obligations. But when our firm is all set up, I will leave.'

Despite my efforts to avoid the subject, a few months later I had to give in to Shirin and discuss her plans for marriage. Faramarz had received his bachelor's degree and was getting ready to leave for Canada. They were intent on getting married before he left so that he could apply for Shirin's residency permit as well. I was against her dropping out of university, but they assured me that it would take approximately a year for her residency application to be processed, which would give her ample time to finish studying for her degree.

It was painful to think about being separated from Shirin, but she was so happy and excited that I did not allow myself to express the slightest bit of sadness. We held their marriage ceremony and a short while later Faramarz left. He would return when Shirin's residency had been arranged and she had finished her degree. We would then have a proper wedding celebration and the bride and groom would leave together.

I felt that in spite of the hardships, I had met my responsibilities. My children had studied well, started their own lives and were successful. But I also felt empty and purposeless, just as I used to feel right after the final exams at school. It seemed there was nothing left for me to do. I thanked God more than ever before for fear that he would think I was ungrateful and would punish me for it. And I consoled myself that fortunately there was still time; Shirin would not be leaving for at least another year. Still, I could not ignore the dark clouds of old age and loneliness that cast their shadow on me.

CHAPTER TEN

The closer we got to the time Shirin would go to Canada, the more depressed and anxious I became. I tried to be less attached to my children, I didn't want to cling to them like an old, busybody mother and make them worry about me all the time. I tried to socialise more, widen my circle of friends and find new ways to fill my free time of which I had more and more as the months passed. But finding new friends at that age was not easy and I didn't have much of a relationship with my family. Mother was very old and living with Mahmoud. She would not agree to come and stay with us occasionally for a few days, and I would not go to Mahmoud's house, therefore I seldom saw her. Mrs Parvin had aged too and was no longer as energetic and active as before. But she was still the only person I knew I could count on if I ever needed help. Faati had been sad and sombre ever since Firouzeh had got married and left Iran. We weren't as close as we used to be; it was clear that she somehow blamed us for the pain she suffered being separated from her child. I had regular gatherings with my former women colleagues and I still occasionally saw Mr Zargar. He had remarried a few years earlier and seemed happy.

The only time my thoughts and worries ebbed was when Parvaneh was in Tehran. We talked and laughed and travelled back to the happy days of our youth. That year, her mother had been taken ill and she was spending more time in Iran.

'After Shirin leaves, you'll have to rent the apartment and spend a few months a year with each of your children,' she said.

'Absolutely not! I will not lose my independence and self-respect; and I have no intention of intruding on my children's lives. It is no longer practical or appropriate for several generations to live together in the same house.'

'Intruding? They should love it and be grateful!' she argued. 'They should want to make up for all the hard work you did for them.'

'Don't say that! It reminds me of my grandmother. She used to say, "Raising boys is like frying aubergines, it takes a lot of oil, but then they have to render a lot of oil." I have no such expectations of my children. I did it for myself, it was my duty. They don't owe me anything. Besides, I really do want to keep my independence.'

'Independence to do what?' she argued. 'To sit at home all alone and for them, in peace and with a clear conscience, to forget you?'

'That is nonsense,' I said. 'Every single revolution in the world was because people wanted independence. Now you expect me to simply give up mine.'

'Massoum, time passed so quickly and the kids grew up so fast!' Parvaneh said. 'Those were wonderful days; I wish they would come back.'

'No!' I exclaimed. 'I don't want even a single hour of it to come back. Thank God, those days have passed. And hopefully the rest will pass just as quickly.'

The hot summer days had arrived. I was busy preparing Shirin's dowry and Parvaneh and I often went shopping together or found some other excuse to spend the day together. On one of the hottest afternoons, I had just lain down to rest when the unexpected and unrelenting sound of the doorbell made me jump. I went to the intercom and asked who it was.

'It's me. Hurry up and open the door.'

'Parvaneh? What's the matter? We were supposed to meet later this afternoon.'

'Are you going to open the door or do I have to break it down?' she screamed.

I buzzed the door open. In the blink of an eye she was upstairs. Her face was flushed and there were beads of sweat on her forehead and on her upper lip.

'What has happened?' I asked. 'What is the matter?'

'Go inside, go!'

Stunned, I stepped back into the apartment. Parvaneh tore off her headscarf, threw down her manteau and fell on to the sofa.

'Water, cold water!' she gasped.

I quickly brought a glass of water and gave it to her.

'I'll bring you some sherbet later,' I said. 'Now, tell me what has happened. You're killing me!'

'Guess. Guess who I saw today!'

I felt my heart drop to the floor like a rock and my chest emptied. I knew. Her behaviour and the state she was in had drawn an exact image of thirty-three years ago.

'Saiid!' I said in a choked voice.

'You minx! How did you know?'

We were again two adolescent girls whispering in the upstairs room at Father's house. My heart was pounding just as it had then and she was just as excited and restless.

'Tell me! Where did you see him? How is he? How does he look?'

'Wait! One thing at a time. I went to the pharmacy to pick up my mother's medications. The pharmacist knows me. He had a visitor. They were standing behind the counter, but I couldn't see his guest's face, he had his back to me. His voice sounded familiar and because his hair and figure looked attractive I was curious to see his face. The pharmacist's assistant gave me the medications, but I couldn't leave without taking a look at that man. I walked up to the counter and said, "Hello, doctor. I hope you are well. How many sleeping pills can one take in one day?" Imagine! What a stupid question. But it made his guest turn around and look at me with surprise. Oh, Massoum, it was him! You can't imagine how I felt. I was so flustered.'

'Did he recognise you?'

'God bless him, yes! He is so clever. After all these years, he recognised me despite the headscarf, the manteau and the coloured hair! Of course, he hesitated at first, but I quickly took off my sunglasses and smiled at him so that he could take a good look at me.'

'Did you talk?'

'Of course we talked! Do you think I am still afraid of your brothers?'

'What does he look like? Has he aged a lot?'

'The hair on his temples is completely white; the rest is salt and pepper. And he was wearing pince-nez glasses. He didn't wear eyeglasses back then, did he?'

'No, he didn't.'

'Of course, his face has aged, but he doesn't look all that different,' Parvaneh said. 'Especially his eyes; he still has the same eyes.'

'What did he say?'

'The usual greetings. He first asked about my father. I told him Father died a long time ago. He offered his condolences. And then I boldly asked, "So where are you living these days? What are you doing?" He said, "I lived in America for a while." And I asked, "You mean you don't live in Iran?" He said, "Yes, I do. I came back a few years ago and started working here." I didn't know how to ask him whether he was married and had children or not. I just said, "And how is your family?" He looked surprised, so I quickly added, "I mean your mother and sisters." He said, "Unfortunately, Mother passed away some twenty years ago. My sisters are married and have their own families. Now that I am in Iran and alone, I see more of them." I pricked up my ears. It was the best opportunity. I asked, "Alone?" He said, "Yes, my family stayed in America. What can one do? The kids grew up there and are accustomed to that life; and my wife didn't want to leave them." Well, I had most of the information and I thought it would be rude if I asked any more questions, so I said, "I am happy I ran into you. Please write down my telephone number. If you ever have time, I would be happy to see you again."'

411

Dismayed, I asked, 'He didn't ask about me?'

'Yes, wait! As he was writing down my telephone number, he said, "How is your friend? Are you still in touch with her?" I could barely contain my excitement. I said, "Yes, yes. Of course, she too would be happy to see you. Call this afternoon, perhaps we can arrange to see each other." You would not believe how his eyes suddenly shone. He asked if it would be all right. I think he is still scared of your brothers! I said, "Of course it would be all right." Then I quickly said goodbye and I drove here as fast as I could. It was only God's will that I didn't have an accident. Now, what do you think?'

A thousand thoughts were dancing around in my head. They were really dancing; they wouldn't slow down for me to figure out what I was thinking ...

'Hey ... where are you?' Parvaneh asked. 'What should I tell him if he calls this afternoon? Do you want me to make plans for him to come tomorrow?'

'Come? Come where?'

'Either to my house or here. Just find out what Shirin's plans are.'

'What day is tomorrow?'

'Monday.'

'I don't know what she will be doing.'

'It doesn't matter. We can meet at my house. Mother will be sleeping and oblivious to everything.'

'But why should we make plans? Forget it.'

'Don't be a sissy!' Parvaneh chided. 'Don't you want to see him? In spite of everything, he is an old friend. It's not as if we are doing anything wrong!'

'I don't know,' I said. 'I'm so confused I can't think straight.'

'That's nothing new! When have you not been confused?'

'My brain doesn't work. My hands and knees are shaking.'

'Come on! Stop acting like a sixteen-year-old.'

'That's exactly it,' I said. 'I am not sixteen any more. The poor man will be terrified to see what I look like now.'

'What rubbish! We are not the only ones who have aged. He

has, too. Besides, according to Khosrow, you are like a carpet from Kerman, you keep getting better with age.'

'Stop it! We both know we have grown old.'

'Yes, but what's important is for others not to know. And we shouldn't let on.'

'Do you think people are blind? It's obvious how much we have changed. I don't want to look at myself in the mirror ever again.'

'Stop it! You talk as if we are ninety years old, when in fact we are only forty-eight!' Parvaneh said.

'No, my dear, don't fool yourself. We are fifty-three.'

'Bravo, excellent!' she quipped. 'With your mastery of maths, I am surprised you didn't turn out to be another Einstein.'

Just then, Shirin walked in. Like two guilty kids Parvaneh and I stopped arguing and quickly pulled ourselves together. Shirin kissed Parvaneh on the cheeks and without paying much attention to us she went to her room. We looked at each other and burst into laughter.

'Remember how we used to hide the papers the minute Ali walked into the room?' I said.

Parvaneh looked at her watch and cried, 'Oh my God! Look at the time. I told my mother I would be gone for only fifteen minutes. She must be worried sick.' Putting on her manteau, she said, 'I won't come back today. If he calls, I will ask him to come to my house tomorrow at six, it's safer there. But you should come earlier ... well, I will give you a call.'

I went to my bedroom and sat in front of the dressing table. I took a close look at my face in the mirror and tried to find remnants of the one I had when I was sixteen. I carefully examined the wrinkles around my eyes that deepened when I smiled. There were two distinct lines that started at my nostrils and stretched down to my lips. The beautiful, round dimples on my cheeks, which according to Mrs Parvin were an inch deep when I smiled, had transformed into two long grooves running parallel to the lines flanking my mouth. My smooth, radiant skin was now pale and sagging and there were faint spots on my cheeks. My eyelids were no longer taut and dark circles detracted from the brightness of my eyes. My lush, reddish-brown hair that used to cascade down to my waist was half as lavish, short, thin and awkward, and in spite of regular colourings its white roots were showing. Even the expression in my eyes had changed. No, I was no longer the beautiful girl Saiid had fallen in love with. Perplexed, I was sitting there searching for myself in the mirror when Shirin's voice brought me back.

'What's the matter, Mum? You have been entranced by your own face for an hour! I have never seen you so fond of a mirror.'

'Fond? No! I want to break every mirror there is.'

'Why? As the saying goes, "Break yourself, for breaking a mirror is wrong." What do you see in it?'

'I see myself, my old age.'

'But growing older has never bothered you,' she said. 'Unlike most women, you boldly talk about your age.'

'Yes, but sometimes something, perhaps even a photograph, takes you back in time. You look in the mirror and suddenly realise how different you really are from the image you have had of yourself. It is so cruel. It is like a free-fall.'

'But you always said every age has its own beauty.'

'Yes, but the beauty of youth is something else.'

'All my friends say, "Your mum is such a lady, she is so gracious."'

'My dear Shirin, my grandmother was a kind woman. She didn't have the heart to describe some girl as ugly. Instead, she would say the girl was amiable. Now your friends don't want to say, "Your mother is run-down," so they say I am gracious.'

'Mum, it's so unlike you to talk like this,' Shirin said. 'To me, you are always the most beautiful woman. When I was a little girl, I always wanted to look like you. I was jealous. Until just a few years ago, people looked at you more than they looked at me. I was always sad that my eyes weren't the same colour as yours and my skin wasn't as fair and smooth.'

'Ridiculous! You are far more beautiful than I ever was. I was always so pale that people thought I was sick. But you, with your lively eyes, beautiful wheat-coloured skin and those dimples are something else.'

'Now, what made you think about your youth?' she asked.

414

'It's a function of age. When people reach my age, their past takes on a different colour. Even the bad days seem nice. When we are young, we think about the future, about what will happen next year, we wonder where we will be in five years, and we want the days to pass quickly. But when we reach my age, we see no future ahead of us, we have in fact reached the peak, and we turn and look to the past.'

Parvaneh called late afternoon and said she had made the arrangements for six o'clock the following day. I spent the entire night in feverish excitement. I kept telling myself that it was best for Saiid and me not to see each other, that we should each hold on to the memory of the other's youth and beauty. I remembered how during all those years each time I wore a beautiful dress and liked my reflection in the mirror, I wished I might run into him at the party or at the wedding or out on the street. I always hoped that if we were to ever meet again, it would be when I was at the peak of my beauty.

Early the next morning, Parvaneh called. 'How are you feeling? I didn't sleep a wink last night.'

'Oh, we are so alike,' I said, laughing.

Then she quickly started to give me instructions.

'First, colour your hair.'

'I coloured it only recently.'

'It doesn't matter, do it again; the roots didn't take the colour too well. Then take a hot bath. Afterwards, fill a big bowl with cold water, add plenty of ice and stick your face in it.'

'I will drown.'

'No, idiot! Dip your face in it several times. Then use those creams I brought for you from Germany. The green one is a cucumber mask. Put it on your face and lie down and rest for twenty minutes. Then wash it off and smear on a good amount of the yellow cream. And be here at five so that I can fix you up and put on your make-up.'

'Fix me up? I'm not a bride!'

'Who knows, you may become one,' she said.

'You should be ashamed of yourself! At my age?'

'Age again? If you talk like this one more time, I swear to God I will beat you.'

'What should I wear?' I asked.

'The grey dress we bought together in Germany.'

'No, that's an evening dress. It's not appropriate.'

'You are right. Wear the beige two-piece. No! The rose-coloured shirt with the lighter-shade lace collar.'

'Thanks,' I said. 'I'll think of something myself.'

Even though I never had the patience for too much fussing, I pretty much followed all of Parvaneh's instructions. I was lying down with the green mask on my face when Shirin walked into my room.

'What is going on?' she said surprised. 'You are really pampering yourself today.'

'Nothing is going on,' I replied casually. 'Parvaneh insisted that I use this mask and I thought I would give it a try.'

She shrugged and walked out.

I started getting ready at three-thirty. I carefully blow-dried my hair, which I had already set in curlers. One by one, I carefully put on my clothes. I looked at myself in the full-length mirror and thought, I weigh at least ten kilos more than I did back then ... How strange that when I was skinny, my cheeks were plump, but now that I am heavier, my face is half as full as it used to be.

Every outfit I put on had something wrong with it. Soon, there was a heap of shirts, skirts and dresses on the bed. Shirin leaned against the door frame and asked, 'Where are you going?'

'To Parvaneh's house.'

'All this fussing is for Aunt Parvaneh?'

'She found a few of our old friends and she has invited them over. I don't want to look old and ugly.'

'Aha!' she exclaimed. 'So the rivalries of your younger days still continue.'

'No, it's not rivalry. It's a strange feeling. Seeing each other will be like looking in the mirror after some thirty-odd years. I want us to still see some of what we looked like all those years ago; otherwise, we will be complete strangers to each other.'

416

'How many are they?'

'Who?'

'Aunt Parvaneh's guests!'

I was flustered. I had always been a bad liar. I mumbled, 'She found an old friend and the old friend will bring along whoever else she can find. So I don't know if there will be one person or ten people.'

'You never talk about your old friends. What is her name?' Shirin asked.

'Of course, I had friends and classmates, but I was never as close to them as I was to Parvaneh.'

'It's so interesting,' she mused. 'I can't imagine what my friends and I will look like thirty years from now. Think about it! We will be a bunch of doddering old people.'

I ignored her comment. I was trying to think of an excuse in case she said she wanted to go with me. But as usual, Shirin preferred to be with people her own age or even stay home alone rather than be in the company of 'doddering old people'. In the end, I wore a chocolate-brown linen dress with a cinched-in waist and brown high-heeled sandals.

It was past five-thirty when I arrived at Parvaneh's house. She carefully appraised me from head to toe and said, 'Not bad. Now come and let me fix the rest.'

'Look, I don't want you to make me look gaudy and gussied up. I am what I am. After all, I have lived a life ... and what a life it has been.'

'You are beautiful just as you are,' Parvaneh said. 'I will just add a touch of chocolate-brown eye shadow, a little eyeliner and a bit of mascara. And you should put on some lipstick. You don't need anything else. God bless you, your skin is still as smooth as a mirror.'

'Yes, a cracked mirror.'

'But the cracks don't really show. Besides, his eyes are weak. We can even sit inside where it's dark and he won't see much.'

'Stop it!' I chided. 'You sound like you are trying to pass off shoddy goods! We will sit outside in the garden.'

At exactly six o'clock, we both jumped at the sound of the door-bell.

'I swear on my mother's life he has been standing outside for the past ten minutes waiting to ring the doorbell at six o'clock sharp,' Parvaneh said. 'He is in a worse state than we are.'

She pressed the button on the intercom to open the main door and started towards the garden. Halfway, she stopped and looked back. I was still standing there. She waved to me to follow her, but I couldn't move. I watched through the window as Parvaneh led Saiid to the table and chairs in the garden. He was wearing a grey suit. He was a little heavier and his hair was salt and pepper. I couldn't see his face. A few minutes later, Parvaneh walked back inside and snapped, 'Why are you still here? Don't tell me you want to walk out carrying the tea tray, like a bride-to-be!'

'Stop it!' I pleaded. 'My heart is about to burst out of my chest. My legs froze and I couldn't follow you.'

'Oh, my poor little baby! Would you like to grace us with your presence now?'

'No ... wait!'

'What do you mean? He asked if you are here and I said yes. It's rude, come on. Stop acting like a fourteen-year-old.'

'Wait ... let me get a grip on myself.'

'Ugh! What am I supposed to tell him? That the lady has fainted!? It's impolite; he is sitting there alone.'

'Tell him I am with your mother and that I will be right there. Oh my God! I didn't even say hello to your mother!' And I dashed towards her mother's bedroom ...

I would have never believed that at my age I would feel that panicked. I always thought of myself as someone sensible and sedate, someone who had experienced life's ups and downs. Over the years, there had been many men who had expressed an interest in me, but not since my adolescence had I felt that nervous and flustered.

'My dear Massoum, who is here?' Mrs Ahmadi asked.

'One of Parvaneh's friends.'

'Do you know her?'

'Yes, yes, I met her in Germany.'

Just then I heard Parvaneh call out, 'Massoum, my dear, come join us. Saiid Khan is here.'

I looked at myself in the mirror and ran my fingers through my hair. I think Mrs Ahmadi was still talking when I walked out of her bedroom. I knew I shouldn't allow myself time to think. I hurried out into the garden and in a voice that I was desperately trying to stop from shaking I said, 'Hello!'

Saiid jumped out of his chair, stood up straight and stared at me. A few seconds later, he came to himself and gently said, 'Hello!'

We exchanged a few casual greetings and soon sounded less nervous. Parvaneh went back inside to bring some tea and Saiid and I sat facing each other. Neither of us knew what to say. His face had aged, but the look in his fetching brown eyes was the same look I remembered and had felt weighing on my life for decades. Altogether, he seemed more settled and attractive. I was hoping he had the same impression of me. Parvaneh came back and we continued with routine bits of customary conversation. Gradually, our reunion became warmer and we asked him to tell us where he had been and what he had been doing all those years.

'I will tell, if everyone tells . . . ' he said.

'I have nothing to tell,' Parvaneh said. 'My life has been quite ordinary. After I graduated from school, I got married, had children and moved to Germany. I have two daughters and a son. I still live in Germany, but I spend a lot of time here because my mother is ill. If her health improves, I will take her there with me. That's it. You see, nothing interesting or exciting has happened in my life.' And then she pointed to me and said, 'Unlike her.'

Saiid turned to me and said, 'Then you should tell me about your life.'

I looked beseechingly at Parvaneh.

'For the love of God, don't say anything!' she said. Then she turned to Saiid and explained, 'Her life story could fill a book. If she starts now, she won't be done until well after midnight. Besides, I know it all and it will be boring for me to hear the entire story again. Instead, you should tell us about yourself.'

419

'I graduated from university a little later than expected,' Saiid said. 'And I was exempt from military service, because my father had passed away and I was my mother's only son and considered to be the head of the household. After university, I returned to Rezaieh and with the help of my uncles I opened a pharmacy. Our circumstances improved, the value of my father's properties increased, I helped my sisters get married, and then I sold the pharmacy and moved back to Tehran with my mother. A few of my old classmates had decided to start a pharmaceuticals importing company and I joined them as a partner. Our business grew and we started manufacturing cosmetics and healthcare products as well.

'My mother kept insisting that I take a wife. I finally gave in and married Nazy who was the sister of one of my partners and had just finished school. Eventually, we had children, twins, a pair of mischief-makers. It was so difficult raising them that I decided I didn't want any more kids. After the revolution, everything was a mess and the future of the company was unclear. When war broke out, our prospects became even more uncertain. Nazy's entire family was leaving the country and she got it into her head that we should leave as well. The borders were closed, but she insisted that we leave illegally. Still, I resisted for two years until the situation improved. By then my mother was gravely ill; I think the sorrow of knowing that I would soon leave Iran hastened her death. I was terribly depressed. I sold everything we had. The only wise thing I did was that I kept my shares in the company. We first went to Austria; Nazy's other brother was living there. And we stayed until we had the necessary documents to go to America.

'Starting from zero was difficult. Regardless, we stayed and settled down. The children were happy. It took only a couple of years for them to become completely American. Nazy wanted to improve her English, so she forbade us from talking Persian at home. As a result, the boys almost entirely forgot their mother tongue. I worked morning till night and we had a comfortable life. I had everything except happiness. I missed my sisters, my friends, Tehran and Rezaieh. Nazy had her family and friends around her

420

and my children were happy with their friends at school and in the neighbourhood, but they were living in a world that I had never experienced and knew nothing about. I felt alone and alienated.

'When the war ended, I heard that the situation here had improved and a lot of people were coming back. So I came, too. The company was still in business and the market wasn't all that bad. I returned to work. I felt much better and was in good spirits. Soon, I bought an apartment and went to bring back Nazy, but she wasn't willing to return. She had the perfect excuse, the kids ... Well, she was right. It was no longer possible to tear them away from a culture they had blended into. In the end, we decided that because I could make more money in Iran, I would stay here and work, and Nazy would stay there until the boys grew up. This is how our life has been for the past six or seven years. Now, the children have grown up and moved to different states, but Nazy still has no intention of coming back to Iran. Once a year, I go to see them for a few months ... the rest is loneliness and work. I know it's not a healthy life, but I haven't done anything to change it.'

Parvaneh was kicking me under the table and looking at Saiid with a mischievous, scarcely concealed smile that I knew all too well. But I felt sad for him. I had always hoped that at least he would end up happy, but it seemed he was lonelier than me.

'Well, it's your turn now,' he said looking at me.

I told him about my rushed marriage to Hamid, his kindness, his political activities, his years in prison and his execution. I talked about my work, about going to university and about all that I had suffered because of my children. Then I told him about the recent years, about my children who had settled down and about my own life that was finally almost quiet. We talked like three dear friends who had come together again after many years, and we forgot the hours passing.

The sound of the telephone ringing made us jump. Parvaneh went to answer it. A few seconds later, she called out, 'It's Shirin. She says it's ten o'clock!'

421

'Where are you, Mum?' Shirin said angrily. 'It seems you are having a really good time. I got worried.'

'It's all right if for once you are the one who is worried,' I said. 'We were busy talking and lost track of time.'

As we were leaving, Saiid said, 'I will drive you home.'

'No, she has her own car,' Parvaneh said with her usual brashness. 'You are not allowed to talk without me present.'

Saiid laughed out loud and I glowered at Parvaneh.

'What? Why are you glaring at me again?' she said. 'Well, I want to know what you two talk about ... You see, Saiid Khan? She hasn't changed a bit. When we were kids, she was always saying, "Don't say this, it's rude; don't do that, it's improper." Fifty years later, she is still doing the same thing.'

'Enough, Parvaneh!' I chided. 'Stop saying all this nonsense.'

'Well, I say what is on my mind. I swear to God, if I find out you two have seen each other behind my back, I will punish you. I have to be there, too.'

Saiid was still laughing. I bit my lip and said, 'Of course, you will be there ...'

'Then, why don't we plan our next gathering now? And don't tell me you don't want to see each other again.'

To put an end to the discussion, I said, 'Please come to my home next time.'

'Aha, that's good,' Parvaneh said. 'When?'

'Wednesday morning. Shirin leaves for the university at ten and she won't be back until late afternoon. Come for lunch.'

Parvaneh clapped her hands and cheerfully said, 'Great! I will ask Farzaneh to come and stay with Mother. Is Wednesday all right with you, Saiid Khan?'

'I wouldn't want to trouble you,' he said.

'It is no trouble at all,' I said. 'I would be delighted.'

He quickly wrote down my address and telephone number and we parted with plans to see each other two days later.

I went home but had not even changed my clothes when the telephone rang. Laughing and ecstatic, Parvaneh said, 'Congratulations! The guy doesn't have a wife!'

'Of course he does. Did you miss that long story?'

'The story was about a separation, not a marriage. Didn't you get it?'

'The poor man ... You are so mean. God willing, his wife will come back and their life will get back on track.'

'Come on!' Parvaneh said. 'After all these years, I still don't know if you are really stupid or just pretend to be.'

'My dear, they are officially husband and wife,' I argued. 'They have not legally separated, and there was no mention of a divorce. How can you allow yourself to so hastily judge people's relationships?'

'Let's see, what is the definition of a separation?' she stubbornly maintained. 'Is it a separation only after you sign a piece of paper? No, my dear. When it comes to emotions, preferences, lifestyles, time and place, they have been separated for seven years. Use your brain, do you really think in that open society the lady is sitting all alone, crying her eyes out over a man for whom she won't even make a quick trip to Iran? And do you think for seven years this gentleman has lived as innocently as Jesus Christ with only the memory of his beloved?'

'If this is the case, then why don't they legally separate?' I asked.

'Why should they? The woman is too smart to do that. She has a mule who works, makes lots of money and sends it to her. And he is a trouble-free mule ... he doesn't need lunch and dinner, and he doesn't need his clothes washed and ironed. She would have to be an idiot to give up the goose that lays the golden eggs. On his part, the gentleman has either not wanted to marry someone else, or he has assets overseas, half of which he would have to give to that woman in case of a divorce. And so far, he has not seen the need to do that.'

'My God, the things you think about!'

'I have seen a thousand similar cases,' Parvaneh said. 'Saiid and his wife may have different circumstances, but they have one thing in common with the others: this husband and wife will never be a husband and wife for each other again. You can be sure of that.'

*

I prepared for Wednesday with a youthful energy that I thought I had long lost. I cleaned and tidied up the apartment, cooked and tended to myself. What a wonderful day the three of us had together. And so our gatherings continued, dominating my life.

I felt young again. I took care of my appearance, wore make-up and bought new dresses. Sometimes, I even pilfered Shirin's closet and borrowed her clothes. The world had taken on a different colour. There was a new purpose to life. I worked and did everything I had to do with passion and excitement. I no longer felt lonely, old, useless and forgotten. I looked younger. The wrinkles around my eyes were less obvious. The lines around my mouth were not as deep. My skin looked fresher, more radiant. There was a pleasant feeling of anticipation in my heart. The sound of the telephone ringing had a new meaning. I would instinctively lower my voice and answer the call with vague and broken words. I avoided Shirin's inquisitive eyes. I knew she had noticed the changes in me, but she didn't know what had brought them on.

A week after our meetings started, she said, 'Mum, ever since you found your old friends, you seem to be in much better spirits.'

Another time she joked, 'Mum, I swear there is something suspicious in your behaviour.'

'What do you mean by "suspicious"? What am I doing?'

'Things you didn't do before. You pamper yourself, you go out a lot, you are cheerful, you sing. I don't know, you're different.'

'Different how?'

'You're like someone who is in love; like a little girl.'

Parvaneh and I thought it wise to introduce Saiid to Shirin. At my age, it was unbecoming to sneak around and to be terrified of her seeing me with him. But we had to come up with a reason for his visits. After several discussions, we decided to introduce him as one of Parvaneh's family friends who had recently returned to Iran from abroad and work was the reason we were occasionally meeting. Coincidentally, Saiid had translated several articles into Persian and he had asked me to edit them for him.

Shirin saw Saiid on a few occasions. I was curious to find out what she thought of him, but I didn't want to make her suspicious. Finally, she broached the subject herself.

'Where did Aunt Parvaneh find him?'

'I told you, he is a family friend,' I said. 'Why?'

'Nothing ... he's a good-looking old man.'

'Old man?'

'Yes, he is very refined and gracious,' she said. 'He doesn't match Aunt Parvaneh.'

'You are so rude! All of Aunt Parvaneh's friends and relatives are dignified.'

'Then why is she the way she is?'

'The way she is?'

'Well, she is a little crazy.'

'You should be ashamed of yourself!' I chided. 'You shouldn't talk about your aunt like that. Is it bad that she is cheerful and funny and makes everyone feel young?'

'Yes! When she is around, you are too peppy and perky and the two of you are constantly whispering to each other.'

'Are you jealous of her? Can't I have even one friend?'

'I never said that! I'm happy to see you so energetic and in good spirits. It's just that she seems to forget how old she is.'

Over the summer, the three of us saw each other at least every other day. It was early September when Saiid invited us to a garden estate he had bought north of Tehran, near Mount Damavand. What a beautiful and memorable day. The mountains reached up to the sky and the breeze brought the chill of their snow-covered peaks. The air was clean and fragrant; the small leaves on the slim branches of the white poplars that circled the estate fluttered like large sequins, changing colour under the brilliant sun. When the breeze gusted more strongly, the flickering leaves sounded like a crowd of thousands applauding you, life and the beauties of nature. Alongside the narrow streams, clusters of petunias were lolling in their own sweet scent. The trees were laden with heavenly fruits. Apples, pears, yellow plums and fuzzy peaches glistened under the sun. There had been very few occasions in my life when I had wished time to stop. That day was one of them.

The three of us were so happy and comfortable together. The veils of caution and unfamiliarity had dropped and we talked freely. Like my other half, Parvaneh would say the things I found myself incapable of verbalising. With her friskiness and candour, she made us laugh. I could not control my laughter. It was as if it was rising from the deepest particles of my being and blossoming on my lips; its sound was pleasing and foreign to me. I asked myself, Is this really me laughing like this?

Late in the afternoon, after a long and refreshing walk, we sat on the villa's high terrace that had a view of the magnificent sunset. We were having tea and pastries when Parvaneh started.

'Saiid, I have to ask you,' she said. 'All these years, Massoum and I have wondered why you disappeared after that night. Why didn't you come back? Why didn't you send your mother to ask for her hand? You could have avoided all the hardships you both endured in life.'

I was stunned. Until that moment, we had avoided talking about that night because it would have embarrassed me and certainly made Saiid uncomfortable. I looked at her and gasped, 'Parvaneh!'

'What? I think we have grown close enough to be able to talk about everything, especially about something this important that changed your destinies. Saiid, you don't have to answer if you don't want to.'

'No, I need to explain,' he said. 'As a matter of fact, I have wanted to talk about that night and everything that happened, but I didn't want to upset Massoum.'

'Massoum, is it going to upset you?' Parvaneh asked.

'Actually, I wouldn't mind knowing . . . ' I said.

'That night, oblivious to everything that was going on, I was working at the pharmacy when Ahmad suddenly burst in and started shouting obscenities. He was very drunk. Dr Ataii tried to calm him down, but Ahmad attacked him. I ran over to pull the doctor away and Ahmad lunged at me and started beating me.

426

Everyone in the neighbourhood came running. I was shocked and mortified. Those days, I was so shy that I wasn't even comfortable smoking a cigarette in public, and there was Ahmad shouting that I had led his sister astray. Then he suddenly pulled out a knife and people ran and dragged me out from under him. Before he left, Ahmad threatened that if he ever saw me around there again, he would kill me. Dr Ataii said it was best if I didn't go to work for a few days and allowed things to calm down. Besides, I was not doing too well. I could hardly move and one of my eyes was so swollen that I could not see out of it. Still, my wounds were not serious. It was just my arm that needed a few stitches.

'A few days later, Dr Ataii came to see me. He said that every night Ahmad was going to the pharmacy completely drunk and creating a scene. He had said, "If people stopped me from killing that filthy dog here, no one can stop me at home. I will kill that shameless girl and make that bastard grieve for the rest of his life." Meanwhile, Dr Tabatabaii told Dr Ataii that he had been called to your house and that you had been badly beaten and were in terrible shape. Dr Ataii said, "For the sake of that innocent girl, go away for a few months. Then I will talk to her father myself and you can go with your mother and ask for her hand."

'A few times I came and stood outside your house late at night, hoping that I would at least see you behind a window. In the end, I dropped out of university, went home to Rezaieh and waited to hear from the doctor. I was thinking that we could get married and you could live there with my mother until I got my degree. I kept waiting, but there was no word from the doctor. Finally, I came back to Tehran and went to see him. He started telling me that I had to continue my studies, that I was just starting out in life and that I would soon forget everything that had happened. At first, I thought you were dead. But then he told me that your family had quickly married you off. I was devastated. It took me six months to finally pull myself together and go on with my life.'

The cool days of mid-September heralded the coming of autumn. Parvaneh was getting ready to leave for Germany. Her mother was in better health and the doctors had said it was safe for her to travel. The three of us were sitting in the garden at Parvaneh's house. I had wrapped a thin shawl around me.

'Parvaneh, this time I am sadder about you leaving than ever before,' I said. 'I will feel terribly lonely.'

'May God hear what is really in your heart!' she said. 'You two prayed and pleaded with him to get rid of me! But from now on, every word you two exchange you will have to write for me in a letter. Even better, get a tape recorder and record all your conversations.'

This time, Saiid didn't laugh. He shook his head and said, 'Don't worry; I have to leave, too.'

Parvaneh and I suddenly sat up straight and I gasped, 'To go where?'

'I have to go to America. I always go at the start of the summer and spend three months with Nazy and the boys. This year, I have been putting it off. To be honest, I just didn't want to go ...'

I sank back in my chair. All three of us grew quiet.

Parvaneh went inside to bring more tea. Saiid used the opportunity to put his hand over mine, which had remained on the table, and said, 'I must talk to you before I leave; but alone. Meet me for lunch tomorrow at the restaurant we went to last week. I will be there at one. You must come.'

I knew what he wanted to say. All the love we had felt for each other so many years ago had reawakened in us. Nervous and filled with apprehension, I walked into the restaurant. He was sitting at a small table at the far end of the room, gazing out of the window. After the usual greetings, we ordered lunch. We were both quiet and deep in thought. We couldn't finish our lunch.

Finally, he lit a cigarette and said, 'Massoum, by now you must know that you were the only true love of my life. Destiny put many obstacles in our way and we both suffered deeply. But perhaps destiny wants to make up for it all and show us its other face. I am going to America to finally settle things with Nazy. Two years ago, I told her that she would either have to come to Iran and live with me or we would have to get a divorce. But neither one of us did anything about it. Now, she has opened a restaurant and it seems to be doing well. She says it is to our benefit to live there. Regardless, we finally have to decide what we want to do. I am tired of this uncertain and unsettled life. If I am sure of you and know that you will marry me, many things will become clear for me and I can comfortably decide and firmly follow through with it . . . Well, what do you think? Will you marry me?'

Although I had expected this, and from the first day I saw him again, I somehow knew he would one day ask this question, still, my heart sank and I couldn't speak. Even in my thoughts, I didn't know what answer I should give him.

'I don't know.'

'How could you not know? After thirty-something years you still cannot make a decision for yourself?'

'Saiid, my children . . . what will I do about my children?'

'Children? What children? They have all grown up and gone off to live their own lives. They don't need you any more.'

'But they are very sensitive about me; I'm afraid this would upset them. Their mother, at this age—'

'For the love of God, let us for once in our lives think only about ourselves,' he said. 'After all, we have a share in this life, too. Don't we?'

'I have to talk to them.'

'All right, talk to them, but let me know as soon as you can. I am leaving a week from Saturday and I can't delay the trip any more; especially because I have to stop in Germany for a business meeting.'

I went straight to Parvaneh's house and told her everything. She jumped up and screamed, 'You traitors! You finally did it. You finally said what you had to say without me there. I waited more than thirty years to see your reaction the minute he proposed to you, but you betrayed me!'

'But, Parvaneh—'

'It doesn't matter, I will forgive you. But for the love of God, get married in the next few days, before I leave. I must be there. This has been one of my greatest dreams.'

429

'Please, Parvaneh, stop it!' I cried. 'Get married? At my age? What would my children say?'

'What would they want to say? You gave them your youth, you did everything for them. Now you have to think about yourself. You have the right to have someone in your life to grow old with. I think they would actually be happy for you.'

'You don't understand,' I said. 'I am afraid they would be embarrassed in front of their spouses. I have to think about their honour and reputation, too.'

'Enough!' she shouted. 'Enough with all your talk about honour and reputation. I am sick of it! First you were worried about your father's honour, then your brothers' honour, then your husband's, and now your kids' ... I swear if you say it one more time, I will throw myself out of this window.'

'Huh? Which window? Your house has only one floor.'

'Did you expect me to leap off the Eiffel Tower for the sake of Your Excellency's concerns over honour? Besides, you will not be doing anything dishonourable. Many people marry several times. Give yourself the chance to at least spend the rest of your life in peace and happiness. After all, you are a human being, too, and have some rights in this life.'

I spent the entire night thinking about how I should tell my children. I tried to imagine how each of them would react and what they would say in the best and worst case scenarios. I felt like the teenage girl who stands in front of her parents, stomps her feet and says, Yes, I want him; I want to marry him. Several times, I decided to give up on the idea entirely, to close my eyes to Saiid and to live my life as I had lived it before. But his kind and gentle face, my fear of loneliness, and the honesty of an old love that had stayed alive in our hearts stopped me. Turning away from him would be difficult. I tossed and turned all night, but it was useless.

Parvaneh called early in the morning.

'Well, did you tell them?'

'No! When did you expect me to tell them? In the middle of the night? Besides, I still don't know how.'

'Come on! It's not as if they are strangers. You are always talking to your children. Don't tell me you don't know how to tell them something this simple.'

'Simple? What is simple about it?'

'Tell Shirin first. She is a woman and she would understand better. She doesn't have that silly red-blooded zealousness that men have when it comes to their mummies.'

'I can't! It is so difficult.'

'Do you want me to tell her?'

'You? No! I have to find the nerve to do it myself or give it up altogether.'

'Give what up? Have you lost your mind? After all these years you have found your love and now you want to give him up? And over nothing and for no good reason? In fact, why don't I come over and we can tell her together. It's easier that way. Two against one ... we can deal with her better. We will even hit her if we have to. I'll be there around noon.'

After lunch, Shirin got dressed and said, 'I have to go see my friend Shahnaz for little while. I will be back soon.'

'But my dear Shirin, I came to see you,' Parvaneh said. 'Where are you going?'

'I am sorry, Auntie, I have to. It's for an assignment we have for the summer term. If I finish it in time, next term will be my last at the university ... I will be back by the time you two wake up from your afternoon nap.'

'It's not proper for you to leave when your Aunt Parvaneh has come to see you,' I said. 'She is only here for a few more days.'

'Auntie isn't a stranger,' Shirin said. 'And I wouldn't go if I really didn't have to. Take a quick nap and brew some tea. On my way back, I will buy the cake Auntie likes and we can sit out on the balcony and have tea and cake.'

Parvaneh and I lay down on my bed.

'Your story is just like a movie,' she said.

'Yes, an Indian movie.'

431

'What's wrong with Indian movies? Indians are people, too, and things happen to them.'

'Yes, strange things. Things that are highly unlikely in real life.'

'It's not as if movies made in other countries are any less strange or more likely to happen in real life. What is that big American guy's name? ... Arnold. He single-handedly destroys an entire army. Or the other one who drops six hundred people with a karate kick, jumps out of a plane and on to a train, and then leaps on to a car and flies into a ship and en route clobbers three hundred people without so much as a scratch on him ...'

'What's your point?'

'My point is that God, or destiny, or whatever you want to call it, has offered you a beautiful chance. It would be very ungrateful of you if you don't make the best of it.'

We were sitting out on the balcony when Shirin arrived with the cake.

'Oh, it has got so hot again,' she panted. 'Let me go change.'

I looked desperately at Parvaneh, but she motioned to me to stay calm and sit tight. A few minutes later, Shirin joined us. I poured some tea for her and she started chatting with us. Parvaneh waited for the right opportunity and then she said, 'My dear, how would you like to go to a wedding?'

'Wonderful!' Shirin exclaimed. 'I am dying to go to a decent wedding; one of those with plenty of music and dancing, not like the ones at Uncle Mahmoud's and Uncle Ali's homes. But who is getting married? Are the bride and groom gorgeous? I hate ugly brides and grooms. Are they cool?'

'My dear, talk properly,' I said. 'What does "cool" mean?'

'Cool means hip and trendy. It's a great word. You just don't like it because it's an expression young people use.' Then she turned to Parvaneh and said, 'Thank God Mum didn't end up being our Persian literature professor; otherwise, we would have to talk with highbrow pomposity.'

'See what a sharp tongue she has?' I said to Parvaneh. 'You so much as say one word, she will come back with ten.'

432

'Oh, stop arguing over nonsense,' Parvaneh said. 'I'm late, I have to get going.'

'But Auntie, I just got here!'

'It's your own fault,' Parvaneh said. 'I told you not to go.'

'But you didn't say whose wedding it is.'

'Whose wedding would you like it to be?'

Shirin leaned back, savoured her tea and said, 'I don't know.'

'Well, what if it's your mother's wedding?'

Shirin spat out her tea and keeled over laughing. Parvaneh and I looked at each other and tried to smile. There was no end to Shirin's laughter. It was as if she had heard the funniest joke.

'What is the matter with you?' Parvaneh chided. 'It's not funny!'

'Yes, it is, Auntie. Picture Mum in a wedding dress and a veil walking into a marriage ceremony with a hunchbacked old man with a cane! I guess I would have to hold the bride's train! Imagine the tottering groom trying to put a ring on the bride's wrinkled finger with his shaky hands. Just picture it! Isn't it hilarious?'

Humiliated and angry, I looked down and wrung my hands.

'That's enough!' Parvaneh snapped angrily. 'You talk as if your mother is a hundred years old. You young people have become so rude and inconsiderate. And don't worry, the groom is not tottery at all. As a matter of fact, he is far more handsome than your Faramarz.'

Shirin gaped at us and said, 'Well, don't be so insulted! I saw the scene in a movie. Now, what exactly did you mean?'

'I meant if your mother decides to get married, there are some very eligible men she could choose from.'

'For the love of God, Auntie, stop it. My mother is a lady. She has two daughters-in-law, two grandchildren and soon she will be giving away her beloved and only daughter.' Then she turned to me and said, 'By the way, Mum, Faramarz said my Canadian residency is almost ready. He will probably come to Iran during his holidays in January so that we can have our wedding celebration and leave together.'

This was about my daughter's wedding; I had to show some

433

interest. But all I managed to do was shake my head and say, 'We will talk about it later.'

'What is it, Mum? Are you upset because I said you are old? I'm sorry. It's all Auntie's fault. She just says things that make me laugh.'

'Why does it make you laugh?' Parvaneh snapped. 'In the West people get married even in their eighties and no one laughs. As a matter of fact, their children and grandchildren are happy for them and celebrate. And your mother is still a young woman.'

'Auntie, you have lived there for too long. You've become completely Westernised. Things are different here. I for one would be embarrassed. Besides, my mother is not lacking anything in her life to want to get married.'

'Are you sure?'

'Of course! She has a lovely home, she has her work, she goes on trips and holidays, Massoud has gone to a lot of trouble to make sure she receives her pension, and both her sons provide for her in every way. Besides, after I get married, she is going to come to Canada to help me take care of my children.'

'What an honour!' Parvaneh said indignantly.

I couldn't listen to them argue any more. I got up, gathered the dishes and went back inside. I saw Parvaneh talking fast and Shirin glowering at her. Then Parvaneh picked up her handbag and came inside. As she was putting on her manteau and head-scarf, she whispered, 'I told her our needs in life are not limited to material things, that we have emotional and sentimental needs, too. I told her the gentleman who has visited us here a few times is the one who has proposed marriage to you.'

Shirin was sitting there with her elbows on the table, holding her head in her hands. When Parvaneh left, I went back out on the balcony. She looked at me with tears in her eyes and said, 'Mum, tell me Parvaneh was lying. Tell me it isn't true.'

'What isn't true? The fact that Saiid has asked me to marry him? Yes, it is true. But I still haven't given him an answer.'

She sighed with relief and said, 'Oh, the way Aunt Parvaneh said it, I thought it was a done deal. But you won't do it, will you?'

'I don't know. I might.'

'Mum, think about us! You know how much respect Faramarz has for you. He always talks about what a moral, decent and selfless lady you are. He says you are the kind of mother before whom one should kneel. How am I supposed to tell him that my mother is hankering for a husband? If you do this, you will shatter the image we have had of you and have worshipped all these years.'

'I am not planning to commit a crime or a sin for any of you to question my character,' I said firmly.

She got up, shoved her chair aside and ran to her room. A few minutes later, the beeps on the telephone indicated that she was dialling a number. I was sure she was calling Massoud, and I said to myself, The storm has started.

An hour later, Massoud walked in looking distraught. I was sitting out on the balcony and pretended I was busy reading the newspaper. Shirin was talking to him rapidly, but in a low voice. After a while, Massoud joined me outside. He was frowning.

'Well, hello!' I said. 'Nice of you to come for a visit.'

'Sorry, Mum, I have been so busy with work that I can't tell night from day any more.'

'Why, my dear? Why do you get yourself all tangled up in useless administrative work? Weren't you supposed to start your own firm and pursue your art and architecture? Your personality is not suited to this job at all. You look a lot older and I haven't heard you laugh in such a long time.'

'I'm too deep into it. And Atefeh's father says it is our devout duty to help.'

'To help whom?' I asked. 'The people? Do you think you would be helping society any less if you worked in your own field? As a matter of fact, you had absolutely no experience in management for them to offer and for you to accept this position.'

'Let it go for now,' he said impatiently. 'What is all this nonsense I hear from Shirin?'

'Shirin says a lot of nonsense, which one are you referring to?'

Just then Shirin walked out with the tea tray and sat down next to Massoud. It was as if she wanted to clearly delineate the two

435

fronts. 'Mum!' she griped. 'He is talking about some man propos-
ing marriage to you.'

They both stifled their laughter and gave each other a sideways
glance. I was furious, but I tried not to lose my temper or my self-
confidence.

'After your father's death, a number of men proposed to me.'

'I know about all of them,' Massoud said. 'Some of them were
stubborn beyond belief. You were a beautiful and complete woman.
Did you think I didn't notice their eager looks and the way they
pursued you? Like all other children in the same situation, I used
to have nightmares about you marrying a stranger. You don't know
how many nights I lay in bed and imagined Mr Zargar's murder.
The only thing that kept me calm was my trust in you. I knew you
would never leave us to follow your heart. I knew you were the best
and the most sacrificing mother in the world and that you would
never exchange us for anything and would always choose us over
everything. I don't understand what has happened now and how
this man has affected you so much that you have forgotten all
about us.'

'I never have and I never will forget you,' I said. 'And you are
a grown man, so stop talking like a boy with an Oedipus complex.
As long as you were young and needed me, it was my duty to dedicate my life to you. I don't know to what extent that was the right
thing to do, but I knew that young boys like you and Siamak
wouldn't easily accept the presence of a stepfather, even if he was
a great guide for you and helped me through the difficulties of life.
At the time, the only thing that mattered to me was your comfort
and happiness. But now, the situation is very different. You have
all grown up, I have done my duty to the best of my ability and you
no longer need me. Don't you think that I finally have the right to
think about my own life, to make decisions for my own future and
to do what makes me happy? In fact, it would be easier for you, too.
You will not have to deal with the problems of an ageing, lonely
mother who will naturally become more demanding and testy as
time wears on.'

'No, Mum, please don't say that,' Massoud said. 'You are our pride and honour. To me, you are still the most precious person on the face of the earth and to my dying day I will be your slave and do whatever you need or want. I swear, the only reason I haven't come to see you in a few days is because I have been so terribly busy, but all my thoughts are with you.'

'That is exactly what I mean!' I said. 'You are a married man and a father and you have a mountain of problems and responsibilities, so why should all your thoughts be with your mother? All three of you have to think about your own lives. I don't want to be a cause for worry, an obligation, or a burden. I want you to see that I am not alone, that I am happy and that you don't need to worry about me.'

'There is no need for that,' Massoud argued. 'We will not leave you alone. With love and respect, we want to be at your service and will try to make up for a tiny bit of all that you have done for us.'

'My dear, I don't want that! You don't owe me anything. I just want to live the rest of my life with someone who can give me the peace and tranquillity I have always dreamed of. Is that a lot to ask for?'

'Mother, I am surprised at you. Why can't you understand how dreadful a plight this will be for us?'

'A dreadful plight? Would I be doing something immoral and ungodly?'

'Mother, it would be against tradition, which is just as bad. News of this is going to explode like a bomb. Do you realise what a scandal and embarrassment it would be for us? What would my friends, colleagues and employees say? Even worse, will I ever again be able to hold my head up in front of Atefeh's family?' Then he quickly turned to his sister and said, 'Shirin, make sure you never mention any of this in front of Atefeh.'

'And what will happen if she finds out?' I asked.

'What will happen? She will lose all the respect she has for you. The idol I have made of you for her will shatter. She will tell her parents and everyone at the ministry will find out.'

'So what?'

437

'Do you know what they will say behind my back?'

'No, what will they say?'

'They will say, "At his age, Mr Manager has a new stepfather. Last night, he put his mother's hand in the hands of some good-for-nothing jerk." How could I ever live with the shame?'

There was a lump in my throat. I couldn't talk any more; I couldn't stand them talking like that about my pure and beautiful love. My head was throbbing. I went inside, took a couple of painkillers and sat in the dark on the sofa, leaning my head back.

Shirin and Massoud talked for a while longer out on the balcony. Massoud wanted to leave and they came back inside. While seeing him off, Shirin said, 'It's all Aunt Parvaneh's fault. She is just clueless. Poor Mum would never even think of such a thing. She talked Mum into it.'

'I never liked Aunt Parvaneh,' Massoud said. 'I always found her to be vulgar. She never observes decorum. That night at our house, she tried to shake hands with Mr Maghsoudi! The poor man was so flustered and upset. You can be sure if Aunt Parvaneh was in Mum's place she would have remarried a hundred times by now.'

I got up, turned on a small lamp and said, 'This has nothing to do with Parvaneh. Every human being has the right to decide how to live his or her life.'

'Yes, Mum, you have that right,' Massoud said. 'But would you want to exercise it at the cost of your children's honour and reputation?'

'I have a headache and I want to go to bed,' I said. 'And I think you are late. It is best that you go see to your wife and child.'

Despite the sedatives I took, I spent the night restless and agitated. Conflicting thoughts flung me back and forth. On the one hand, the knowledge that I would be hurting my children made me feel guilty. Massoud's tired and troubled face and Shirin's tears would not let me go. On the other hand, the fantasy of freedom beckoned to me. Oh how I needed for once in my life to unchain myself from all responsibility and to fly free in this big world. My heart's desire, the love I felt for Saiid, and my fear of losing him again were crushing my heart.

Morning came, but I didn't have the energy to get out of bed. The telephone rang several times. Shirin answered, but the caller hung up. I knew it was Saiid. He was worried, but he didn't want to talk to Shirin. Again the telephone rang; this time Shirin said a cold hello and then rudely barked, 'Mum, it's Mrs Parvaneh, pick up.'

I picked up the telephone.

'So now I am Mrs Parvaneh!' she said. 'Shirin almost swore at me!'

'I am so sorry. Don't take it to heart.'

'Oh, I don't care,' Parvaneh said. 'But tell me, how are you?'

'Awful. This headache just won't go away.'

'Does Massoud know, too? Is he taking it as badly as Shirin?'

'Much worse.'

'What selfish kids! The only thing they don't care about is your happiness. They just don't understand ... It's your own fault for always sacrificing yourself and giving in to them. They've become so impudent they can't even imagine that you have rights, too. Well, what are you going to do now?'

'I don't know,' I said. 'For now, let me pull myself together a little.'

'Poor Saiid is half dead with worry. He says he hasn't heard from you in two days. Every time he calls, Shirin answers the telephone. He doesn't know what the situation is and whether he should talk to her or keep his distance for now.'

'Tell him not to call. I will call him myself later on.'

'Do you want the three of us to go for a walk in the park later this afternoon?' Parvaneh asked.

'No, I'm not in the mood.'

'I'm here for only a few more days and Saiid is leaving soon, too.'

'I can't, I really don't feel well,' I said. 'I can barely stand. Tell him I said hello. I'll call you later.'

Shirin was leaning against the door, looking furious, and listening to my conversation. I hung up and said, 'Do you want something?'

'No . . .'

'Then why are you standing there like hell's doorman?'

'Wasn't Mrs Parvaneh supposed to run along and leave? Isn't she clearing out of here?'

'Watch your mouth!' I snapped. 'You should be ashamed of yourself, talking like that about your aunt.'

'What aunt? I have only one aunt, Aunt Faati.'

'Enough! If you talk about Parvaneh like this one more time, you'll have it coming! Do you understand?'

'My apologies!' Shirin said sarcastically. 'I didn't know Mrs Parvaneh enjoyed such a lofty position in your eyes.'

'Yes, she does. Now, leave. I want to sleep.'

It was around noon when Siamak called. It was strange. He never called at that hour. Shirin and Massoud must have been in such a hurry to give him the news that they hadn't even waited for him to get home from work. After an icy hello he said, 'What is all this I hear from the kids?'

'All what?' I asked.

'That you want to get hitched.'

Hearing my own son speak to me in that tone was excruciating. Still, I firmly said, 'Is there a problem with that?'

'Of course, there is a problem. After a husband like my father, how can you even speak another man's name? You are being unfaithful to his memory. Unlike Massoud and Shirin, I will neither lose my honour nor do I find it strange that a woman your age would want to get married. But I cannot stand by and allow the memory of my martyred father to be mired in muck. All his followers look to us to preserve his memory, and you want to bring some tramp to sit in his place?'

'Do you hear yourself, Siamak? Which followers? You talk as if your father was a prophet! Not one in a million Iranians has ever even heard of your father. Why do you always boast and exaggerate? I know the people around you encourage you and, being

440

simple and gullible, you enjoy playing the role of a hero's son. But, my dear, open your eyes. People love creating heroes. They make someone big so that they can hide behind him, so that he will speak for them, so that in case of danger he will be their shield, suffer their punishments and give them time to escape. And that is exactly what they did with your father. They put him at the head of the line and cheered him on, but when he ended up in prison, they all ran away, and when he was killed, they denied having ever had anything to do with him. And afterwards, they only criticised him and listed his mistakes. And what did all your father's hero-isms bring us? Who knocked on our door to ask how the family of their hero was faring in life? The most daring and fearless among them barely mumbled a hello if they ran into us on the street.

'No, my son, you don't need a hero. I could understand your obsession while you were a boy, but now you are a grown man and you neither need to be a hero, nor do you need to follow one. Stand on your own two feet and rely on your own intelligence and knowledge to choose the leaders you want to support, and the instant you think they are heading in the wrong direction, take back your vote. You should not follow any person or ideology that asks you to blindly accept everything. You don't need myths. Let your children see you as a man with a solid character who will pro-tect them, not as someone who still needs to be protected.'

'Ugh! ... Mum, you never understood the magnitude of Father's greatness and the importance of his struggle.'

Every time he wanted to make a giant of Hamid, Dad would become Father; as if the word dad was too small for that titan.

'And you never understood the misery I suffered because of him,' I said. 'Son, open your eyes. Be a realist. Your father was a good man, but at least when it came to his family he had weak-nesses and failings, too. No human being is perfect.'

'Whatever my father did, he did it for the people,' Siamak argued. 'He wanted to create a socialist country where there would be equality, justice and freedom.'

'Yes, and I saw how the country he looked to, the Soviet Union, was ripped apart after only seventy years. Its people were ill for the lack of freedom. The day that country was dissolved, I cried for days, and for months I asked myself what exactly did your father die for? You never saw the citizens of that superpower's southern republics who came to Iran desperately looking for work; you never saw how bedraggled, confused and ignorant they were. Was that the Medina he gave his life for? I am happy he never lived to see what became of the mainspring of his hopes.'

'Mother, what do you know about politics and political issues? And besides, I didn't call to argue with you about this. The problem is you and what it is you are planning to do. I really cannot bear to see anyone take my father's place. That's all.'

And he hung up.

Arguing with Siamak was useless. His problem was not me, his problem was his father, and I had to be sacrificed before that idol.

Late that afternoon, Massoud, Atefeh and their adorable son who always reminded me of Massoud's childhood came to the apartment. I took my grandson from Atefeh and said, 'My dear Atefeh, welcome. I haven't seen this fair-haired boy in a while.'

'It's all Massoud's fault,' she said. 'He is so busy at work. Today, he cancelled a meeting and came home early. He said he wanted to come visit you because you were not feeling well. I hadn't seen you for a while and I was bored at home, so I forced him to let me come, too.'

'You did well. I missed you and this little boy.'

'I'm sorry you haven't been well,' Atefeh said. 'What is wrong?'

'Nothing really,' I said. 'I just had an awful headache, but these kids make it sound so much worse. I certainly didn't want to cause you any trouble.'

Massoud said, 'Please, Mum, it is no trouble at all. It is our duty. You have to forgive me for having been so busy lately that I have neglected you and not taken care of you.'

'I am not a child for you to take care of me,' I said dryly. 'I am still on my feet and you have your own wife and child to take care of. I don't want you to leave work and come here just to perform your duty. It makes me even more uncomfortable.'

With a quizzical look on her face, Atefeh picked up her son who had started crying and went to change him. I got up and went to the kitchen, my usual refuge. I busied myself washing some fruit, giving Shirin time to comfortably update Massoud on the latest news so that they could plan their next move. Atefeh quickly returned to the living room and was desperately trying to figure out what their cryptic and hushed conversation was about. Finally, as if she had overheard enough, she said out loud, 'Who? Who is getting married?'

Flustered, Massoud snapped, 'No one!'

And Shirin rushed to his rescue and said, 'Just one of Mum's old friends whose husband passed away a few years ago. Now, in spite of having sons- and daughters-in-law and grandchildren, she has got it into her head to get married.'

'What?' Atefeh exclaimed. 'I can't believe some women! Why doesn't someone tell them that at their age they should be thinking about doing good deeds and properly observing their prayers and fasts. They should be turning to God and thinking about their hereafter. And here they are, still preoccupied with their whims and fancies ... unbelievable!'

I was standing there holding the fruit bowl, listening to Atefeh's eloquent sermon. Massoud looked at Shirin and avoided my eyes. I put the fruit bowl on the table and I said, 'Why don't you just tell the woman to buy a grave and lie down in it?'

'What sort of comment is that, Mum?' Massoud chided. 'A spiritual life is far more rewarding than a material life. At a certain age, one should strive to experience this sort of life, too.'

My children's attitude to my age and to women my age made me realise why women never like to reveal how old they are and keep their age to themselves like a sealed secret.

The next day, I was getting ready to go to Parvaneh's house when Shirin walked into my room all dressed and ready and said, 'I am coming, too.'

'No. There is no need.'

'You don't want me to go with you?'

'No! As far back as I remember, I always had a guard. And I hate having a guard. I suggest you all stop behaving this way; otherwise, I will head for the mountains and deserts where none of you will ever find me.'

While Parvaneh packed her suitcases, I told her everything that had happened.

'It is unbelievable how our kids want to quickly send us off to the other world,' she said. 'I am surprised at Siamak. Why can't he understand? What a fate you have had!'

'Mother used to say, "Everyone's fate has been predetermined, it has been set aside for them, and even if the sky comes down to earth it will not change." I often ask myself, What is my share in this life? Did I ever have an independent fate of my own? Or was I always part of the destiny that ruled the lives of the men in my life, all of whom somehow sacrificed me at the altar of their beliefs and objectives? My father and brothers sacrificed me for the sake of their honour, my husband sacrificed me for his ideologies and goals, and I paid the price for my sons' heroic gestures and patriotic duties.

'Who was I, after all? The wife of an insurgent and a traitor or the wife of a hero fighting for freedom? The mother of a dissenter or the sacrificing parent of a freedom-loving fighter? How many times did they put me on the highest heights and then hurled me down on my head? And I deserved neither. They did not elevate me because of my own abilities and virtues, nor did they cast me down because of my own mistakes.

'It is as if I never existed, never had any rights. When did I ever live for myself? When did I ever work for myself? When did I have the right to choose and to decide? When did they ever ask me, "What do you want?"'

'You have really lost your nerve and confidence,' Parvaneh said. 'You never used to complain like this. It's unlike you. You must stand up to them and live your own life.'

'You know, I don't want to. It's not that I can't, I can, but there is no pleasure in it any more. I feel defeated. It is as if nothing has

444

changed in the past thirty years. Despite everything I suffered, I didn't even manage to change things in my own home. The least I expected of my children was a little compassion and understanding. But even they were not willing to consider me as a human being who has certain rights. I am valuable to them only as a mother who serves them. Remember that old proverb, "No one wants us for ourselves, everyone wants us for themselves." My happiness and what I want is of no significance to them.

'Now, I have no passion and enthusiasm left for this marriage. In a way, I have lost hope. Their attitude has tarnished my relationship with Saiid. When those who I thought were closest to me, who I thought loved me, whom I raised with my own hands, talk like this about me and Saiid, imagine what others will say. Imagine how they will drag us through the mud.'

'To hell with them!' Parvaneh said. 'Let them say what they will, you shouldn't listen to any of it. Be strong, live your own life. Despair does not suit you at all. Your solution is to go see Saiid. Get up and call that poor man. He has been going out of his mind with worry.'

That afternoon, Saiid came to Parvaneh's house. She no longer liked to sit in on our conversations and went about her own work.

'Saiid, I am terribly sorry,' I said. 'It is impossible for us to get married. I have been condemned to never experience happiness and a quiet life.'

Saiid looked devastated.

'My entire youth was destroyed by this fateful love,' he said. 'Even in the best of times, deep inside, I was sad and alone. I am not saying I never paid attention to any other woman, I am not saying I never loved Nazy, but you are the love of my life. When I found you again, I thought God has finally given me a blessing and in the last half of my life he wants to show me its joys. The happiest and most peaceful days I have known were the days we spent together these past two months. Now, not having you is difficult. Now, I feel lonelier than ever before. Now, I need you more than ever. I am asking you to please reconsider. You are not a child, you are no longer that sixteen-year-old girl who needs her father's permission, you can decide for yourself. Don't let me fall again.'

My eyes were brimming with tears.

'But what about my children?'

'Do you agree with what they are saying?'

'No. Their logic is worth nothing to me. It is based on selfishness and self-interest. But with this mindset they will condemn me and they will suffer, they will be confused and dejected. I have never been able to stand seeing them heartbroken. How could I now do something that would make them feel shame, humiliation and sorrow? I will feel guilty for being the cause of their spouses, colleagues and friends looking at them with scorn and disdain.'

'They may feel like this for a while, but they will soon forget.'

'What if they don't? What if it stays in their hearts for the rest of their lives? What if this damages the image of me they have in their minds?'

'It will eventually return to what it used to be,' Saiid argued.

'What if it doesn't?'

'But what can we do? Perhaps this is the price we have to pay for our happiness.'

'And I should make my children pay it? No. I cannot.'

'For once in your life follow your heart and set yourself free,' he pleaded.

'No, my dear Saiid ... I am not one to do that.'

'I think you are using your children as an excuse.'

'I don't know, perhaps. Perhaps I have lost my nerve. What happened was very insulting. I didn't expect such a harsh reaction from them. Right now, I am too tired and depressed to make such a big decision for my life. I feel a hundred years old. And I don't want to do anything out of spite or to prove my strength. I am sorry, but under these circumstances, I cannot give you the answer you want.'

'But, Massoum, we will be lost to each other again.'

'I know. I feel like I am committing suicide, and it is not my first time ... But do you know what is most devastating?'

'No!'

446

'The fact that both times it was my loved ones who contrived this kind of death for me.'

Parvaneh left.

I saw Saiid a few more times. I made him promise to make amends with his wife and to stay in America. After all, having a family, even one that was not warm and intimate, was better than not having one at all ...

After I said goodbye to him, I walked home. A cold autumn wind was blowing in gusts. I was tired. My burden of loneliness felt heavier and my steps more unsteady and weak. I wrapped myself in my black cardigan and looked up at the grey sky.

Oh ... what a hard winter lay ahead.